SAXBY FOR GOD

To Anne & David

Best Wishes

Richard

Also by Richard Haley
THE SATURDAY PEOPLE

RICHARD HALEY

SAXBY FOR GOD

HUTCHINSON OF LONDON

HUTCHINSON & CO (*Publishers*) LTD
3 Fitzroy Square, London W1

London Melbourne Sydney Auckland
Wellington Johannesburg Cape Town
and agencies throughout the world

First published 1974

© Richard Haley 1974

*This book has been set in Baskerville type, printed in Great Britain
on antique wove paper by Anchor Press, and
bound by Wm. Brendon, both of Tiptree, Essex*

ISBN 0 09 118640 4

CONTENTS

For my Father and Mother

PART ONE

MAN OF DESTINY

I

It began on a cold clear day in the spring of 'sixty-seven.

'Meet Esther Moore.'

She looked too good for us. Attractive. Dark, shoulder-length hair. Grey eyes, level gaze, discreet smile. Grey mini-dress, crisp white collar and cuffs.

Not what we were accustomed to at Singleton Fisher, not by light years. I rose smiling from behind my desk. Martin looked as puzzled as I felt.

'Hello, Mr. Saxby,' she said calmly.

I saw why she smiled with her mouth shut. Teeth. Big upper ones. They instantly destroyed the cool balance of her face.

'Bob, please.' I made the smile go crinkly. 'Unless you really want to be formal.'

'Bob, then.'

'Bob, like me, is also an accountant. Which is rather like saying Picasso and Annigoni are both artists. He's the ideas man. It'll take you about half an hour to see what I'm driving at.'

'Sounds ominous.'

'Sinister's the word, dear. He won't be really happy until the office staff consists of five computers and him.'

'He can't get the past out of his mind,' I told her. 'Look at those twenty-eight-inch trouser bottoms. He can't forget those halcyon days when everyone in General had a quill pen and an abacus.'

I stopped. This wouldn't do. Not in front of the children. Certainly not in front of a new shorthand typist. But she wasn't like the others. You just couldn't imagine her hammering away in a pool with that other lot. She smiled, prominent teeth carefully concealed, directly into my eyes. She knew. That she puzzled me.

'Right, Esther. You're to look after Bob and I in that little room that connects our offices. There'll be plenty of work, but I think you'll find it interesting. Give priority to anything to do with the weekly management meeting. You've done committee work, I believe—minutes, etc.?'

She nodded. You were convinced.

'Splendid! Our search is over. Shall you have Esther first, Bob?' His eyes skimmed across her firm high breasts before innocently meeting mine.

'I'd sooner she saw to you first. I'm pretty sure what I've got for her will keep her occupied most of the afternoon.'

We'd been at it ten years. Sometimes they suspected, sometimes they even tittered, but our maturity, our unsmiling demeanour, always left them finally uncertain. But not her. She knew she puzzled me and she wasn't fooled by innuendo. Her steady gaze passed from me to him. Wasn't fooled and wasn't even going to pretend she found it funny. He led her away. I felt fatuous.

'I don't get it,' I said. 'On top of everything else she's got A-levels.'

'You've been at the personal files.'

'I've got to know the bitches. X-factors make me uneasy. Why isn't she an air hostess or something?'

'*Very* strange.' Martin poured himself some claret. 'And the tight-lipped smile only enhances the mystery. Of course, it's only to cover those spectacular teeth. When women smile inscrutably it's always teeth. Esther, prominent ones, the Empress Josephine, rotting ones, and the Giaconda, clearly, no bloody teeth at all.'

'Titillating,' I murmured. 'That sudden flash of wet, prominent teeth.'

'Madly titillating. She disturbs me. I could imagine a girl like her having pubic hair as soft as gossamer.'

'And spiky nipples.'

'Fantastically supple legs.'

'Yes,' I said. 'I shan't be happy till I know why she's working for a dirty little sod like you.'

We drank coffee, gloomily watched one of those Lego office blocks going up across the road.

'Simon's coming back,' he said.

'He comes back every year.'

'He's coming back for good.'

'If he does, I go.'

'Don't be a bore.'

'Did the old man tell you?'

'Who else?'

'Why not me?'

'Oh, for God's sake . . .'

'He'd better come off it, Martin. I won't stomach it much longer. I run the bloody place and I want to know what the bastard's up to.'

'You really are the biggest bore of all time.'

'Why's he coming back? Jesus, don't we wire enough money out?'

He sighed, settled back in his chair, began to light a small cigar. 'Oh, go on then, have your ritual mouth-froth.'

'I will *not* work with that supercilious drunken sot breathing down my neck. Not now.'

He took a copy of the *Financial Times* from a nearby rack, put it up between us. A few minutes later I threw my napkin on the table.

'All right, all right—get on with it.'

He watched me through blue smoke and sunlight, the network of wrinkles deepening into the inevitable smile, put down the paper.

'He'll always bypass you. The old man. You'd better get used to it. I'm one of them and you're not.'

'No need to be sadistic. Just give me the hard facts.'

'Simon's not well. He's going to a drying-out farm in Scotland and then back to S.F. to settle down.'

'The Governor said *that*?'

'No. He said he'd caught some foreign bug that needed specialised treatment. And believes it, I swear.'

'Definitely believes it. Never alcoholism, by God. Not a Fisher. It's only human beings who get the drink habit.'

He hesitated, slowly stubbed out the cigar.

'I want you,' he said, 'to ask the Governor to let Simon have a spell in your office until he's back in the saddle again.'

I stared at him. I couldn't speak. I got up, scribbled my name over the Diners' Club chit, and started out of the room. Halfway up Cloth Hall Street I said : 'No.'

'The old man's doddering. He's doddering and Simon's the legitimate heir. You've got to get him fenced in.'

'No.'

'Bob, what did you expect? You must have known he'd come back in the end.'

'You're wrong. I thought he was a born remittance man. I thought when the Governor died it'd be me and you running it, and sending him his whisky money out till he killed himself.'

'You're supposed to be a politician. You're supposed to be able to cope with changing situations and work out fresh plans quickly. Can't you see the power of good it would do you with the old man?'

'Yes, but I just can't do it.'

'You've got to. And you know it. You don't fool either of us.'

I came to a halt outside the swing doors of the entrance hall, so depressed, in the clear spring air, I didn't want to go back in.

'All right,' I sighed. 'Give me time. I'll think about it.'

'Good man!' The faint eternal smile deepened. 'I knew you'd see reason, repellent calculating swine like you.'

'Lay off, Martin—I'm not in the mood.'

'Still, we've brought you a long way. Not far enough to suit me, but at least you don't go white and kick filing cabinets now.'

' "Why did he do it?" they wondered in later years. "This devoted almost saintly friend who seemed to want nothing in return." '

'Dear boy. Your betters seek subtler rewards. The Professor Higgins thing, don't you know. They all said it couldn't be done and I did it. Or very nearly.'

Six o'clock. Building silent except for one discreet electric typewriter worked at such speed it sounded like radio static.

'Such devotion!'

'*Oh!*' Her head jerked. 'You startled me. I thought you'd gone.'

I didn't quite believe her. The eyes had widened, but if she'd really been startled wouldn't her mouth have opened on the teeth?

'The answer to an administrator's prayer. A secretary who can't have enough work.'

'It was almost finished.'

'Not the whole report?'

She nodded.

'My dear girl, I didn't expect it at least until lunchtime tomorrow.'

'I'm awfully sorry, but I'm afraid there's nothing I can do now to stop it being ready before nine-fifteen.'

I laughed : 'You mustn't dream of apologising.'

But approval was tinged with suspicion. What was there in it for Esther Moore? She had A-levels, and her A-level intelligence must already have told her that Singleton Fisher didn't pay A-level money or provide A-level jobs. So why was she here, working over? She was a variation in the unvarying pattern; it fretted my accountant's mind.

'Well—I'm off.' I ignited my warm crinkly smile. 'But you feel free to stay. I'll ask the night man to keep looking in on you.'

'I'm coming too now. I'm at the end of a page.'

A few more seconds' radio static, she flicked out the foolscap sheet. I helped her into a short fawn raincoat. She smelt very clean.

It all seemed innocent. Too innocent. I knew all the gambits backwards. I wasn't twenty. Christ, I wasn't even thirty. Suddenly, in the middle of the small talk, I said : 'Perhaps I could give you a lift home. To make up for the overtime.'

She hesitated. 'Heylands Avenue. Rather a detour for you.'

'How would you know that?'

'You are *the* Bob Saxby?'

'Go on.'

'I've read about you. In my father's files.'

I stopped outside the front door, watched her. She almost laughed then, lips briefly forced apart by the tips of the large upper teeth.

'Don't be alarmed, he's not the Chief Constable. He's a lecturer. Social science. Takes it all frightfully seriously. He keeps neat little files on the more prominent people in any kind of politics. You're in the promising newcomers' section.'

It was the best thing I'd heard all day. Her father had me in his notes. Some anonymous chalk-fingers, whose job it was to know, had twigged about Saxby. It was like an omen, and I believed in omens. And luck.

The kicks were killed by suspicion. Too neat. It was so bloody neat it was like the sort of play critics dismiss as Well-made.

'This is all very disquieting. I can see I'll have to be a model boss if everything's going down on paper.'

We began to walk along Cloth Hall. She shrugged. 'I don't believe it would make much difference. He thinks you're very clever but he doesn't like you. Or your politics. It comes out in the summing-up.'

You really had to hand it to her for a fresh twist. Masterly. My father thinks you stink, but what are you doing after the election?

'Tell me two things. Has he always been a lecturer, and has he ever tried active politics?'

'Yes . . . and no.'

'That's why he doesn't like me.'

We'd reached Spinner Gate. Time for the big fat moment of truth.

'Are you in a tearing hurry?'

'Not particularly.'

'Care for a drink?'

'Oh . . . all right.'

Yes. Flirtation. I just caught the glint of triumph, the minute down-turn of lips. It was there and gone, but I was waiting for it. Behind the gentle crinkly grin.

Poor kid. Poor young kid. If you got all the bitches of twenty-odd together whose nipples had stirred at the sight of kind, cheerful, boyish-looking Bob, they'd stretch the length of Town Hall Square. She was really good—terrific that air of inscrutability. And the father gambit. But it was always age that told in this particular game, the thousands of extra days. And it was always me who won. Strictly in the Hemingway sense, where you lost at the same time. For a few seconds I was badly depressed.

I looked across the city, the buildings tinted red before a setting April sun—the Greek temple and the Gothic barn, the Palladian hall. Saxby-town, Martin sometimes called it. It was always good for a lift.

I turned back to lead her over to the George. This time I caught an almost brooding look, a faint sullenness, as if she resented the attention going off her. A possessive one.

The George was half-full of men I was on nodding terms with. They consumed the body in the short raincoat, but there were no knowing smiles. I'd been here with too many girls, in ones, in pairs, in little giggly bunches. I was old Bob Saxby—family man, top-flight administrator, keen party-type—and I was as safe as Slater sodding Walker.

'What's the in-drink then?' I said cheerfully. 'Vodka?'

'I'd like a dry Martini.'

'Ah, of course. The 'thirties are the vogue now, aren't they?'

'Are they?'

I got a cigarette case out and wished I hadn't. As I flicked it open it struck me that Christ I hadn't seen anyone under forty use one for ten years.

'Do you smoke? I don't, but I try to be sociable.'

She smiled faintly : 'I *do*, but I'd prefer one of these.

King-size filter-tips in a gold packet. It had been Gauloises in my day, smoked through an ivory holder. It was lung-cancer statistics now, and being old enough to want to live for ever.

She leaned over the match, I looked at her dark hair, her pink-ness. It was about now that boredom struck, driving me to the dark-ened gazebo, to the ripped dress and the rotated breasts and the ecstatically spreading thighs. Even the Updike stuff if they looked as if they kept it really fragrant.

With her it didn't happen. Maybe it was the A-levels. Or those riveting teeth. They seemed to shatter the impassive balance of her face like loud notes following soft in a Chopin mazurka.

But did I use her or didn't I? I had a little job back at home that was absolutely tailor-made for an A-level intelligence. But would she give trouble when it was time to phase her out? Women with brains were often more trouble than they were worth.

'How did your first day go?'

'I liked doing your report. It's a popular word at the moment, isn't it, rationalisation, but I never really understood what it meant in everyday terms until this afternoon.'

'Most of this well-nourished lot are in a similar state of ignorance, only they've been in commerce all their lives and should know bet-ter. It must be quite a change for you—I understand you came to us from the University library. Whatever made you desert the olive-grove of Academe for the jungle?'

She shrugged : 'Curiosity.'

She covered the teeth up and watched me steadily. Clever stuff—she wasn't talking. No matter, I'd figure it out in the end. I always did.

'Speaking of libraries,' I said, in a voice as bland as crème de menthe. 'Do you know of anyone who might be able to help me with a sort of private library?'

'At Fisher's?'

'At my home. I've had a small room made into a study. Shelves floor to ceiling. I've got a great pile of books I want arranging and card-indexing.'

She sipped the Martini, pretended to think, a fleck of white teeth resting on lower lip. 'I might be able to find someone,' she said slowly. 'Though I'd not like to promise.'

She fenced like a woman of thirty. I wasn't used to having to talk girls into doing what I knew they longed to do. It could be risky going on.

'I rather thought . . . you yourself might be able to help me.'

She pretended to consider this too at length. Then the teeth forced her lips apart in a wry smile.

'Would that mean I'd be working for the party?'

'Tenuously, yes, I suppose it would. Brand you as the worst kind of heretic with your father.'

'Why do you say that?' she said quickly.

At last, an unguarded reaction. I gave her my crinkly grin.

'Your father's as left-wing as Michael Foot. He talks passionately about referendums and political cells. His voice trembles with emotion about Britain's economic links with South Africa. He marches with that curious body of people who only last week went in silent protest over Vietnam from the cathedral to the cenotaph.'

Sudden extreme anger. She'd flushed; her grey eyes were as hard as slate. Her teeth were fully exposed for the first time, in an expression of almost rat-like ferocity. I'd scored a direct hit.

Self-possession was equally swift. She turned away, took out another cigarette. When she looked at me again she'd clamped her face back into its old impassive mask.

'You obviously don't think much of protest marches.'

'I suppose they serve some purpose if they make the marchers feel good. Useless as a form of political expression, of course.'

She didn't reply. She looked away from me with a peculiar dilation of the nostrils, a glance that passed in a subtle sneer over the polished octagonal tables and the fire-basket, the heraldic devices above the chimney-piece and the oak-panelled walls.

I was dismissed. And it stung. I'd made her furious, but she'd risen above it. I wasn't even worth arguing with. I was mature, well-heeled, relaxing in my well-heeled middle-class watering-place, and I wasn't worth the trouble of even trying to convince or win over. It hurt.

I finished my sherry. Did I just look exactly the same as that lot then, for God's sake? The great Bob—upstart, actor, buccaneer, brain. Was there no mark, no aura? With a destiny like mine.

I pulled up. Tall Victorian terrace house, dingy brown paint, narrow, ill-tended garden, half a dozen overgrown sycamores.

I smiled. Exactly as I'd guessed. I could see that gaunt living-room too, the ancient telly with the buckled indoor aerial, the battered table by the window with the piles of exercise books and the yellowing copies of the *New Statesman*. I could smell the St. Bruno, hear the worn needle raggedly thundering *Schubert's Ninth.*

Hear those fluting Fabian Society voices.

'I thought it would amuse you.'

I turned. A-level women—they could tell you were smiling without seeing your face.

'A house full of talk,' I said. 'Wine parties every Saturday night and no one wanting to go home. And that's a compliment.'

Her face softened wryly. 'You're right. It's a house full of talk.'

We sat in silence in the blue gathering dusk.

'I hope he won't take it too badly, your father, you being brought home by an unsavoury character like me.'

'I'd better not tell him. I'm certain he'd see it as a fate much worse than death.'

We were buddies again, we could even lightly joke about chalk-fingers. I could even get back to my book-listing now, if I wanted to. But I didn't.

'Esther, I must be off. My life runs to an exacting schedule.'

'The assiduous Mr. Saxby.'

I winced. 'It's not fair—you know all these things about me, but I know nothing about Esther Moore.'

'Perhaps there's not much to know. What is it tonight—the municipal?'

'And the Grand Spring Bazaar. And the Chanctonbury Tea Club.'

She was playing for time, willing me to bring the books up again. But I didn't think I was going to.

Difficult to know why. She was sharp and she was attractive, and that was a dangerous enough combination, but I took risks with young girls all the time. Risks I could calculate as precisely as those the Fisher salesmen took on the roads, who drove hundreds of miles a week.

But there was more to it than that. Something I could sense. Perhaps it was envy. Of her actually belonging to the 'sixties. Just now and then some girl in a city street, a face here and gone, would remind me how badly I'd wanted to belong to the 'sixties too. I sometimes wondered if anyone could possibly ask more from life than to be single and twenty-odd while all that colour and music was going on. That music. That fantastic music and those words.

The artistry. The irreverence and the candour and the freedom. And the fancy dress. Above all I envied them those brilliant symbolic clothes.

More than any other decade the intelligent young had made the 'sixties entirely their own, and if I let her get too close it might all become too unbearably *Lucy in the Sky with Diamonds*.

Anyway, my instincts told me to pull out.

'I'll see you tomorrow,' I said cheerfully.

'I'll index your books.' She looked startled. As if the suddenness had taken her by surprise too. 'That is . . . if you'd really like me to.'

'Well . . . that would be splendid. If you're sure it wouldn't bore you to death.'

I hadn't expected it but I couldn't turn down a direct offer now. Otherwise she'd think she attracted me so much I was running away. I could read them like a balance sheet. And I didn't want any silly archness in the office.

'How would Sunday afternoon suit you?'

It didn't have to be Sunday afternoon but if she was forcing the game she might just as well do it at my convenience.

'Oh . . . all right.'

'Have you got transport?'

'Mother's car.'

'Good. Would you meet me at the Westbury Club then about two-thirty? I always have to call in there on Sundays. I sometimes get delayed. If I've got you as an excuse I'll be able to get away without seeming churlish. Do you know it—lavatory brick building near the junction. Tell them you're my guest—they'll point me out. We can go on home then and you can meet Gwen. And the books, of course.'

I smiled ruefully. They worked harder if they thought you weren't happy at home. Convince them that if it wasn't for Emma and Gwen it would be you and her standing hand in hand at life's gateway and they worked like Fanny Cradock.

'I'll be there at half past two.'

'Splendid ! But wait—about payment . . .'

'It doesn't matter. I'll make the party a present of it.'

Quite. I'd be reward enough.

'Well, thank you. Thank you very much.'

'Good night, Bob.'

She looked at my face as she got out. Not into my eyes, but at the whole of my face. It puzzled me—it was a hungry look. It didn't fit in with crushes and flirtations.

I watched her until she was out of sight behind the forest trees of Transport House. I was playing with fire this time. Definitely. Not that I hadn't got the water-buckets handy.

What if she were a nymph? An intelligent middle-class nymph? It would be nice to have my books in exact order, but what if she threatened to tell Gwen I'd had it off with her in the Gestetner room?

Too late now. I had a warm feeling in the guts. Several weeks of intensive flirtation with a wily practitioner. It was going to be fun. I hadn't had a difficult one for over a year now and life could be very tedious.

Even at my speed.

2

'Penelope Sharpe wants to do a profile on you. Can you rustle up some details? What drew you to politics, how you rose commercially, what makes you tick—you know the sort of thing.'

'Is she the one who turned out that deathless piece of prose entitled *The Assiduous Mr. Saxby*?'

'Yes.'

'God.'

'I thought it would please you. It's the second write-up in two months.'

'I am pleased. Her kind of flattery's exactly what I need at this stage. It would just be nice to read something perceptive and accurate about yourself now and then, even if it didn't pull punches. I'd give a lot to get my hands on Lecturer Moore's notes.'

'Lecturer Moore?'

'The disapproving father of this delicious new girl. Keeps great files on local talent.'

'Ah—I remember. How very thorough. And the girl's to index your books. Fallen for you, of course.'

'Heavily.'

'When does she start?'

'This afternoon.'

'Jolly good! If we can talk her into dinner she can crack away for hours.'

'Quite. But watch her. She's got it pretty bad.'

'Oh, very well, dear.'

Emma ate her egg, lost in her thoughts. Soon I'd have to be more cautious about discussing my girls in front of her.

Sunday breakfast. Best meal of the week. It was a heavy meal that did away with lunch—we ate it in the living-room off an old inlaid oval table. The kitchen annexe was too workaday, the dining-room seemed too formal. In here we could listen to Gwen's rousing records—the Wagner overtures and the *Karelia* and the *Pomp and Circumstance Marches*—and after breakfast we could play table games with Emma. The living-room also had the best view of the pool and the ornamental trees.

It was my single break from sustained, constructive thought. No office, no politics—you could think as you liked.

Dear Miss Sharpe—I understand you'd like a few personal notes to work up into one of your charming profiles. How kind! Well, here they are, just as they came into my head. You're the expert, you'll know exactly what I'm trying to say.

Career then. In a nut-shell I'm the brains at Singleton Fisher. And I owe it all to the younger Fisher—Simon. Of course, I've worked hard as well but without him I couldn't have got where I am today. I loathed the sod so much I swore I'd run that bloody show round him. And now I do.

'Are you seeing young Dowling?' Gwen said, taking her glasses off.

'Playing billiards with him.'

She pursed her lips, gazed up at galleon clouds in a clear sky.

'I saw Paul on Wednesday. Of the *Standard*. I'd got him a vase. While I was there I showed him a couple of Peter's *Forward!* articles.'

'And he paled beneath his tan.'

'He did rather wince. But he agreed they showed promise. However, to be brief, I finally got him to say that if Peter would develop a proper journalistic style they'd consider the occasional article about the problems of the region. Absolutely non-partisan, of course, and he *must* be crisp. He did grudgingly admit that he had a very good grasp of the local set-up.'

'Great stuff, Gwen.'

She smiled. 'Will it help?'

'Just what I need.'

Emma had begun to stack the breakfast things on a nearby trolley. 'We're going to play Woodland Happy Families today, Daddy.'

Hate and imagination. Those are my qualities, Miss Sharpe. Hate got me going but can you believe how much imagination you'd need to give a grotty old dump like Fishers' star quality? And to see yourself as the man of the West Riding. Good big thinking, eh?

Gave me hell in my youth, of course. We were poor, I got away from it all at the pictures. Audrey Hepburn, Grace Kelly, Ava Gardner—Christ, they have a lot to answer for. I wanted the girls in my own life to be the same. Remote, ethereal, adoring. Giving an impression of depths and a subtle quirky humour.

Needless to say they never did. They just kept catching colds or saying their feet hurt or could they please have a Cherry B.

I'd have accepted it in the end. That girls weren't really like Jean Simmons. But just to confuse things I met Maggie. Of the endless silences and the curious inward smile. Of the fantastic knack of saying the very thing that would have the utmost impact on a glamour-hungry mind. Maggie, of the large brown-tinted nipples and the body that smelt ever so slightly of dank undergrowth.

'Do it, Poppa.' Emma began to giggle. 'Go on—do a rhyme.'

'Mm. Let me see now. Mr. Stoat had a shocking sore throat.'

She gave a tiny shriek of laughter.

'Go on—another.'

'Mr. Mole—fell down a great hole.'

'Another!'

'Mr. Frog—treats his wife like a dog.'

She laid her head on the table, honey-coloured hair spreading across its glowing surface, weak with mirth. 'Go on, go *on*—another.'

'Mr. Hedgehog—gets stoned on egg-nog.'

'Now, Bob,' Gwen said mildly.

'What does stoned mean, Daddy?'

But it was no good. In the end she turned out to be just as much an illusion as Grace and Audrey and Kim. It was them she modelled herself on, for God's sake!

Poor Maggie. We loved each other so much and I hurt her so badly. So badly in fact that it scared me. And I over-reacted. I played safe and married Gwen Endersby—straight sex, push, ex-

pertise, materialism and no nonsense about love. And a walking political machine into the bargain.

'Please have you got Mr. Shrew, Daddy?'

'No, Emma. Please have you got Master Shrew?'

'Oh, Daddy! How do you always know?'

An empty marriage. The finest asset any would-be politician can have, Miss Sharpe. But what about love, you'll surely ask, gazing mistily at that waistcoated little sod of a dog of yours. Exactly. And me working class too, where the urge for love is bred into you.

Can you wonder I'm so ambitious? However far I get in politics, and let's not beat about the bush, I'm obviously going to hit the jackpot, it will always be measured against what I really needed. Shining eyes, a hand on my cheek. Poor bloody Bob.

'Daddy, please have you got Mr. Hedgehog?' She glanced daringly at Gwen and added: 'Who gets stoned on egg-nog.'

How badly I wanted a woman to love, Miss Sharpe, after a couple of years of Gwen. You'd never think it, would you, to see us looking so right for each other at the meetings. But affairs were out because by then I couldn't do without politics. And in Beckford it's not possible to have both.

'Daddy, why do you *always* win?'

Her face was contorted with rage. She hurled the last card at me, which flashed over the glossy surface and on to the floor.

'Emma, *really*!'

'I can't help it, Em, I'm just lucky. And anyway, I've only got one more trick than you. Come on, let's play Chinese Checkers instead.' It was the only game I could swing in her favour without arousing her suspicions.

'Oh, all right. But you can't have pink.'

Your dog, my daughter, Miss Sharpe—both innocent objects of such complex and powerful forces of love. Sometimes it seems that in Emma I'm trying to create the kind of woman I always wanted and never found. I can't wait for her teens, for those lengthy tours of Europe we'll take together, for the reading schedules, the trips to theatres and art galleries and concert halls. She'll eclipse even me one day, it's clear she's got my kind of mind, and then she'll be gone, but for a short time, for a handful of years, she'll belong entirely to me. And like your dog she'll never see it as anything else but natural affection.

What makes me tick, what drew me to politics? Self-knowledge,

Miss Sharpe. You see, you don't understand how you feel about that bloody dog, but I know exactly how I feel about my daughter.

I know my success was founded on hate, that fear induced an empty but astute marriage, that I split my nature down the middle between wife and daughter—Gwen for sex, Emma for love. I know that I'm ambitious, calculating, cynical and as hard as granite. And I know that I've the imagination to do for Beckford what I've done for Singleton Fisher.

A man who knows himself so well, Miss Sharpe, and who can make such a satisfactory mix of such unpromising ingredients is a natural politician. Art of the possible, don't you know. Or to put it Edward Fitzgerald's way—'We are all mad, but with this difference—I know that I am.'

'Pink wins!'

'Are you *sure* you couldn't have won?' Delight fought suspicion in the flushed face bent over the checker-board.

'I hadn't a price, Em.'

Gwen said : 'I really think you'd better be making a move, Bob.'

'Right. See you later, my dears.'

'Bob, you'll remember those notes for Penelope's profile, won't you? Most important.'

I smiled. 'I've already begun to toy with ideas.'

Beer, cigar-smoke, ancient leather, green baize, dust motes in sunshine.

'Bob!'

'Gentlemen, good morning! What will you have?'

Gwen had said not to bother whose round it was, just keep buying them drinks. She and Pop had also advised me never to try to talk to too many members at once. Select three, talk to them at length, select a different three next time. It was the trenches with Garnett Holdsworth today, lack of incentives for businessmen with Henry Symes, and the offer of an opening at Singleton Fisher for young Myers, recently made redundant.

Finally, it was billiards with Peter Dowling. Tall, broad-shouldered, arrogantly graceful. Flared tweed jacket and long blond hair. 'TRAGIC DEATH OF UNDER TWENTY-FIVES CHAIRMAN,' you could hear Martin murmuring. 'Decapitated in Motor Rally.'

'Ready for your trouncing then?'

'Half a sheet says I beat you into the ground.'

'Nonsense!'

He set the white balls up for the string.

'How's the driving?'

'Doing the Cherry Tree Farm run at three. Father says I'll shag her out before Christmas. Cock, of course, engine on her like she's got.'

I began helping him to beat me into the ground. I'd always had luck with games. The hardest part was playing to lose narrowly enough to make them feel good. I only allowed myself an occasional modest victory. Damn good sport, Bob, as well as having an open hand.

'I liked your *Forward!* article this month.'

He coloured slightly, went on to make a four-cannon break.

'Merely a few scribbled paragraphs. Forgot I'd promised to do it till Wilton rang me up the other night peeing himself.'

I tittered. He was lying. He'd breathed heavily and worked hard over it, those recondite words he'd decked it out with were a give-away.

I pocketed the red, carefully fluffed an in-off.

'Mind if I make a single criticism?'

'Of course not.'

This time he didn't finish his break, the words came straight out, clipped, irritably polite.

'I thought you'd want me to be honest.'

'Naturally.'

'This is simply an impression I got as I read it.'

He said nothing. He slashed the red into a centre pocket; it sounded like a shot-gun.

I spoke slowly. 'Well, frankly, I thought you were slightly above the head of the average member. Awfully well done, but . . . do you not suppose, just a little too good for *Forward!*?'

He botched the cannon a child could have made, even pocketed his own ball. He looked up, unable to stop himself smiling.

'I *thought* that might be the trouble, don't you know. I did my best, but writing down's so impossibly difficult.'

'Exactly. But don't forget, they haven't all had the benefit of your wide education.' I lowered my voice. 'And let's face it, none of them have your grasp.'

'Decent of you to speak so frankly. I'd a shrewd idea I'd set my sights too high. So bloody hard, writing down.'

'It must be.'

I began a modest break. He'd had more than his share of straight praise from Wilton and the other hacks. Another dollop wasn't going to make any impact. So it had to be praise packaged differently. I'd annoyed him, then gratified him. He'd remember me.

'Peter, I showed Paul Watts of the *Standard* a couple of your articles the other day. He thought they showed considerable promise. In fact he rather thought they might be able to use some of your work—the occasional article about regional economies, business prospects, etc. He certainly thought you knew your stuff.'

If he missed any more shots the game would be mine by default.

'Forgot to chalk me blasted cue! Bit of a rag, don't you think, the *Standard*?'

'Ah, well, it is a provincial paper, isn't it? And you'd really have to force yourself to write down because the *Standard* goes into every possible kind of home. Watts suggested you studied the articles of other outside contributors . . .'

'Oh, I don't know, Bob. Knocking out a few lines for *Forward!* is one thing, but I don't honestly know that I could find the time to write kids' stuff for the *Standard*.'

'No . . . no, I see that. You've a lot on with the UNDER TWENTY-FIVES and your work. I merely thought . . .'

'Of course, if he's so *anxious* for decent articles . . .'

'Peter, don't you think it would reflect favourably on the party to have you in the *Standard* now and then?'

He sighed, set the red up for me. 'Oh, well, you bounder, if it's a question of my loyalty to the party I suppose I shall have to.'

'Good man!'

Well pleased with the morning's work, I applied my concentration to the now virtually impossible task of losing the game.

'Jesus, who's the dolly?'

I glanced through the nimbus of the powerful lamps to the viewing bench opposite. It was Esther Moore. Impassive as ever, she sat in a corner of the bench, alone. I wondered how long she'd been there, how I'd managed to miss her. I wondered if she'd been listening in. It didn't matter, but if I'd known she'd been there I'd have done my stuff with Peter some other time.

'Esther! Hello! You should have announced yourself. Have you got a drink?'

25

She smiled, close-lipped. It was a hot April day and she wore a simple sleeveless mini of navy blue, broken at the throat by a stiff white jabot Her hair was slightly bouffant and fastened at the back. She looked very pink and clean.

'My secretary,' I told him. 'She's going to catalogue my text-books.'

'Hell's teeth, what do you pay them to get that kind of talent?'

I whispered a curse. He liked what he saw. And if he wanted her he'd get her. He'd wrecked too many of my past cosy friendships. But I particularly didn't want her to be another notch on his belt. Which was a bad sign.

By a stroke of genuine luck I contrived to give him the game by a single point. We put up our cues and walked over to her.

'Peter Dowling,' I said. 'Our hard-working U.T. Chairman. Peter, Esther Moore, my hard-working Girl Friday.'

'And what do you do when you're not working hard, my dear?'

I'd seen girls flush with pleasure at that particular note of languid charm.

'Work even harder.' She briskly retrieved the hand he'd not yet released. 'Now that Bob's talked me into doing his books.'

His smile congealed. He wasn't used to rebuffs. But if he got one it simply made his pursuit more relentless. I knew.

'One day I'll find out how Bob can make every female in sight work her fingers to the bone for him.'

Behind the affability there was an unmistakable bitchiness. For some reason girls liked it.

'Perhaps it's his way of making work so interesting,' she said evenly, without smiling.

'Is *that* all it is?' I said, in my silly-ass voice. 'And I thought it was my fatal charm all the time.'

The tension had to be reduced. She did a good hatchet job, but it mustn't go too far. It was important that I wasn't linked in his mind with a girl who might give him a bad time. If he wanted her he'd better have her, because I wanted things from him.

Fortunately it was time for his rallying. He smiled tightly.

'You must bring Esther to our Bazaar Dance, Bob.'

As if I could keep her away. She was being so bloody with him it was almost certain they were going to wind up in bed together.

But when I turned back from seeing him off it wasn't him she was watching, it was me—with the same hungry look I'd seen in the car. It didn't bode well, but imagine being one up on Viscount Dowling.

I pulled in at the kerb, followed by the girl in her mother's tiny car. Emma was at the gate in a yellow dress with daisies on.

'Stay there, Daddy ! *Stay there!*

She climbed on to a rustic bench and then on to the garden wall. 'Catch !'

She hurled herself into space. I caught her, whirled her round and round till she screamed with laughter, tossed her over my shoulder. I turned to Esther, gave her my sad, wry smile. What could you do when there were kids involved?

'Her *pièce de résistance*.' I put her gently down. 'She can revolve hula-hoops and leap from a moving swing too. But she likes to start the show with a bang.'

'Are you Esther Moore?'

She gazed up at the girl's white jabot, at the aureole of her long dark hair against the spring sunlight.

'Yes—I am.' She sounded as if she'd not had much to do with small children. Uneasy. Bright. 'How did you know?'

'Mummy said you were coming. It's a pretty name.'

'Well . . . thank you, dear.'

'This is Emma,' I told her. 'Six and a quarter. The quarters are very important at her age.'

'What a pretty dress.'

'Can *I* help you with Daddy's books, Esther?' She grinned, casually took hold of her hand.

The girl didn't like it. She stiffened. You'd have thought she'd been touched by someone she found physically repellent. She looked down with a rigid smile.

I said : 'I'm sorry, darling, but it's all very complicated and you'd just be in Esther's way.'

'Is she staying to dinner then? Will you stay, Esther? We're having chicken and sauté potatoes.'

The girl hesitated, the tips of large square teeth on lower lip.

'I'm sure Mrs. Saxby is far too busy to make meals for a total stranger.'

'Dear girl, would-be M.P.'s wives spend a quarter of their lives making meals for strangers. Do stay—if you'd like to, that is.'

I opened the front door. I saw her looking at the taper-legged telephone table and the fan-back Windsor and the gilt-framed Victorian water-colours of the hallway.

'Bob!' Gwen opened a door. You could hear teacups rattling, assured feminine voices. 'This is Miss Moore, of course.'

'Esther—please.'

'Very well—Esther. And I'm Gwen. Jolly nice of you to give your time up, dear. So important for Bob to get his books in order. It's essential for him to be able to collate his facts quickly. For his speeches, you know.'

'I'll do what I can with them.'

'Splendid! Now, Esther, I know you're not one of us—Bob told me; that's why I think it's so decent of you to help him out. But if you want to come to any of our do's we'll be delighted to have you. And we won't try to convert you, I promise. The U.T.s have some marvellous disco sessions.'

'The welcome mat's already down, Gwen,' I said. 'Peter Dowling's seen her.'

'Ah, I *see*. I'll say no more. But remember, Esther, you're our privileged guest.'

The craftsman. No one could generate warmth like Gwen, not even me, we always turned her loose on youngsters toying with the idea of joining the U.T.s, she was a sort of political Billy Graham. I could see she regarded Esther as a real challenge.

Gwen went briskly off to join her ladies. I smiled wistfully at the girl—if only it was you and me, baby, instead of me and her. But the girl turned away with a sharp distracted movement. It went oddly with her normal composure. So did the look of utter wretchedness she'd turned away to hide.

It disturbed me. If she was a neurotic it really wasn't a good idea to play her along. I wondered how quickly she'd be able to do the books.

'I'll get my brief-case,' I said. 'I've made a few notes.'

I went in the living-room. I sensed her follow me as I fished through the bag, could imagine her looking at the decanters and the balloon-backs and the cabinet and the oil-paintings.

'Victoriana.'

'Mainly. We cheated with the telly and the gram.'

'But this cabinet's William and Mary, isn't it?'

I was getting used to the things she knew.

'Clever stuff! Gwen's grandfather gave us it.'

She passed on to the inlaid table, the one we'd eaten breakfast off.

'My favourite possession,' I said. 'Not that I care much about objects. Never at home to enjoy them.'

'Another present?'

'No. Gwen picked it up for a fiver. She found it in someone's cellar covered in bags of plaster and jam jars. She felt guilty about paying so little, but they thought she was some kind of nut to want it at all.

'You see, she buys antiques semi-professionally. It began as a hobby but people liked the stuff here so much they asked her to look for pieces for them. She's making quite a thing of it. Just as well really because my income will probably drop if I ever get to the Commons.'

I always went into detail with them about Gwen's activities, smiling ruefully. How bound up I was in the web of marriage, a young daughter, a career partly dependent on my wife's earnings. How was it possible to break away, to follow the dictates of my unhappy heart and walk hand in hand with them towards a Warner Brothers sunset?

It made them want to do things for me, that smile, fill tea-urns, address manifestos, sell jumble. Impassive as ever, she crossed to the french window, lit one of her king-size.

'You're lucky to be so highly organised.'

The inflection of contempt was so subtle you hardly knew it was there. It depressed me. She casually lifted the radiogram's lid. It depressed me even more to see an L.P. of *The Pirates of Penzance* on the turntable.

Gwen bought all the records, but how fatuous to point it out. Even though I wanted to, wanted to tell her I *knew*, knew all about Radio One and Sergeant Pepper and Bonnie and Clyde. Knew and longed for her salad days with a wistfulness that was only too genuine.

I smiled cheerfully. 'How square can you get?'

It was better upstairs, in the working atmosphere of my study, with its newly fitted shelves and its leather-topped desk, and the great jumble of books on the floor crying out to be given order.

'Bagehot,' she said. 'May . . . Campion . . . Redlich . . . Ilbert— have you actually *read* all these?'

I nodded. 'If you're aiming at Westminster it's as well to know the drill, I suppose.'

'They look very dull.'

'They are dull. The Commons is dull. Have you been in the Chamber?'

I picked up an old Order Paper.

'An average day—a Bill about Disused Graveyards. Docks and Harbours. Money. The Tees Valley and Cleveland Water Bill.'

I tossed it aside.

'Committees are coloured by the dullness of the dullest member. And yet things happen in committees. You learn to play them, when to appear to give in on one thing to get your way on another, when to be agreeable, when to be tough. Dullness is the price you pay for being involved in the most engrossing activity known to civilised . . .'

I broke off. That was no way to talk. You talked about the honour of serving and all the other meaningless crap, not your own complex kicks. And I always did with the rest. But she wasn't like the rest.

'You said you'd made some notes.'

'Ah, yes, the notes.'

I explained how I wanted them separating into subject order and then alphabetical order within the subject, with each title and author on a large index card on which I could enter my own comments.

She picked a paper-back up.

'*Geography of World Affairs*,' she said. 'Is that Geography or World Affairs?'

She smiled then, showing the big teeth for once. It shattered the balance of her face but I liked it a lot better than when she was being Jeanne Moreau. It was pointless playing at mysteries with someone who was old enough to know there weren't any.

'You're teasing me, aren't you? You know perfectly well what it should be. If not, toss a coin.'

Still smiling, we made a start on the books. My spirits lifted as the first handful were shelved and their titled lettering gleamed in the sunlight. Work had always been my anodyne. But it was also good to be one up on Dowling, to know that if I made a pass at this odd contemptuous girl I'd only get a technical rebuff.

'What made you go right?' she said after a while. 'Instead of left.'

I watched her until she stopped rummaging among the books and looked at me.

'What makes you think there might ever have been a choice?'

She watched me steadily, shrugged.

'Men of all types join both parties these days. Robert Maxwell, for instance . . .'

'But this is Beckford,' I said. 'And I work for Singleton Fisher and I married an Endersby. How can you think I might ever have been a left-winger?'

'There must have been a time when you didn't work for Singleton Fisher and hadn't married an Endersby.'

What did she know? What could she have found in chalk-fingers' notes? That I had working-class parents? What did that prove? Men of my upbringing could notoriously go left or right. Apart from that the record could reveal nothing. I'd once lived and breathed the Labour Party, but I'd never been a member and there was nothing in writing. Only Maggie knew about the left-wing phase. Maggie and a handful of friends now scattered across the world.

The door-bell chimed.

'The Bazaar Committee.' I glanced reluctantly at my watch. 'We'll have to continue this intriguing chat over our chicken dinner. Do you mind if I leave you to it now?'

She smiled. 'If I did would you send them away?'

She began to climb the folding steps with more books. I didn't believe in pretty girls with secrets. I'd been around too much, *les illusions* had been too long *perdu*. But the youth was still father to the man and I had to admit that I wouldn't like to see her go until I'd solved her riddles. Wouldn't like to see her go at all, in fact. But she would inevitably—to elegant bloody Dowling.

3

'I told him straight. "Mr. Simon," I said, "that Stock Book isn't no part of my duties. Never has been, Mr. Simon." So then he says, "Well, see here, Lambert, *I'm* telling you to get it up to date." So I looks at him. Not saying nothing, you understand, just looks at him. "Mr. Simon," I says, very quiet, "I mustn't touch that Stock Book without Mr. Saxby gives the word. Mr. Saxby's in charge of all that side of things." '

'You're a troublemaker, Lambert.'

'Eh?'

'A troublemaker, a gas-bag and an idle old sod.'

'Now look here, young Bob . . .'

'It wouldn't have taken half an hour.'

'Look, if he'd *asked* me . . .'

'He did ask you . . .'

'Ah,' he cried triumphantly. 'That's it, that's just it. He didn't ask me, he *told* me. Like I were a sample lad. Got right up me back. Now *you'd* have asked. "Percy, old chap," you'd have said, "would you be good enough to look on at the Stock Book till Joseph returns?" Not that he's going to be back overnight and his face that colour. Made me feel queer, seeing him cower again the fire like that . . .'

'Percy, there's plenty to do so go and do it and stop wasting my time. And that's bloody well *telling* you.'

He broke into a hoarse grating laugh.

'Ah, I can take it from thee, Bob. You've been here man and boy and we understand each other. But I won't take it from him.'

'Don't talk wet, Percy, he's the boss.'

'*Old* Mr. Fisher's my boss. And he'll see me through to my retirement, I'm thinking.'

'Percy,' I said. 'Sod off.'

'All right, all right, I know when I'm not wanted. Only if he upsets folk when he just comes in for a day or two what'll it be like when he's back for good?'

'Had your ear against keyholes again, I see.'

He cocked his close-cropped head on one side like a gun-dog, gave me his cunning squinty smile.

'Well, you watch him, Bob lad, if he does come back. It's always your department he pokes his nose into most. And whatever you decide to alter he always seems to be crabbing it—I've noticed that particular. You watch him, son.'

'You've got an hour to do the Stock Book, the Lot Book and the Stamp Book. If they aren't up to date when I come upstairs I'm firing you.'

He went off, his hoarse laughter echoing in the corridor. Martin had been hovering at the ante-room door; he came over, sat on the edge of my desk.

'I always seem to be queuing up behind homespun Percy Lambert to see you these days.'

I sat back.

'Isolate a single man from the ranks and cultivate him, you said. The way Napoleon used to do. Christ, I bet he never had a French Percy talking his gammy leg off.'

The perpetual faint smile deepened slightly.

'Still—it worked.'

I got up, turned round to the window. It was sunny spring weather with clean white clouds. The trees in the square seemed to be wrapped in green nets.

'Yes. I must admit I learn more about what goes on down the line in this place in ten minutes with him than I could find out for myself in a week.'

'He's one of a dying breed. A kind of wool trade equivalent of the Army's old sweat. Knows every dodge.'

'He's superb as a deliberate leak. I can just casually mention an idea for improved work-flow up there, and inside a couple of days I know whether the lads are going to wear it or not. If not, I can say I'd already had second thoughts about it; if they will, I can put it straight into practice.'

'And preserve your reputation for always making the right decision.'

'Yet none of them think he's a creep.'

'That's because they really think you're one of them. Working-class boy makes good and all that rubbish.' He smiled ruefully. 'You've an instinct for the camaraderie. You're at home among those foul mugs of ginger-coloured tea and the Woodbines and the fish and chips.'

'I had a great many fishermen uncles. They all drank mugs of ginger-coloured tea.'

He came over to the window and we stood for a while in silence.

'Bob, when are you going to see the Governor about Simon?'

I sighed. 'Today, I suppose. Knowing that you'll ask me twice a day till I've got it over.'

'You did agree it was an astute move.'

There was a faint rustle behind me. I turned round; it was the impassive Esther dressed in her grey office dress with the white cuffs and collar, placing various impeccable pieces of typing in my tray.

'Esther—buzz the Governor and ask him if he can spare me half an hour, will you?'

She nodded, went back to her office.

'Good man!' Martin said.

He was dressed as he'd been dressed fourteen years ago. They might even have been the same clothes, like him they looked durable enough—black jacket, striped trousers, tall collar starched like porcelain, stout black boots. He read on for fully three minutes before turning his bleak pale blue gaze on me.

'Yes, Robert.'

'Governor, you're looking remarkably fit and well today.'

In fact he looked as if he'd just caught sight of his backside. It was a system of opposites with the Governor. He rarely smiled at anyone except at Christmas, just in case you got above yourself; it followed that the more you pleased him the more po-faced he became. And nothing pleased him like a shovelful of flattery.

'I don't feel at all bad for an old man, Robert.'

'Governor, I simply can't think of you as old. To me, you look a man in the prime of life and have done ever since I joined the company.'

'And when would that be? Ten years ago?'

'Nearer fifteen, sir.'

'Fifteen, eh.' He picked a cigar up from the Benares ashtray and re-lit it. 'Just so.' He gazed at me unwinkingly for about ten seconds in silence. 'You didn't look the type who'd turn me out on the street. You seemed a nice polite boy.'

Some time ago I'd had a professional efficiency study made and pushed through a scheme for making all the clerical offices open-plan, so that there was a better work-flow from desk to desk. In a battle that had raged for weeks I'd finally talked the old man into relinquishing his original office so we could knock its walls down and square off the big new room.

Being turned out on the street, as he put it, was his single joke. He suddenly emitted three bird-like cries. When you'd been with the firm a number of years you twigged it was laughter.

I began to bray like a car engine refusing to fire, at the same time rocking and shaking and even clutching hold of his desk as if I might lose my balance.

Livid with delight, he turned abruptly back to his reading, which

34

I now saw was a copy of my latest management report.

'Mm. I can't go along with everything here, Robert,' he said heavily. 'But I must admit you appear to have detailed the main lines of my thinking rather well.'

'Thank you, sir.'

'I fear I shall have a number of objections to raise, even so.'

'But, generally speaking, don't you think we should push ahead with the bulk of it? The economies are beginning to show positive results and when the expense of the change-over . . .'

'It's the only way,' he said, in a voice like sonic boom, 'in these difficult times. Expenses cut to the bone so we're as competitive as it's possible to be. So many will not rationalise, do you see. They say : "I must sell at this margin to meet my expenses," not—mark it well, Robert, *not:* "Now where can I cut my overheads to reduce my margin?" Looking at it from the wrong angle, if you follow me.'

'Right as always, Governor. If only more of your contemporaries would move with the times as you've done we shouldn't be seeing so many fine old businesses folding.'

'Indeed.' His face was dark with pleasure. 'You see, my boy, all these things that seem so new to you young fellows—rationalisation, intensive cost-cutting, planned work-flow—they've all passed through my mind in past years. But I'm an old man, Robert, and I know the value of caution. Oh, I know what it's like to want to rush the fence, but I also know from long experience that when you're dealing with workmen and staff in a very old firm it's a case of softlee, softlee, catchee tiger. That's why I sometimes seem to be opposing your enthusiastic schemes.'

He fished a small gold container that held a box of matches from his waistcoat pocket, then glared irritably through his window at the city's skyline, as if the angular white buildings that were beginning to obscure the Gothic sheds of his youth were a personal affront.

'As it is,' he growled, 'Simon and I both think we must beware of going too fast. Simon frankly believes that things are changing faster than necessary. The memos, for instance—he's still not struck on the idea of jotting down one's reply in longhand on the original.'

'As a matter of fact, Governor, it was Simon I wanted to see you about.'

'Eh . . . eh . . . eh?'

For a moment he looked very old and very confused. He'd forgotten, for all his briskness and his buzzers and coloured door lights, that I was here for a definite purpose.

'Miss Moore asked you to spare me a little time, sir.'

'Yes, yes, *yes*!' he cried. 'It was about the report, wasn't it?'

'Well . . . no, sir, it was about Simon.'

'Then why on earth didn't you say so right away? Oh, good lord—I have a luncheon appointment in ten minutes.'

'What I have to say won't take more than five, sir. I wanted to suggest that when Simon comes back for good he might care to share my office for a while.'

'Share your office?'

'I rather thought that as practically every aspect of the firm's activities are touched on in my office it might well be as useful a way as any for him to take up the reins.'

He gazed at me in astonishment.

'Really, Robert, don't you think after his years of travel in the producing areas Simon must know more about the firm's activities than any of us?'

I arranged my face into a look of boyish guilt.

'Governor, you always seem able to see through my little machinations. I suppose I shall have to confess that I was hoping to have first call on his vast stock of knowledge of the areas. But I had thought also that I might be able to help him settle in by outlining the new procedures at this end . . .'

Mollified, he scowled. 'I *see*. For a moment you sounded as if you were preparing to break in a school-leaver. However, I grasp your reasoning—yes . . . yes, I daresay your department would be as good a point as any for him to embark once more on the stream of our prosaic backwater. Yes, very good. I shall put that to him. But, Robert, don't trouble him with *detail*.'

Martin spread a napkin on his lap, broke a crusty roll. 'What did God have to say then? Did he accept your supplication?'

'Graciously condescended to offer it up to the Only Begotten.'

'Good show! Did he keep you kneeling long?'

'Only long enough to assure me he'd forgotten more about cost-cutting than I'd ever know. But just as my forehead touched the ground for the third time he was kind enough to tell me I was rather good at putting his ideas into practice. We even had The Joke.'

'The Joke! Why, that must be three times in as many months.'

'Four. The Joke's having a banner year.'

'You'll be telling me he laughed next.'

'Something made him cry out. If it wasn't The Joke it must have been piles.'

Grinning, he poured himself a glass of claret and began to eat a thick game soup. I rarely ate anything at lunchtime except a straight steak, two green vegetables and a glass of water. He'd once said we ate like an ascetic and an alderman.

'Good work, Bob. It couldn't have come easy.'

'Trouble is, the old devil *still* makes me feel I'm about nineteen. He sits there with his big bushy eyebrows in front of those paintings of his father's father and nothing seems to have changed since the day I came.'

He watched me in silence as the waiter began to serve the main course, in my case the modest sirloin, in Martin's the cutlets and French potatoes, the creamed carrots, the onion rings in batter.

He poured more wine. 'The Governor thinks he's God, ergo he *is* God. And because he's convinced he's God people can't help an instinctive feeling of awe in his presence.'

'Which just proves how second-rate he is. He might *look* as tough as those men in the oil-paintings, but he can't hold a candle to them. They deliberately fostered the mystique of Fisher infallibility as a business gimmick, but he just believes in it. They *never* believed in it, they only believed in themselves and their talents.'

'Bob, if you were the product of a talented family with a successful business already built up wouldn't you be tempted to think you were something pretty special?'

'Not if I was such a lousy businessman. If he'd got an *ounce* of flair . . .'

He smiled, his face deepening into a network of wrinkles. 'But the firm's prospered under his leadership.'

'Of its own volition. It's like a West End hit. Top-flight actors create the original roles and then a year later the second stringers take over, but the money keeps on rolling in.'

'Even second-string actors must have very good basic skills. The Governor's got genuine qualities. He's got an instinct for picking the right men to do the real work—you for instance, and Garbutt. And he can grasp new ideas, even if he never has any of his own.'

'Oh, yes, he's particularly good with other people's ideas.'

'All right, so all ideas become his property, but he will at least act on them. And he looks good. You and I know this business couldn't survive today without hard-faced crafty swine like you and Garbutt, and we know a lot of our activities are only just this side of the law. But we've got the old lad fronting for us, with his high collar and his black boots, and we've still got the indestructible reputation of merely wanting to turn an honest copper. The trade tends to think of Singleton Fisher as a carriage and pair—they don't know about your jet engine. They will, one day.'

'And what good will it do me? The trade'll think it's the Fishers themselves who've modernised so cleverly. A second-rate old man and a drunken layabout. And the Fishers'll be in complete accord, Christ, that's what really rankles, the Fishers'll be absolutely convinced it's all been their own work.'

The waiter removed our plates. Martin asked him to bring apple charlotte and coffee.

'You're being bloody boring,' he said mildly.

'Well, I'm the brain, for God's sake. They're just names. They'd hardly be in business at all if it hadn't been for my methods.'

'There is no point in criticising the Royal Family. The Fishers are there and that's that. It's their firm, their money, their mystique and their hired brains. You either accept it or you get out.'

'Perhaps I'll do that. I could go to Artfiber tomorrow and make some real money.'

'If real money was what you were after. Oh, come off it, what good could Artfiber do you politically? The Fishers need you and you need the Fishers, so stop whining.'

'It's easy to recommend a stiff upper lip when you've never had anything to whine about.'

He sighed, poured coffee from the glass flask, lit one of his small cigars.

'You're not just boring me,' he said, 'you're depressing me. *Every* time I think you've really got it out of your system you start whipping yourself up again. You regress like a five-year-old.'

'Look . . .'

But he'd picked up a back number of *Punch* from the window-ledge and would not listen to me.

Walking back along Cloth Hall Street to the office, I broke the silence.

'All right, I regressed. I've spent half the morning listening to a second-rate old man explain my ideas to me and I regressed.'

'You're ten years on, Bob.'

'And don't forget I'll have that other drunken clown actually sharing my office in a couple of weeks.'

'You're ten years on and you're a politician. By now nothing should make you lose your cool.'

'I'm worried,' I said. 'That's really the trouble. The old chap's got to retire soon and what then—Johnny Walker for boss.'

'Don't be naïve. We know he's a layabout but the trade doesn't. As far as the trade's concerned he's been doing the producing areas like other father's sons. The boozing's irrelevant—the trade's always winked at the heavy drinker. If anything, the travel and booze will have enhanced the mystique. Don't worry, old lad, we'll sell him to Beckford all right. Give him something to play with and work round him, the way we do with the old man.'

'I wonder if he really will stop drinking.'

He paused at the entrance-hall steps, the faint smile deepened. 'You know, I think there's a good chance. They're a tough breed and they have an instinct for survival. If he gives himself chance he might find that work's more fun than fun.'

'It'd suit me.'

He watched me steadily. 'Right then, let's get him fenced in. This is your acid test. If you can force yourself to work in harmony with him in the same office the bad old days really will be behind you.'

I nodded wryly. We got into the lift.

'To be fair,' he said, 'it's a long time since I've seen you quiver with rage in quite that grand Russian manner you used to have. I was certain I'd come in one day and find him lying by your desk with a paper-knife through his heart.'

'Next, I'd like to talk about stock wools. In particular the N.A.S.A.s.'

'I can't see why,' Garbutt said. 'As I see it, you add the books up and we worry about the wool.'

'Roy, I'm not trying to tamper with the technical side . . .'

'Damn right you're not!'

'At the same time, having costed every sale of N.A.S.A.s over a twelve-month period, I can tell you we broke even on two-thirds of them and made a loss on the rest.'

He flushed. 'Look, everyone *knows* they don't make much.'

'They don't make *anything*.'

'All right, we know that, we all know it. Dammit, we stock them because some of our people want a few now and then. The same people, I might add, who buy big weights of the types that give us a good profit.'

'They're a loss leader, then?'

'You can cut that fancy talk right out. We stock them so we can offer our people a complete range. They come to us for N.A.S.A.s, they come to us for hundred bale lots of Cape.'

'Well, I think they'd come to us for the big stuff whether we stocked N.A.S.A.s or not. They come to us because we've got them. If we hadn't got them they'd get them where they could, but they'd still come to us for shipment wools *if* the price was right. Believe me, it's the new economics of this trade.'

'Look, I'm not arguing with you. My decision is that we go on buying. Governor, may we have your opinion?'

'Robert, you really must leave the question of the actual buying and selling to we technical chappies. We've always prided ourselves on our range.'

'Quite right, Governor.' Garbutt flushed again, in triumph this time. 'We're *renowned* for our range.'

'With respect, Governor, each year we buy several hundred N.A.S.A.s and other oddments, ship them, insure them, finance them, warehouse them and sell them at a loss. Money senselessly tied up. Now keeping a wide range was all right in the 'fifties but these days we've *got* to concentrate on certain money-spinners. Let some smaller firm without our overheads dabble in N.A.S.A.s. My point, I repeat, is that if we're right on price we'll get all the business we need without using N.A.S.A.s as sweeteners.'

'Look, *I* want to go on buying them, the Governor wants to go on buying them and ten to one the others want to go on buying them, so that's that!'

Predictably, the rest of the managers all nodded in righteous indignation.

'Robert, it's not entirely *money*. It's part of our service. We're known in the trade for our range. People respect us for our wide knowledge.'

I said : 'Darcy, Pepper kept a wide range of stock wools because they thought people expected it of them. You could ask them for anything and they'd have it lying in a warehouse somewhere. They

40

were *very* respected. They were the most highly respected firm in town just before they went into voluntary liquidation.'

A long embarrassed silence, broken only by the sound of Esther's pencil calmly recording what we euphemistically called the feeling of the meeting. Men's eyes met mine and skated away, as if they'd caught me talking to myself in the street. The Governor began a woodpecker tapping of his battered silved cigar-case on the table, a sure sign of extreme irritation.

Abruptly Garbutt spoke. 'The meeting's agreed that we continue buying N.A.S.A. wools into stock. Put that down, Esther.'

'Oh, come, Roy . . .'

'You keep your bloody nose out of it !'

'Enough !' The Governor's cigar-case crashed down on the table like a gavel. 'Roy, I will *not* have the language of the tap-room in front of this young woman. Robert, you seem to revel in thrusting Darcy, Pepper down our throats. You seem to bring it up every week.'

I spoke slowly this time, and in a gentle faintly aggrieved tone.

'I'm sorry, Governor. Perhaps I worry too much. I was very upset to see a fine old family firm like Darcy go down because they hadn't concentrated on priorities. Roy, no one can move wool like you can—I find it hard to believe you need to use N.A.S.A.s as a lever.'

He flushed yet again, this time with suspicious pleasure. I'd set in motion two aspects of his powerful sense of pride. He wanted to go on buying them because I was against it—that was his basic reaction. At the same time he couldn't bear to think that if the meeting forced my agreement I might then believe he really couldn't sell as well without them.

'Roy,' I said quietly, 'shall we leave the decision till next week?'

'Oh, all right. For God's sake let's get on. The bloody . . .' He glanced guiltily at the old man. 'The stuff doesn't sell itself while we're all argy-bargying round this blessed table.'

'Leave it over ! Leave it over ! It'll give me time to study my source analysis,' the Governor boomed obscurely.

Garbutt fell back in his chair and reverted to staring glassy-eyed at Esther's bosom. The other five or six managers began a fretful discourse about their point of view. I listened with cordial indifference. Garbutt was their leader and what he said went.

I sensed the girl watching me. She was isolated from the rest of us at the opposite side of the great circular table. Cool and capable in her white-cuffed grey dress, she skilfully projected her usual aura of mystery. No wonder Garbutt was spellbound. I detected hostility in her steady gaze. I wondered if it was the trappings of capitalism that upset her—our talk of liquidity and margins and interest rates, the stark quest for money. It was a far cry from the crystal reaches of pure socialist theory, the gentle ebb and flow of academic life.

I liked it, the disapproval, it rubbed at my nerves like Bartók. She was intelligent enough to be aware of my skills and it flattered my ego.

Despite herself, she was attracted to me, and pretty girls being attracted to me had always given my performance a top gloss; some of my best speeches had been made to an adoring U.T. on the third row. The meetings had always been the best part of Singleton Fisher : since she'd come I waited for them with the eagerness of an actor awaiting his cue.

It was time to cut off the N.A.S.A. wrangle. 'The next item, gentlemen,' I said firmly, 'is the matter of a possible further reduction in the clerical staff. I'm convinced that by normal retirements and wastage we could steadily cut back on one clerk in three.'

'It'll be like a flaming sweat-shop,' Garbutt said, the light of battle beginning to rekindle in his small bloodshot eyes. 'It'll be like mailorder.'

'But they'd get more money, Roy. They'd get a proportion of the displaced clerk's salary.'

'And half his work each.'

'They'd sooner work at pressure than have time dragging. I remember when *I* was in General.'

'*Robert!*' The old man's voice clubbed the room into silence. 'Before we start on that I want to settle this matter of a tea machine in the sample room. You *must* see that the men won't have it. I'm astonished you thought it practical. The men like to infuse their own tea in those . . . ah . . . great pots. It would be out of the question to expect them to have tea in *plastic* cups from a *machine*.'

'With all due respect, sir, I can't agree. We pay an elderly man several pounds a week to do little else but make tea. A tea machine would fulfil the same function and save us a wage . . .'

'No, Robert ! The men would walk out !'

'Like Armley Gaol !'

'Like a concentration camp !'

42

'Like a bloody bus station !'

Having loosed a hare that all could instantly spot, give full vociferous chase to, and satisfactorily annihilate, I sat back in my chair looking hurt.

'The tea machine,' said Martin, in the silence of my office, 'was a plant.'

'Exactly. They were so pleased to beat me to a pulp over that one they let me have the cut-back almost out of pity.'

'And the N.A.S.A.s. That was masterly, Bob. You've beaten Garbage over that one.'

'I fancy we'll be able to slip it past quietly next week. I'll find something else he can wipe the floor with me about, to take his mind off it.'

'Poor Garbage. So cunning in some ways, so simple in others. He walks into the trap every time.'

'He half knows it too. His instincts warn him the trap's there but he can never see it till he's in it. That's why he gets so vicious.'

He crossed to the window and opened it on the distant roar of traffic and the warm, faintly scented spring air.

'What a lout the Garbage must have been as a lad. You can see him at the back of the class glowering at the clever devils like you. You can see him coming alive twice a week when he was allowed to boot leather about. And now he's getting his own back. Somewhere deep down he always suspected real life was selling things to other great louts, and now he's got seven thousand a year and an automatic four-point-two to prove it, not to mention that string of used-looking dolly-birds he does frightful slobbery things to on the back seat. He's paying them all back, those clever sods who looked down on him from the commanding heights of mere academic brilliance, and he's paying them back through you and me.'

I joined him at the window.

'And it puzzles him because we don't seem to envy him like his sidekicks do,' I said. 'How can we possibly face life without boxes of cigars and crates of Scotch and a different jump every night? I have considerable respect for Garbage, even while looking on in fascinated horror. No one can keep shop like us but without Garbage and the money those fantastic appetites force him to pull in there'd be no shop for us to use our talents on.'

'Your talents.' He smiled ruefully. 'This firm's you and him. He makes the money, you make the money work. Even Garbage can't entirely convince himself all you really do is tot the books up.'

'He gets bloody high marks for trying.'

He set off towards the ante-room door.

'By the way,' he said. 'Devaluation—do you think there's anything in the rumours?'

'Harold's scotched it, hasn't he? We're supposed to be back on course and picking up speed.'

'I know, but people keep bandying the word about and it worries me. Maybe we ought to start thinking carefully about covering currency.'

'Right, we'll talk to the banking lads.'

'Perhaps we'll see you at the Bazaar Dance?'

She smiled faintly. 'And the Bazaar.'

'And the Bazaar?' I looked up from my desk.

'Gwen asked me if I'd mind helping out.'

'She *would*! She jolly well would! Oh, really, Esther, we can't expect you to put a full day in up there. It's just not on. I'll speak to Gwen. Doing my books is more than enough, without slogging it out at the Bazaar.'

'I've promised,' she said, a little too quickly. 'I've been assigned cigarettes and chocolates.'

'Oh no. It won't do. We can't expect that from a non-member. It's more than decent of you, but ...'

'She can't get anyone else. The girl who was going to do it's gone down with appendicitis.'

Her eyes widened : her mouth fell open on the large teeth. My hostility startled her, coming as it did after those cosy moments in my study and drinks at the George Hotel, after what amounted to a tacit acceptance that a state of flirtation existed.

But this was something entirely different. This was something she'd deliberately engineered, despite what she'd said about Gwen, and I didn't like it. I controlled my flirtations like I controlled everything else in my life.

I watched her steadily for a moment, then went back to signing my letters. I'd let it ride. If I went on trying to force a veto she'd immediately assume she was getting under my skin. She had to be played with dexterity.

I didn't like it.

I liked it.

4

'The Chairman of the 'Fifty-eight Committee,' I said. 'The facts.'

'Golf,' she said. 'Plays a fair game. Only hobby outside politics. His wife has the antique bug. Not any old tat though, she knows the best.'

'Chelifer collection?'

'You *could* mention it. Don't push it if he's not personally interested. He likes to talk as if he's in the know about national politics, Pop says, so let him ramble. The rest—his record, committees—you'll have read up.'

'An hour ago.'

'He likes you. And Pop's given you the build-up. But give him the full treatment, you'll badly need him next spring.'

'They're a national disaster!' cried the Chairman of the 'Fifty-eight Committee. 'And the reins of state must be wrenched from their grasp.'

'CHAIRMAN OF POLITICAL COMMITTEE ON OBSCENITY CHARGE', I could imagine Martin murmuring. 'Indecent exposure before packed bazaar.'

'Need I list their failures? Squeeze and freeze, S.E.T., Corporation Tax, continued flights from the pound, *another* rebuff from General de Gaulle? Can anyone in this room think of *one* major issue on which this luckless Government has made the right decision?'

He smiled wryly at the crowded room without speaking until he'd got the kind of silence you had in a Hitchcock film after the murder noises had stopped.

'And worse to come, ladies and gentlemen,' he continued in a subdued voice. 'For only yesterday I heard strong rumours of heavier taxes yet, of a savager deflation still, of even . . .' his mouth suddenly twisted as if he had to overcome a profound distaste to speak the next word at all, 'of even devaluation.'

He took his glasses off, a weary doom-laden gesture. I wondered if I ought to have a pair made with plain glass, as a prop.

'What nightmare is this?' he cried. 'What terrible precipice are

45

we hovering above? What fearful rock is the ship of state bearing down on if there can even be speculation that the mighty pound, a *reserve* currency, is itself in danger?'

A packed, silent room. Feathered hats, flowered hats, hats bearing half-pounds of artificial fruit. I wore my funeral of an employee face, women wore keep death off the road faces, men wore Normandy-landing faces, U.T.s wore Outward Bound faces.

Esther's face was as impassive as ever.

I let my eyes meet hers at last. She'd never stopped watching me throughout the speeches. Now, perversely, she looked with the rest towards Mr. Vereburn.

She wore a summer dress of muted greens and oranges and yellows, her dark hair had been tied at the back into a soft green bow. She stood behind a U.T. stall in sunlight from a high side window. She looked very pretty.

She'd turned up early that morning, had put a smock on and had thrown herself into setting up tables in the tea-room. The older women had thought she was a new U.T. and had promptly accepted her with preoccupied gratitude. The girls of her own age had been wary.

They didn't know why they were wary. Like them, she was unmistakably middle class. Perhaps it was the almost unnerving containment, the total absence of shyness among a completely strange group, perhaps they sensed a superior intelligence and were made uneasy.

But they knew she was different. And their reactions were like radar echoes of my own. She *was* different. Different enough to be dangerous. And she had to go, books or no books. She'd been found guilty of forcing the pace.

What normal girl could want to stand at a cigarette stall for the whole of a fine spring day, simply to be in the same room with a married man on the verge of total commitment to public life?

'Do you agree—a layabouts' charter?' he demanded. 'Do you agree?'

A violent wind seemed to blow through the feathers and the fruit. They agreed.

'Come, ladies and gentlemen, we want men we can trust in Downing Street.'

'Hear, hear!'

'To hold our head up in the world again.'

46

'Hear, hear!'

'A reduction in the fearful burden of taxes.'

'Hear, hear!'

'Freedom of choice in the schooling of our children.'

'Hear, hear!'

'Then, buy, buy, buy at this splendid bazaar and you'll not only be helping to get all those things, but filling your pantry at the *same time*!'

He bowed, waved his hand in deprecation at the prolonged and tumultuous applause, and sat down. Soon afterwards the proceedings were wound up and the room reverted to its earlier confusion —Constituency Men to stack chairs, tea-ladies to don smocks and elderly women to rummage balefully through brilliantly coloured woollies.

Cocktail-hour music stole raggedly through the speaker system; I regarded the scene dourly from behind the clip-on smile. My idea of hell was a permanent Grand Spring Bazaar, buzzing with tunes from *The King and I*, foetid with the scenty pong of middle-aged female flesh and haunted by Councillor Turman's smile, a smile that Martin had once said reminded him of Bacon's screaming popes.

The moment Turman let go of the Chairman of the 'Fifty-eight Committee, I slid my hand under his arm.

'Excellent speech, sir.'

'Ah, Bob!' He looked relieved to see me. 'Didn't let you down, I trust?'

'We always pull the big spenders in if we're lucky enough to get you to speak for us. This room would have been half empty if it hadn't been for you.'

His eyes shone with pleasure.

'Bob, do you think we could escape from the customers for five minutes. The heat, you know.'

'Our little office. Perhaps I could offer you something a little stronger than tea.'

'You certainly could, my boy!'

I led him upstairs and into silence, past the darkened and sheeted billiards tables to the private office.

'Brandy, sir, I believe, half and half with soda.'

'You've a valuable memory, Bob.'

'Thank you, sir. Here's your good health. How's the handicap?'

47

'Try to keep my form, you know. But what time have men like us to spare for developing a really decent game?'

I modestly inclined my head.

'By the way, you talked about devaluation as if you'd heard it was more than a rumour.'

'Nigel Marten-Greene. You met him? Fine fluent speaker. Came over for dinner last night.'

'*Really?*' I put my visibly impressed look on. He put his head back, half-closed his eyes, passed a hand delicately over immaculate grey hair.

'Close friend of the Shadow Chancellor. They dined together Sunday. Ludgate's certain they'll eventually devalue. Part of their over-all strategy.'

'Didn't know they had one.'

He laughed shortly. 'Good, that, very good. I was speaking in the loosest possible way naturally.'

'Do you think it would be all bad—a devaluation?'

'Do you?'

I'd asked for that. He looked blandly on, but his eyes were watchful. He might be the kind who spoke one way and thought another, or he might have meant exactly what he said downstairs.

'There's an all-party school of thought that thinks the rate's at an unrealistically high level.'

'And are you a member?' He poured himself another lavish brandy.

I decided on the truth. It sometimes worked, even in politics.

'I believe I am. It might be better than all the tinkering around they're doing. Bound to increase exports, I should think, and cut back on home demand. And if it brought us more into line with the other currencies it should spike the French argument that it's our high rate that keeps us out of the Common Market.'

'Yes, Bob, I can see all that, but it's this business of confidence. It is a reserve currency.'

'Perhaps it's time to get out of world banking then and turn ourselves into a straight industrial nation.'

'Perhaps. There's no doubt it's getting to be a remarkably difficult role to sustain. Though I personally believe it should be sustained.'

But he smiled amiably; I felt he respected my outspokenness.

'Well, Bob, if they *do* devalue I'm not saying it won't help us.

48

Could give us the best of both worlds—an improved balance of payments and a stick to beat them with at the next General.'

'Shall we defeat them, do you suppose?'

He gave me the hooded look again.

'I shall be at the Commons in May, as Marten-Greene's guest. He's giving a luncheon party for Ludgate and Chanctonbury and one or two others. Ask me when I get back.'

'My word! I certainly shall, sir.'

'As far as Beckford goes I think we've got a good chance of East. North and West are hopeless, of course, but a hard struggle might give us South.' He gave me a direct glance. 'With the right man up you might just sway the balance.'

'Oh yes—we've got to find a man of the right calibre.'

Someone like the brilliant Bob Saxby, for instance. But they liked modesty, particularly in men as outstandingly able as I. Perhaps, my tone suggested, if the other candidates all suddenly had seizures there might then be a faint chance for me.

'Well, Bob, must be off.'

I took him by the arm.

'It's been an honour,' I said simply. 'Thank you so much. And do give Mrs. Vereburn our warmest regards. Did she know, by the way, that Gwen's been given the chance of handling Miss Charlotte's furniture?'

'Really! The Chelifer stuff. By jove—yes, I'll tell Nancy.'

'If she'd like Gwen to take her over there any time she only has to ring.'

There was someone outside the door of the office. I'd felt a minute upward pressure on one of the floorboards I stood on. I'd noticed it before now and then when the games room was in use.

'Excuse me, sir, one moment.'

I took a single stride to the partly open door and flung it back.

Outside stood Esther.

'Oh!' A hand flew to her breast. 'Oh, Bob—you gave me such a start. I was just going to knock.'

'Oh.'

I was convinced I'd startled her: but not that she'd just been going to knock. How long had the floorboard wobbled—seconds . . . or minutes?

'Gwen sent me. She's very sorry to disturb you, but Emma's feeling ill. Gwen wondered if you could take her home fairly soon.'

49

We watched each other. She had a perfect alibi but just how long had she been listening in?

'Oh—I see.' I gave her the crinkly smile. 'Thank you, dear.' I turned back to the Chairman. 'Sick offspring, sir—I've been called to the rescue. This is Esther Moore, one of our helpers.'

'Jove, Bob, you've got some remarkably pretty gels in Westbury. How do, my dear. Thank you so much for the splendid work you've put in. Fight the good fight, eh, fight the good fight. "Hard pounding," to quote the—ah—the—ah—Duke of—ah—of—ah . . .'

'Wellington,' she said calmly.

'Ah—quite—Wellington. Quite so. Bless me soul, brains *and* beauty, Bob, eh? Yes, Wellington it is, my dear, as you say.'

With a faint smile she walked away from us. We watched her go in silence, and I wondered if he felt he'd missed out too, on that world of new erogenous zones and flowing hair and wistful music and bright clothes. Standing there, among our yellowing piles of old manifestos and campaign posters, her glowing youth seemed to inflict a similar sadness on us both.

Downstairs, the stalls had been virtually looted and the hats, like tiny galleons, were beginning to sail steadily towards the calmer waters of the tea-room. I found Emma in the kitchen, perched on a table near the door looking crestfallen and pale.

'Sick?' I said grimly.

She nodded. Her bottom lip trembled slightly.

'Jelly and cream?'

She nodded again.

'How many lots?'

'Five.'

'How many lots did Mummy know about?'

'All except three.'

The typical almost absent-minded cunning forced a laugh down my nose. She smiled tentatively back.

'You've been very very naughty, haven't you?'

'*Extremely* naughty,' Gwen said. She stood at my side, holding a teapot the size of a small dustbin. 'Particularly when exactly the same thing happened last year.'

'Sorry, Mummy.'

'Then do as you're told in future, young lady. It's a good job we were near the sink, that's all I can say.'

'I'll take her home, Gwen.'

'Better still, take her along by the river for half an hour. There's nothing much here now except the clearing up.'

'All right. Come along, naughty Emma.'

Before we left I thanked the tea ladies for their work at charming length, assuring them that the real slog was always in the kitchen, and inviting them to have a drink with me at the Bazaar Dance. I gave them all, plain and pretty alike, a faintly suggestive smile, a watered-down version of the smile I gave their daughters. The sort of smile that Martin had once said projected a thoroughly tasteful hint of dick.

'Esther, I have to go now. I can't begin to thank you for your work. Are you mobile?'

'I'll get a Circle. Mother needed her car today.'

'Come along,' I said cheerfully. 'Couldn't possibly let you go home by bus after all this.'

It had grown hot, with the humidity of diffused May sunlight through a fine haze. The clubhouse stood near private houses on a main road; the air was heavy with the odours of their gardens, the smell of newly turned earth, of sap and grass clippings and opening bud.

I shivered. I didn't like spring. It reminded me too much of poor Maggie, of that old desperate search for happiness and glamour.

'Are you coming to the river too, Esther?' Emma said, shyly eager.

'That depends on your daddy, dear.'

'Might as well. Fresh air wouldn't do you any harm either.'

It was a good chance to do a thoroughly tasteful hatchet job.

We entered the woodland that skirted the bank. It was bright without leaf cover. The river flowed rapidly with the spring rains and it gave a freshness and movement to the air. Emma's colour was already coming back.

'I could hardly believe you'd find time from all that public duty to walk in the woods,' the girl said.

'I suppose I'd better confess to moments of uncontrollable impulse,' I said. 'I'm flawed. Week in, week out, I can throw myself into campaigns and bazaars and committees and tea-club talks, and then all at once something snaps. Suddenly I feel I must live, have fun, spend entire half-hours on river banks. Cackling wildly to myself I rush across to the island in Westbury Lane and shriek at passing cars : "Loveliest of trees, the cherry now, is hung with bloom along the bough. About the woodlands I will go. To see the cherry hung with snow."

'But no one ever takes any notice or stops, except occasionally to ask me where the Calor Gas Company is or how to get to Cleckheaton.'

Emma was jumping up and down between us.

'Was that a poem?' she said. 'Was that a poem?'

'It was indeed, Em.'

'I know one. Listen—"Humpty Dumpty sat on a wall, eating fresh bananas. Where do you think he put the skins? Down his best pyjamas." '

She looked up expectantly from Esther to me.

'Mm. I think I prefer Housman, Emma, to be scrupulously honest.'

Suddenly Esther snorted with laughter. And then again. I looked at her. She was almost trembling with the effort of self-control, but a moment later she was forced to give in to natural laughter. It was something I'd not seen before.

Her face seemed to fall apart. When she smiled the teeth had always broken the balance of her features. Open laughter made her face seem to distort and melt like a crushed rubber mask of outstanding goofiness.

But it wasn't off-putting. It should have been, but it wasn't. It simply increased her attraction to the point of giving me a telltale flicker across the guts. I half-wished I hadn't seen it.

She stopped laughing, her jaw muscles white and clenched with the effort. I knew now why she rarely laughed—she despised those melting features herself. The normal inscrutable mask represented a continuous concentrated effort. She was like an actress exploiting a gamine look or a sexy voice; she was pushing a characteristic to its limit. The relentless pursuit of an appearance she could live with impressed and faintly chilled me.

'Laugh at Emma at your peril,' I said. 'She'll say it all over again now.'

Emma did so, running ahead and shouting, emphasising certain words and screaming with laughter. But the girl only smiled now.

Depression seeped across my mind. Youth. God, how well I knew the scene—the silences, the poses, the world weariness. I'd taken girls in, girls had taken me in—only youth could be fooled, only youth had the freedom and the time for make-believe. I walked on forlornly beneath budding trees. What a pathetic figure I seemed, telling myself she had to go. As if she wouldn't go anyway. I only had to solve the rest of her riddles. I only had to make her life ordinary by my scepticism and my ageing presence and she'd run a mile.

'I thought Mr. Vereburn rather sweet. He really sounded as if he believed all his slogans and half-truths.'

Emma had run off into the distance, the white of her pants showing beneath the blue dress now and then like a rabbit's bob.

'He does believe what he says, Esther, and most of what he says makes sense.'

There was a dangerous temptation, with a woman of her intelligence, to be as cynical with her as it was possible to be with Martin.

'Surely he doesn't go on like that in private.'

I remembered the moving floorboard; but she was smiling innocently.

'I trust you're not darkly hinting at wheeling and dealing in smoke-filled rooms,' I said. 'The sum total of our private conversation is that Vereburn believes the right man could win the party South.'

'You, for instance.'

I hesitated warily. 'Everyone knows I wouldn't refuse to let my name go before the Selection Committee. Along with about six others, two at least of which have the university background I lack.'

We came to a small clearing round which stood a grove of silver birch, now hung with crimson catkins. The mossy ground gave way to a stretch of river-sand which sloped gently beneath a shallow part of the river.

'Can I paddle, Poppa?'

'All right. Five minutes.'

'Will you come, Esther?'

'Next time, dear.'

She took her sandals off and walked squealing into the fast-flowing water. All at once I shuddered, to see her standing in the hard spring light against shimmering water and the forest trees of the opposite bank. It was like the inexplicable emotion aroused in me by certain piano phrases heard in silence late at night.

The girl's voice, curiously harsh, cut across my absorption. 'But it'll almost certainly be you. As Prospective Candidate?'

I turned back with an effort. 'I know the division and I know the people. I'll give them good service. And the machine knows I'm entirely serious about politics.'

'But what if you aren't selected? Or are, and get beaten? Will you try somewhere else?'

'No. If I don't get South I shall invite the good people of West-bury to second me on to Beckford Council.'

She looked puzzled. So much so that she forgot to be impassive and let the tips of her teeth appear.

'I thought you wanted to be a career politician. All those books, the planning . . . I thought you'd want to be a Junior Minister at least.'

'No. I want to be a perfectly ordinary M.P. for a single term and then I want to devote myself to Beckford Council. If they'll have me, of course.'

'I don't understand. All that studying—aren't you being a trifle excessive?'

'Any kind of political ambition needs homework. I feel that if I had a decent run at Westminster it might convince Beckford I'd be a long-term asset to their Council. I've always considered my real future lay with Beckford.'

It was a public duty statement and I was using my public duty voice, a voice Gwen had advised me to base on the timing and warm breeziness of Kenneth More's; we taped the soundtracks of his old films off television. The girl turned irritably away.

She lit one of her long cigarettes. I lay back full length on the sand. The smell from the river hit me.

The dear, dead days. I looked at the distant bridge; from it when we'd been sober Maggie and I had just been able to define the shapes of fish among the glittering shallows. One evening she'd suddenly begun to hum the rippling music Schubert had written to evoke trout in rippling water. I'd not trusted myself to speak for minutes.

Later, I found out that the Quintet theme was her father's favour-ite piece and that he'd once arranged it for a brass band, and that apart from the top twenty it was the only tune she knew.

I sat up. The girl was motionless, gazing wretchedly at the flowing water.

'We'll have to go,' I said.

The river smell had been an omen, and I believed in omens. I didn't want to know anything else about her and I didn't want her around me any more.

I helped Emma to dry her feet; we set off back to the car.

'Shall you come to the dance?'

'Yes.'

'Shall I pick you up?'

'I'd sooner you didn't.'

'I understand. It wouldn't look well to your parents. Do they know what you've been up to today?'

'No.'

'Esther . . . I don't honestly want you to do any more party-work for us.'

She watched me steadily. 'Gwen . . .'

'I know. I'll speak to Gwen. Her enthusiasm sweeps her away.'

She shrugged. 'All right.'

'Oh, dear.' I smiled the crinkly smile. 'How churlish I seem. It's simply that I don't believe it would be ethical for you to get involved with the inside stuff. Of course, we'll always be delighted to have you to the dances and U.T. do's.'

'And the books?'

'Oh, well, let's leave the matter of the books for the time being. But please don't think I'm ungrateful. I only wish we had more U.T.s who worked half as well as you.'

We regained the bridge; my car stood beneath the trees. We both paused, both looked down at the clear fast water. She shrugged again, a delicate coltish movement of her body in the soft-coloured dress.

'All right, Bob—if you're not happy about it. Perhaps I should join the U.T.s.'

She looked at me sidelong, my eyes were cold behind the grin. It was said to tease, I knew the contempt she had for the party and its works. And she knew I was warning her off.

She proceeded now at her own risk. If she tried to go on with the game I could legitimately get rough. And I could get very rough.

5

She came into the bedroom naked from the bath. I put my arm round her, squeezed a large firm breast.

'There's nothing,' I said, 'quite like a handful of warm moist talcumed bubby.'

'No time for that, old chum, you're due back there again in half an hour.'

'Three minutes is all I'll need in this heat.'

She held a dark green dress against her body, hurriedly stuffed it back in the wardrobe.

'You'll neeed all your energy for dancing with the tea-ladies.'

'Not if I stick to slow foxtrots. Go on—adopt some riveting dalliance position.'

'If it's all going to be over in three minutes you can't expect the dance of the seven veils.'

I pulled a clean shirt on. She'd be game if I was. I watched her fasten herself into girdle and bra. I still liked the feel of her body, I still liked the vigorous *Après le bain* look of it, and I still liked entering it. Which was pretty good, after ten years.

I slipped on the jacket of my nice dark suit, adjusted a striped tie neatly in its blinding white collar, filled my old-fashioned case with hospitality cigarettes. I looked down for a moment at evening shadow inching over close-cut turf, at Emma playing by the pool.

So much love-making, so little love. She'd twigged in a flash, the girl. No wonder she thought I was wide open for a take-over bid. Nice Bob Saxby trapped in a loveless marriage. Goodness, how sad.

I turned away. The trouble was sometimes it *was* sad, on a hot, odorous spring evening. But then, it was only to be expected. After all, I'd married her for what she was, she'd been the finest horse for the course—healthy, sexually inventive, a walking political machine. I recalled how two or three days ago it had struck me that never once had we ever said—'I love you'.

How shocking, how obscenely calculating it would seem to the girl. Gwen's happiness, of course, would mean nothing to her. The fact that our marriage worked perfectly wouldn't be the point at all.

Gwen was humming the theme from the *Die Meistersinger* overture—proof that she was extremely happy. I looked at my watch, sighed. Time to go. It worked. It worked like a computer. Gwen for sex and Emma for love, and ambition filled the gaps. It was only now and again, on spring evenings, that I had a brief sentimental urge for the sort of love the girl would believe it was impossible for a man as nice-looking as me to live without.

'Whose idea were the gift-boxes?'

'Mine.'

'Congratulations.'

'You know, it made the biggest return on its outlay of any other stall.'

'Do you suppose you could talk Norman into believing it was his idea?'

'Good thinking. I'll do it.'

'Are you off now?'

'Yes, I'll see you later. I want to give the kids a big thank you.'

'Invite them to supper next week as a gesture. Nothing elaborate —booze, coffee, patties, records.'

'You're in cracking form tonight. I wish I'd had that three-minute jump now.'

'Ask them for Wednesday. Quiet day on the antique front.'

'Right. I'll spontaneously think of it as I'm chatting them up.'

'And don't forget your new chum. She's a dynamo, that one.'

I paused on my way out.

'That reminds me,' I said. 'I wish you hadn't talked her into serving on, Gwen. She's not even a member.'

Puzzled, she stood watching me with her dress half-zipped. '*I* didn't talk her into anything. I merely complained about being short of a girl and she promptly volunteered.'

'Quite. In order to flirt with me.'

'Don't they all?'

'She's getting oppressive. I see her every day at the office, don't forget. I'm just afraid it might start to look naughty once the members have caught on she's my secretary.'

'Naughty! *You*, naughty? After ten years of chatting up? My dear man, how can one girl possibly stand out among that mob that never stops flocking round you?'

Her voice rose in amazement. She'd virtually built the Bob Saxby we presented to the ward, that clean-cut, drip-dry, deodorised all-purpose male we clipped a crinkly smile on and sent knocking at

57

council-house doors. The image was now exactly right; if it hadn't been she'd have re-jigged it inside twenty-four hours. I was being faintly absurd.

'All right, all right, just don't encourage her any more. She's got it bad and she could be trouble.'

She shrugged, began to brush her hair.

'Very well. It's a pity though. She's a real worker.'

I stood on the lawn in the late sun.

> *'One, two—three-four-five,*
> *Once I caught a fish alive.*
> *Six, seven—eight-nine-ten,*
> *Then I let it go again.'*

Emma was skipping in the drive. I walked across to watch her. I remembered the way she'd looked by the river, standing against the hard light in her short dress. Poor Esther. It was always the same with single girls who fancied you, they always saw your wife as the sole obstacle. They never really got the hang of the kids.

'Catch, Daddy!'

Emma swarmed up on to the wall as I came up to the gate.

'All right, but this has to be the *last time*. You know what Mummy thinks about little girls leaping about like monkeys.'

I caught her and held her in the crook of my arm for a moment. She grinned, squinting into the late sun, one tombstone second tooth dwarfing the milk teeth.

'Bye-bye, Poppa. Bring me some streamers and a paper hat. A green one. And put them on my bed-table, won't you, in front of Mr. Noggs? You won't forget, will you—just in front of Mr. Noggs.'

I got into my car, blew her a kiss, pulled slowly away. It was always the same with single girls. All they could tell was how little you loved your wife, never how excessively you might love your daughter.

'Great!' I said. 'Absolutely fantastic! We've made *half as much again* as we did last spring, and that was one of the best we've had. Thank you very much, all of you.

'Do you know what Mr. Vereburn said? How does South always seem to have the keenest U.T.s? Easy, I told him, in South we involve our U.T.s. We don't just ask them to do the dirty work and then tell them to go away and play, like certain other divisons do. We've made it an absolute rule that if they share the work then they must share the decisions. And that's why our bazaars go with such a bang. Right, friends?'

'Right, Bob.'

Heads nodding enthusiastically on every side. Except one. Hers.

'Well, I simply don't know how to thank you enough for all that marvellous graft. Look, this calls for a celebration—how about coming to my place on Wednesday for a bite of supper? And bring all your pop records—we'll have a right old rave-up. There'll be plenty of hard stuff for them that drinks, and non-stop coffee for them that don't, and hot snacks, and you can come when you like and go when you like. All right? You'll honour me with your actual presence? Good—I'll buy a pair of ear-plugs!'

Their approval was almost tangible, like radiated heat. Laughing and nodding, they began to drift away to where the men in the band were setting their equipment up. Only Esther remained. She wore a plain white shift with a high collar flecked in silver and her dark hair had been drawn from her face and fastened at the back with a large white bow. We watched each other; the battle for Bob was still on.

'Full members only?' she said ironically. 'At your soirée?'

Before I could reply we were joined by Peter Dowling—all flared tweed and flowing golden hair.

'Esther—I'd be honoured if you'd enter my name on your dance-card.'

She smiled so warmly at him it made him flush. It was against the rules for her to smile like that, it showed too much of her large teeth. The band struck up, he swept her away, she didn't look back.

New gambit—show Saxby how much he's missing. She never let up.

'Hundred and fifty more than last year. Fully. *Not* including the dance.'

'Yes, we've done well, Bob.'

'That gift-box idea of yours was an absolute winner, Norman.'

'BANK CASHIER ON ASSAULT CHARGE,' Martin had once whispered. 'Interferes with girl during Hokey-Cokey.'

He looked at me with faded blue eyes, began to pack a great pipe with Three Nuns.

59

'Oh, was it my idea?'

'Well, it certainly wasn't anyone else's.'

He puffed smoke out deprecatingly.

'I can never tell when we're all jawing round a table. The ideas just seem to arrive. You think it was my baby, then?'

'I *know* it was. I remember wishing I could dream them up as easily as you seem to.'

'Mm, odd that. I can never tell where they come from when we're all jawing round a table.'

'They come from you, old lad, most of them, despite friend Turman hogging so much of the credit.'

'Well, we did better with me as Bazaar Secretary than we did last year with him, didn't we?' he said, demurely venomous.

'The proof of the pudding's in the eating, Norman. He just isn't an ideas man.'

I glanced out sharply at the dance-floor, certain I'd catch her watching me. But she was smiling into Dowling's eyes, and from the way he was gazing at her she'd been smiling into them ever since they'd begun to dance. For one so young she really did have style.

I took my cheerful leave of little Norman and began to work my way round a room now filling with older members, squeezing an elbow here, patting an arm there, asking after health, thanking people, occasionally kissing an elderly woman on rouged cheek in the filial manner Gwen assured me I'd brought to a peak of artistry.

Then I saw them again. The music had altered and they were now doing one of those jerking modern dances, all subtle footwork and waving arms. I tried to turn away, but couldn't.

Their beauty knocked the breath out of me. They glowed with youth, their sheer physical aura seemed to bathe the rest of us in reflected radiance. The colours of them, of their skin and hair and clothes, and the contrast of their gyrating bodies, of her high breasts and illusive fragility against his hard maleness and his broad arrogant shoulders, filled me with a sudden unbearable envy.

And I craved it terribly for a moment—that wistful land of Twiggy and yellow submarines and frilly shirts and Steve McQueen.

I made some excuse to leave the old women, to get away from the dance, from them, jerking and swaying and smiling at each other. I stood in the entrance-hall, a place that echoed with the special sadness of dance music at one remove, trying not to think about them having it off together, of red lips crushed against pale, soft flesh clamped against hard muscle, gold hair mixed with dark. Because they would have it off together sooner or later, they were too right for each other not to.

Or would they? Wasn't that exactly what I was meant to think, that I didn't turn her on any more and he did?

I didn't know. Right then all I knew was that for the first time she'd turned *me* on. If the bitch was still playing games she'd won the set.

Upstairs, in the bar, I bought my tea-ladies the drink I'd roguishly promised them. Then I sat down at a small table with Olga. Olga was a tease. She was very pretty and she looked very available. Squeeze me, her buttocks seemed to say, like those plastic liquid-soap dispensers, and some men had done. Her outraged scream, I'd been told, could be heard on the other side of Westbury Lane.

I bought her drinks and flirted with her. Like all art it looked more convincing than real life. For our own good reasons we'd both developed latent acting talents, and I'd never seen her in better form since the night she'd tempted poor Alderman Brighouse into risking a handful. Bob Saxby, a potential M.P.—this was the big time. We talked softly, as if we were alone in the room, faces almost touching.

Later, when the girl came into the bar with Dowling, she stopped short as if she'd reached the end of a rope. For all her self-possession she hadn't been ready for me and Olga. I never once looked directly at her, but I saw from my eye-corners that radiant smiles had given way to bright ones, volubility to mere chat.

The honours were even and the game was still on. It was important I knew.

'Peter—how did you make out with Watts?'

'Oh . . . told me to send my *Forward!* articles along to him. Depending on what he's pleased to call getting my hand in he might commission two or three articles later on.'

'Splendid! Your this week's article had a much simpler style than usual. Pity you have to write down, of course, but there it is.'

'Get my hand in, by God!' he drawled. 'Fellow's got delusions of grandeur. How about that, Esther, being told to get your hand in for a comic like the *Standard*.'

Even praise of his writing didn't cheer him up. The evening had gone all wrong for him. For some inexplicable reason she'd suddenly stopped gazing into his eyes and smiling at him and hanging on his words.

'Well, Peter, he needs humouring, you know. If you've got the only decent paper for a ten-mile radius you do tend to think of yourself as a sort of village Rees-Mogg, I imagine.'

'Father says it's the best balanced paper in Yorkshire,' Esther said coolly, face turned outwards towards the dance-floor.

'That's not saying so damned much, is it?' he muttered.

'Can I have this dance, Esther?' I said. 'It's some sort of medieval gavotte known as a quickstep.'

I was angry with her for using Peter. I'd need him badly next spring; I didn't want him to remember it was me who'd introduced him to a girl who'd given him the run-around.

The band was playing *June is Busting Out All Over*. I moved on to the floor with her. He stumped moodily off towards the bar.

'Just in time,' she said.

'For what?'

'To stop Peterkin turning ugly.'

'Is something bothering him?'

She smiled wryly, looked away. She wore no scent. Her only smell was that of new clothes and hair washed in plain soap. Clever stuff —she'd still smell fresh when the scents of the other women were staling. I could feel the warmth of her flesh through the white dress and I remembered how badly I'd wanted to hold her when she'd danced with him. So badly that I'd not have allowed myself to dance with her at all if it hadn't been necessary to seperate them.

'You dance very well,' I said.

'So do you. You must come here often.'

'Alas, my style is frozen at that distant point in the early 'fifties when they were still writing songs you could foxtrot to. When they still had dance-halls with sensible orchestras, such as Dick Steeton and the Steetones. Never missed a Saturday at one time.'

'In your suèdes and your collarless corduroy jacket,' she said. 'Smoking your French cigarettes.'

I suddenly shivered. I could feel my short hairs prickling.

'How do you know that? How can you possibly know?'

I'd almost stopped. It made her miss a step and our bodies briefly collided. She gave me a startled glance.

'Well, how *do* you know?'

People danced on every side; it wasn't easy keeping the wide public duty smile clipped on.

She shrugged. 'Didn't everyone wear things like that in the good old days? And smoke Gitanes bleu?'

'Corduroy jackets might have been the rage, but only mine had no collar. It was a fashion twist all my own.'

'It must have been a good guess.'

A week ago she'd asked me why I'd gone right instead of left. Tonight she knew the exact clothes I'd worn fifteen years ago. Who could be telling her these things about me? And why?

'How's Bob?'

'Wilting. How's Gwen?'

'Ready for bed. You don't suppose any of your girl-friends are going to hold it against me for actually dancing with my own husband?'

'Not if I look thoroughly bored.'

'By the way, you've omitted to take Dolly Waterhouse in your arms.'

'Christ, so I have! You don't suppose . . . just for once . . . ?'

'No. The Alderman's too important to us. We don't want her telling him you danced with everyone but her.'

'All right, I'll trundle her round. The B.O.'s in full strength, I imagine.'

'I've rarely known it worse.'

I nodded cheerfully at Mrs. Turman. 'You callous, bloody swine,' I murmured.

'I'll ignore that. Don't forget, I've had Turman and the home-made lager half the evening. Another thing—before you swirl off with Dolly—keep a seat in the car free for Esther, will you?'

I smiled. How crashingly obvious. But then, the evening was almost over—she had to act quickly.

'I thought she'd come in Mummy's.'

'She's not allowed to use it for nights out.'

'What about Viscount Dowling?'

'Drink. Too much for safety, she says.'

'Safety of what? Her life or her honour?'

'Don't go on. She is your special chum.'

'I *knew* she'd be in my car tonight. You won't listen to me, but I just knew.'

'I shall worry now,' she said, grinning. 'About you driving off into the night with her and never coming back.'

'All right, *be* smug. I've a good mind to let her seduce me just to teach you a lesson.'

The music ended, we finished our dance. Not far away stood Dowling, flush-faced, glaring sullenly at the balloons that were starting to fall. At his side, like an ice-maiden, stood the now totally indifferent Esther.

'But I must admit,' Gwen said, 'that if a gorgeous creature like young Peter had wanted to take *me* home when I was her age I'd have been too swept aside to even know he'd had a couple.'

'You don't surprise me—fast randy cat like you were.'

'*Beast!* Ah, *Dolly*—Bob's just been asking about you . . .'

It had become cold and very clear. The lights of the ring road flickered in the valley like diamonds on black velvet. On one side of us was a dense screen of poplars which cut off a private nursing home; on the other, the reservoirs, two dark sheets of water on different levels—one feeding the other down a narrow stepped gully. The faint roar of water boiling down that gully was the only sound.

The scene had been set with my usual efficiency and now I waited. I'd deliberately dropped Gwen off at home before going on with the girl, just as I'd deliberately drawn to a halt on this quiet road.

'Why have you stopped?'

I took a leaf out of her book and shrugged without speaking.

'You had to go out of your way to drop Gwen off first,' she said.

I didn't reply and the noise of the water began to grow again in the silence. I could remember that sound from the days when I'd gone about with Maggie. We'd often crept up to the embankment above the reservoirs, usually after we'd been to the Tatler to see the sort of film that left us excitedly convinced I was going to make the grade as rapidly and dramatically as Bill Holden or Gregory Peck. We'd made love to that roaring gully sound. Roaring water and rasping breath.

'Why have you stopped?'

I made no reply. A moment later she laid a hand over mine. As it rested there, soft, warm, faintly moist, I ran through the final details rapidly.

Very slowly I began to raise the hand on which hers lay. Then suddenly, when our hands were level with my face. I jerked hers

64

savagely off. I rounded on her, took hold of her and kissed her so hard teeth ground against teeth. I pinned her body down, dragged open her raincoat, clamped my hand straight over her breast. At the same time I began to press my abdomen roughly and obviously against her thigh. Then I waited, for the moment of shock to pass, for the frenzied struggle, the blind panic, hands clawing in fear.

She was amazingly strong. I'd always suspected the sturdiness masked behind the apparent fragility of slenderness and soft hair and delicate features, but she almost broke free at the first attempt, even though I'd been ready for her. First the head frantically trying to shake itself free of my clenched arm, then the hand scrabbling at the one that clamped her breast, then the legs kicking and squirming against the obscene pressure of my abdomen. It was all working out perfectly.

It took me perhaps another fifteen seconds to see I'd got it all totally, diabolically wrong. She *was* struggling, struggling with every ounce of her strength—but not to get away from me. The hand I'd been certain was tearing at mine was actually clenching it more firmly against a breast that itself was being pushed even harder against it. The mouth that finally dragged itself away did so only to apply those large square teeth with more pressure still. Her thighs didn't squirm for release but for more closeness.

Her mouth came against mine again and again, her arms began to tighten round me like steel bands. I was astounded. She'd chased me, and I knew she wanted me, but nothing she'd said or done had given me any idea about all this. Dazed, practically reeling beneath the onslaught, I automatically continued the routine I'd planned.

Then I slackened. She went on, holding and kissing me, but when I sat there completely still she finally released me. She sighed heavily, sat back on the seat. I could see her profile against the paler darkness beyond the car, black as a woodcut, the bluntish nose, the slightly open mouth, the flowing hair.

It hadn't worked. I rarely misjudged a situation these days and being so utterly wrong about this one had given me almost as big a shock as I'd been certain I was going to give her.

'All right,' I said at last. 'I'll make it nice and simple for you— *get out of my bloody hair!*'

'Bob . . .'

'Christ, you ought to be running terrified down Water Lane now.'

'What do you mean?' she cried. *'What do you mean?'*

'I was trying to scare your pants off, you silly bitch!'

'I don't know what you mean!'

'Is that what you wanted—rape? You must have been scared, you *must* have been.'

'I . . . I was *surprised*. At the suddenness. But I didn't mind it. Not you. Not you. I wanted it. It was the same for me as it was for you. I couldn't help it either . . . Oh, Bob . . .'

'For God's sake, shut up! It was not, repeat not, blind passion. It was a deliberate plan to scare you off. For good.'

After a while she said : 'Is that the truth?'

'Yes. I gave you the gypsy's warning this afternoon, *and* you know it, but you persisted in playing the fool.'

There was a prolonged silence. The sounds of cascading water slowly grew again as she smoked half a cigarette. 'I don't believe it.'

'Why? Because I smile so nicely and kiss old ladies? I thought you were brighter than that lot.'

'I am,' she said in a low voice. 'I know all about your popular image. But I don't believe the man you really are could be capable of something as vile and calculated as that.'

'Then you've been fooled by the image behind the image.'

'Oh, *Bob*.' Her voice broke. 'Can't you just admit you wanted to do it? I'm sorry. Most of it *was* my fault, but please don't pretend you did it on purpose. At least be honest . . . so . . . so we can decide what to do . . .'

'Stop!'

She moved away in alarm.

'Don't start that! Don't! *We* are not doing anything. *You* are getting out of my hair. Tonight. Understood?'

'Oh, *please*, you're not like that. I know you're not like that . . .'

'How do you know? How can you possibly know?'

'Because . . .'

'Go on.'

'Because I can tell. Beneath all that empty charm I can tell there's something genuinely decent.'

'Stroll on! Bloody stroll on.'

'You sound like him when you speak like that. Like Peter Dowling.'

'You've researched me. And don't give me that nonsense about

Daddy's dossier. That wouldn't tell you about the left-wing phase or the collarless jacket.'

'They were chance remarks . . .'

'Rubbish. You've dug deep and hard. You came to Fishers' fully armed and you made a set for me right from the start. You were between boy-friends and it looked a good way of relieving the boredom of that intelligent mind. Let's see what makes Saxby tick. Let's see if he can be tempted. Let's see if he catches if we throw.'

'Oh, *stop*! *Please* stop. You can't begin to understand how wrong you are.'

'It's a game. Research Saxby for kicks and then, very mysteriously, begin to drop little odd facts into the chat that'll make him wonder, that'll intrigue him, that'll perhaps even titillate him into an affair. Then if he makes it to Westminster there'll be all the kinky satisfaction of recalling the first time he made a grab for your knockers in Water Lane.'

She was shuddering. It was exactly the reaction you'd expect from a decent young girl and I knew I was totally wrong. Not that it mattered if it got me rid of her.

'Look, bitch, don't kid yourself this is the start of anything. You'll know all about enemies of promise, won't you, with your A-levels? Well, I've got more promise than anyone you'll ever meet, and booze hasn't caught me, or prams in the hall, or a difficult youth, and you can be absolutely certain I'll never be caught by any dangerous slags like you . . .'

'Oh, *please*!'

It was a genuine cry of pain. I switched the engine on, did a jump start, drove rapidly down to the main road. What could the truth about her possibly be that I couldn't even begin to guess at?

At Heylands Avenue I leaned over and pushed her door open.

'Goodbye,' I said. 'I hope you're going to leave me alone now. I'd hate to have to get really rough.'

'Do you?'

'Do *you*?'

'It always makes us sleep well.'

'It's got the edge on Horlicks.'

We abandoned our nightclothes in the darkness and drew together to begin that highly refined series of caresses and manipulations.

'You were a long time,' she murmured, shuddering slightly. 'I imagined all sorts of abandoned scenes in parked cars.'

She turned away with a slow fluid motion, so that I could stroke her breasts and the insides of her thighs from a new angle, fitting her body against mine like an interlining.

'This must be the acid test then. If I can't make the grade I'll clearly have been having it off with Esther.'

'Having it off indeed! Where do you hear these things?'

'Esther—who else?'

She chuckled; we languorously adopted new positions, so that it was she, breasts rubbing against my shoulder-blades, who now stroked my chest and thighs, softly drew fingernails across my abdomen.

'I gave her the hard word tonight,' I said. 'As I'd imagined, she was rather keen to hold hands in Water Lane.'

She gently bit my shoulder.

'Pity—she was a worker. Need you have been quite so ruthless?'

'You don't take her half seriously enough. Believe me, she's trouble.'

'Oh, Bobbie, what chance has she against a man of the world?'

Again we turned in slow motion, face to face this time, each of us using both hands in a dozen well-rehearsed pressures and contrasting feathery touches.

'I shall want to begin soon. *Very* soon in fact.'

'Which way?'

'Like . . . this, this time?'

'Lovely! And your legs . . . like that?'

'You are a beast. It plays havoc with certain muscles.'

'Mind-blowingly sexy, though.'

'Where *do* you hear these things?'

Finally we began. Our sex-life had always been very good, we'd worked on sex like we'd worked on everything else, few people could have wrung more pleasure from it. Tonight, entering her sumptuous flesh was pure contentment. Everything was finished with the girl and I was back to normality, back in the exact context of a life that had been planned in detail years ago. Our grinding bodies sparked no love, it was just straight sex, but it was very good sex, the best-quality article, as befitted a man who'd carried off the Endersby girl and fully proved himself as a money-spinner, a home builder and a man of ambition. I was safe with old Gwen.

The rigid shudder of her orgasm was within seconds of my own. Exhausted, we lay on our sides, our bodies resting inwards one against the other, sexual craftsmen exulting in the skills won from a lengthy, painstaking apprenticeship.

I shut my mind down and fell asleep with her soft heavy body in my arms. But it was the girl I awoke thinking of, kissing me as Gwen had never kissed me, with the ferocious desperation of emotional depths beyond Gwen's nature.

I'd gone wrong with Esther. I should never have kissed her. She wasn't going to bother me any more, but it was going to take a long time to forget being kissed like that.

6

'Strange animals, women.'

'Oh, do get out, you old rubbing-rag.'

'Take the missus. Pictures. Big feller—John Wayne. This woman locks him out of the bedroom. Big feller says : "If you don't open this door I'll smash it in."

' "No !" she shouts. So he smashes it in.

'The wife *wouldn't* stop talking about it. "*You'd* never do a thing like that," she says, reckoning to laugh but sour-graping as well, know what I mean? "Not in a thousand years. You're just not romantic, Percy Lambert, and you never have been."

' "Maybe not," says I. "Maybe not. And I'll tell you for why. *He* can go about kicking doors down 'cause he doesn't have her getting him up at six o'clock to get it painted and back on its hinges. 'Cause that'd be his first job if he were wed to a stupid nagging cow like you." '

Percy was a card. He knew it and waited for hearty laughter with the confidence of a professional comic. For once I could raise little more than a chuckle.

'Are you not so good, lad? You don't seem quite your cheery self today.'

'I'm all right, Percy. Just got rather a lot on my plate at the moment.'

I'd woken up jumpy. I tried to gain confidence from my large desk, from the battery of phones and the intercom box. Only the Governor, Garbutt and I had intercom boxes. Usually I only had to slide behind this desk to feel in command, to feel I was exerting that intangible influence that gave the firm its focal point of brisk efficient industry. Today I felt dwarfed by it, dwarfed almost by my own former achievements. I felt vulnerable.

'I understand the young feller's coming back today.' He flicked his head back scornfully. 'Wouldn't you know it—couldn't start on a Monday like anyone right in the head.'

'You'll have to keep your nose down now, you idle old git.'

'Ah—like his dad for that. Eyes in his backside. Might not be no good for nothing else but always knows who's having a smoke up the lav.'

It was always the same, meeting him at intervals. It threw me back like nothing else could these days. Back to a nicer Bob, back to a man who'd seemed genuinely outgoing and capable of normal love, a man who'd seemed to care about people as individuals, to be a man of ideals. A man aware of an ability to lead but who'd still considered it of supreme importance the led were consulted.

But that Bob hadn't been tested.

I got up restlessly and gazed out through my high, privileged window. That was before he'd tapped the wells of hate. And perhaps if I'd never known him they'd never have been tapped, I might still be on nodding terms with the old Bob.

Not that hatred hadn't done me proud. My whole way of life was founded on it, and what was more I was clever enough to know it. I was that enviable creature, the well-adjusted man. Most of the time I could get along perfectly well with the man I'd become. It was only when Simon appeared that I found myself measuring the man I'd become against the kind of man I'd once wanted to be. And getting depressed about it.

'How long do you think he'll stay this time then, eh, Bob? A month? I'll lay you half a sheet he's gone again the end of May.'

'You'd better sod off, Percy. I don't want you here when he comes —you're not his favourite person.'

'Happen you're right. He'll be round soon enough to see how much string and sticky tape the lads are using.'

But as he moved to the door it was suddenly flung open and Simon

Fisher himself walked in. After ten years of strenuous leisure the prodigal son was back for a heaped-up plateful of fatted calf.

'Hello, Robert.'

'Simon, how nice to see you again.'

'Lambert.'

' 'Morning, *Mr.* Simon.'

They eyed each other warily, like tom-cats who'd inflicted equal damage on each other in past battles.

'Lambert, every time I return to the office I seem to find you taking up Mr. Saxby's time in some way.'

'Ah, well, *Mr.* Simon, it was necessary for me to look at the Prog. Book which happened to be on Bob's desk, whereas normally it reposes in the warehouse office.'

'Prog. Book?'

'Progress Book. It's what Bob had drawn up special to follow every parcel of wool right from being bought to being sold, for every department. But you'd not know about it, sir, would you, with having been away so much?'

He stood near my desk wearing his squinty half-smile. I'd never known anyone with quite his flair for respectful insolence.

When he'd gone Simon sat down slowly on top of the desk I'd had brought in for him.

'I thought we were supposed to be cutting the number of books down,' he said. 'Not spawning more.'

'It replaces six deprtmental record books,' I said. 'It goes from department to department every morning for entering, and Lambert looks after it. It's a kind of instant encyclopaedia of the firm's operations.'

'It doesn't seem a very sound idea to me. If no department's personally responsible for it, no one will trouble to enter it very well, I should have thought.'

'We've built a number of safeguards into it.' I said. 'And of course it was basically the Governor's idea.'

'Oh. I see. Then if Father wanted it it was obviously necessary.'

I held out some papers. 'Perhaps you'd care to see the details of this afternoon's meeting.'

I watched him read. Like his father, he hadn't changed much in a decade. There was no grey prematurely streaking his black polished-looking hair and he had the sallow Fisher complexion—

71

in his case it effectively masked the marks of prolonged drinking. The only clue to his alcoholism lay in the minute red lozenges on his cheekbones and the insect-wing vibration of the hand that now held a lighter to a thick cigarette. His blue chalk-striped suit was well pressed and very fashionable—both father and son had a showy way with clothes.

'This rationalisation programme you all seem so hysterical about. I should have thought one of the first things it ought to do would be to weed out impertinent time-savers like Lambert. '

'Oh, well, Simon, it's hardly a matter of finishing anyone. It's a longish-term thing of not replacing certain men if they should leave or retire.'

'There's no sentiment in business, Robert, particularly when lay-abouts like Lambert are involved.'

'I . . . had always thought of Percy as a loyal and reasonably hard-working employee.'

'*I* had not.'

The door to Esther's little ante-room was ajar. Through it I could see Martin watching me, his face serious for once.

Simon tossed the papers down. 'I hope you're not trying to change everything for the sake of change. I see the memo question still hasn't been decided. I can't honestly see why the system should be changed there.'

'At present a girl spends half a day typing memos. If everyone scribbled their answers on the original memos she'd only spend an hour and a half.'

'And spend the time gained powdering her nose, I fancy.'

'I . . . did suggest a number of duties which could occupy the time gained. In those notes.'

'And this business of the N.A.S.A. wools, Robert. I do wish you accountant chappies would try to realise that the buying and selling of wool is a skilled matter that simply cannot be found in a text-book.'

'The watchword in modern business is concentration, Simon.'

He walked over to my desk. I saw his slightly yellowish eyes moving over it restlessly, over the buttons and the phones and the electronic calculator.

'I understand from Father you suggested some kind of briefing.'

'Ah . . . yes. I thought that if you'd care to sit in here for a month or so I could run through the broad outlines of the administrative system with you. Some of the changes have made a great deal of difference to the way things work.'

'I'm *quite* aware of that. It seems a reasonable idea, though I daresay a couple of weeks would be ample. However, I must ask you to let me borrow your desk for that period. I find it impossible to work without a decent light over my shoulder.'

'Oh, God—sit down.'

'My desk! For Christ's sake, my bloody *desk*!'

'Look, sit down and don't say a *word* for five minutes.'

'I'm going. This is it. He can stuff his bloody firm.'

'Yes, yes.'

'Let him run it the Fisher bloody way.'

'Look, just sit there till I've finished this and then we'll talk about it sensibly over lunch.'

'You heard him. I saw you in Esther's room. "Oh, Robert, get rid of Lambert," "Oh, Robert, you mustn't change things for the sake of it," "Oh, Robert, I must have this desk because I need the bleeding light over my bleeding shoulder." '

'So—what's a desk?'

'The straw that broke this camel's bloody back, that's what.'

'It'll only take an hour to get your phones re-sited. It's only temporary.'

'That's not the bloody point! It's my office and my bloody desk and I'm the bloody brain.'

'If you're the brain start thinking then.'

'Sod the Fishers. I'm going.'

'Go then. Let Artfiber snap you up. Let the Fishers run you down.'

'They can't do that. Not if I leave clean.'

'Oh, come off it. I'm not talking about Artfiber. Vereburn, Dowling, Telleyman—that mob. If you want the nomination you need old man Fisher telling them what a grand lad you are. If you leave he won't.'

'If I leave this firm it'll sink without trace in five years, do you know that?'

'Yes—but they don't. And even if it did sink they'd never connect it with you going. They have the name, the mystique and the money, and they're never going to twig about accountants being the new men.'

'It's no use, Martin, if that sod's back for good it won't work.'

73

'It'll have to work. You need them exactly as much as they need you.'

'I'll take the chance.'

'Not in this town. Vereburn's one of the Gov's oldest friends. Even with the Governor for you you might only just scrape the nomination. Without him you haven't a cat's chance.'

'Oh, *hell*!'

The waiter brought a full bottle of St. Julien.

'I insist on you sharing this,' Martin said. 'If you don't calm down you'll bring your migraine on, and there's the meeting after lunch.'

I let him pour me a glass and I didn't quibble when he ordered me jugged hare with all the lavish trimmings he usually had. We ate in silence in the tranquil costly atmosphere of the George's upper room, in the window-seat, with the blind down against another day of sunshine.

Finally he said : 'You're not on your own, you know. We're all going to suffer with him being back. Wait till he starts on Garbutt at the meeting.'

I shook my head. 'He's always twice as bad with me.'

'He always was. And look where you are today.'

I sighed, pushed my plate away, sat back in my chair.

'I sometimes wish I'd never known Simon Fisher. Or you, come to that.'

The smile deepened the network of wrinkles.

'It must have been destiny, old son.'

'My entire working career is based on hating that sod. How do you think it feels to know that?'

'I can't imagine. I've never hated anyone. On the other hand I'm not a top-flight accountant, a potential M.P. and the future strong man of Yorkshire.'

'I get so *depressed*. Sometimes I wonder if *any* of it's what I really wanted.'

'I should think you're in a state of reaction to that towering rage you've just been in.'

'It all seems so decadent somehow, forcing myself to stay because I hated him so much.'

'Dear, dear, what kind of evil Svengali-esque figure does that make me, seeing it was my idea that you should.'

'Don't,' I said. 'I really am pretty brassed off.'

'As you know,' he said, 'sympathy has never been one of my qualities.'

'Let's not kid ourselves,' I said. 'I nourished a hate object and you talked me into it. We've neither of us much to be proud of.'

He lit one of his small Dutch cigars; poured coffee from a glass flask. His face was striped by the bars of light through the blind and I could see his deep-set eyes watching me through blue smoke.

'You were an idle bastard,' he said. 'You were an idle bastard full of half-baked left-wing ideas. You were clever and you were a born leader, but if you'd left Fisher's you'd have done nothing.'

'You can't know that. I might have done just as well in quite a different way.'

'Rubbish! Simon and I were part of your destiny—I wasn't joking. You were a drifter and you know it, a spouter of working-class twaddle. But there were worthwhile things in you and fate placed you in the best place to exploit them—Fisher's. Where could you ever duplicate such spectacular inequality than in the wool trade? Where else could you have found someone as idle and wealthy and arrogant as Simon to bring all that hatred out? And where else would you have found someone like me to suggest how that hate could be refined into booster fuel? Fisher's was your forcing ground.'

'That's the trouble,' I said. 'I feel as if I've been so . . . so manipulated.'

He shook his head. 'You chose it, Bob. It might have been my so-called decadent wisdom, but in the end it was your choice that you stayed and deliberately used him to goad yourself on. And as far as I'm concerned if you chose it then it was the right way for you to go. Some people are made by the people they come into contact with; you're one of them. And not to put too fine a point on it, I think after all these years you ought to accept it and stop snivelling.'

We returned to the office the long way round. On fine days he always liked to walk through the gardens in Town Hall Square trying to decide which of the typists he'd most like to sleep with.

'All right,' I said. 'I'll stop snivelling.'

'Dear boy, you working-class types are born snivellers. I make allowances for it. To be fair, I must admit Simon is *not* an easy person. Twins, be God!' he said, glancing round. 'Imagine being in a massive bed with two who looked exactly the same.'

'I'll get my phones moved tomorrow.'

'Good man! And try to be *nice* to him, Bob. After all, you owe him everything. Doesn't it seem sad that the only real point of his existence has been to make you the remarkable man you are. Heavens above, you can see half her buttocks, look. You know, I sometimes think if you'd been born a Fisher and him a Saxby, handy-dandy, the situation would have been exactly the same. You're pecularly similar in many ways.'

'All ready, Esther?'

'Yes. Martin asked me to remind you about currency-covering. Rands mainly. He's worried there might be a snap devaluation. We'd make a heavy loss on South African wools.'

'We would too.' I made a note. 'Right, consider me reminded.'

'He definitely thinks we ought to cover but says will you do the talking.'

'Be like the bloody Civil Service working here.'

'Roy!' The Governor's cigar-case crashed down on the big round table. 'I will *not* have that kind of language in front of this young woman.'

'I'm sorry,' I said doggedly. 'But whenever you buy or sell on a big scale you must consult me or Martin. *We've* got to find the money and *we've* got to know the position of the money every hour of every working day. It's going to be the only way to keep ahead in this difficult trade, believe me, complete efficiency and being able to turn our money over faster than the next man. I'm sorry, Roy, but you've got to get used to the bits of paper.'

He snorted and turned away in disgust, to the sycophantic smiles of other, lesser managers.

'Is that all then, gentlemen?' the old man said.

'Not quite, sir. I'm sorry to bore the technical men with more financial matters, but Martin and I aren't happy about sterling. They could devalue. We're thinking about South African wool bought in South African currency. We believe we ought to cover our purchases forward.'

'Jesus H. Christ!' Garbutt muttered, in a voice just too low for the Governor to catch.

'It would cost money, Robert,' the old man called.

'A snap devaluation would cost a great deal more, sir.'

'It would be a disgrace!' Simon cried. 'They devalued the last time they were in power.'

'Quite so, Simon.' Mr. Herbert scowled fondly at his son. 'Monstrous, absolutely monstrous.'

'Governor, I'm a busy man,' Arthur Bratton broke in querulously. 'I don't even know what covering currency means. Can't we be spared these irrelevant details?'

'If it's money we should all know what's happening, Arthur. Covering forward means we buy the rands we'll need to pay for our wools with in advance of the actual cash settlement. In other words, if the pound was devalued in between Roy buying the wools and us actually settling the invoices, we wouldn't have to make up a nasty shortfall out of our own pocket.'

'Surely you've got that wrong, Robert,' Simon said. 'Surely if this appalling government devalues sterling the country we're buying from will have to take the loss, not us. Obviously we're not going to pay more than the original purchase price, but it will be in sterling that will buy less *outside* the U.K. It will be the suppliers' bad luck. That's the whole point of devaluation—to get our imports more cheaply.'

Silence. At first I thought they were as embarrassed as I was. But then Garbutt began to nod vigorously. And then the other managers. Finally the Governor.

It was one up to Garbutt. He knew who was right and who was wrong. He was nodding to annoy me. The Governor nodded because a Fisher was never wrong, even when he was wrong. The rest nodded because Garbutt nodded.

Martin gently kicked my ankle.

'Oh dear, am I mistaken? How stupid of me. For some reason I thought it would make imports dearer and exports cheaper. Getting the balance of payments into equilibrium and all that. Evidently I've gone astray.'

A curious thing happened then. Those tiny booze lozenges on Simon's cheekbones suddenly began to glow a deeper red. I watched him, smiling genially, and after a moment he turned curtly back to his scratch pad.

I was puzzled. He'd let me off the hook. For the past two years he'd only attended two or three meetings a year; I'd grown to dread them. He'd picked me up over every item, argued with me, sneered at me, made me look a fool before tittering Garbutt. And because a Fisher was never wrong, and because Martin had kicked my ankle almost raw, I'd always in the end accepted the humiliation of defeat. And it hadn't made me feel any better to know that my own ideas would be adopted the moment he'd left Beckford again.

'Well, gentlemen,' Martin said. 'Do we cover or not?'

'Not much point if it's the suppliers who lose on the deal,' Garbutt said. He grinned maliciously. 'I think we ought to table a motion that in future the finance department gets its facts right before it wastes our time.'

'We must cover, I think,' the Governor called. 'Whoever stands to lose. In any case we must retain the goodwill of our suppliers. What will it put on the price?'

'About a fifth per cent, we believe.'

'Then cover for a month and we'll review the situation in June. I really must go now, gentlemen, if we're quite finished.'

'The Garbage had a field day.'

'But why did Simon let me go free, for the first time in living memory?'

'That was *very* odd. I wonder. He's been to the drying-out farm, he wants to make a comeback, and he's older. Perhaps . . . perhaps he's just beginning to realise he's got to live with you, just as you've got to live with him. Somewhere beneath all that Fisher confidence he must *know* you're good.'

'Correction—good at putting his father's ideas into practice.'

'You handled him very well. I was proud of you.'

'I did grovel rather nicely, don't you think?'

'Keep it up, old son.'

'Stay there, Daddy! Stay there!'

'No, Emma! Mummy gets so cross about it. You promised me you wouldn't do it any more.'

'I'm *here* now, Daddy. If I don't jump I'll only have to climb down again.'

She settled it by launching herself into space. I caught her, shook her gently, tried to ignore the ingratiating tombstone grin.

'Look, young lady, *no more jumping*.'

'Don't worry about Mummy, Poppa. She's in the kitchen.'

'It doesn't matter whether Mummy can actually see you or not. She doesn't like it and neither do I.'

'Ian and Gregory jump off the wall when *their* Daddy comes home.'

'But they're boys. You're a girl.'

'And so does Sandra.'

I sighed. Not only did Sandra jump off walls, she climbed trees, fought boys and hurled half-bricks at dogs. I let the matter drop as usual. I liked catching her. After the sort of day I'd had in the office I liked to see her grinning face close to mine.

'There's someone to see you.'

'Who?'

'Guess.'

'Lady or gentleman?'

'Lady. She's got a pe-pe-peculiar hat on.'

'It must be Mrs. Fisk.'

'No.'

'Mrs. Luke then.'

'No.'

'I give in.'

'Esther!'

She was sitting on the Windsor chair in the hall. She was wearing a navy-blue straw hat oddly like a man's trilby, and a soft grey coat with two buttons at the neck and two just below the bust. As with all her clothes the effect was simple, dramatic and exactly right. She watched me impassively.

'Hello.'

'Hello.'

Gwen came briskly across the hall. 'Ah, Bob, you're home at last. You're late. Have you eaten? Esther's been waiting ten minutes. Anxious to help with the canvassing, bless her.'

'Jolly good!' I slipped on the breeziness like an old kid glove, adjusted the mechanical smile. 'No, I haven't eaten. Give me five minutes for a sandwich, Esther.'

I gave her a bleak rapid glance and walked quickly into the kitchen, where Gwen was already cutting bread.

'Hell!'

'Oh, Bob, it'll wear itself out in a month or so. They always do.'

'Gwen, I wish you'd get rid of her. You don't take her seriously enough and never have done.'

'But what trouble could she really cause, against two people like

79

us? Unless you actually seduced her, of course. And let's be brutally honest, dear, what normal well-bred girl would really climb into bed with a married man when it came to the crunch?'

'Exactly. Most normal well-bred girls wouldn't. But she's not like the rest. She's odd.'

'Well—I let her in because she looked exactly what you needed for getting people to listen on doorsteps.'

'All right, don't bother about it now. Mrs. Telleyman—she'll be in the committee room tonight. The facts.'

'Terrifically keen on all-round family men. You've probably gathered that. Push your modest charm and go on a bit about the value of the family group. Her main hobby's the party, but this morning Helen Walsh mentioned she was very keen on Proust.'

'*Ah*. Good! Good! One of the $\grave{A}$ *la Recherche* brigade, eh?'

'I'm glad something pleases you. Who was Proust anyway? He sounds foreign. Did he write about politics?'

'Well—he *was* foreign and he *did* write.'

'Your calls, Bob. Miss Charlotte for one. Mustn't take her for granted. The rest are the ones the others can't get anywhere with. A Mr. and Mrs. Henry—there's always some bizarre reason why they can't go.'

'Yes, I remember her.'

'Then Osgood.'

'Christ, what is it now?'

'The statue in Town Hall Square. Thinks it should have stayed. Says there'll be nothing of old Beckford left.'

'Right—I'll tell him if he'll turn out and vote for us I won't let Turman touch the horse-trough.'

'Then Mrs. York.'

'Ah—Mrs. York.'

'Won't cross the doorstep unless you personally ask her to vote and you personally drive her to the polling station.'

'What has Turman done to deserve me?'

'Your day will come.'

'Right. Where shall I drop you?'

'Bob ...'

'Nothing doing, Esther.'

'Will you let me speak? Please.'

'I can give you thirty seconds.'

'I wanted to say how very sorry I was.'

I looked at her. She was gazing miserably down the drive. She looked very fine in the mannish straw hat with her long black hair falling straight down from underneath it and hanging loose. Finally she turned to me with a wan smile. I switched off the engine.

'I mean it. I was a fool. I deserved the things you said. I'm very sorry.'

'I see.'

She turned away again.

'I'd better admit you attract me. A lot. Too much. I won't go on about it. You're married and you've got your career—I want you to try and believe I'm not irresponsible, that I can't see what . . . what cheek it would be to try and involve you. I'm not like that, honestly, whatever it seemed on Saturday. I'm not like that at all, and I'm sorry for being stupid.'

I suppose I should have stayed cautious even then, when I remembered the determined and skilful play she'd made for me. But I believed her, instantly, because what she'd just said exactly matched the kind of woman I'd always been certain she was. She was too sensible, too intelligently middle-class for out-and-out folly. The rich and the poor could lead messy lives, but people like she and I had responsibilities, we were the ones who trained for careers, sensibly educated our kids, looked out for elderly parents, scrupulously settled tradesmen's bills. We lived our entire lives by reason's dismal light.

'I believe you, Esther.'

She turned back to me with a wretchedness she didn't bother hiding, and I smiled at her, a genuine smile, not the clip-on one.

'Would you mind driving me to the Circle bus-stop? I've said what I wanted to say. I don't want to take your time up.'

I glanced at my watch.

'Do you *want* to go canvassing?'

'I . . . wouldn't want you to think I was still chasing you.'

'Come along then. It's good fun and it really is much better with two people, particularly when one of them looks like you. I'll run you home later and we can talk things over properly. If you want to talk things over, that is.'

'I'd like that. And . . . I'd like us to be friends, if that's still possible.'

'Nothing I'd like better.'

'Good *evening*, Mrs. Henry. Here we are again about the Municipal Election.'

A vague-looking elderly woman stood on the step wearing a hat, pinafore and slippers, as if uncertain whether to stay in or go out.

'Election? I thought we'd had it.'

'No, dear, I'm afraid it's fully a year since the last one. Now the Party's candidate this time is Arnold Turman again. I'm sure you'll know he's just completed what we all consider to be a very successful term of office.'

'Oh—has he?'

'Here's his manifesto and here's his picture.'

'He looks like one of the three wise monkeys, doesn't he?'

I turned on my braying laughter.

'Well, just between the pair of us, Mrs. Henry, I always thought he had more than a look of Dr. Crippen, but seriously he's a very sincere, hard-working sort of person and we're all anxious to see him re-elected.'

'Oh . . . righto then,' she said, closing the door. 'Good night.'

'Shall you be voting for us on Thursday, Mrs. Henry?' I said quickly.

'Thursday? Oh, well, that's a funny night, Thursday. Jack works over on a Thursday.'

'We'll send a motor.'

'He's not home till half past eight.'

'We could have a car here at five and twenty to nine. *And* we'd bring you back.'

'What about Buster?'

'Buster?'

She pointed to a small, grey, repellent dog that was slobbering quietly over her slippers.

'He frets if one of us isn't with him. He's delicate.'

'Bring him along by all means.'

'He doesn't like that polling place. Someone stood on his little paw last time he went. Didn't they, Bustie, Bustie, Buster? Stand on his little paw?'

It seemed to explode. It barked hysterically, it leapt in the air, then it ran backwards and forwards into the kitchen over and over again, colliding every time with a piercing yelp into some object that filled the impenetrable gloom with a reverberating gong-like sound. Finally, its claws skidding across highly polished linoleum, it tore out into the back garden and began to scratch savagely at a weather-beaten plaster gnome.

'There!' she said. 'He can't get it out of his little mind.'

I sensed the girl backing none too slowly till she was round the corner of the house. 'Mrs. Henry, we'll come for you at twenty-five to nine and I give you my word one of our helpers will make absolutely certain no one foolishly stands on Buster's little paw.'

'Oh, all right then.' She watched the scrabbling dog anxiously. 'If you give me your word. I wouldn't want him to have to go through that again. He's highly strung, you know.'

'Yes, he's obviously a very sensitive little chap. Thank you, dear. Put your cross next to Turman at the little booth, and you'll tell Jack as well, won't you? Turman. T-U-R-M-A-N.'

Hidden round the corner of the house, the girl dabbed her eyes with a handkerchief. I grinned, glad in a way I'd missed the earlier, profoundly titillating part, where her face would have melted like wax round those large square teeth. Glad but sorry.

'First lesson in canvassing.' I wagged my finger. 'Never laugh at the customers, even if they answer the door wearing nothing but a bowler hat.'

It was a good moment. It was like the first afternoon at my home when we'd worked so well together on the books. It was a very clear evening, and from the heights of Chelifer Crescent we could see Westbury's neat estates and the spires of the two churches and the park and the split-level reservoirs with a Canaletto definition.

I genuinely liked the activity of canvassing, and it was nice to have a pretty girl in a mod hat at my side. A girl who wasn't going to give me any more trouble.

As the evening passed on I knew it had been a mistake; I should have let her go home. After Mrs. Henry it tended to be people like truculent little Osgood, who could be talked into giving us his vote by a hand on heart assurance that I cared as much about ornamental lampstandards as he did, or attractive housewives who liked my wistful crinkly smile—ordinary people who were up against the man Gwen and Martin had made of me, the man who'd developed the skills of cajolery over a decade with a tableful of tough men once a week, a man who was fighting a local election for Turman purely as a dry run for a General Election he one day hoped to fight for himself.

It was too inhibiting to know she grasped it all so well, the mechanics of persuasion and flattery and charm, grasped it and stood in judgement on me, as coldly as the man I'd once been would have stood in judgement on the man I'd become.

She became quieter as we passed from door to door, quieter and more unsmilingly polite.

It was a large house in a quiet tree-hung road overlooking Westbury Park. It had high walls and iron gates. The words CHELIFER HOUSE were carved one on each side into the pillars of the gateway.

The gate swung open with a whine. Esther looked about her. Through the trees the lawn was knee-high. It had once been a garden of geometric formality; now the shrubs were tangled and shot with glints of viscous-looking water, and the pavilion was a decayed ruin.

'Who lives here?'

She looked at the massive rectangular house. It was Victorian but built in the style of Queen Anne with a meticulous and loving care that extended to white panelled doors with Grecian pediments and raised stonework round multi-paned windows.

'Miss Charlotte Chelifer.'

'Of *the* Chelifers?'

'Daughter of Chelifer the second.'

'You can't mean it.'

'She's incredibly old.'

I grasped an iron bell-pull in the shape of a falcon's head; suddenly she looked alarmed. Bells tinkled in the distance, but the door was opened almost straight away, very slowly, by an incredibly bent old woman with high cheekbones and violet-coloured eyes and white hair drawn back into a bun. She must have seen us in the drive.

'Bob! My dear boy! Do come in. And who is this sweet child? One of your U.T. friends, I suppose. My dear, you must forgive the condition of my house.'

'Don't worry about Esther, Miss Charlotte. She'll be too thrilled with your treasures to notice a spot of dust.'

Our heels clipped slowly on the ornamental tiles of the hall as we followed the slight, twisted figure past the ponderously ticking long-case clock and the sombre oils. I glanced at the girl. She looked tense. She'd been almost rudely distant in the face of Miss Charlotte's charming welcome.

'In here, Bob. I did at least contrive to dust this today.'

It was the drawing-room, that beloved haunt of Emma. It was decorated in faded reds and golds and greys, and it had Abbotsfords and vases and rosewood cabinets stuffed with Victorian knick-knacks. On several surfaces there were sepia tints of Miss Charlotte as a young woman. She'd been very beautiful. It was incredible to think that this brave bent old woman had once possessed flesh as soft and sweet as Esther's, hair as glossy, a body as desirable. It was as difficult to see her young as to see Esther withered and old.

'You're not to worry, Miss Charlotte. I don't know how you manage at all, on your own.'

'It won't be for long now, Bob dear. But . . . I'm afraid it's going to be a terrible wrench.' She turned to the girl. 'Has Bob told you I'm selling my house to the Gas Board for offices? I was born here, Esther.'

She rested a yellowing, claw-like hand on the other's. I thought the girl was going to faint. She suddenly swayed, half-closed her eyes.

'Esther, are you all right?'

'Yes . . . yes.' She withdrew the hand the old lady's rested on and held it to her forehead. 'Only a headache . . .'

'Oh, my dear! Can I make you a cup of tea . . . ?'

'No!' she said abruptly. 'No, thank you so much, Miss . . . Charlotte. I'll be perfectly all right in a little while.'

'Do you want to sit in the car? There's brandy in the glove compartment.'

'No, it's all right, Bob, really. It's passed now.'

I didn't press it. One learnt to be discreet when young women had sick headaches.

'I'm sure I'm to blame, Miss Charlotte,' I said. 'I've led her a merry dance along the garden paths. When are the gas-men coming, by the way?'

'September. An old friend of mine at York has invited me to live with her. I'm going to spend a fortnight with her in June.' Her faded violet eyes passed forlornly over the glowing surface of a nearby table; she caressed it with a hand she couldn't open properly any more. 'It's a little trial. If we can get along together we shall pool our resources and set up a permanent home.'

'Grand! I think you're doing exactly the right thing.'

'Will you do an old woman a favour, Bob?'

'Just name it.'

'You see, I made my plans and forgot about the Act of Parliament clock. Do you know what an Act of Parliament clock *is*, Esther?'

'Something . . . something to do with a tax on clocks,' she said in a low voice.

'Yes! How clever you are! It's not a very pretty object, but my nephew Robin would like it. And now I've arranged my holiday, quite forgetting that he'd written to say he'd like to collect it on June the third . . .'

'Say no more.' I cut her gently off. 'I'll come round and open up for him.'

'Would you, Bob! He travels such a lot, you see, it wouldn't be easy for him to change his plans.'

'Consider it done.' I took out my diary.

'Thank you *so* much. Two o'clock, dear, if that would be all right.'

'Gwen's got a key, I believe?'

'Yes.' She chuckled. 'Yes, she'll be able to finish her inventory in fine style without me waylaying her into endless chats about Victoriana.'

I took hold of her withered old claws. We'd always been very fond of each other. She was fond of Gwen too, but she knew somehow that I'd never loved Gwen. She knew a lot about living without love.

'Are you *sure* you're happy about Gwen buying you up? You don't think you should go to a dealer?'

She smiled up at me. Her teeth were ivory-coloured and uneven but they were still her own.

'Oh, we understand each other. I wouldn't want those dealers round telling me what a hard time they'd have getting rid of it. Don't worry, Bob, Gwen and I know the value of everything. In our own friendly way we drive some very hard bargains.'

'I can imagine. You're not a Chelifer for nothing. All the same, it's a fantastic stroke of luck for her.'

I glanced at Esther. She was staring fixedly at our clasped hands. She still looked pale and unwell.

'We must go, Miss Charlotte.'

'Tell the exquisite Emma I've decided that when I leave here the very special music-box shall be hers. Don't forget, the very special one. She'll understand.'

'You're very kind. She'll miss you terribly. We all will.'

'What did you think of her?'

'I liked the house.'

'But Miss Charlotte?'

'She seems . . . a very fine person.'

'Why are you afraid of her?'

She gave me a quick startled glance, began to walk away down the dark funnel of the drive.

'You *are* afraid, aren't you? I thought you were going to drop when she took your hand. Why?'

'You spent a great deal of time with her,' she said quickly. 'I can only assume she's someone very special in the party.'

'You're wrong. She merely votes for us. The Chelifers never gave money to political parties. Anyway, she's none to give.'

'None?'

'The original Chelifer made it, the second one spent it. On the Stock Exchange mainly. The mills were heavily mortgaged when the group bought him out—they went for pin-money. Charlotte and the other girls came out of it with small trusts. At least, not small before the first war, but a pittance in 'sixty-seven. She's broke. I spend time with her because I like her.'

She smiled wryly.

'You can't believe there are some people I actually like for themselves, can you?'

She looked across the garden.

'Do you really like her, or are you just flattered because you get on so well with a Chelifer?'

That was why she'd been aloof with the old lady, it was left-wing disapproval of Chelifer splendour, of people who'd made a lot of money by employing a great many workmen to look after machines for sixty hours a week. But that didn't explain the fear.

'No,' I said. 'I just like her. I like her courage and her manners and her kind heart.'

'Mr. Saxby!'

'Mrs Telleyman—how *nice*!'

'MULTIPLE SEXUAL ASSAULT ON TEA CLUB CHAIRMAN,' Martin had once said. 'Found Unconscious in Corsets on Waste Ground.'

'Shall your man win, Mr. Saxby?'

'A rubber stamp, Mrs. Telleyman. What we're really after is a high poll. We *must* get the voters poll-conscious for the next General —that's what I'm forever drilling into the youngsters.'

'Ah, yes, the General. You'd allow your name to go forward, I understand.'

I glanced modestly at my highly polished shoes. 'Well . . . yes, I *had* been encouraged to hope there might be some sort of chance of adoption.'

She liked me but she was nobody's fool. Fiftyish, well preserved, metallic-looking, she seemed to vibrate with energy. She owned several very successful unisex boutiques, all managed by long-haired, floppy-tied young men who looked deceptively languid. She'd seen men with style too often to be easily impressed.

'I should imagine there'd be possibilities,' she said carefully. 'Family man of your background.'

'Thank you,' I said quietly. 'As an ordinary family man, Mrs. Telleyman, I see it my duty to help other ordinary families. I think I can say I've reached an age to have faced most of the problems they have to face.'

'You've lived in Westbury a long time.'

'All my life. I like to feel I've learned a lot about Westbury people and their problems.' I laughed delicately. 'Pity I'm not a writer. I feel sure I could have done something on a Proustian scale with the fascinating types I've met.'

Her eyes snapped back from the bustle of the committee-room.

'Oh—you're a Proust fan then?'

'An absolute addict, I'm afraid.'

'Really! How very interesting! I should never have suspected— such a hard-working practical man like you.'

'Does this mean . . . you too?'

'Dote on him. Ever since I was sixteen.'

'Well, *really*!'

'What a coincidence!'

'Ah, Mrs. Telleyman, if only we could re-create all the people we meet in our work as the Master did. How did he put it . . . something about seeing hundreds of characters for a novel, ideas begging him to give them bodies, like the ghosts in the Odyssey asking Ulysses for a drink of blood to bring them to life.'

She flushed almost girlishly.

'Why, Mr. Saxby, you must have steeped yourself in his work. *Such* a memory. In fact you share that with him—wasn't it at one of his grand Paris dinners that he held the table spellbound by quoting an entire page of Loti from memory?'

I'd no idea. I was hoping to be able to make a little look a lot till I'd had time to do some homework. I wondered if I'd really taken her in. She handled men who tried to say the right things every day, searching questions would be second nature, despite the girlish flush. I knew nothing of Loti, but I knew what most sixth-formers knew about Proust—that he'd divided his later life fairly evenly between Paris and the coast. Should I risk it?

'I wish I did have his kind of memory, Mrs. Telleyman, but it really does fall very much short of his. I confess that until now I'd always imagined he made his celebrated Loti quotation at a dinner-party in Cabourg.'

The respectful hush told me luck had been with me. As usual.

Beneath us, in the darkness, we could hear the steady roar of the upper reservoir endlessly debouching itself into the lower. She smoked one of her long cigarettes.

'Thank you for stopping. It must have seemed a risk.'

'I believed you. Earlier on.'

'I meant it.'

'I know. Talk about it if you want to.'

'I'll help you with the election on Thursday, if you still want me to, and I'll finish indexing the books. After that I think I'd better go.'

'Perhaps that would be the best thing.'

'It's too upsetting.'

'*Did* you come to Fisher's because I was there?'

She nodded. I saw her eyes gleam in the pale light.

'Do you want to talk about that?'

'No. I'm sorry.'

'Might be better if you did. How do you know so much about my distant past?'

'Don't, Bob, please. I can't talk about it. I know a lot about you. An awful lot. And I deliberately tried to attract you. But it's over now. I've been a fool.'

I hesitated. 'I shouldn't say this, I suppose, but if it's any consolation I wish I'd met you as you are now ten years ago.'

I could sense she was trembling.

'Will you kiss me?'

It grew so silent after those whispered words that the roar in the gully seemed so close it was as if we'd soon be engulfed by the water itself.

'You disappoint me, Esther.'

'Just once. That's all I ask and then I shall go. I know it sounds silly and selfish, but I'm not being devious, I'm asking you openly.'

I wondered where the harm lay. A single chaste goodbye kiss. She attracted me, but nothing more—yet. Perhaps I'd lost the ability to fall in love again. I believed her, that she was going. I was touched and flattered. The situation had an appealing element of *Brief Encounter*. Where was the harm?

I turned to her. I felt her arms go delicately round my shoulders and I pressed my lips on to her faintly moist ones. She smelt of soap and new cloth and she barely moved in my arms. It was odd kissing someone so gently on the lips. Gwen and I had never kissed like that. Our kissing was limited to the open-mouthed kind that would stimulate us to an even intenser pitch of sexual frenzy. Our mouths were for rubbing nipples with, for biting at shoulders, for nuzzling the insides of thighs. We'd never kissed as the girl and I kissed.

I'd kissed poor Maggie like that though. There'd been burnished afternoons in silent houses when we'd not made sexual love at all but had simply lay clenched together, naked, mouth on mouth, for hours.

The girl couldn't have found a more disquieting way to kiss me. Had she bared her teeth at me like Saturday I'd have simply brushed her lips and withdrawn, but she held me lightly and passively and I didn't want to let her go.

I'd never been more disorientated; I only had to close my eyes to be engulfed by those sunlit days near rivers and in silent afternoon bedrooms. I felt numb with longing.

I began to draw the zip down that ran almost to the hem of her dress. It wasn't sex but nostalgia. It was a yearning to hear her breath change rhythm, as Maggie's had, to feel a nipple stir. It wasn't stimulation I wanted but closeness, the illusion of an old dead love.

Her legs slowly parted; I put my hand between her thighs. I'd never known a sadder smell than the odour I suddenly released. It was the odour of youth at its most overwhelming and it filled my head like a drug. And like a drug it released me from anxiety, it let me relive the only time I'd ever known genuine happiness.

Her passivity had started it, her movements began to end it. Passive, she'd been a Maggie-substitute and I'd been willing to let her go on holding me; active, she became a woman in her own right with her own urgent desires. Her thighs trembled and her arms had begun to grip, her lips were falling away from her teeth and tongue. I was back in the present again, her dangerous present, where she could still be a threat to the work of a decade.

I drew the zip back and stopped kissing her. She kept her arms clamped tightly round me for fully a minute, trying to force me to react to her, but at last she let me go and sank against the seat. Her hat had fallen into the back of the car and her hair hung over her face. She took her cigarettes out unsteadily.

'Bob . . .'

'You're not just a bitch, are you? You're the E-type.'

'*Bob!*'

'You only want a goodbye kiss, but you just happen to be wearing your easy-feeler. This is the end of the affair, but you don't actually *stop* me groping you.'

Her hand shook so badly she dropped the cigarette. She picked it up, ground it out, began to light another, the flame on her lighter flickering as if it was in a draught. 'That was cruel.' I could hardly hear her. 'Why did you say that? *I* didn't do anything to make you open my dress. If I had I'd feel I deserved it, but all I did was kiss you.'

'Look, I *know* women. I'm not some tenderfoot like Dowling. You could have stopped all that if you'd wanted to. You didn't encourage me, but you didn't stop me, and I'm merely flesh and blood.'

'Don't you think I meant it? Don't you believe I wanted to end it?'

'Oh yes, I believe you meant it. As much as women like you ever mean anything.'

I made towards the ignition.

'It's dreadful. It's appalling to be attracted to someone as vile as you.'

'It's the image, do you see. I told you before about confusing the actor with the man.'

'No.' She took her head. 'No. The way you are with *them* always sickened me. But here, the two of us, do you have to be so hard . . . so knowing. Can't you just be *yourself*?'

'Myself. This marvellous, decent, kindly Bob who lives beneath the bastard who lives beneath your very own friendly neighbourhood politician.'

'You must hate yourself. With your brilliant mind and what you once were, there must be times when you utterly loathe yourself, there *must* be.'

'Yes,' I said. 'And some of the nicest people I know are nobodies.'

7

I let myself in and went up to my little study. It was close on eleven o'clock but I had an hour's reading to do before I turned in. If it hadn't been for her I'd have managed two.

I sat down heavily, drew up the latest textbook.

How did she *know*? How *could* she know about the times when I hated myself? And who was she crazy about, for Christ's sake, me or a man who'd lived four thousand days ago? How could she possibly get so emotional about what time had done to me when she'd never known the man time had done it to?

'Hello. Are you immersed or can I come in?'

'Hello. Yes. No.'

'Oaf. If you really were immersed you wouldn't even answer. How did the canvassing go?'

'The sods know when the election is, that's the main thing. First steps in politics—always make sure the sods know when the election is.'

'How was Esther?'

'I refuse to discuss Esther. If I told you of yet another attempt at seduction in Water Lane you'd only start laughing.'

She started laughing. 'Oh, Bob, you do go on about that poor moonstruck girl. Mrs. Vereburn called, by the way, just after you'd gone.'

'Really! About the antiques?'

'I'm taking her over to Chelifer House next Wednesday. Meanwhile, I showed her our bits and pieces and I'm afraid she . . . er . . . fell madly in love with the oval table in the sitting-room.'

'Oh, God.' I sat back with a sigh. 'You know, I don't mind selling my soul to the devil to get on in life but I do object to selling my one favourite piece of furniture.'

'We don't *have* to let it go.'

'Sell her it. Sell her it, but make sure she knows we wouldn't do it for anyone else. Tell her it's because I admire her and that ale-cart she's married to so much.'

She smiled faintly. 'I'd rather been thinking on those lines.'

It hadn't been my day. I poured out two brandies. She sat on my desk in a blue housecoat humming the slow movement from *Beethoven's Seventh*. She looked vibrant and happy.

And I envied it, the happiness she got from being married to the man she'd always been quite convinced I was—that cheerful, sexy, right-wing live-wire who drove a Mexico-brown two-litre Rover and brought best-quality bacon home once a month. It was happiness based on an illusion and it seemed unfair. I'd been clubbed out of my illusions years ago and now I was surrounded by people like Gwen, who thought I was exactly like her, and Esther, who was convinced I was a fine noble soft-centre inside a tough shell, and Mrs. Telleyman, who believed my soul thrilled as sensitively as hers did to *The Guermantes Way*. I was beginning to wonder if anyone was ever going to know the real Bob Saxby any more. Even if he could be made to stand up.

'Bob, Alderman Girling's dying.'

'Poor old boy. I liked Girling.'

'They told Pop he won't last the week.'

'Who'll take his place?'

'Definitely Turman, Pop says, assuming he wins on Thursday.'

'It'll mean a by-election.'

'For a seat Pop's always had in mind for you in case you didn't get to the Commons. He says at this stage we really must have a stop-gap.'

'No,' I said dismally. 'Not Charles Algernon Breasey. I can't take any more today.'

'It's got to be, Bob. He's ideal. A decent manager, absolutely safe, and so starry-eyed about it he'll do as he's told.'

'I'm going to close my eyes and put my hands over my ears.'

93

'Pop . . . Pop thought it would be a nice touch if you proposed him.'

'*Zowie!*'

She pursed her lips, frowned, put the heavy glass down with an irritable click.

'I honestly don't think you try hard enough with Chas.'

'How can you say that? I give him exactly the same treatment as the others. I talk to him, buy him drinks.'

'Well, *I* think he feels you aren't as matey with him as you are with them.'

'Oh, come off it . . .'

'Do you ever put your arm across his shoulder or give his knee the confidential Saxby squeeze?'

'If you go on, I'll vomit.'

'Exactly. Look, Bob, we all find him repulsive, heaven knows I don't envy you, but if you're going to clap the others on the back you shouldn't leave Chas out.'

'Oh, all right, Gwen, don't go on. Look, he'll be at the Spinners' on Thursday—I'll spend the time between now and then steeling myself to touch him.'

'Good man! I'll tell Pop to get things moving then, shall I?'

'Just make sure the Alderman's absolutely dead, old chum. It creates a nasty impression lobbying when they've still got the odd lungful of breath left.'

At midnight I put *Yorkshire—A Study in Depth* down, marked ready to take up again at six a.m. sharp, turned off the lamp, went out on the landing. Downstairs an ormolu clock began to chime the hour, the chimes falling rapidly on top of each other in a soft flurry of sound.

I went into Emma's room, looked down at her in the bar of light from the landing. She was asleep, still wearing a pair of enormous sunglasses, mouth open on crooked teeth. There was a nursery clock on her bedside table; it had been dropped in the bath and now rotated its hands visibly. It was always hours fast, the dwarf who tapped a diamond with a hammer working with the furious energy of the demented. Next to the clock there was a pencil and a piece of paper.

My Saturday, it was headed, in shaky block letters, and then went on: *Last Saturday I went to the grand spring bazaar with*

94

*Mummy and Daddy. There was a Jumbel sale. Daddy bought
a book about greeks. A man talked about polatics. Daddy does a lot
of polatics. Daddy is great.*

Other men, at the end of a bad day, turned to saunas, or old films,
or Teilhard de Chardin. I turned to Emma. It all in the end came
back to Emma.

Without Emma there'd be no code. And without the code there'd
be others hurt as Maggie had been hurt. After a day like this it had
been almost unbearably tempting to let Esther Moore into my life,
to try once again for a relationship that worked. Only it wouldn't
have worked.

I picked her limp hand up and held it against my cheek. It was
lonely, always living above the cloud-cap of other people's illusions
about me, but there *was* a real Bob Saxby, and one day Emma
would know and understand his complexities. And love him.

And maybe in the perfection of that relationship I'd assuage
the emptiness and disappointment of these long sad years. Perhaps
in the balanced happy creature I'd help her to make of herself
there'd be a sort of atonement for what I'd done to Maggie. And
myself.

I kissed her and went on to my own bed, calmer in spirit than
I'd been for a week.

'Ah, well—you know *why* we're not in the Common Market, don't
you? It all goes back to when de Gaulle was over here running that
Free French affair during the war. Well, he got as he wanted to
run the whole bloody issue, don't you see, and in the end Winston
had to tell him to sod off. He didn't hang about, Winston, if someone got up his back he told them to sod off out of it.'

'Percy, you're getting up my back, so sod off out of it.'

'Don't talk to *me* about politics, Bob . . .'

'I wasn't.'

'I've lived through it, lad, do you see, and I've studied it as I've
gone along. Oh, I'm not saying as how you haven't studied your
books and that, but you haven't lived through it like I have. Take
the Common Market. Now *you* thought it'd be all right, didn't
you, with Harold and George Brown going across yonder. *You*
thought we'd soon be knocking it into shape for them, but I *knew*
it wouldn't . . .'

'Because of Winston telling de Gaulle to sod off.'

'Mark my words, Bob, that's what Simon's trying to do in here. He's trying to run *your* show. Having to give your desk up, it's a bloody disgrace, you want to tell him a few home truths.'

'Don't push your luck, Lambert, just because you've been here forty years. You can be replaced, you know, all we need is a school-leaver or a reasonably intelligent pensioner.'

His grating laughter echoed in the corridor; a moment later Simon came in. He was wearing a new mohair suit, as dressy as those worn by private eyes in trendy television serials. He'd looked tired since he'd been dried out; the fashionable clothes made him look more so.

'Good morning, Robert.'

'Good morning, Simon. How are you?'

He settled heavily into my chair, began to glance indifferently at the *Financial Times*.

'Robert, I believe you take some sort of an interest in politics.'

He began to light one of his thick cigarettes with his insect-wing tremor.

'Well . . . yes,' I said guardedly from behind my attentive smile. 'It does take up a good deal of my leisure time.'

'Perhaps you could tell me when the party will choose its candidates for the next General Election.'

'Next year. Starting in spring it'll take about six months before they're all adopted.'

'I'd rather thought of putting myself up for one of the constituencies. They'd be keen to take a man like me, I shouldn't wonder —travelled, commercial background and so on.'

'Simon, what a splendid idea! Just the type the party needs!'

'Perhaps you'd outline the procedure. One loses touch.'

'But of course! I'd say the best thing would be to bowl along to your local headquarters and let them know you're willing and able. You *are* actually a member, I suppose?'

'Well—ah—matter of fact never actually signed one of their bits of paper. Always voted for them, naturally, whenever I happened to be in the U.K.'

'Ah. That could make it a little bit awkward. They do rather expect you to be a member. Of course with you being away so often that's been impossible. Shall I speak to the chaps at Central Committee? Obviously we could speed the process up for someone of your background.'

'That would be quite unnecessary, Robert. No doubt my close personal friendship with Sir Alfred will be sufficient entrée.'

I hesitated. 'Well, frankly, Simon, I don't honestly believe Sir Alfred's got quite the pull he makes out.'

'Oh, come, he's party spokesman. He's quoted almost weekly in the local rag. He's on all the committees.'

'Well . . . yes. Oh dear, this is rather difficult, particularly as he's such a close personal friend of yours, but in local politics it's not always the man who's in the paper most who has the most pull. Of course, he's rather a character, with his spats and his dicky and his amusing grey bowler, and you can always rely on him to give the press a good safe statement. But he's not chairman on any of the committees, you know, and the real say does lie with the chairman. I think your best bet would be Gerald Fearnley.'

'Fearnley! That superannuated ironmonger. You can't possibly be telling me he carries any real weight.'

'I'm writing a monograph,' I said. 'Pricks I Have Worked For.'

He rarely laughed outright. 'Where do I go to be an M.P.!'

'You go to Sir Alfred, of course, and he signs you up, and next week you're in the House thumping the Despatch Box and playing bloody hell about wild-cat strikes.'

'Well, well—I must confess I could never quite see Simon as a kisser of babies.'

'Cheeky sod! He lolls at my desk in his executive mohair and he has the brass-faced arrogance to assure me the party'd jump at him. Not a word about *my* aspirations. And he must *know* I'm putting up. The old man sees Vereburn two or three times a week.'

'He knows, Bob. But how can mere intelligence, charm and hard work compare with being born a Fisher?'

'Christ, he isn't even a *member.*'

'Now I'd say that was *rather* an obstacle to winning a nomination. Even for a Fisher.'

'However, I could imagine how you'd advise me to play it and I thought, well, we're stuck with the pillock now, I'll do what I can to let him down as gently as possible. So I warned him right off that meddling crap-heap, Sir Alfred, and told him to try Fearnley. And much good it did me. "Fearnley," he says, "what possible weight can a superannuated ironmonger have?" I could have kicked his bloody teeth in.'

'Poor Simon. Absolutely no instinct for genuine power. That's what you get with ten-year holidays.'

'Well, let him go to Sir Alfred and see where that gets him. Central Committee's collective boot up his backside if I'm any judge.'

Martin poured coffee from the glass flask and lit one of his Dutch cigars. Through the smoke the wrinkles deepened in an approving smile.

'Well handled, Bob. You did right to drop it when he wouldn't take sound advice. He'd have thought you were sour-graping. Let him find out the hard way. But I think when he's finished licking his wounds your best move would be to pull all your stops out and try and talk him into council politics.'

'What a ticket! I can see it all—a vote for Simon Fisher is a vote for youth, vigorous government, a lower rate and a completely fresh policy for the Baths and Wash-houses Department.'

'Now don't be naughty, Bob. This politics idea is just what we need for him. If we can get him the council and the Chamber of Commerce and the Sunshine Homes to play with we'll be able to work in peace.'

'Yes . . . good thinking. I hadn't seen it quite that way.'

He gave the waiter his Diners' Card, watched me in silence while the bill was prepared.

'Is he really being a trial to you?'

'About once a day he makes me so wild I have to go to the wash-room to cool off. But mostly he works quite well and listens carefully to what I tell him. In fact, he's put himself in charge of the rand-buying.'

'Ah—I was going to check that with you. You covered yesterday's sale?'

'Yes. I was showing him the drill and it obviously took his fancy, ringing the dealing-room and ordering great blocks of currency. We've decided it's to be one of his jobs. Not that his enthusiasm extends as far as working out the requirement. He leaves that to Saxby, the well-known accountancy chappie. Still, it's a job less for me, though I'm not sure I'd just as soon do it myself and be certain of it.'

'No, no, let him have a crack, Bob, if he wants to. Then if he makes a balls of anything it's his own money he'll be losing.'

'But isn't a Fisher never wrong?'

'Perhaps, but if he made a bad mistake with Fisher brass he'd never make another.'

We came out on to the street.

'Savour it,' he said. 'Him wanting to try his hand at politics and administration. He doesn't know it, but it's an admission that your life has more to offer than his has. He envies your life-style, or why would he try to imitate it? You've won, old lad.'

'You always knew it would work out like this, didn't you?'

'Always. If I could keep that temper of yours in check I knew it would work out like this. And I've a shrewd idea that from now on Simon'll gradually come to accept you for the master you are.'

' 'Afternoon, Robert.'

'Why, Governor, this *is* an unexpected pleasure. How are you?'

'Oh, not too bad for an old man.'

'Governor, it's simply not possible for me to think of you as an old man. You look exactly the same as when I joined the firm all those years ago—a man in the vigorous prime of life.'

Pleased, his face darkened.

'Just on my way out. Chamber day, you know. Simon not here?'

'He's in General, investigating the stationery expenses, which he believes are excessive.'

'Quite so. We spend a fearful amount of money on paper. He'll be fully on top of things in here now, of course.'

'Fully. But then, Governor, you know the old saying—like father like son.'

He gave me a ferocious scowl of pleasure.

'Perhaps he's divulged to you his wish to offer himself to the party?'

'He has, sir, and I think it's an absolutely first-rate idea.'

'Jump at a man like Simon, I shouldn't wonder.'

'Absolutely *jump* at him!'

You needed total concentration on Polling Night. You had about two hours to taxi all those people who wanted transport up to the polling-station and back, and you had to do it at a time of the year when the streets were full of children. And you couldn't just drive, because this was a little event for the old ladies and they expected their moneysworth of cheerful chat. And you couldn't just drive and talk because you had to be on the look out for party members in other cars so you could pass information down the grape-vine.

That's how it was all evening, trip after difficult trip, chat upon chat, an endless series of dear old ladies, until all at once, as darkness began to filter across the blue dome of the spring sky, it was nine o'clock and all over. But not for us. For us, cheeks burning with the throb of excited blood, it was time to adjust our rosettes, turn our motors towards the city, and converge like Z-cars on Spinners' Hall.

I'd been with her all evening, but I only seemed to see her for the first time as I handed our Declarations of Secrecy to the policeman in the foyer. I had to wait a moment for him to scrutinise them, and then I saw her, her eyes large and forlorn, her sad impassive face with its frame of long dark hair isolated from the background with a sudden intense definition.

I knew later that Polling Night had ended it. Never before had she seen me so engrossed in any activity that I didn't know whether she was there or not, and it was too much for her.

I saw her once, and then I forgot her, because I had to get in as quickly as possible to see how the Count was going. Afterwards I realised I must have seemed like a compulsive gambler with a fistful of counters as I pushed eagerly through the big doors. Certainly nothing I'd done in a decade gave me as much of a kick as the sight of those crowded tables in that great room.

The Counting Room was the entire floor of the Spinners' Hall, now gutted of its rows of seats. It was too vast even for the seventeen long ward-tables ranged across it, but I loved the drama of its arena effect. Even the Count for a municipal election had a certain grandeur set against soaring organ pipes and the damask and gold of the high ceiling and the shields and cherubs of the balcony supports.

There was a good public turn-out too, and those crowded front rows of the balcony gave the atmosphere an immediacy and tension.

I could never thread my way across the Spinners' or hear those people in the balconies calling encouragement down to candidates without seeing it all as it would be the night I fought the next General for South.

I stood at Westbury table, watching the local government clerks check and re-check the bundles of ballot-payers. Poor Turman's smile became more fixed and bird-like than ever on Polling Night and my sympathies went out to him. Elections were nothing to do with the real business of politics, but it was the atmosphere of the tables that really main-lined the drug. You waited at those tables to find out if people liked you enough to vote for you. Your intelligence assured you it was simply the party they voted for, not you, but deep down in your guts and blood you were convinced it was people liking you enough.

One day it would be the big time and I'd be in Turman's shoes. I'd have kissed babies, ogled married women, patted old ladies on the arm, and here I'd be, knowing it was all what comics call business, but still hoping as naïvely as any would-be school captain that people would care enough to turn out and put a cross opposite Saxby.

'I declare Mr. Oliver Newton to be elected councillor for Daisy Edge Ward.'

Suddenly, at the next table, about half the people standing round it began to applaud. After a time-lag and frenzied signs to the balcony sporadic clapping broke out up there too. It was the first result.

I turned to watch; I saw Esther again. She was conspicuous among that engrossed excited crowd by her total indifference.

She stood apart from us, in her grey empire line. She seemed to be watching the clerks with the papers, but I could see that her gaze bypassed the group to travel sombrely on without focus into the darkened depths of the massive stage. Wretched, as I realised later, because I got more of a charge from a ballot-box than I did from her.

'Chas, my dear chap!'

I forced myself to take his arm. It gave to the touch and seemed to go on giving, like foam rubber.

He peered through his bottle-top lenses from my face to the hand clasping his arm, eyes sluggishly lighting at the unusual gesture.

'Oh, *hello*, Bob, didn't see you come in.'

'Glued to the summaries, eh? Are we winning?'

'It's closer than I'd expected but I'm almost certain we're in. The opposition thinks so too, by the cut of his face. Looks a bit of a bleeder, doesn't he? Suits him, the red rosette.'

I chuckled heartily. Encouraged, he began to mutter a lavatory-joke about the Prime Minister. Braying with laughter I forced myself to put my hand across his shoulder. It seemed as if there was no bone there either, just stronger foam rubber. He gazed up almost tremulously, as if he were a U.T. girl I'd made eyes at, and twitched his nose above that minute obscene moustache.

'Chas, old son. I'm particularly glad to see you tonight—I wanted a word with you about poor Girling.'

We regarded each other gravely.

'Poor old chap,' he said. 'Shame that. Passing across before they could even tell him who'd won Westbury.'

'Maybe that's just how he'd have wanted it, Chas, to pass across right in the middle of it all.'

He smiled uneasily, unconvinced. He was scared, he didn't want to pass across in the middle of anything, he didn't want to pass across at all, ever. I guessed at hardening arteries, swimmy turns, doctors telling him to lay off salt and alcohol. I had an overwhelming urge to soliloquise at length about Girling, the human condition, death, and my profound doubts about a hereafter, but I could see Gwen watching me with a faint smile. I comforted myself with one of Martin's headlines—'PORKSHOP PROPRIETOR FOUND IN POOL OF BLOOD—Shop Assistant helps Police.'

'Now then, Chas,' I said in a low voice, 'I know it doesn't seem quite the thing to talk this way so soon after poor Girling passing across, but you know how vital Pop thinks it is to plan well ahead. Between you and me, if Arnold's re-elected tonight he'll almost certainly be made an alderman. And that'll mean Westbury vacant again, as you know.'

He nodded conspiratorially. Old China hands, we brought our heads closer together.

'Well, Chas.' I tried not to breathe too deeply. 'In brief, Pop asked me who the next strong man of Westbury was going to be. "Pop," says I, "there's no doubt in *my* mind. Old Chas Breasy." '

There was a bad moment when I thought I'd presented the whole thing with too much style. The colour fell out of his face as if he'd had his throat cut and his breathing began to rasp like a saw-blade. I found myself instinctively bracing myself to catch him.

'Why, Bob,' he whispered at last, in a hoarse agony of delight, 'this *is* a shock. I'd never imagined . . . This *is* a surprise. Why, it had never occurred to me . . .'

Except in his wildest dreams. I sighed. Right then I didn't see how we were going to sell him to the machine, let alone nice young housewives on doorsteps.

In a voice vibrant with friendship I said : 'I'd like to propose you myself, Chas, if I can talk you into standing.'

And then I saw her again—for the last time that night. Our eyes met. Hers were filled with revulsion, revulsion so powerful as to leave her open-mouthed with shock. I caught a single glimpse of naked horror, and then I was distracted by the cheering and clapping that broke out round me. A distant answering fire began to sound from the balcony; I made haste to join in. Arnold Turman had been returned for Westbury.

'Your turn next, Chas,' I said warmly. 'Always a place for a man like you in the council chamber.'

It was the exact truth—it pleased us both. I gave his shoulder a final squeeze that still didn't locate bone, then pushed my way across to have a ritualistic go at Turman's hand.

'Where's Esther, Bob?' Gwen said. 'She was with you when you first came.'

I glanced quickly across the room. I just saw her, pushing her way through the crowd towards the entrance. She was like a swimmer desperately trying to make the beach before her strength went. She ran up the broad shallow steps without looking back, then plunged through the doorway. The great panelled door, which a policeman had held open for her, swung heavily into place.

It was a poetic and fitting end to the affair.

8

'What's happened to Esther?'

'She walked out on me on Polling Night. Remember?'

'Then you shouldn't have been so off-hand with her.'

'Look, chum, I *wanted* to get rid of her.'

'Don't you see her at the office?'

'Every day. We are polite with each other but cool. At any moment I expect her to hand her notice in.'

'What about your book-listing?'

'That's all over. Martin's hoping she'll help *him* now with, his leather-bound collection of eighteenth-century pornography.'

'Seriously, Bob, there are still dozens left.'

'Then you bloody do them.'

'You shouldn't have sent her packing with a job half done.'

'Yes, well I got pretty damn sick of being sexually assaulted in Water Lane.'

She began to giggle. 'You are an idiot! How long will you be at Miss Charlotte's?'

'Half an hour. I'll go straight up to the Club.'

It was a perfect spring day and the racemes of the laburnums were like frozen rocket-bursts. The freshly cut lawn stretched in sleek perfection to a distant woven-board fence and every so often a breeze struck rainbows out of the thin plumes of water tossed up by the rotary spray. Emma sat by the pool with her friends.

'Daddy! Knock, knock.'

'Who's there?'

'Ewart.'

'Ewart who?'

'Ewart a beautiful morning!'

They fell flat on the grass, helpless with mirth. It gave me a spasm of pure happiness.

She jumped to her feet and ran across to me, freckled and brown-legged by now, in a red and white checked dress.

'Where are you going, Poppa?'

'Miss Charlotte's.'

'Oh, *Daddy*. Can *I* come? Please say I can come.'

'Not today, lovey—sorry. You're going to Granny's with Mummy, remember.'

'Oh, *please*, Daddy! I love going to Miss Charlotte's!'

'She won't be there, Em. She's on holiday. I'm just going to help a gentleman with a clock.'

'Oh, *please*—I can play with the paper-weights.'

I took hold of her hands. 'Now look, Emma. I've got something to tell you. A little while ago Miss Charlotte told me that when she leaves Chelifer House, if you're really good, she's going to give you the very special music-box.'

Her mouth fell open.

'The *very* special music-box? Not just the *special* one. The one that plays the *St. Antoni Chorale*?'

'The *very* special one.'

'She's going to give me it for ever?'

'If you're really good.'

'Oh, *Daddy*!' She pulled her hands from mine and began to jump up and down. 'Oh, *Daddy*!'

On days like this it was almost possible to think of Emma as Emma. Not as my daughter, or a focal point of a kind of love that had never had a proper outlet, or as a make-weight for my deficiencies, but as Emma—the person, the individual inside that collection of atoms that now delighted my senses. Because what she was and what she would be, her genetic structure, her intelligence, her charm and the talents she would develop, her happiness even, must have sprung from my complexities. She was the phoenix who'd risen from the ashes of my dreams. And how wonderful it would be to be her—an unflawed Saxby, capable of happiness without hate, a perfect product at the end of a tortuous assembly line. She'd never know how lucky she was to have been raised in the superb framework that only a man as knowing and bitter and disappointed as I was would be capable of erecting.

I'd taken my jacket off against the heat and now wandered through the grounds in shirt sleeves. The nephew had been and gone; we'd carefully loaded the Act of Parliament clock into his estate car. Elderly, courteous, he'd stood in the drive for a moment looking up at the great rectangle of Chelifer House for what he'd told me would probably be the last time while it was still in the family.

'Can you imagine that oak table, blazing with silver and glass?' he'd murmured ruefully. 'She had a dinner-party every Wednesday night up to 'thirty-nine. Holidays with Aunt Charlotte were the high spots of my young life. I've never known anything grander. It makes me so nostalgic, Mr. Saxby. Oddly enough, Aunt Charlotte thought it very small beer—*she* was nostalgic for the days before the Kaiser's war, when they had a complete household staff. My grandeur was her candle-ends.'

When he'd gone I should have gone. Days of shimmering heat that smelt of hot grass and apple blossom were bad for me, they reminded me too keenly of Maggie and idle humming days of trout-stream and moorland.

It had been a day like this when we'd walked to Saddal along a route that first skirted the river and then went up by footpaths through wooded slopes. I could remember the way sweat had trickled down my face and the sound of my own voice in shady clearings and those long exciting silences of hers. Suddenly she'd stumbled and almost fallen; when I'd turned I'd seen that her eyes were full of tears. Of happiness. She was smiling and crying at the same time and I'd never seen a woman so happy. Or ever did again.

I should have gone but I wandered through Miss Charlotte's grounds, wading in knee-high grass, passing under dense sycamores, until I came to the flaking statues and terracotta eagles that brooded over the wilderness that had once been a formal garden, with a long narrow pool and stiff sentinel shrubs.

I stood on the causeway above the pool and looked down through a hole in the slime. The years had been kind to me; in that dark surface I looked little different from the man I'd looked a decade ago.

He'd been a nice boy, the old Bob. He may have been a bit of an idler who'd watched too many celluloid fairy-tales, but he'd had a good heart. And he'd cared too, not just about Maggie, but about people. People who lived in the same road, who passed you in city streets, who sat round you in cafés. To the old Bob people living happy and fulfilled lives had been something worth working for.

But then those three—Maggie, Simon Fisher and Martin. And ever since, nothing had been the same. And ever since, there'd always been the feeling my life might have been better without them. In real terms.

Suddenly a car turned in through the distant gateway. Puzzled, I waded back through the long grass to the green funnel of the drive. A blue Hillman passed me and shortly after turned into the forecourt. I began to walk after it. When I reached the forecourt it was standing before the front door. I paused; a woman began to get out.

I started to shiver as if someone had touched my neck with cold steel. Her hair had been parted in the centre and drawn with slide-rule precision over her ears and into a perfect bun on the nape of her neck. She was wearing a claret-coloured satin dress, long-sleeved and skin tight in the bodice, and relieved at the neck by a stiff white frill. The enormous skirt, flounced and falling bell-like as if supported by a crinoline, cleared the ground by a bare couple of inches.

The shivering stopped. I'd always been a child who'd gone in fear of dark bedrooms and graveyards at dusk, but apparitions didn't drive round in D-registered Hillmans.

Which left the question of who the hell was she and why was she dressed in Victorian gear? And then I wondered if it was something I shouldn't have seen. I couldn't begin to understand why oddly dressed young women should be calling on Miss Charlotte on Saturday afternoon, but conceivably she and Miss Charlotte might regard it as none of my damned business.

But why didn't she know Miss Charlotte wasn't at home?

I turned to go, but my foot slipped on the hot grass and touched the gravel, which crackled like firewood. The woman, her hand on the falcon's head bell, spun round. We stared at each other.

It was Esther.

'Bob!'

'Hello . . . Esther.'

'Bob, I didn't expect to see *you* here.'

'I was absolutely convinced I wasn't going to see *you* here.'

'I've come to ask Miss Charlotte if she'll lend me one of her ornamental fans.'

'Ah,' I said. 'That explains everything.'

She smiled faintly. 'I can see how peculiar it must seen. It's the Victorian garden-party. St. Mark's. Mother does the Vicar's secretarial work. That's why I was roped in.'

'I *see*.' I walked across the forecourt. 'Well, I'm sorry to disappoint you but Miss Charlotte's on holiday.'

'Oh—is she?'

'And *I'm* here because her nephew was picking an Act of Parliament clock up.'

'Oh . . . so he was . . . yes, I remember now.'

'Or could it be that you never really forgot?'

We watched each other. She began to finger a cameo brooch that anchored a black ribbon round her neck.

'What exactly do you mean, Bob?'

'Exactly what you think I mean.'

'That I'm here this afternoon because you are?'

'You heard Miss Charlotte ask me to come and open up for him that night.'

She watched me steadily.

'You conceited fool!'

Suddenly she turned and went back to the car. She got in and began to yank yards of billowing satin in after her, briefly revealing white stockings and shoes. She slammed the door, then stared up at me through the open window.

I'd only seen her angry once before and I'd forgotten how hard and ugly it made her face, how rat-like those prominent teeth.

'You . . . you conceited oaf! You conceited big-headed oaf! As if *any* woman could be attracted to you once they *really* knew you. Look, I don't care *what* you believe, I came here to borrow a fan.'

She ground the key in the ignition, began a jolting three-point turn.

It rather looked as if I'd got it all wrong. It rather looked as if she was going to the Victorian garden-party and had cleverly re-called how Miss Charlotte's cabinets were stuffed with exquisite fans. It rather looked as if I were a conceited big-headed oaf.

The car performed its last lurching manœuvre, began to set off down the drive.

'Esther!'

She swerved slightly but went on gathering speed. I shouted again. And again. About halfway down the drive, after I'd shouted yet again, she brought the car to a grating standstill.

I ran after her. She didn't look up, she looked straight ahead, hands clenched on the wheel.

'I just wanted to say I was sorry.'

'All right. Goodbye.'

She'd not even put the hand-brake on; the car began to slide away again.

'Also that I'd like to get you a fan, or let you in to get your own. She wouldn't mind.'

The car jerked to a halt—she'd stalled the engine.

'My God! My God! You wouldn't dare, would you—go in there with *me*. After all the terrible things I've made you do in parked cars. You poor thing—what do I have to do to prove how evil I am?'

'I'm very sorry, Esther. I'm a conceited big-headed oaf.' I took out a large door-key. 'Take it. Go in there and select any fan of your choice and let me have the key back on Monday. Goodbye.'

On the afternoon Maggie and I had walked up to Saddal we'd dis-covered a pool among the hills beyond the village—we found out later that the locals called it Star Pool. It was deserted; we'd taken a chance on swimming naked. Sometimes now the smell off water on a hot day, or French tobacco, or the sound of an old Nat King Cole record would pluck me back to that moment when she'd taken her few clothes off and stood above the pool on a rock. All at once she'd brought her arms up in a wide curve that embraced the glassy water and the hills, the sun, the trees—me. All this. It could make my heart quicken even now. All *this*.

Entering Miss Charlotte's was like plunging into that pool. After the heat, a chill that touched the bones. More disturbing, a fleeting impression of verve, of expectancy, of the brilliance of my youth's gold.

We glanced at each other in a brown musty silence broken only by the ponderous ticking of long-case clocks. I was alone with her again. Yet it was me who'd stopped the car, me who'd talked her into coming back. And the anger—that had been no act.

But I was alone with her, and now that we were inside this dark quiet house I couldn't forget that the old lady had somehow frightened her, that she'd almost passed out when Miss Charlotte's dry yellow hand had touched her. Could she really have wanted to see her again? Alone.

'Here we are.'

I walked into the faded red and gold of the drawing-room. There was a rosewood cabinet between the windows of the opposite wall that was filled with things like card-cases and fans. I opened it. It released an odour of old ivory and verdigris and cigars, as dangerous as alcohol in its fleeting stimulation of indefinable desires.

'Take your pick.'

I turned round. She was standing quite still in the middle of the room, watching me.

'You'd have made a very fine Victorian girl, Esther.'

She turned abruptly away and crossed to the marbled and mirrored chimney-piece.

'Mother would love these vases.'

'Gwen talks about Classical Mortuary Urn shape. Also conjures with various names, such as Coalport and Minton. Note the grey background to the flower sections; it's the restraint that counts. If they had white backgrounds the colours would be too strong. I'll ask Gwen to reserve them until your mother's seen them, if you wish.'

She picked up a smaller vase from a loo table, one of a pair with courting couples in a rustic setting. 'Sèvres?'

'You could be forgiven for thinking so. Some of the Coalport imitations were close enough to fool Sèvres themselves. No, they're just good country pieces from the early part of the era. Nothing's been changed since the house was built and precious little's been added.'

We sounded like Gwen or Mrs. Vereburn or Mrs. Telleyman, making our elegant middle-class noises. When we talked like this it was difficult to believe I'd held her breasts and put my hand between her pungent thighs. But I had, and there didn't seem to be any other way we could talk any more.

She moved about the room, stroking leather bindings and Berlin woolwork and wine-coloured wood, and picking up and setting down objects—a silver writing-set, ivory chess-men, a pastille-burner in the form of a castle.

'You can imagine the fantastic break it'll be for Gwen to market this lot.'

'The pictures—are they of value?'

'Frinks mainly. Ever hear of the Frinks? Pair of itinerant artists who presented themselves at just such houses as this and would stay nearby, chatting the maids up and knocking out family portraits. Good solid work, like everything else here. They'll sell.'

'I suppose I'd better choose my fan.'

'Do you want to see the tapestry?'

'Tapestry?'

'In the room over the way.'

We walked across the hall, my scalp still tingling slightly at the swing of pendulum and the rustle of satin. There was a harpsichord in one of the upper rooms—I half-expected to hear it play.

'The Vicar of St. Mark's,' I said. 'He's quite an operator.'

'The garden-party was never much of a success till he came. It's something different every year now. This time it's eighteen-fifty-one and we all have to dress accordingly. Mother says it's a total sell-out.'

'Bang in the middle of the Victoriana boom. Good thinking. He's got the luck too, landing weather like this.'

'Oh, he's definitely in the Saxby class,' she said wryly. 'Sermons full of trendy metaphors.'

'I know. I've been along once or twice to study his style. I did rather get the impression that only the most switched-on of the Lord's mansions would do for St. Mark's congregation. When the Great Hippy came to give them their last fix.'

I stood her before the tapestry; it ran the length of a wall. It depicted part of the Beckford legend—the great savage dog that had terrorised outlying farms. One night it attacked some coach travellers stranded by snow, and was clubbed to death by one of them, a giant of a man, who then strode off into the night never to be seen again.

It was the clubbing incident we were looking at. The dog dominated the entire room and its evil seemed to impregnate the atmosphere. Its fangs dripped and its eyes glowed like neons. In its anguished efforts to avoid the massive flailing club it seemed almost to leap off the wall.

I could never look at it without a wave of gooseflesh. I sensed her move closer to me.

'It's horrible!' she whispered. 'It's *dreadful*!'

I heard the tremor in her voice; my earlier doubts came back—how could she possibly have faced this silent musty house on her own?

'The young man who supervised the weaving also saw to the dyeing of the yarn. It's hardly faded, has it?'

'Did he do any more?'

'No. He was a designer in the Chelifer mills. The old man encouraged him. Miss Charlotte's got the full-scale cartoons he made for the entire legend. It was to go all round the room. Like keen young men in every age he couldn't resist doing the exciting bit first.'

'He died?'

'He died. Coughed his poor bloody lungs out at twenty-four, while Chelifer Two lived mindlessly on to hurl away a fortune.'

'You've got a thing about moneyed ignorance, haven't you?'

'Have I?'

'It's one of the few chinks in your armour.'

'Well,' I said. 'You seem to be the Saxby expert.'

'I'd better go now, Bob.'

'All right. Go get your fan.'

'I'm sorry.'

We watched each other.

'What for?'

'Because of the silly way things have been since I came to Fishers.'

'So am I . . . Esther.'

'You were right. About me remembering you'd be here this afternoon. You're always right—that's why I got so angry.'

'I see.'

'I hoped you'd still be here. It would be quiet here and there'd just be the two of us. I wanted to have one more try at saying sorry.'

I put my hand out and laid it against her cheek.

'Let's share the blame,' I said. 'Let's share the blame and put the past behind us, where it belongs. Above all let's try to be friends.'

'I'd like that. I can't tell you how much I'd like us to be friends'.

'Come on then, we'll drink to it. One drink and then we'll go, before the swinging vicar throws the refreshment tent open for tea and cannabis.'

It was a lovely room—high, rather narrow; plain white walls relieved by velvet curtains of faded royal blue, falling from gilded rails and hanging from gilded rings. A heavy oak table was always kept fully extended, a dozen well-spaced chairs of square Regency shape always in place, a candelabra always in position at each end. On a sideboard against one wall stood the silver—chargers and flagons and pear-shaped coffee-pots : on a rosebud chiffonier against another stood the heavy fruit bowls, the engraved high-necked decanters, the wine glasses. A romantic portrait in oils of each Chelifer girl by the ubiquitous Frinks smiled down from the wall exactly opposite each window.

'The silver and glass are the only things that shine now,' I said. 'Cleaning it's her hobby.'

She picked up a sherry glass engraved with vine leaves and standing on a twisted stem. Then she sat down in a band of sunlight at the foot of the table and placed it in front of her. She could have been a Chelifer girl herself sitting there, with her meticulous hairstyle and her wine-red satin, her smiling prettiness. I picked up a sherry decanter and slowly filled her glass, the sounds of liquid trickling and glass tinkling magnified in the heavy silence. Then I filled another glass and walked to the far end of the table. I raised my glass to her and drank. It was a one-off situation and I was old enough to be able to give it the reverent attention it deserved.

'How nice of you to call, Mr. Saxby. We see you only too seldom.'

'Then I must apologise for an absence that prevented me for so long from beholding a lady so decorative.'

'Pray, what news do you bring?'

'News, dear lady? I bring news of that remarkable edifice so rightly named the Crystal Palace.'

'Mr. Saxby, *do* continue. But quickly !'

'It gleams like a diamond, Miss Esther. And inside—but where am I to begin? Why, before entering the Palace is there not that stupendous sight to be seen of a piece of coal weighing four and twenty tons? Before stepping a foot inside, ma'am.'

Her mouth twitched. 'A piece of coal of such proportions must indeed have been quite breathtaking, Mr. Saxby.'

'And within, dear lady, *within*! Phosphorescent *matches*, elixirs of sarsaparilla, a champagne manufactured from *rhubarb* stalks, an elastic chest-expander, an artificial *nose* . . .'

'Mr. Saxby, I'm quite overwhelmed!'

'But then, Miss Esther, the *commodes*. An entire area devoted to *commodes*. The proportions! The elegance of the marquetry! Nay, those chamber-pots could only receive fitting tribute from the pen of a Keats . . .'

How rarely she laughed as she began to laugh now—with an abandon that dissolved those impassive features like melted wax. In all the hours I'd spent with her I'd only seen her laugh like that three times. I'd never known anyone who lived in such an aura of sadness. Or mystery. Yes, mystery. With extreme reluctance I had to admit that.

Afterwards, I took the glasses carefully away to wash them. When I returned to the hall she was sitting in the tiny room Miss Charlotte called the parlour. Miss Charlotte spent most of her time in here. There were several well-worn ladies' chairs of the armless type, a battered Sutherland and a work-table in which she kept her jewellery, apart fom the costly pieces. You looked out on to the solid greenery of a beech hedge that screened off what was left of the vegetable garden. Emma loved this room, with its Aladdin's cave of trinkets, and I think of all the rooms I'd seen this one was the most peaceful.

I looked down at her in silence while she took out one piece after another to gleam in the sunlight—bird brooches, flower brooches, a snake bracelet, a silver locket, a brooch in the form of a tiny Gothic window, shell cameos from Paris, mosaics from Florence, coral from Naples, quartz from Cairngorm, malachite from Derbyshire, Whitby jet. She gravely scrutinised each item before placing it on the Sutherland's glowing surface.

'I really shall have to go, Esther,' I said gently. 'I'm promised at a U.T. tennis tournament in half an hour or so.'

'Oh, dear.' She sighed, glanced at her watch. 'I'll have to fly.'

We went out into the hall.

'Thank you, Bob.'

She raised the lid of a music-box, shaped like a medieval chest with linenfold panels. A simple version of the *St. Antoni Chorale* began to tinkle in the hot still air.

'Look, Esther, in a couple of months this place'll be full of computers sending out gas-bills for No pounds, no shillings, no pence, payment now due. If there's anything else you want to see a few more minutes aren't going to make any difference.'

'Could I see her bedroom?'

'Of course. As you surmise, it contains the best pieces of furniture. It's the door facing you at the far end of the landing. I'll wait here.'

Her eyes came quickly up to mine in wry acknowledgement of my caution, and she gave a slight nod. Then, lifting the great skirt on white shoes and stockings, she began to climb the wide staircase.

I opened the front door for when we left, fitting the key into the mortice lock. From the gloom of the hall there was an impression of the white light of a furnace out on the forecourt, an impression enhanced by the incoming swells of heat, heavy with the odour of viburnum and dandelions and scorched grass.

I thought of the way she'd looked at the top of that long table; it filled me with a strange almost pleasant melancholy. I was glad she was back, that we were to be friends again. It wouldn't last, but it would be nice to indulge myself in that quick intelligence for a few more weeks. We'd be all right, we both had stacks of common sense. We'd both made mistakes in the past, but we were exposed to greater temptation here than we'd ever been in the car and we'd neither of us put a foot wrong.

'Ready, Esther? I really will have to go now.'

Ten minutes had passed. At the end of another five I called again, louder and more urgently.

And then I remembered that Miss Charlotte's bedroom door closed itself automatically, and that because she slept so badly the room had been soundproofed, the windows double-glazed. The girl couldn't hear me and could genuinely have forgotten the time—I remembered how she'd immersed herself in the trinkets.

I suppose I should have been suspicious after all that had gone before, but I wasn't. I was cautious, because of the circumstances, but I still believed she wouldn't consciously do anything foolish.

I was certain she'd simply become preoccupied with the bedroom furniture.

And I was right. When I opened the door she was standing not far away in front of a chest of drawers. On top of it, to one side, stood a sepia-tinted photograph in a silver frame of Miss Charlotte as a young woman in a short fur cape and muff; on the other side, a matching photograph of Miss Charlotte's fiancé—a dark-haired handsome man with humorous eyes. Between the faded pictures stood a mother-of-pearl box with an ornamental key. The girl had opened it and was looking inside. It contained, as I knew, a tiny mourning ring fashioned from strands of two separate shades of human hair, fair and dark, picked out with tiny seed pearls and mounted on a carved jewel of Whitby jet.

A moment later she turned to me. I was accustomed to the habitual sadness, but I'd never seen her look so utterly desolate. She seemed as if about to speak, but no words came, and I saw she was swallowing.

'Passchendaele,' I said. 'Poor fellow. She never married. He must have been someone rather special.'

She picked the ring up from its little bed of oyster velvet. Suddenly I saw tears glistening on her eyelids.

I hadn't seen a woman weep like that since I'd told Maggie I was jacking it in. And Maggie would have wept over a mourning ring, in the unlikely event of her knowing what it was. She'd not have thought there was anything excessive or faintly absurd about fifty years of remembrance.

And Maggie would have married me, even if I could have shown her home-movies of the misery I'd have brought her.

But it was a long time since I could have been touched by a mourning ring. It was a decade since the days of 'Bob, Maggie—always' written on glass mats, and she and I walking hand in hand towards the future to the sound of *Moonglow*—a future full of places in the sun and houses on hills and white-haired directors giving young Saxby his big break.

I put my hand lightly on her arm. I'd meant to jolly her along with a few cheerful words. Before I could speak she threw her arms round my waist and put her head on my shoulder.

'Oh, Bob . . .'

The action seemed to blow my defensive system flat, it acted like the kind of drug that melts the protective barrier the brain keeps between itself and the subconscious. I could feel her tears through my shirt, the heat of her body mingling with mine. I put my arms round her.

In the next few moments, in a room as soundless as a recording studio, the slightest wrong move could have broken the mood. If she'd uttered a single extra word it would have been over. Or if the dress had been as complicated as a genuine period dress.

But it was held by simple press studs and hooks; it fell from her body in seconds, and so did the stiffened waist-slips that supported the skirt.

Too soon she was naked, too soon the satin dress in a billowing heap at her feet, too soon an old sense of wonder at the first sight of an unknown body attached to a face I'd come to know so well. And by then the first acrid threads of her odour had crept into my brain; I was through the sound barrier of my obsessive prudence.

At first I thought she just wanted nearness. At first I thought it might be like the last time in the car.

I drew her down behind the chintz curtains of Miss Charlotte's brass bed. Her face was flushed. She wouldn't look at me and she lay completely passive in my arms. It could have been Maggie I held on one of those distant afternoons.

And all I really wanted from her was that, despite expanding flesh—to feel her pliant young body against my maturing one, to keep her head buried against my shoulder, to ward off the utter folly of it all by engulfing myself in a past I'd never wanted to leave. It was my mind that revelled in her nakedness, not my body, and for a while she seemed to sense it in the passive way she reacted to my hand on her narrow waist and on her breasts.

It should have been a warning, her lack of movement; that and the buried face and the extreme modesty. The moment I touched her between those pungent thighs her teeth suddenly clashed against mine and she went into the rigid shudder of an orgasm that lasted for seconds.

I was hurled out of my past and into her present. I moved away from her in alarm, watching her fluttering eyelids and listening to the rasp of her breathing.

'Are you . . . all right?'

Eyes tight shut she pulled me nearer and covered my mouth with her open one. A few seconds later she said : 'Will you . . . do it . . . now?'

She was trembling. She spoke through clenched teeth to keep her voice under control.

'Look . . .'

'No! Don't speak. Please. Just . . . just do it . . . darling. *Now.*'

Everything told of total inexperience—the awkward way her legs spread to take me, her inability to guide or control, the tension, the tight-closed eyes. I wasn't surprised when her forehead furrowed and her eyes opened wide with a sudden anguished ecstasy.

It scared me. I wanted to stop, to move away from her. I didn't want it. Not that. If she'd been around it wouldn't have been quite so bad, but that was too much. Far too much.

But her strong arms were clamped round my back now and she was rapidly learning how to lock her limbs in mine. And there was my own body to fight against now, not just hers, a healthy body that had been subjected to the heat of a baking spring day, whose moist flesh was sticking to her moist flesh, a body that had been tantalised by satin, stimulated by breasts and thighs so startlingly different from those it had become accustomed to.

Her mouth had fallen open on square wet teeth, the shyness was forgotten before the rapid approach of a new climax. Her eyes were open so wide there were bands of white round the grey irises. She began to utter small almost yelping sounds that broke the studio silence at faster and faster intervals and fell without echo into the sunlit void.

I'd never been in greater danger, and I knew it. Wet teeth and total abandon—as if that wasn't enough without the knowledge that I—incomprehensibly—had been chosen to be the first to enter her body.

Then the rigid uneven shaking began and I let it take me into my own orgasm, and for a few seconds we both shuddered together like a single body. To the sound of her long tremulous moan.

A dead palpable silence. Not even a clock or a distant lawn-mower. Not even the drone of an insect.

She lay on her back, her hands resting one inside each thigh as if to comfort an area where pain would certainly have replaced ecstasy, eyes closed again, head to one side because of that awkward bun of hair. Her odour was distasteful to me now and her flesh had

117

acquired a faint used grittiness. The same heat that had provoked such intense desire now provoked sweating petulance.

'You were a virgin.'

She lay without a flicker of movement, as if she hadn't heard.

'Why me?'

Finally, she opened her eyes, moved them slowly from the flowered chintz canopy to my face.

'Bob ...'

'Look, if you were so determined to stay a good girl why didn't you wait for your nice graduate to come along? For Christ's sake, the way you chased me I thought you at least knew what *happened* in bed.'

She winced, turned away.

'Please, Bob,' she whispered. 'Please don't talk.'

'Look, *sleeping* with you would have been bad enough, let alone ... oh, Esther, you little fool, can't you see how unfair you've been? You shouldn't have let it happen. Can't you see what a heel it makes me? Why? Tell me *why*?'

'Oh, *please*! Please, Bob, I've waited so long ... please! Explanations won't do any *good*. I *wanted* it. And now I want you to give me this little bit of time without being harsh with me.'

'But *why* have you waited so long? You've *got* to tell me, Esther —I'm out of my depth. You've got to tell me the truth so we can sort it out. If you'll tell me the truth I'll help you all I can, I promise.'

She began to cry. I remembered then that it was her first time, that she was only a kid. Compassion stirred in me; I reached out and stroked her arm. She was right, she ought to be allowed those moments of peace and reflection, other women were. Even though it was all so terribly wrong—I the wrong man, this the wrong place and hers surely the wrong reason. It would all *have* to be sorted out very soon, but it was only common humanity to give her fifteen minutes to herself.

I lay back again, glanced at my watch. I had to remember to take the towel away and launder it. I had to make sure nothing was left lying about. I mustn't forget to leave the bed-curtains exactly as we'd found them. I wondered if what was left of the afternoon was worth salvaging for the U.T.s. Perhaps I ought to go straight home and say the nephew had delayed me.

The girl and I had better leave separately and when the coast was clear. Would they have missed her at the garden-party? Would she have told them where she'd gone?

9

'So the wife's father said to me : "Percy, if I hear of thee running thy ferret elsewhere I'll break thy bloody neck." Strangely enough, Bob, he broke his own not six months later falling down the lavatory steps at the Travellers' Rest. Ironic, that, I always used to say, most ironic.'

'I bet that's exactly what he said as he sailed through the air.'

I shooed him away, grabbed my brief-case, and set off along the corridor, trying not to forget to ignite my smile at passing typists and clerks.

What if Bob Saxby got to be known as the kind of man who ran his ferret elsewhere? What if that muck-rake Breasey somehow cottoned on about Chelifer House? It'd be the same as having it read out over *World at One*.

But nobody'd seen us—I was positive. I'd checked the garden and the road before I'd even let her out of the house. I'd washed the glasses, I'd remade the bed, I'd taken the towel home and returned it. And I'd seen a fortnight pass without incident. I must be in the clear.

She was sitting in her usual isolated position at the big round table, in the grey dress with the white collar and cuffs. She gave me a brief impassive glance as I burst in then looked back at her shorthand pad.

'Apologies for lateness, Governor. Last-minute crisis.'

'Don't think of it, Robert. With the quiet season almost upon us we're scarcely overburdened with technical matters.'

What was I going to do about her? For Christ's sake, what did I do, what did I say? I couldn't go on much longer behaving as if nothing had happened. Or hoping she'd settle it by leaving Fisher's.

'There's not a lot from the cash department, Governor,' Martin said. 'Apart from the running question of covering rands. Does the meeting feel there's still the danger of a devaluation?'

'Governor, your friend Mr. Vereburn had lunch with the Shadow

Chancellor recently,' I said. 'He told me that Ludgate's still certain it's bound to come.'

'Really, Robert.'

'What do you reckon it costs?' Garbutt grunted, his voice heavy with star-salesman's boredom.

'About a fifth per cent.'

'Four bob a hundred because of a rumour?'

'That's nothing to what it would cost us if there was a ten per cent devaluation, Roy,' Simon Fisher said. He'd recently begun to adopt a ringing, didactic tone. 'What happens, do you see, is that if the rand wasn't devalued equally it would cost us ten per cent more on our invoice values, if we weren't covered. I believe some of you aren't at all sure what the full implications are.'

He began to appraise us of them at length, for the benefit of ignorant and knowledgeable alike. I could have knocked him down. He would talk now for five minutes; when he'd finished the meeting would have lost what bit of steam it had. Normally I didn't mind him waffling on, but today, just to give my mind a rest from worrying about Chelifer House, I'd positively longed to lose myself in a tough, lengthy, acrimonious session.

I shielded my scratch-pad from all but Martin, then scribbled across it : *Jesus Christ All Bloody Mighty!!!*

I heard him sigh, but I was too angry to care. Eyes were growing heavy beneath the merciless rise and fall of Simon's voice, and tending to rest surreptitiously on Esther's bosom. I saw her white naked body beneath me, lurching into those orgasms. A hankie? Could she possibly have dropped one? Or a hairclip? There must have been a lot of concealed ones in that elaborate hair-do. What if Miss Charlotte found a comb and asked Gwen where she thought it might have come from ?

At last Simon let go of us.

'Thanks for a full and necessary clarification, Simon,' I said briskly. 'It's the sort of thing we all need to keep in the front of our minds.'

The Governor cleared his throat, scowled warmly at his son.

'Well, gentlemen, after that timely warning there can be no question about it. We cover. Now, what next? It *is* a thin morning.'

I was going to change all that; I was just about to speak when Simon cut in again.

'I want to say a word about lateness among the weekly staff,' he said. 'Several mornings recently I've driven in *especially* early to find staff arriving anything between five and fifteen minutes late. I'd have thought, Robert, as you insist on having such a large measure of control over General, you'd have made it your business to ensure they do the work they're paid for.'

We watched each other across the table. I became aware of Martin's knee tapping against mine. I looked down and saw that my hands were clenched and bloodless.

'I . . . see,' I said at last. 'Yes . . . serious matter. Glad you brought it up—lateness can soon erode a firm's efficiency. Make a note to remind me about it, Esther.'

'Perhaps *I'd* better give you something to pin on the notice-board, Miss Moore,' he said. 'I don't want anyone to be in any doubt about our feelings over the matter.'

'Request the meeting's indulgence.' Garbutt began to scrape his chair back. 'If the main items are finished with I've a great deal to do.'

It was exactly what I'd feared—boredom, the men who mattered getting the hell out of it, me back with Chelifer House.

'I'd be grateful if you didn't go just yet, Roy,' I said. 'I've got something to say I'd like all of us to hear.'

'For God's *sake*!' he cried. 'We've had rands and lateness, what's the next burning issue going to be—how much bloody petrol we're all using?'

'*Roy—language!*' The Governor's cigar-case hit the table so hard it made the ashtrays jump.

Simon's booze lozenges turned on like pilot-lights; I recalled that he'd spent the whole of an afternoon recently combing through the transport-clerk's book. Garbutt had scored a direct hit.

'I'm afraid I shall have to insist that you stay, Roy,' he said, in cold fury. 'Because I happen to believe matters like lateness—*and* petrol bills—should not be allowed to snowball.'

'Quite so!' the Governor growled. 'Like liquid gold. You fellows sign a forecourt bill and forget that someone has to foot it at the end of the month.'

Garbutt turned away in disgust. He could be more outspoken than any of us, secure in his costly talent. Unlike me, he wanted nothing from the Fishers but money. But even he wouldn't mix it with a Fisher. Inside Garbutt was the loutish uncomprehending boy who'd fathered the self-confident braggart he'd become—a boy

who in the end would always be cowed by intangibles like authority and class and self-perpetuating mystiques.

'All right,' Garbutt said, turning ominously to me. 'If you've got
something on your mind say it and say it fast.'

'Very well,' I said. 'I'll be brief. I'd like to know what the meeting thinks about us taking Quentin Fotherby's over.'

I loved that particular quality of silence, the silence across No-
Man's-Land before the dawn.

'Mother of God!' Garbutt cried. 'He's doing a *Planemakers*!'
The Governor was so taken aback he forgot to assault the table.
'Robert, can you be serious?' he said at last, his voice quavering.

'I've been expecting this,' Arthur Bratton said. 'I knew he
wouldn't be happy just turning everything here upside down.'

'I'm only surprised it took him so long.'

'Aren't you getting on a bit to be a whiz-kid?' Garbutt
demanded.

'Robert!' the Governor cried. 'You bewilder me. Can you not
remember that only last winter the question of our size was dilated
on for fully a month? Why, you yourself were adamant that once
our procedures were rationalised we'd be exactly right to remain
medium.'

'I remember it very well, Governor. And I haven't changed my
mind. But it occurred to me recently that Fotherby's is the only
small firm that overlaps part of our operations so precisely . . .'

'Look.' Garbutt had suddenly reddened, I was glad to see. '*Your*
job is the money. Who sells what in this trade is something you know
sod-all about, so don't waste our time . . .'

'Come off it, Roy, the days when accountants simply added books
up are gone forever. We have these meetings so that we *all* know
what's happening. Fotherby's parallel part of our business and you
know it.'

'So what? Are you trying to say we're missing out on the firms
they trade with? Look, friend, they've had their outlets as long as
this firm has, if not longer.'

'Quite. Quite so. Really, Robert, don't you think you're out of
your depth here?'

'Then convince me I'm wrong, Governor. I may not be a technical
man but I can see perfectly well that Fotherby's aren't going anywhere. As I see it they can either sell out as a going concern or they
can slowly grind to a halt.'

'Robert, have you any idea of the sort of money it would cost to buy a gold-plated firm like Fotherby's out? Assuming they'd let us.'

'I *could* make an inspired guess,' I said gently.

Garbutt said : 'Well, *I* think you're trying to get us out of our depth. Last winter you were drilling it into us that we were exactly right as we were. How is it you want to start buying Beckford up all at once?'

'*One* small take-over, Roy. All right, let's assume a group takes them over. Do you think a group would be happy to just go on servicing Fotherby's traditional outlets and making a bit of steady money? Don't you think some bright spark might suddenly see it as the thin end of the wedge to drive into *our* business? The sort of cash and time a group has it might well be worth it, even if it meant selling at less than cost for a while to undercut us.' I shrugged. 'Well, has it happened before or hasn't it?'

'Too imponderable, Robert . . .'

'Rubbish !'

'Airy-fairy . . .'

'Accountants' talk . . .'

But Garbutt had now begun to light a truncheon cigar with great deliberation, a sure sign that he was set for the morning. With luck we'd even be late for lunch.

And I'd be able to get that girl's white naked body out of my mind. I'd hardly even *seen* her for the past five minutes.

'Gentlemen,' I said in an aggrieved tone, 'you're all being very scathing, but I'm still not convinced . . .'

He ate his Quiche Lorraine in disapproving silence; I picked in-differently at my grilled steak and green beans. It was a dark sultry day, the sort of English summer day that can depress you even when you're in good spirits. And I hadn't been in good spirits for a fort-night.

'What's biting you?'

'The weather.'

'Oh, no, this is more than the weather. You've been like a cat on hot bricks all week. I wasn't impressed by your performance in there.'

'Fotherby? Well, I didn't mean to spring it on you, but we neither of us had a minute to compare notes . . .'

'No, not Fotherby. If you want to take Fotherby over, I'll back you—you're usually right. No, I mean Simon, and you know I mean Simon. First you scrawl blasphemies about him and then you bunch your fists at him like a drunken bricklayer. For heaven's sake, when are you going to grow up?'

'Lateness,' I said. 'Lateness, stationery expenses and petrol bills. Just once a week, for a couple of hours, we manage to get all that expensive talent in one room, and he bleats for ten minutes about devaluation.'

'And bleats very well. Very well. At least he's done his homework about devaluation now, which was more than he'd done a month ago. At least he's off the bottle and getting himself involved. All right, he's a damned bore, and he gets in the way of the real business, but he happens to own the firm and we happen to need him.'

'Like we need lung cancer . . .'

'Bob . . .'

'They'll leave. I got that clerical team together and they're bloody good workers. I don't give a sod about them being a bit late if they get the work done; and they do. If he starts going on as if it's nineteen-thirty-five they'll tell him where to stick his firm.'

'Bob, he was born to middle-class wealth and he's always had it drilled into him he's superior . . .'

'Can he sell it on the open market? His superiority? I can.'

'Then use your superior skills in guiding him into a sensible and useful role. The mark of a top man is the way he can make people do what he wants them to do without them being aware of it.'

He poured out coffee from the glass flask, selected and lit one of his small cigars. I looked on irritably.

'As usual,' I said at last. 'Everything you say has the profoundly annoying ring of common sense.'

The network of wrinkles finally deepened.

'I'll say no more. To be fair, you have him on your back all day and you're doing better than I gave you credit for. It was just that I didn't want you at loggerheads with him on this particular day.'

'Why?'

'He might want something from you this afternoon and I'm anxious for you to be at your urbane best. I was talking to the Governor just before lunch. Translating Fisher hints and euphemisms into brutal English, I rather gather that when Simon selflessly offered to let his name go forward as a possible prospective candidate for a division, Headquarters wheeled as one man and gave him their collective boot in his goolies.'

I had a mouthful of coffee—it expended itself in a fine spray all over the George's snowy tablecloth. I'd not laughed for days and the almost hysterical way I laughed now was a response to the tension of the past two weeks. Martin watched me, one eyebrow raised in a pained smile.

'You're a cad, sir.'

'Christ, it's like Laurel and Hardy. You know for half a reel he's going to fall on his backside and it still has you in the aisles when he does.'

He chuckled. 'Reading between the lines I understand Fearnley told him a bit of ward-work wouldn't do him any harm.'

'Just what I told him.'

'Mm.' His deep-set eyes rested thoughtfully on me through the plumes of smoke. 'Why not take the plunge and offer to show him the ropes at Westbury? Now, don't start frothing at the mouth, it's obvious you'll only really get him going if he's under your wing.'

'Oh, all right—I'll speak to Pop. A Fisher's a Fisher, he'd look good in our literature. It might be worth helping him with a council seat to have him on our committees.'

'Could do you a power of good. In the end he'd need you for both his firm *and* his politics. You couldn't go wrong.'

Later, as we walked back along Cloth Hall, I said : 'Thanks, Martin. It's a bloody good idea. I don't deserve you.'

'My wife tells me that, only the emphasis is different. Now look, Bob, one thing more, don't let Simon get so bound up in his politics he forgets about things like covering those rands up.'

'Don't worry, I watch him like a hawk.'

His hand, trembling like an electronic oscillator, put a match to what must have been his fifth cigarette since lunchtime. At last he stopped pacing up and down the office and stood in front of my desk. 'Robert,' he said reluctantly. 'I'd like a word with you on a personal matter.'

I smiled the wide clip-on smile.

'Of course, Simon, fire away.'

'This—ah—political business. I—ah—saw the chaps at Headquarters. Awfully keen to have me as a candidate eventually, but—ah—not just at this moment. They agreed it was absurd, of course, man of my experience, but it seems Beckford people are distressingly insular. Seems they—ah—feel they must see one around for a year or two before they can bring themselves to accept one. Ridiculous, but there it is.'

'*Ludicrous*, man of parts like you.'

He looked paler than usual and more weary, a fatigue that went oddly with the fashionable dark blue mohair and the thick soft tie. He was still locked in combat with his alcoholism; for a month I'd watched his dogged struggle with growing admiration. Today, I could have seen him back in Port Elizabeth or Adelaide, rotting his guts out on treble Scotches. He hadn't got up my nose like this since his last return to Beckford.

'Gerald Fearnley.' He wrenched out the name of the man he'd once dismissed as a superannuated ironmonger. 'Thinks a spell in local politics essential. I'm not really very keen to fight for council seats against gas-fitters and shopkeepers, but it seems to be the price one has to pay to get into civilised politics.'

'I think you're very wise, Simon.'

I turned my chair away from the partially open door to the annexe, where I could see Esther moving about. *She* was the real culprit; but for her and her damned white shuddering body I'd not be in a state where he could get up my nose.

'Simon, why don't you let me show you the ropes over at Westbury? I think you'd find them a nice bunch of people. No riff-raff. I needn't say how pleased we'd be to have you.'

'There's a by-election coming up in Westbury, isn't there?' He turned casually away and glanced down at the city square. 'Now you mention it the thought had crossed my mind I could perhaps be proposed for that.'

I tried not to think of the spray of coffee over the tablecloth.

'You know, the one thing that really goes down well in Westbury is someone who can't wait to get started. Oh dear, if only you'd told us earlier. You see, Simon, these things have to be arranged such a long time in advance. I'm afraid the by-election candidate was chosen quite soon after poor Girling passed . . . died. Chap called Breasey.'

'The meat-pie man?'

'The meat-pie man.'

'Oh, but surely they'd prefer me to a meat-pie man. Couldn't he be asked to stand down for me?'

'There's nothing I'd like better,' I said gently. 'Unfortunately the nomination's in now. Between you and me, it was a case of Buggins's turn—Breasey's the oldest of party hacks. I really am very sorry, but don't forget, another spring, another seat. Shall I get my colleagues together to meet you? Just the handful that matter. We could get together at my house, if you like, and mull things over in peace.'

'Oh, very well, Robert. I'll try and find a spare evening during the next two or three weeks.'

'Have you all got a drink? Splendid. Now tonight we're having a little nomination meeting upstairs for old Chas. I'd regard it a personal favour to me if you'd all come up later and cheer him on a bit : he's done a lot for this club—it won't take up more than fifteen or twenty minutes of your time.

'Meanwhile, I'd like to give a short talk about that word the papers are bandying about almost every day. Devaluation.

'Right then, let's take as a very simple analogy a shop in the high street. Now the manager of this shop feels that it isn't doing as well as other shops round about, and eventually he decides that it may be because his prices are higher than prices in other shops. So he decides to lower his prices. And having taken the plunge he goes on to lower his prices until his goods are not just as cheap as goods in other shops but even cheaper.

'In other words he gives himself a competitive edge.

'As I said, I'm oversimplifying, but let us assume that Britain is that shop and overnight its prices are dropped. Now before I go over the pros and cons of this complex matter, I should point out that it's unlikely the party we serve would ever countenance taking such a step. I think the reason will be obvious to you when I've given you all the facts ...'

Yes, clear as bloody crystal the way I pegged facts along the party line. On I went, bromides for nice young people who came from nice bright homes that had a nice bright Cortina in the drive. Who trusted old Bob because he looked just as solid as their dads did, who told them about political matters in a straight simple way they could understand, who said exactly what their dads had always said—that the other lot simply weren't up to the task of government. You could turn out and fight for a man like old Bob, because he was decent and generous and clever and well heeled; and if old Bob thought this was the right party where was the need to think it out for yourself?

Such enthusiasm, such keen faces. I was coming across at full pitch tonight, doing the Kenneth More bit an absolute doddle—the crinkly smile, the warmth, the voice that backed the Isle of Skye documentaries. It was like sleep or a meeting-room battle—you couldn't worry about Esther Moore's naked body when you were in front of a roomful of people.

I talked on, giving a special grin to a plump new U.T., reminding myself to tell Peter Dowling later that I was sorry to sound so pedestrian, but the others simply hadn't got his remarkable grasp. Where was he anyway? I'd seen him earlier. The heavy cloud had still not lifted; there were a few people in deep shade against the blind wall.

Then I saw her. Sitting next to him in the gloom, watching me impassively. I suddenly felt so utterly depressed I could barely sustain the cheerful smile. Oh God, was it back to square one then, back to getting me hung up over Dowling, elegant hulking Dowling with his golden hair and his sideburns and his full red lips.

And his damned youth, shining with the hostile brilliance of sun off a polished shield.

I glanced at the key words Gwen had written for me on an envelope, then began to smile—at different faces this time, middle-aged ones, my slow-travelling honest-John gaze lingering fractionally on certain women. Then I let my hand sink into the boneless tissue of Breasey's shoulder.

'Ladies and gentlemen, it's a pleasure and a privilege to nominate my good friend of ten years' standing—Mr. Charles Algernon Breasey—as prospective candidate for Westbury ward. I do so in the certain knowledge that if Chas wins next week's by-election, we shall be sending into the council chamber one of our ablest, most devoted, most industrious members.'

I paused, to give the silence a deeper edge, then began again in a lower voice.

'Can anyone here tonight call to mind a more deserving candidate for office than the amiable Chas? Need I remind you of the long selfless years spent running our club? Or the fact that he looks after our U.T.s like everyone's favourite uncle? Or the fact that he's one of the first to volunteer whenever tedious jobs need doing?'

I began to raise my voice. 'There must be those among you who are asking themselves in a puzzled way, "But why are we only asking Chas to serve now? Why haven't we asked such an obviously devoted man to serve years ago? Have we not fallen down in our duty to the community, and indeed to Chas himself, in not giving our city the benefit of his wisdom and industry so much sooner?"'

'The answer, ladies and gentlemen, is yes—yes, we have fallen down in our duty, and we've fallen down out of entirely selfish personal motives. Because I can only imagine that in past years when there have been other seats to contest, and our executive members have put their heads together, with the intention of prevailing upon the worthiest of our number to serve, they have first thought of Chas only to think at the same time . . .' Spacing my words, I gave my voice its full vibrant tone ' *"But how shall we possibly manage without him here?"* '

Gwen had finally figured the angle, the best way to gloss over those ruthless years of party indifference. The minute she told me I'd known it was something I could work up into a winner. Breasey suddenly gulped and began to snuffle into a handkerchief. I saw Pop Endersby's swift upward glance of admiration from further down the table, saw eyes begin tenderly misting in the small audience. I was in cracking form. You had to be very very good to give people a lump in their throat over Charles Algernon Breasey.

I paused, my hand still submerged in his shoulder, a pause which lasted a fraction too long due to my catching sight of Esther and the coldest gaze I'd ever seen in my life.

I worked my way through the knots of people, shaking hands, squeezing arms, asking precise questions about jobs and illnesses, hobbies and children, and listening to the answers with an absorbed smile. All at once I came upon her, alone, sitting on a bench at the side of the room. 'Oh . . . hello, Esther.'

'Hello.'

'I . . . didn't expect to see you here tonight.'

'Peter called for me. We're going to a barbecue near the river in a few minutes.'

We watched each other. She wore an off-white shirt and a sort of waistcoat of light green tweed, black pants, a silk scarf. From one hand hung a black, wide-brimmed Spanish hat. The sort of crazy get-up a pretty girl looked superb in. My imagination instantly constructed that enviable scene—a flaring orange fire against the heavy cloud-cap, frying steaks, swirling water, guitars, wine, laughter, a dozen happy voices singing about yellow submarines and when I'm sixty-four. Dowling. And her, looking impassively on, who'd yelped and shuddered and emitted an odour that had nearly choked me.

'I hope . . . you have a nice time.'

'Thank you.'

'Would you have gone to the barbecue if he hadn't been coming here first?'

The words seemed to come of their own volition. Startled, I glanced round to make sure I wasn't overheard. She turned away, ostensibly to smile at Dowling, who was coming towards us. But I'd seen the pain.

And I saw the barely perceptible shudder when he touched her.

She was sitting in the room she'd furnished with antiques, in the pool of light from a standard lamp, tea things beside her on a small table. Just like any other suburban mum.

Only she wasn't like other suburban mums and I only ever saw her sitting doing nothing when something was wrong. When Emma was ill or she'd bought a piece at too high a price.

'Something the matter, Gwen?'

'How long's it been going on, Bob?'

My heart lurched. She'd been up at Chelifer House today seeing the old lady.

'I don't quite . . .'

'Fluke.' She cut me off. 'Nothing you'd neglected, letter from the nephew.'

'*Gwen, I've no idea what you're blathering about!*'

'Look, I am *not* a suspicious woman and you know it. She insisted on reading the nephew's letter; I was barely listening. But he went on and on about the clock stopping when you put it in his car and refusing to start since. Some drawn-out joke about it only being right twice a day. It stopped at two-fifteen.'

I had fast wits, but I couldn't find an answer to that one. The nephew's lateness had been my excuse for cutting the U.T. tennis tournament. It had seemed bullet-proof. I might have known such a chatty bastard would write a long chatty letter the minute he got home. I began to flush, aware that having said nothing even for a second was already an acknowledgment of guilt.

She took her glasses off, snapped them down on the table.

'Esther, of course. It could only be sex that'd make *you* leave the U.T.s hanging. Oh, you *fool* !'

'You're jumping to conclusions, Gwen.'

'Am I? Am I? I can trace that girl's movements on that particular day in half an hour flat if I set my mind to it, so *come off it!*'

She could too. Didn't she brief me every other day on people like Vereburn and Dowling and Mrs. Telleyman? I decided right then to abandon puzzled innocence. We were realists. Tacitly admitting my guilt, I sank down heavily into the opposite armchair.

'A *girl*,' she muttered. 'A girl in her twenties. Oh *really*—how *could* you be such a fool? If you must behave like a tom-cat why couldn't you have found some discreet tart your own age !'

'Gwen . . .'

'Ten years ! Ten years of tea-clubs and dances and bazaars and selling you to the machine, and you have to jeopardise *everything* by seducing some fool of a girl.'

'Gwen, going on like this isn't going to help matters. I'm sorry . . .'

'Sorry ! Look, my lad, Pop and I have made you linchpin in this ward. Next spring there's a good chance the Selection Committee's going to find for you. Don't you think you can go round living the sort of messy life other men live. You belong to everybody. And if you want to make the Commons, and take over the reins in Beckford, you'd better stop seducing silly girls and find some tart who can keep her trap shut.'

'Is that all you're bothered about—the politics? Doesn't it matter about us? Christ, aren't you even *hurt* ?'

The echo of my voice lingered in the room, shrill with incredulity. She turned away so that all I could see was her profile in the lamp's glow, hard and black, like one of those five-minute cut-outs they do on seaside promenades, every line and blunted angle telling of sturdy common sense.

'I'm disappointed,' she said. 'I hoped you'd be satisfied with what I could give you. Oh, I'm not stupid, I know you're attractive and how much temptation you're exposed to. All the same, I hoped you'd be satisfied. For my sake *and* the party's.'

'But mainly the party's.'

'I can get over it better than the party could in the unthinkable event of it finding out.'

I'd been flung off-balance. I was like those overweight people who lived on a permanent diet, who flew to their bad habits at times of stress. Only my over-indulgence had been all those films I'd consumed in my throwaway youth, and it was in celluloid terms I was instinctively thinking, in which scenes of unfaithfulness were the high drama, with tears and recriminations and bitter words and broken hearts.

But our relationship had never been anything like that. We'd never, in all our time together, ever said—'I love you.' We'd married for a number of excellent reasons; love hadn't been one of them.

Her reaction to the affair was an exact comment on our marriage. Hadn't she always said, only half-jokingly, that if I was ever stupid enough to play around, to make sure the woman was one of us, over thirty, and married to a man who was getting *his* share somewhere else.

I went across to the sideboard.

'Drink?'

'Oh, Bob, you've been a bloody *fool*! Can you *imagine* the mischief she could make if she turned against you?'

'Gwen, I'm *sorry*.'

'Sorry! What good's that? Do you realise, if Pop heard a whisper of this he'd drop you tomorrow. If there's one thing he sees red about it's public men who can't mess about discreetly. He doesn't mind affairs, just stupidity.'

'For Christ's sake! Pop says this, Pop says that. Pop knows every bloody thing, doesn't he?'

'Well, he wasn't so far wrong about you. He once said you had the sort of brilliance that often went with instability.'

It stung. By God, it stung. He was the best judge of men in the business, but I'd been certain he'd never been able to see behind my protective colouring. I'd been certain he saw me exactly as she saw me—able, clever, materialistic, totally partisan.

I said : 'Look, don't give me that about him dropping me. He *can't* drop me—he's spent too much time grooming me for stardom. You both have. You and Pop need me as much as I need both of you, so don't let's have *that* kind of talk.'

'Don't be silly,' she said flatly. 'He *would* drop you, and you know it. If *he* found out he'd assume others in the machine might find out, and he couldn't afford to let the machine think he was condoning your behaviour. Not Pop. It's the machine that really has the power, Bob, not you or me or Pop. They do the work and they pick the man.'

'Do they want a brain?' I cried. 'If they want my brain and my drive and my research working for them they'll have to accept the body that goes with it. All right, the body makes a mistake—what the hell difference does it make to the top-flight brain they're getting? What do they want—me or some sexless nobody with a bit of paper from Sheffield University?'

'The machine hasn't reached your level of sophistication,' she said. 'Yes—as a matter of fact they *would* prefer a sexless nobody with a degree to a clever man who seduces typists in deserted houses.'

My hands suddenly began to tremble so badly it made the glass ring against the decanter. So far the pace of my life had just managed to keep panic at bay; now it engulfed me. Oh, they would, they would, there was no question of that, the machine had elderly ladies for cogs and clean-limbed U.T.s from nice homes and respectable little men who played bowls and spoke at Sunday schools. I sipped the brandy, but the throbbing nerves in my guts seemed to swell up against my stomach and I almost retched.

I leaned over, my hands on the sideboard, and breathed deeply, sucking air into my lungs till the nausea passed. Then I sat down opposite her and tried the brandy again. After a few minutes I began to speak, slowly and carefully.

'Gwen, I'm sorry. I'm sorry for upsetting you and I'm sorry for the sheer bloody stupidity of it. This is the truth—she's never stopped chasing me since she first laid eyes on me. I tried to tell you what a dangerous pest she was, but you never believed me.

'I simply cannot make her out. Honestly. She's peculiar. I know it sounds crazy but she seems to know everything about me going back years and years, politics, career, everything. Even down to the clothes I wore in the early 'fifties.

'And—well, she got through my defences. It's *never* happened before, you know that, but she chased me till I couldn't run any longer. She turned up at Chelifer House out of the blue. It was . . . a single incident. I won't go into it or try to justify it. I just ask you to forgive me, if you can, and to help me to get her off my back. I mean that.'

She picked up my heavy brandy glass, held it against the light, looked thoughtfully from it to me and took a sip. For the first time in two weeks I began to relax. She'd always reacted instantly to plain speaking.

I was glad it was out. Glad that she was so realistic, so intensely practical, glad that we weren't in love. Gwen would sort it out. She'd never in her entire life been moved by mourning rings or June sunlight coming down behind mist or Gregory Peck having to leave Audrey Hepburn in Rome; on the other hand it would take a lot more than me seducing Esther to break her up. We inhabited different planes of sensibility, Gwen and I, but for a man going somewhere she was the very best there was. That was why I'd married her, so there'd be no happiness or unhappiness, no jealousies or nostalgia or pain. Old Gwen would help me to fence it in.

'All right, Bob,' she said at last. 'I believe you.'

She smiled ruefully. 'I'm disappointed. Very disappointed. No good pretending otherwise. But it's done now. And you *did* try to warn me and I *should* have listened, so I'm prepared to accept part of the blame. But this is it, Bob, it must never happen again.'

'It won't—believe me.'

She watched me steadily in the half-light, nodded. 'All right then. Could anyone *possibly* know about that caper at Miss Charlotte's?'

'Absolutely not.'

'Good. How does she know all these things about you?'

'I haven't the remotest idea.'

'Very well, never mind about that for the time being. Now the important thing is that you don't drop her.'

'*Eh?*'

'Under no circumstances.'

'You're losing me.'

'Look, if you drop her like a ton of bricks she'll resent it. And she might resent it so badly she'll do something utterly fatal. *I'm* a woman and I know what women can do.'

'You're wrong, Gwen. She's an intelligent, responsible girl, you've said so yourself. She'd never try to damage my chances. She's been stupid, but she'd not be spiteful.'

'*I'll* be the judge of that. I don't think it was very intelligent and responsible to compromise a man committed to public life, do you? It seems to me anyone who's so determined to get an old hand like you into bed could turn bloody-minded.'

I made no reply. She was running the show. And hadn't Esther, suddenly taken up with Dowling again to spite me?

'No, you must keep in with her, involve her in your activities. Let her hang about till she gets so bored she goes for good. It might takes months, but it's the only way. And you must be nice to her, as nice as you possibly can. But firm about keeping your distance. In other words, you'd have an affair if it wasn't for all the trouble it'd cause. But you mustn't let her feel rejected, that's essential. If it grinds to a halt through boredom there won't be any trouble about her bitching things up for us, she simply won't be bothered.

'But don't ever be alone with her again. If you *have* to run her home, go the busy Welshman Road way, and remember from now on I'll be watching you both like a hawk.'

Later, we looked in on Emma. I felt shame then for the first time, looking down at her in the band of light, the shame I should have felt before Gwen. And I knew it had been the shame, like the panic, that I'd tried to fend off with furious activity.

So much for my ideal woman. So much for the only really worthwhile part of my unsatisfactory life. So much for the happiness I'd determined to give her, for the talents she'd develop in the right way at the right time, for the complete adjustment to a complex society.

Even Emma, liable to be damaged as few other children might be damaged by a fallen idol, even the vulnerable Emma hadn't been a strong enough protection against that girl and her body.

But Gwen would make it right. She leaned over and kissed Emma on the forehead, then she looked up and smiled at me. It was as reassuring as the second drink. There was nothing we couldn't sort out between us

We undressed. 'I've got an idea,' she said. 'How would it be if you were to arrange a meeting with her somewhere? Westbury Park maybe, or Daisy Edge Woods. On a Sunday afternoon. And take Emma with you. You could do your little sad act with Emma playing by the stream. Appeal to her sense of decency. Put your cards on the table and ram home the sob-stuff about your duty to the family. But ask if she'll please go on seeing you and helping you with your work.

'Better soft-pedal *me*.' She laughed shortly. 'They never care a damn about the poor wife. But she seems to like Emma and Emma thinks she's wonderful. What do you think?'

It was good. A girl who'd weep over a mourning-ring ought to react well to a mixture of Emma in sunlight and my quiet voice at its elegiac best. Emma had failed to act as my conscience, let's see if she would act as the girl's.

It was good.

I O

'What's this one then, with the big leaves made up of five smaller leaves?'

'A...a...a horse-nut.'

'Horse *chestnut*. Good shot, though. Now—what about this twisty one with the tiny uneven leaves?'

We walked in single file along the diagonal pathway that cut down through the densely covered slopes of Daisy Edge Woods to the valley floor. We could hear the brook running against the faintly tropical chatter of birds, and through breaks in the foliage, a long way below, we sometimes glimpsed it, as blinding in the sun at the angle of our approach as white-hot metal in a trough.

I had dressed carefully in a quiet jacket and cavalry twills and Emma had never looked better in a French blue shift and a white sun-hat with a curly brim. I practised my sad brave smile. It was a good day for being elegiac.

At the next break in the trees we saw the bridge. She was already there, looking down at the water.

'Esther...!'

The echo of Emma's shrill voice seemed to float in the air like a bubble. The girl looked up. She wore a close-fitting trouser suit in pale green canvassy material and her dark hair hung loose. She looked very fine, alone on the bridge, searching the foliage with an uncertain smile.

I thought of her white body emerging from the yards of rustling satin, a body I'd never seen attached to a face I'd come to know as well as my own. How narrow her waist was, how firm and high her breasts. She'd smelt so strong in the hot silent room and she'd been so scared. I heard her yelping faster and faster, saw her eyes open so wide there were bands of white round the iris, felt the pain of those square wet teeth against mine.

I picked my way down the pathway behind Emma. That's all

there'd ever be now between me and that strange pretty girl on the bridge. Memories. Sex in the head.

And yet I felt curiously happy. Perhaps it was the sun and the unaccustomed leisure and being with Emma. Perhaps it was the release from anxiety. Her body would never lie beneath mine again, but balanced against that was the security of my political future, the end of panic and shame.

And we'd still be together. I was certain she'd want to stay with me whatever the terms. I'd be able to go on having her with me in complete safety. It wouldn't be easy but nothing could go wrong now. And hadn't I anyway become expert at zoning my life? Gwen for sex and Emma for love. Perhaps now the girl for friendship. Genuine friendship. She'd go in the end, nothing was surer, but for a while we might be able to give each other sanctuary.

We finally emerged on to the pathway skirting the brook.

'*Esther!*'

Emma darted towards her, put both arms round the girl's waist and gazed up at her face. There was an almost unbearable poignancy in the sight of their bodies merging among the shafts of light and the oily pools of shade. It was like certain gramophone records of the 'fifties you could no longer bring yourself to listen to—the exact music of youth that evoked exactly the dead joys and hopes of youth.

Emma broke away and ran across the bridge, her feet drumming on the boards. The girl waited for me, smiling slightly, the tips of her square teeth showing against her lower lip.

'Hello, Esther.'

'Hello, Bob.'

'Thanks for coming.'

She shrugged; we began to cross the bridge. When we reached the other side Emma had scrambled up on to one of the heavy posts the rails were connected to. 'Catch, Daddy!'

She hurled herself confidently into space and I did so stylishly, pleased by the unexpected chance of underlining the felicity of my home life. I went on to swing her round and round until her body flew out at right angles to mine and the wood echoed with her laughter. 'There.' I put her down at last. 'You're witnessing the polished team-work of months. Even so, Emma, I thought jumping was supposed to be forbidden. Tomboyish, Mummy says. You're just a little show-off.'

'Like her father,' the girl said softly.

I grinned. 'Ah, well, self-projection's essential in my line of country.'

We walked on, Emma running ahead, until we came to a point where the brook emptied into a pool the locals called The Tarn. The girl and I sat down on a rough wooden bench. Emma helpfully began to hum a tune and dance to it, affecting indifference but eyeing us every few seconds to see if we were watching.

'Dvořák?'

'It does rather sound like one of the Slavonic Dances. She won't show off to any old rubbish.'

The girl laughed, took out her cigarettes.

After a while, I said : 'I wanted to speak to you.'

'Oh.'

'I wanted to ask you to help me.'

I turned to her. She was gazing straight ahead, across the sheet of water, her lips ruefully pushed out a little.

'Look, Esther.' I nodded at Emma. 'They don't come much brighter. I bet she's not much different from you when you were six. And when you were six I've no doubt you adored your father. I don't know your parents, but I can guess at clever outgoing people who gave you the sort of imaginative upbringing your kind of mind needed.'

I paused, let the low murmur of my voice be overlaid by the sound of the brook running into the pool, the bird-song, Emma's humming. The girl finally tossed her unsmoked cigarette into the water and gave a single nod.

'I'm working class,' I said. 'As you know. I came from nothing. I was the first Saxby to go to work in a collar and tie. I won't bore you with it, you'll have read all those late 'fifties novels for your A-level English. My people understood me so little they just let me go my own way. And here I am, I suppose, with the money, the house and the gear. But I wasted years, And I went through some frightful patches. And with my kind of brain I'd have been twice as far along the road if I'd been directed by parents like yours. It's the waste that sickens.'

I paused again. Emma, flush-faced and beaming, had now begun a series of rather uncertain *entrechats*; her hat had fallen over one ear.

I went on, the gentle voice in the television documentaries about alcoholism. 'I want it different for her, Esther. I want to give her the background your parents gave you. I want to spare her all the frustrations and bitterness. She's got talent and she's very much like me, which means she'll not be satisfied if she can't achieve her full potential.

'She's also very sensitive, like most intelligent children. Very dependent on a strong parental structure. I . . . I suppose what I'm trying to say is what a criminal waste it would be if anything going wrong between me and Gwen spoiled her development. It would put her back a lot further than working-class ignorance put me back. It could stop her dead.'

At last she turned to me; I gave her my crinkly avuncular smile. She watched me steadily.

'I've been waiting,' she said in a low voice. 'Ever since that afternoon. To see just how you were going to package it.'

Emma was exhausted by now and lay spreadeagled on the turf, the sun-hat covering her face. The girl smiled bitterly and gave a nod that took in Emma and the pool and the sunlit woodland. 'Full marks, Bob—that little vignette had a touch of genius.'

I'd known. I'd known almost from the first word she could see the homework. But this was how Gwen had insisted it should be put across and I was determined to play it straight. I gave her a hurt look.

'Don't be like that, Esther. I meant it. I'm at greater risk than most men. I'm well known. If anything went wrong with my marriage it wouldn't go wrong quietly and the innocent would suffer. Emma, in other words.'

'You know, I don't think you *could* do anything that hadn't been worked out in advance.'

'Oh, come, we had to sort it all out, for both our sakes. I've just been trying to find the right time.'

'We could have stayed in the office any lunchtime to talk it out.'

'I . . . wanted to get away from the pressures of the office. Right away, where there'd be no distractions.'

'Except, Emma. Oh, *Bob!*' A single tear glistened in one of her eyes; she rubbed it away angrily on her sleeve. 'Can't you even be yourself with me *now*, after . . . Have you *any* idea of the anguish *I've* gone through about your family and your ambitions? Oh, for God's sake, you can't believe I *want* an affair with you!'

'But that's just it. Of course you don't. And I don't want you to either, a fine girl like you with your life in front of you. I . . . blame myself for . . . Chelifer House. But . . . you attract me,' I said in a low voice. 'Very much.'

That at least was the exact truth. In the V of her jacket I could see the upper plains of her breasts. Bra, pants, the trouser-suit—there were four flimsy garments between me and her young white body, and I ached for that studio silence and the pungent heat of that curtained bed. I could sense her moist pubic hair against my hand. 'I thought we could help each other not to be foolish. For Emma's sake.'

'So you arrange to have Emma dancing on the grass. As if I'm so mean and vicious I might try to damage your chances.'

'Esther . . .'

'You just can't believe it, can you? That I *couldn't* hurt you. Whatever happened.'

Depression hit me like shock-wave. I'd known I was right about her and Gwen wrong. And the man I'd once been was as sickened as the girl by the careful way I'd set the meeting up. The man who'd known about spontaneity and unhappiness and pain. That man pitied her.

But then there was the man I'd become. Who owed so much to so many, to Pop and Gwen and the machine and Emma. Above all to Emma. A man who felt compelled to protect himself even though he knew the enemy didn't exist, who felt compelled even to arrange the raptures and miseries of youth into some kind of order, so that the world would be absolutely safe for egomaniacs.

There was a moment when I almost admitted it was a fix. And then I remembered that bad fortnight. Remembered the bald fact that Esther had got me into bed. Remembered, bitterly, that my world was separated from hers by all the things that had happened in my four thousand extra days. I plugged doggedly on.

'Please don't be upset, Esther,' I said gently. 'I never thought for a minute you'd upset the apple-cart for me. Not you. But we couldn't go on like that, could we—not seeing each other and then suddenly seeing each other and being foolish, and then not seeing each other again?

'But . . . but I'd still like us to be friends. Honestly. We both wanted that, didn't we, all along? Couldn't we try and start again as friends and really try to keep it like that?'

'So you can keep an eye on me? So you can be certain I'm not on the loose somewhere, throwing mud at your shining image? So you can keep the situation suitably de-fused. Oh, God, Bob, where does the style finish and the man *start*?'

It was hard to go on smiling, even me, with ten years of bared teeth behind me. I turned away. You didn't hurt easily when you reached maturity but when you did hurt it lasted longer, the mental flesh didn't knit so quickly over the scars any more. When she was done with me and totally immersed in that fresh-faced graduate she was going to marry, I'd still have those words as fresh in my memory as they were now.

We sat there in silence for minutes. Finally, I became aware of Emma's solemn blue eyes a few inches from mine.

'Come on, Daddy—you've been sitting there ages. Esther hasn't seen the iron-water spring yet.'

She turned to the girl. 'The iron-water's bright orange,' she said. 'And you must never let it splash you after a thunderstorm. Anne Bonner's dog *paddled* in it after a thunderstorm and *his* paws have been bright orange ever since.'

I couldn't help smiling.

'It's true, Daddy, honestly! She crossed her heart and touched the date-stone.'

'Tell her to bring it to see you then.'

'She can't do that. She lives miles away.'

'Tell her we'll call then, one Saturday afternoon, to see this dog with the bright orange feet.'

'Oh *you*! I believe her. And you believe her, Esther, don't you? Daddy never believes *anything*.'

'Yes, Emma, I know.'

It should have have sounded snide, but it didn't. Just sad, matter-of-fact.

'Oh, come on, Esther. *I'll* show you the iron-water spring. Don't bother about Daddy. He never believes *anything*. He didn't believe about Christopher Hemmel seeing the ghost of their dog, *or* about Rodney Hindle and that furry spider . . .'

She marched the girl off down to the bridge, still working steadily through the list of things I'd not believed in. I got up at last and began to follow them. I watched them passing hand in hand through heavy shade and diagonal bands of white light and listened to the cadence of their voices in the heavy silence, Emma's shrill laughter. I gazed at Emma's young body as she climbed over root systems that were like shallow flights of steps. There wasn't even going to be friendship then, to go with sex in the head. All I had of her now was her loyalty.

That peculiarly intense loyalty. She reminded me of Maggie. It was beyond me. You had to be nicer than I was to get that kind of loyalty, and you had to be known to be nicer. She only knew me as a tough bastard. Her intensive Saxby researches might have told her I'd been nicer once, but no one could be loyal to an identi-kit.

She was waiting at the end of another bridge. Emma was down at the water's edge, at the point where the iron-water spring gushed at right angles into the brook. She was bravely tossing pebbles into the spring and then leaping back with a shriek in case she should be marked for life by the dreaded orange fluid.

'Esther!' she cried. 'Are you coming to tea, ducky?'

She'd heard the word in some old film, it was a favourite current endearment. The girl suddenly laughed.

'Well, are you?' I said, politely indifferent.

'Oh, no, I couldn't.'

'You jolly well are, Esther.'

Emma scrambled up through the rails of the bridge. 'We're having lamb chops and new potatoes and salad. And Daddy will give you a glass of sherry and we'll put *The Mikado* on.'

Beaming, confident of a delighted acceptance, she took hold of the girl's hand. It was none of my doing. I'd built the afternoon round Emma, but lamb chops hadn't come into it. Emma simply didn't want to be parted from her and Esther knew it. She looked from Emma's eager face to my totally neutral one. She smiled uncertainly.

'It's very kind of you, but I really will have to go home.'

'Oh, *please*, Esther—I've not seen you for weeks. We'll play you *Peter and the Wolf* as well.'

Then she threw her trump-card down. 'And if you like, you can wind up my music-box that plays the *St. Antoni Chorale*.'

It couldn't have survived without Emma's gay prattle. The situation had been irretrievable. We were too hurt and we'd gone too far. It must still have been there, the urge for uncomplicated friendship, but we were both too dispirited to take any new initiative. And if we'd parted then it would have been for good.

But for Emma the rest couldn't have happened.

Any of it.

PART TWO
DESTINY REVEALED

I I

'What's on your agenda, then?'

'The garden till four, the U.T.s till five, home for dinner. Then Mother Telleyman, then Norman about the dance, then a bit of long-term planning with Pop. Then home to pull the guts out of three newspapers and four periodicals. Then bed.'

'Nice easy day.'

She wasn't joking. Not with the sort of winter and spring we had in front of us.

'Good.' Gwen took her glasses off. 'We can take our time over breakfast.'

I drank my coffee. Life really wasn't at all bad.

'It's London office week soon,' I said.

'I thought it must be.'

'I want advice. Esther's going this year instead of Miss Gleason.'

'. . . I see.'

We watched each other.

'How do you feel about it?'

'How do *you* feel about it?'

I shrugged. 'Seems perfectly safe. It's bloody hard work. She'd be too tired for naughtiness even if she felt like it.'

She picked up the silver coffee-pot.

'Anyway, she behaves herself now, doesn't she?'

'Never puts a foot wrong.'

She glanced out on to the back garden where Emma sat on the swing reading a *Paddington* book, eyes prudently protected against the watery autumn light by enormous smoked glasses.

'I thought Emma might do the trick,' she said.

'I wanted you to know about London well in advance, Gwen.'

She smiled approval. I needn't have told her. It was over now: Endersbys didn't bear grudges. And of course there was no love involved to make her forgiveness of me one of those awkward time-wasting affairs. I'd told her as a sort of atonement, not because of the adultery but because I'd put at risk ten years of inspired En-

dersby toil. Everything was just the same as it had always been—
the same planning, the same teamwork, the same ingenious sex. For
a man wanting to get on you couldn't beat old Gwen.

'Make an excuse to book the rooms yourself, and reserve a single
for Esther and a twin-bedded double for you and Martin.'

I smiled. 'Shrewd thinking.'

'Right, that takes care of London. Now listen, Bob, I think we've
had a bit of luck. Helen Walsh tells me her nephew's almost certain to be engaged by Radio Beckford when it goes on the air. Ex-
perienced in national radio and journalism, keen as mustard on
local radio, engaged to a Beckford girl. He'll be at the dance. Cultivate him—they'll be desperate for material at first.'

'Damned right they will! If I could get in on the ground
floor . . .'

'Quite. But try and draw Oliver Delgin into it if you can. We've
neglected him and he's important.'

'It's not easy. He's so self-sufficient.'

'But very fond of the sound of his own voice.'

'True. I'll work something out.'

'. . . and the little boy said : "Nobody has taken the strawberry
jam, Mummy." ' Emma looked at me gravely. 'Now *we* know who
Nobody was, don't we, Daddy?'

'Yes. Him. He was lying to save his own skin.'

'Oh, *Daddy*, Nobody was the name of the wolf !'

'I thought they called the wolf Alfred.'

'Daddy, you really are quite the silliest person I've ever known.
He was called Nobody, not Alfred. I told you in the story. And the
boy's mummy didn't know the wolf's name was Nobody. *She* thought
he meant *nobody*, and that's why she boxed his ears and scolded
him.'

She pronounced the word as scalded.

'What an absurd name to call a wolf. If he'd been called Alfred
in the first place there'd not have been all that trouble.'

'Oh, Daddy—you are *silly*. I shan't tell you any more. I shall tell
the others instead. They'll understand.'

She stalked across to where the dolls were arranged round an old
tablecloth near the pool and began : 'Once upon a time there was
a wolf who had *such* a curious name. His name was Nobody. Now
you won't forget that, will you? *Some* people don't seem able to

146

remember a little thing like that for a single *minute*.'

Her voice followed me as I worked along the lawn with the edging shears, in those chiselled accentless tones that were such a tribute to Gwen's infinite patience. It made me think ahead to that certain day when I'd see her on my own television, being animated and charming, or open a quality paper and see those confident eyes above a witty, topical column. The Katherine Whitehorn of the late 'eighties.

I thought of that afternoon in the woods last summer, of the sad scene I'd built round her and how quickly the girl had seen through it; I'd felt shabby for days. But over the weeks I'd stopped feeling shabby. I knew now that that had been the quintessential Saxby—manipulating his daughter to protect his career, but using the exact truth.

And I'd never thought of it in quite that way before, but I knew also that ambitious as I was there was no shadow of a doubt in my mind which would come first if either had to be sacrificed—my future or hers. There was never going to be anything about my future that would ever be worth more than the perfecting of Emma's.

It was a situation that wasn't going to happen, but the outcome was positive whether it did or not. I had my code, and I was glad the shabbiness of that afternoon had forced me to re-define it.

She opened the door and got in, shuddering a little against the chill air, hunching a fur collar closer to her neck. I heard the rustle of her dance dress. She'd sideswept her hair and blended it with a hair-piece that fell below her shoulder at the front in a cluster of ringlets.

'You look terrific,' I said.

'Thank you.'

Her wry smile matched my tone.

'Good of you to turn out so early.'

She shrugged.

'I want to get a grip on Chanctonbury before the others get at him,' I said. 'He won't be in Beckford again until the General. There's also a young chap I want to corner who'll almost certainly be working for Radio Beckford when it starts up. And when I've spoken to him I must speak to Oliver Delgin—the two are connected.'

'Delgin—the bald cadaverous one?'

'Who looks as if he keeps a dead whore in an attic.'

She coughed on cigarette smoke; I turned briefly from the road. Her large teeth were exposed in rare laughter.

After a while she said : 'Did you get the draft of the Alderton U.T. talk? I left it in your IN-tray.'

'I did, and a thousand thanks. It's perfect. For a minute I thought I'd written it myself.'

'I imagine you talking to them and it flows out honest-hickory of its own accord.'

'Will you do one for the Daisy Edge Ladies? Bearing in mind that Daisy Edge is snobs' row. They're clannish, reactionary and middle-aged up there, so don't attempt to be constructive. Just make a list of all the things the government's done wrong and work it up into a kind of litany so they can keep saying, "Hear, hear".'

'Concentrated cant.'

'Exactly.'

'What do you want me to do at the dance?'

'Play it by ear.'

I glanced at her again, gazing miserably down at the city, at the sprinkling of neons in office blocks and the necklaces of street lamps, the disc of the town hall clock, suspended mistral-sharp in the cold clear air. She was so pink and young in her evening-out coat and her ringlets, and the night would be so dull if she insisted on making it a job of work.

'Why not just have a night off and enjoy life?'

'If I wanted a night off it wouldn't be at your Grand Annual Dance,' she said flatly.

'Why do you do it, Esther? Why do you do it?'

'I'm not actually hired yet, don't forget.'

'Is there much doubt you will be?'

'Let's say I'm pretty high on the short list.'

'Number one, I should think.'

It wasn't flattery. I squeezed his arm—a middle-sized man with a round sallow face and smooth straw-coloured hair, fashionably dressed. The moment I heard that vibrant unobtrusive voice I knew he was going a long way.

'I've heard a good deal about you from Helen,' he said courteously. 'Are you going to win the nomination, do you think?'

'I hope so. I've been working towards it for ten years.'

'What would your priority be if you were actually returned for South?'

'There's only one thing that really matters in a town like Beckford, and that's industrial diversification.'

He nodded. Like me he tended to work all the time.

'Radio Beckford, Barry. You'll be starting absolutely from scratch?'

'Absolutely. We'll virtually have to put the programmes together as we go along.'

'Do you think there might be any scope for a really good question and answer programme? Something on the lines of taped questions about Beckford affairs from the man in the street answered by a panel made up from someone from each party and a couple of laymen. I know it's been done often by other local stations, but a lot of the attempts sound dull and amateurish. Now if you could put a really decent programme together in advance, with plenty of dry runs, and have it already to go on the air . . . But of course,' I added. 'You'd know whether it would work or not.'

He acknowledged my deference with a faint smile. We could both sense exactly our value to each other. I was a big potential story meeting an intelligent potential interpreter. He glanced at Esther, with her ringlets and her tiered and ruffled dress, intrigued by a relationship his intuition told him went far deeper than that of boss and assistant. I didn't mind it, the curiosity, it did me good with a man like this, to be linked to an attractive and intelligent young girl I might very possibly be having an affair with. She smiled at him warmly for me.

'This deserves discussing at some length.' He glanced at his watch. 'How about a few quiet drinks at the George one night?'

'Good idea!' I reached for my diary.

'You've made an old woman very happy, Bob. Both of you.'

Gwen had talked her into coming out of exile for once. I stood to one side of her chair on the central balcony, like a courtier, in my dinner-jacket, attending an aged royal. The illusion had been continued by the steady stream of elderly men coming to pay their respects. Her hair had been professionally set and her black silk dress brought out the violet of her eyes.

'But the music seems so fast, dear. I simply cannot tell what the tunes are. The dresses are lovely, though. So many styles and materials nowadays. It wasn't like that when I was a gel.'

The band reedily chopped its way through the sort of tunes Vera Lynn had kept the lads going with in nineteen-forty-two. Miss Charlotte thought of the days when she'd been as beautiful as the girl in the brown-tinted photograph, and I thought of the days when Dick Steeton and the Steetones had played here every Saturday night.

The Princess Hall. A gaunt parallelogram with green-painted iron railings in the balconies and cream-washed walls over which had been hopefully hung some coloured drapes and a number of worn-looking tinsel decorations. It doubled as a gymnasium and looked it.

Maggie and I had danced down there week after week. I could remember the tunes—*Begin the Beguine* and *You're the Cream in My Coffee, Moonlight Serenade* and *Stomping at the Savoy*. And we'd got drunk in the same bar.

I shivered with nostalgia. Life had been good then. I could remember the exact sound of that band and I could remember the sound of feet across powdered boards. I could even remember phrases spoken by people dancing nearby and the sad faces of girls at the floor's edge who had not been asked to dance. I'd held the silent ecstatic Maggie in my arms and I'd been happy and in love. Poor Maggie. Poor Maggie and Bob.

'Ah—there's your sweet U.T. friend. Do you see her—dancing with the good-looking boy who needs a hair-cut?'

I watched her circling with Peter Dowling. There was nothing between them now, he'd given up the chase. He was a realist. He'd taken up with a fluffy dumpling of a girl he was almost certainly having it off with. He danced with Esther simply out of hope.

But it still provoked sudden envy to see how well they looked together. Even though I'd known her body and he hadn't.

'Yes, I see her, Miss Charlotte.'

'Is she promised to that boy?'

'Not so far as I know.'

'There'll not be a scarcity of suitors.'

'She's very popular.'

But she was still hung up on Bob Saxby. I'd stopped asking myself why. It was autumn and things finished in autumn. Me and

Maggie, for instance. The sun was casting a long shadow and scarves of mist hung above my lawn, and soon the girl would go.

I'd always be grateful to her. We'd been together almost every day since June but we'd never laid a finger on each other. I sometimes felt it had developed a stronger bond between us than if we'd actually had an affair. The things we actually could do together had been done with a peculiar intensity that had brought me at least occasional flashes of a kind of happiness I'd not known since Maggie herself.

And she'd given me friendship.

'I arranged to have a noggin or two at the George with him, Oliver. I really pushed this idea of an all-party panel for a question and answer programme. I believe our keenness impressed him. Didn't show it, of course, terribly smooth, but he did casually enquire if I'd got anyone in mind for our people. Naturally I thought of you.'

His bald glossy head began to go pale pink. 'You flatter me, Bob. But don't you think it would be rather a waste of time when there's so much legitimate party work to be done?'

'Ah! That's why I didn't actually name you. But I could just imagine that cheerful voice of yours coming over the air. Bit like that Engelmann fellar, I've always thought.'

'I suppose I have done rather a lot of public speaking. And it does sound tolerable on tape I must admit.'

'There you are then! If we could establish you as our broadcaster and it went down well, think of the benefit to the party. We might be able to build you up into a sort of character.'

'I'll certainly think it over, Bob.'

'Oliver, it's only small time, but it could be a stepping-stone to national radio. Or even television. Don't forget, YTV looms on the horizon.'

'I could just imagine Mr. Delgin on television,' Esther said demurely. 'I believe he'd have an awfully good presence.'

'Do you think so, Esther? Do you really think so?'

'WINE MERCHANT ON PORNOGRAPHIC PICTURES CHARGE.' I muttered, as we began to dance together for the first time. 'Horsewhip Produced in Court.'

'You haven't the remotest intention of getting him into Radio

Beckford, have you, let alone the telly? I get the impression those plans are reserved for the great Bob himself.'

'Such cynicism. It puts me in mind of me.'

'But before Radio Beckford goes on the air you'll know if you've been selected or not, won't you? By a Selection Committee composed largely of Mr. Delgin who likes the sound of his own voice and Mrs. Telleyman who's a sucker for Proust and Mr. Vereburn who likes to name-drop and Master Dowling who writes so cleverly for *Forward!*'

'I knew you were eavesdropping. Right from the start.'

'However, you'll look prettier on television than Oliver. Sound better, too. They won't know where Omo finishes and you begin.'

I steered her round the hall, igniting my smile at passing faces. The bodice of her dress had a modern V-neckline that met a wide buckled belt, but the formality of it, and the rich cluster of ringlets falling just below her shoulder, reminded me of that burning buttercup day in the ruins of the Chelifer garden, of the palpable silence of that bedroom and her white body emerging from the wine-coloured satin. We wanted each other so badly we danced almost a foot apart.

But she'd given me this summer. A summer of friendship and sex in the head. Made a middle-aged man happy.

'Thanks for helping me with Delgin and Barry.'

Her grey eyes came up to mine with the sombre scrutiny I'd come to know so well. And care for so deeply.

Inevitably, she shrugged. 'You'll get where you're going with or without my help.'

With her, since that day in the woods, I'd never pretended to be anything but the man I was—a tough machine operator, and I didn't bother to pretend that the complex planning that went into the endless series of lobbying manœuvres was for any other purpose than that of setting up my own scene.

White Cliffs of Dover drew to its melancholy close; the pianist played a few chords of *Small Hotel* to signal the end of the dance.

'What next, Bob?'

'The photos,' I said softly. 'Will you help Gwen to arrange the groups? Leave Chanctonbury and his pals to her—you concentrate on mixing the rest in the ratio of one councillor or committee-member to three nonentities. Makes everyone feel somebody then.'

'I thought, "When everyone is somebodee, Then no one's anybody." ' She showed the tips of her teeth in a faint smile.

'They go to G & S to tap their feet to the tunes,' I said, 'not to be harrowed by the words.'

During the dance the top lights had been turned off and a glass-faceted ball suspended from the ceiling had revolved in the beams of fixed spot-lamps. At the same time the M.C. had played a movable spot-lamp here and there among the dancers. Before we could walk away, the fixed lamps were extinguished. I heard the girl suddenly gasp. So loudly it was as if she'd been given a heavy blow on the back. She gripped my arm. She was looking beyond me to where Miss Charlotte, isolated in the upward beam of the movable lamp, sat in hunched solitary splendour on the central balcony, a faint smile on her wizened face.

It was my doing. I'd arranged for the M.C. to give her a special word of welcome; he proceeded to do so with respectful unction.

And for a moment there had been a slight eeriness about that aged woman in the upward sepulchral light. But the girl was terror-struck. She was trembling. Her lips had fallen open on the large teeth and only once before had I seen her eyes so wide. She darted off then, rapidly threading her way through the groups of dancers towards the supper-room. As if she couldn't bear to watch Miss Charlotte a second longer.

'Ah, Bob—your ladies. How fond Gwen is of that sweet child. They worked so cleverly with the groupings.'

'Yes, they're an excellent team.'

'I do hope they're going to dance. They deserve some enjoyment. Yes . . . Esther is to dance with Mr. Delgin and Gwen . . . with *dear* Mr. Vereburn.'

Enjoyment. From my old station by Miss Charlotte's chair I smiled grimly as my ladies began to do a perfect military two-step. How strange to think of them thrown so closely together : shades of a *ménage*. And Gwen really was fond of Esther. She liked her quick grasp and her willingness. I couldn't have imagined even Gwen warming to the 'other woman', but her heart had always gone instinctively out to a hard worker. The girl had been an idiot, but she was young, and she'd made up for it since. It wasn't in Gwen's nature to look deeper.

It was left to me to wonder. I knew as little about her now as

I'd known the day I met her. She was afraid of Miss Charlotte and she'd been a virgin and she knew things about me that couldn't be found in any record.

I was devoured by curiosity. There was never a day, there was hardly ever a waking hour, when I didn't wonder what the answer was. And lately I'd begun to get the feeling that we were close enough for her to be able to tell me.

At the same time I wasn't really sure I wanted to be told. I remembered my early years, that restless search for mystery and glamour. I remembered the films I'd consumed, the tantalising world that had seemed to be contained in Audrey Hepburn's smile.

I remembered how none of the girls I'd ever known had measured up to the role I'd given them, not even Maggie in the end. There *had* been girls I'd been certain had the indefinable quality I sought, but they were always girls I glimpsed through a train window, or across a bar-room with someone else, or just coming out of a dance hall as I was going in.

And I was a man now, I was in my mid-thirties, I was standing dismally at the threshold of middle age. I was old enough to know there were no mysteries and no glamour. The girl defied solution, but only because I didn't know the whole story, and the solution would be mundane because human beings were mundane creatures. But what if I never knew the solution? What if I deliberately left myself in doubt? Wouldn't I be preserving something genuinely worth while for myself if I let her go out of my life as unexplained as she'd come in? In my youth I'd always sought a mystery, and now was the chance to keep one. If I kept the mystery the memory of this summer would never fade.

We were alone in the car. I'd dropped Gwen off and would be expected home in exactly the time, give or take ten minutes, it took me to drive to Esther's and back along the well-lit Welshman Road. She sat smoking and listening to the radio, which was playing Beatle standards.

'What it boils down to is you taking over in Beckford from Pop Endersby, doesn't it?' she said.

I drove for some time in silence.

'More or less.'

'It wasn't easy to work out. You want to be an M.P. and it fooled me. I was certain it was national politics you were set on.'

'I told you months ago it was Beckford I really wanted to work for.'

'But not control.'

I glanced up from the road. 'Only if all those people who put crosses on paper decide that I shall.'

'You're very clever with people and you're very clever with the party, and once you're into the Town Hall with a safe seat you'll never come out.'

'Agreed. The sort of plans I have for Beckford demand permanence. In fact I'm planning on being in permanently at forty and retiring round about the eighty mark.'

'With a Saxby Mark Two suitably groomed to follow you.'

'It may sound arrogant,' I said, 'but even local politics are getting too complicated for amateurs.'

'Ideally, I suppose they should only be open to keen management types.'

'You know the set-up,' I said. 'Grey area. Traditional industries having to rationalise. Skilled workers tending to leave the district and settling in the development areas.

'We've *got* to diversify our industry. And it's a Herculean task, God knows, but we're further handicapped by having to compete with a nearby development area that can attract new industry with government grants.

'The threat of decline hangs over the entire textile belt—men like Pop Endersby saw it coming as far back as the 'forties. The council spends hours of its time trying to find an answer. It's one hell of a problem and it demands administration every foot of the way. What Beckford needs right now, more than any other time in its history, is a youngish man with imagination and drive, who can handle people, understands finance and does his homework. And it needs him for a long time.'

She snapped the ashtray shut on her cigarette-end. 'A Bob Saxby.'

'Esther, how many men of my type *want* a career in local politics? Most of them are too busy carving their own future out, never mind a city's.

'But I do. And it's lucky for Beckford because it can't do without me. I'm briefed. I'm a Beckford compendium. I get ideas that work and I'm damned good at making sure they're turned into action.

'Most of all I generate enthusiasm. And I'll be able to attract like-minded men. There won't be any dabblers in my team, but men who'll stay and work their guts out because I've sold them a new Beckford. It's got to be me.'

'Then why the Commons?' Her cool voice came out of the shadows. 'You could be in the council now.'

'Partly prestige. It'll give me more authority later in the council. But mainly so I can find out exactly who pulls the regional strings in Whitehall and do some relentless lobbying on Beckford's behalf.'

'A brave new Beckford. I wasn't far out.'

'Make it brave new region. The Maud Report'll be out soon and everybody seems to think it'll be about authorities covering bigger areas. Enormously complex structures that'll demand men capable of complex planning.'

'Of which you're one of the best.'

'You mustn't misunderstand me. This town has its fair share of sound men. But I *know* I could build a team to give it star quality.'

'With Barry to bang the cymbals for you.'

I smiled. 'He's interested, isn't he? I thought you'd notice. I could be the sort of man who really is news and really does make things happen. If I am he'll give me the build-up. If I can develop a top-flight team he'll help to make the thing snowball. If I keep insisting that Beckford's a thrilling place to live in he'll go on telling Beckford. In the end Beckford might start telling the rest of the country. And if we go on telling the rest of the country about Beckford being surrounded by fine open moorland, and being a good place to live in or start a new business in, the rest of the country might start wanting to know more. You actually think of those towns that have got on since the war in terms of the men who've got them on. I'm determined to make Beckford into that kind of town.'

I drew to the side of the main road, a little way off from the drive where she lived. I was glad she wanted to know.

I'd let her in on all of it. For four months I'd never once pretended that every action wasn't precisely calculated, from kisses on old ladies' cheeks to antiques for the wives of party chairmen. She knew that every smile, every handclasp, every bright-eyed speech was part of the Bob Saxby hour.

I'd respected her intelligence. She'd always been able to see through the act so she might as well sit down in the dressing-room. If she was clever enough to see through the greasepaint she was clever enough to know there must be a higher sincerity, a longer term end.

At the same time, I'd realised she couldn't possibly know what it all added up to. She could make inspired guesses but she couldn't know for certain, because no one did, not even Gwen or Martin. Perhaps not even me. I'd always known the shape of the grand design but like most ambitious men I spent most of my time perfecting the detail.

My cheeks burned and I was breathing faster than usual. I'd never defined my future as precisely to anyone as I had to her. It had simply been an abstraction in my mind and suddenly fitting all the pieces together like that had raised me to a rare pitch of stimulation.

I was glad she had it all, Saxby in the round. I was an unhappy and complicated man and I used everything—my family, my looks, my charm, my hatred, my bitterness. But there was a code and most of the time I lived by it, and it seemed to me that the plans I had for Beckford were not without honour.

I wanted her to think so. Very much. I could still remember the things she'd said to me during those ugly scenes in my car and it seemed as if I'd been waiting all summer for this moment.

'I see,' she said.

That was all. When I turned to her she wasn't even looking at me, but looked straight ahead down the silent lamp-lit road. And as the seconds passed on it was obvious she'd said all she was going to say.

Just : 'I see.'

12

Martin cleared his throat nervously.

'The old favourite then. Do we go on covering rands?'

'For God's *sake* !' Garbutt cried. 'If I hear any more of this bloody accountant's talk I'll not come to any more meetings.'

The Governor's cigar-case crashed down.

'Roy, this lady !'

'This is the late 'sixties, Roy,' I said icily. 'Money's a commodity just like wool's a commodity and has to be handled with equal care.

Anyway, Martin and I have to sit through plenty of boring talk about quality claims, so it cuts both ways.'

'Gentlemen, I *deplore* these acrimonious exchanges. You do all work for the same firm, you know.' He turned to Simon with a scowl of doting ferocity. 'What does our devaluation expert say?'

'We must continue to cover,' Simon said firmly. 'I'm not happy about the money market. I was discussing the matter with Sir Alfred only yesterday. As you know he has close family ties with two merchant banks. He said he'd not known the City as jittery in years . . .'

Garbutt gave a soft belch of disgust and we all settled down to the statutory ten-minute lecture on currency, a period I tried to enliven for myself by seeing if I could scribble on my pad, one sentence before he uttered them, such well-loved phrases as 'floating exchange rate' and 'flight from the pound' and 'theory of the Crawling Peg'. Martin alone could see the words. I heard his faint sigh of annoyance.

'Nicely put, Simon,' I said warmly. 'We go on covering then.'

'Just so,' the old man said. 'Now, next business.'

'The London trip, Governor. May Martin and I, *very* briefly,' I gave Garbutt a hard stare, 'run through the changes in system we're anxious to introduce up there . . .'

'Before you go on, Robert,' Simon cut me off, 'it occurs to me that I ought to go up there this time instead of one of you. There are certain aspects of the London office accounting system I should like to examine at first hand.'

I thought fast behind the cordial smile. 'Well . . . come by all means, Simon, we'd be delighted to have your views. But I do rather think Martin and I ought both to be there—the new scheme's a joint effort.'

'Oh, come, I'm perfectly able to stand in for either of you by now. If we all went it would mean four hotel bills—a needless extravagance. We *must* be careful of wasteful expenditure, you of all people ought to be thinking of that.'

I could have kicked him in the crutch. He was sitting against a window, sun shining from behind him made him look as young as the snotty bastard he'd looked ten years ago. It took every ounce of effort to keep me smiling and bland.

'Well . . . yes, you've got a valid point, but the changes are so radical I really do feel we should both go. Another year it won't matter.'

Getting any words out at all had been a feat, but anger had stopped me finding the kind of words that would make our point but also save his face. He lit a thick cigarette irritably.

'Robert, I've been in your office for six months. I can set your mind fully at rest about my competence to stand in for either of you. You and Martin really must get out of the habit of thinking your work is incomprehensible to the rest of us. You are accountants, not nuclear scientists.'

Garbutt and his yes-men began to snigger and even the Governor's face softened into a frown. Esther watched me impassively over her pad. And then I saw the way out. I'd have seen it sooner if I hadn't been trembling with rage. Simon was digging his own booby-trap. All I had to do was keep him talking and edge him towards it. Backwards.

'Do go, Simon, if you feel you ought to be in the picture. I'm sure you're right about standing in perfectly well for either of us. In fact to be honest I must admit it's going to come as something of a relief to whichever of us stays behind. We're not madly keen on midnight oil, you know, new procedures or not.'

'Midnight oil . . . ?'

'The trouble is, you see, that it's not very easy to institute new systems while people are still using the old ones.' I sighed. 'I'm afraid the bulk of the work will have to be done when the clerical staff have gone home.'

'I see. I hadn't *quite* realised there was to be so much time spent on rearranging bits of paper. I'd imagined it would be mainly meetings and group discussions as usual.'

'Ah, yes, there'll be those as well,' I said cheerfully. 'But after dinner it'll be jackets off and down to those bits of paper, I'm afraid.'

'I see. Yes, it hardly needs me around simply to watch you rearrange bits of paper. However, I daresay I could sit in on the meetings and leave the bumf to you and Martin.'

I hesitated. I had him perfectly positioned. Garbutt watched us. Not involved for once, he sensed I was going to catch Simon as I'd so often caught him. Because he was engrossed, the others became engrossed. Everyone waited.

'But Simon,' I said slowly, in a puzzled voice, 'wouldn't that mean four hotel bills after all?'

His lozenges turned on like pilot-lights and he suddenly began to jab his cigarette out into an ashtray. Over and over again, as if he wished it were my eye.

He began to eat whitebait.

'Saxby the sadist.'

'Christ, did you *want* him with us?'

'We need him involved. And you know it.'

'We've got work to do. There won't be time for show-stopping speeches about the state of the nation.'

'It was the dirty way you pulled the rug from under him. You could have saved his face if you'd wanted to.'

'I made the best job of it I could. I didn't notice you rushing to the aid of the party.'

'Don't be snide. You're the brain. You were angry with him so you used a shabby ploy.'

'Angry. I'll say I was angry.'

'Why?'

'Why? Because I've made that bloody firm the best in the business and that arrogant dolt still talks to me like an office boy.'

'So? He's been talking to you like an office boy once a week since April and you've not pulled a nasty trick like that.'

'I'll show the sod. It won't just be that place I run, it'll be the whole town. Give me ten years and it'll be half Yorkshire.'

'Oh, for heaven's sake . . .'

'And one day, when I don't need the Fishers any more, I'll take him on one side and spell it out to him in great detail that everything I've ever done has been to keep my mind off smashing his bloody head in.'

He sighed. 'Oh, Bob. Look, you're a grown man. You *know* you're good. You convinced me years ago you were going to be one of the best things that ever happened to Yorkshire, and in a few years more you'll have convinced everyone else.'

Except her. Depression hit me like nerve gas. Not Esther Moore. The only one it mattered about.

I picked indifferently at the routine steak salad. After a while he said: 'All right, what's biting you? You've not had one of your berserkers for months.'

I watched him, sitting in mellow autumn sunlight, as he poured himself claret and began to eat jugged hare—his usual indulgent repast. I looked at his lined cynical face, at the battered tweeds and the elderly foulard; and guilt intensified the depression. What about him? Ten years of ceaseless encouragement, constructive criticism, humouring, the kind of advice money couldn't buy. Friendship. Hundreds of lunches. Nothing asked in return except that I put no limit on ambition. Without him I couldn't have got where I was, even with Gwen—they'd made equal contributions.

But it wasn't his approval I instinctively sought, but hers, a naïve young girl I'd known since April.

'I'm sorry about the meeting,' I said finally. 'It *was* a rotten trick. Take no notice, I woke up with a monumental migraine—I'm not myself.'

The deep-set eyes rested on mine and I could tell he wasn't entirely convinced. But the faint permanent smile deepened.

'Then have a drop of this claret. It's the kind the late Maurice Healy once said should be drunk kneeling.'

'It won't happen again.'

'I'm half-inclined to believe you. After you've done so well for so long you must disappoint yourself as much as you disapppoint me.'

'I do.'

'Right, drink that, and we'll talk of other things. Rands, for example. You will keep your eye on Master Fisher about that currency covering, won't you?'

'So far he hasn't missed a sale.'

'I wouldn't know how to face Garbage and his men if we ever slipped up on that one.'

'Simon.'

'Yes.'

'Alderman Endersby was asking about you last night. My father-in-law.'

'Really.'

'He did think it was bad luck we couldn't nominate you for the by-election.'

'I still feel a determined effort could have stopped Breasey's nomination.'

'A great pity. But the machinery ...'

'I still can't understand why the machinery couldn't be altered to let me contest a provincial council seat instead of a meat-pie man.'

I was trying to put right the damage I'd done at the meeting. He watched me coldly from behind the big desk that had once been mine.

'We never did have that little get-together we talked about last spring.'

'That's hardly surprising. Your people weren't particularly forthcoming.'

It had been a matter of the greatest delicacy. On two separate occasions I'd got the men who mattered in Westbury to agree on a date when they could meet Simon at my house. In both cases the date hadn't fitted in with Simon's social life. Westbury had lost interest after that and I'd simply had to put the meeting on ice.

The position had been complicated by Simon falling in love, if that wasn't too bizarre a term to describe the belated and expeditious alliances male Fishers invariably made. He was to be married next spring at last, to the daughter of a wealthy cloth merchant, a hefty, cheerful girl who ran a riding school and had a slightly dubious reputation. According to Martin, the younger end of the county set still called her the Yorkshire Cob.

'I was wondering if we couldn't get you to speak to our U.T.s one evening. Decent speakers aren't easy to come by, and there aren't many who've travelled as widely as you.'

He was interested. He was pretending to skim through the *Financial Times*, but I could tell he was focussing beyond it.

'Oh, really, Robert, I don't know that I can spare the time to talk to a dozen teenagers in a club-room.'

The U.T.s were an attractive bunch of youngsters who listened attentively to their speakers and thanked them with great charm. I sometimes used them as bait to entice certain men into membership. If he could do nothing else Simon could speak easily and well. Didn't I know it.

'Simon, you've travelled the world. Don't you think you owe it to their young minds to give them the benefit of your knowledge? They'd be so grateful.'

'Oh, well, if you put it that way I don't see how I can refuse. Heaven knows how I'll find the time.'

'Splendid! How about next Tuesday? Perhaps while you're there you could have a word with my father-in-law about next year's elections. He's very anxious to meet you.'

The spots of colour in his cheeks glowed slightly. The Yorkshire

Cob was beating politics by a short head; once he'd got her out of his system he'd be ours.

Like the Governor, he could watch you for seconds without speaking. He did so now. He'd improved dramatically since his break with alcohol. He'd stopped looking worn out, his eyes shone and he'd put on weight. In my rational moods I could only admire the Fisher toughness.

I could almost feel sorry for him. I knew by now he envied me, envied the pace of my life, the politics, the iron grip I had over every aspect of his own business.

He didn't know it was envy. How could a Fisher consciously envy a hired money-counter? But it showed in a dozen oblique ways. In the way he still wanted to sit at my desk, to stay near the nerve-centre, in his desperate bids to dominate the meetings. There were times now when I felt that deep in his guts and his blood, a dozen years ago, Simon had sensed what I stood for. He'd glimpsed the man standing dimly behind the boy and had reacted with an antagonism neither he nor I had been mature enough to understand.

Perhaps it had always been envy. My hate : his envy. Hate had done wonders for me—perhaps there was hope for Simon. According to Martin, Simon was an essential part of my destiny. Perhaps during this last summer I had become an essential part of his.

Could it be that one day we'd meet on common ground?

'Very well then, Robert,' he said. 'Next Tuesday it is.'

'I've definitely nailed Simon Fisher down to speak to the U.T.s, Gwen. About his travels.'

'Good. I'll roll the red carpet out.'

'That's the idea. Look, I'm having hell's own job to convince him the machine's got to know him before they'll buy him. He wants a safe council seat; sock it to him as tactfully as possible he can't have the one without the other.'

'Leave it to me. The U.T.s are the thin edge of the wedge. Bags of flattery, you say?'

'Trowel job. Don't offer him a drink; he's just stopped being an alcoholic.'

'Right.' She made a note in her big diary. 'Now . . . you're in London next week?'

'Including the final Saturday. We're working Saturday morning and taking Esther to see *Fiddler on the Roof* in the evening. Martin insists we'll owe her *one* night out. It's all any of us'll have.'

'How can Martin Emmott *always* get tickets to things like *Fiddler*?'

'Master of a hundred decadent skills.'

'Bob, while you're away I'm going to start sounding Vereburn, Telleyman, Delgin and so on about next spring.'

'Good. It's about time we went into the overkill stage.'

'Right.' She snapped her diary shut and smiled at me. 'I'll get the dinner out. You will behave yourself in London, won't you?'

'Shall I show you my work-load? I won't even have time for naughtiness, let alone energy.'

It was all over now, finished, dead, buried. Life was exactly the same as it had always been, my own personal machine in full working order, throbbing with the discreet power of a VC10.

'Where's Emma?'

'In the living-room, sulking. I gave her a wigging about jumping off walls. Which wouldn't have been so bad but I'd also given her a wigging about paper golliwogs. When we got home from Morrison's she'd got ten of them in her hot little hand. She'd helped herself, from the sides of ten jars of jam. Ten, as you may or may not know, being the number you send to the jam firm in return for a *metal* golliwog. With a pin on. Stop *grinning*, I want *you* to speak to her. Tell her if she wants a metal golliwog she has to eat ten jars of jam like everyone else.'

She was lying on the floor in jeans and sweater, her honey-coloured hair spread loosely over her back, tying a nail-file with a shoe-lace round the waist of an ancient scruffy bear we called Genghis Noggs.

'What's he supposed to be then?'

'He's been selected by the Queen to be one of her knights,' she said in a flat aggrieved voice.

'What can he *possibly* have done to deserve it?'

'Because he guarded the palace so well.'

'Genghis Noggs couldn't guard a parking-meter.'

'Genghis Noggs captured *ten* enemy soldiers during the night and locked them in the Tower. The Queen presented him with this fine sword.'

'Genghis Noggs couldn't catch a centipede with one leg.'

'Genghis Noggs is the bravest bear the Queen's ever known,' she said irritably. 'And I don't want to talk about it because I'm not friends with Mummy *or* you.'

'What have *I* done wrong?'

'Always going on about jumping off that stupid old wall.'

'Well, you're not supposed to. Anyway, what about those golliwogs?'

'It's not stealing,' she muttered. 'Sandra's got hundreds.'

Perhaps one day, when I was the strong man of the region, and she the Joan Bakewell of the 'eighties, she'd interview me with the same tough but charming objectivity she interviewed everyone else, and people would take us even further into their hearts. I'd always been glad she'd not been a boy. I wasn't dynasty-minded. I'd no desire to perpetuate my name or the kind of man I was, and I could imagine how neurotic a son might be having to stand in my light. But girls were different. I got down on my knees; she glanced at me ruefully.

'Well, it isn't, is it? Stealing?'

'It is really, Em. Those paper golliwogs really go with the jars of jam. They're a sort of reward for buying it.'

'It'd take *months* to eat ten jars of jam. *Years.*'

'Don't be silly.'

'It'd take me a *million* years,' she said firmly. ' 'Cause I never eat any.'

I turned away, but not before she'd seen me grinning. She began to grin too, gleefully, the single tombstone second tooth towering over the milk teeth.

'Now look, Emma, I want you to promise me you'll never do it again.'

'Oh, all right, Poppa. I promise.'

I stroked her hair. She was my daughter. It wasn't right but it wasn't really wrong either, we both had a touch of the buccaneer.

I sighed. Esther would go soon, but there'd always be Emma. And time passed quickly when you lived at my pace, in a handful of years we'd be discovering France and Greece and the Nile together, and making plans for that blinding career she'd have, that would bring so much happiness to so many. It wouldn't do poor Maggie any good, or Esther, and it wouldn't excuse my own deficiencies, but because of those things perhaps, and out of them, one perfectly adjusted woman would emerge—balanced, educated, loving, intelligent and spontaneous.

There'd always be Emma. And it was a lot more than I deserved.

'Daddy.'

'Yes.'

'Don't go to London.'

I was surprised. She'd never questioned my absences before, long or short.

'Why not, Em?'

'Because there'll only be me and Mummy. I might get kidnapped.'

'Oh, come now—you know you'll be all right with Mummy.'

'Don't go to London, Poppa. It's a long way away and you might forget all about poor little Emma.'

She began to suck her thumb. She was tired and she was six, and like most children of six she usually relapsed into babyhood at bed-time.

'I'd *never* forget about poor little Emma,' I said. 'And I can't imagine why you think anyone could kidnap you with the mighty, Genghis Noggs on guard.'

But she'd never minded me being away before, and it made me feel slightly uneasy.

13

'Does it make you nervous? The idea of actually making a speech in here?'

'Petrifies me. Though they say there's rather a sympathetic atmo-sphere, particularly when you make your maiden speech.'

'Would you speak much?'

'Only in any debate on regional affairs. I'd leave the international stuff to the glamour boys. I know *my* brief.'

The Commons was full of aqueous autumn sunlight. Every five minutes or so a guide would march a platoon of sightseers through, but now the Chamber was deserted except for a single policeman standing by the Serjeant-at-Arms' chair. I gazed at the ascending green benches and remembered how it looked on a good working day at Question Time, with the Speaker and his clerks and the famous front bench faces and the packed galleries. I remembered the times I'd sat upstairs with Gwen and imagined myself on one of the back benches, trying to catch the Speaker's eye. Bob Saxby actually addressing the Commons, his words, such as they were, preserved for ever in Hansard.

'It really does mean an awful lot, doesn't it? Getting here. I'd not realised quite how much.'

She watched me forlornly. It was like the night of the local elections when I'd scarcely known she was there at all. From the Robing Room I'd walked her along the Royal Gallery, through the Princes' Chamber and on to the Lords', chattering about Maclise waterglass and Theed bronzes and Pugin fireplaces as if it excited her as much as it had always excited me and Gwen.

'Yes. Getting here's supposed to be the cornerstone of my career, but I shall love every minute of it. Biggest committee-room of the lot, you see.'

I could almost hear the sonorous voice of the Speaker and feel the tension of rising to my feet. I could see the backs of heads and the discs of faces and sense the indifferent amiable silence. And then the Commons slowly became an empty room again, the girl and I standing in watery sunlight in the middle of it.

Suddenly I had that strange rare feeling of being outside myself, almost of looking down at myself from the gallery—a mental long-shot of a forlorn young girl and a confident mature man. I felt an engulfing sadness.

She was the right woman for me at the wrong time. I'd come to accept it as the months passed; but that wasn't the point. If I'd been a free agent, if I could have married her tomorrow, if we could ignore the ten-year barrier, I'd still not have been able to give her anything she really needed. There'd been times when I'd been certain it would have worked. I'd smell her clean scent, or see her watching me, or think of the afternoon at Chelifer House, when it seemed that nothing I'd ever done with my life could compare with the idea of holding her moist naked body in my arms, or walking across moorland with her, or just talking to her.

But this did. I wanted her badly, I ached with longing, but I *had* to have this. I'd fixed on ambition for ten years and it was just like any other hard drug; in the end you could get along without most things but the drug itself.

'They were a sort of Gilbert and Sullivan of architecture, always squabbling. They've never really sorted out who did what with it.

Barry never got on with Gothic, he was a Classical man, both by training and inclination. If the old Palace had burned down fifteen or twenty years earlier we'd be looking at the usual tedious senate house. But it burned down in the Gothic revival and that's the result—a cross between his Classical leanings and his subsequent expeditious leap on to the Gothic bandwagon. "All Grecian, sir," said Pugin bitterly, "Tudor detail on a classic body." '

She smiled faintly. 'But you like it.'

'I like it. It's unique and we've preserved our reputation for oddness.'

'You must work that up into a little set-piece, Bob, for when you entertain visiting constituents. Mrs. Telleyman would be entranced.'

Her voice was wry. I didn't seem able to stop myself today. I gazed at the great limestone building, at the towers and the turrets and the lines of tiny shadowed windows, at the pinnacles which stood against sailing cloud like javelins. There was a keen wind off the Thames and it was autumn, but I knew exactly how it would be on the Terrace in the vertical June sunlight, with the tables and chairs out and the boxes blazing with geraniums. They would visit me, Emma and Gwen, and we'd have afternoon tea and watch the pleasure boats steaming upriver to Putney and Kew. Other Members would stop and have a word with us, and they'd be captivated by Emma and Gwen. Watch the Saxbys, they'll get on.

It ran through my mind like a film. I'd wake up in my small hotel room and on dry mornings I'd walk briskly along Whitehall. I'd see to my mail and have a cup of tea. Hard work on Standing Committees and then Question Time. Dinner, as waning sunlight turned windows to shields of gold, and a glass or two of wine with someone I was cultivating. Weeks and weeks of it.

I'd a good chance. If I could get the nomination I could swing South, I was certain of it, the sort of campaign I'd set up.

'I can see the sense of all those speeches and bazaars,' she said. 'Wanting something as badly as you want that.'

Poor kid—she looked chilled through despite the tweed two-piece and the fur collar.

'Let's go,' I said. 'You must be bored stiff.'

'No, I'm not bored. Really. I wanted to see it all and no one could have shown it me better than you.'

I believed her. She wasn't bored, just dejected by my total involvement. It hadn't been fair to bring her. I should have known it would just be the Bob Saxby show.

We walked along Bridge Street towards Whitehall, seeking a cab. 'How about the National Gallery? We've still got an hour or so.'

She smiled wanly. I'd make it up to her at the National; I'd give her my full attention. I didn't want her to feel neglected, not after the way it had been this summer.

But even then I couldn't keep my eyes off those great buildings in Whitehall against a sky of scudding cloud, or dismiss memories of Snow novels or Eric Coates marches or Churchill's phlegmy voice growling about eleventh hours of eleventh days.

I paid off the cab at the south side and we walked across Trafalgar Square, past the bird-seed men and the knots of people feeding pigeons, dodging spray from wind-blown fountains. The pale autumn sun gleamed feebly off wet flagstones and we were surrounded by a grinding wedge of traffic that seemed to be composed entirely of red buses and black Austins.

I thought of my honeymoon. We'd spent part of it in London, going to theatres and debates, and having lunchtime drinks at the George and the Coal Hole. We'd had rather a lot of deliciously complex sex too, in that cosy hour between getting back to the hotel and sipping the pre-dinner sherries.

I'd enjoyed it, enjoyed it as much as it was possible to enjoy a honeymoon with someone who was such a jolly good chum. But what would London have been like with a woman like Esther? Those lunchtime pubs and Shaftesbury Avenue and Hyde Park. I could imagine. From a depression that suddenly bordered on melancholy, I could imagine.

'*Cornfield and Cypress Trees*,' I said. 'My all-time favourite. Bound to be some sinister clue to the inner me. Have you *ever* seen a picture that lives like that one? Have you ever seen such a sky or such a tree?

'It's like being on a train in summer and the fields of corn and barley and long grass are swirling past—the foreground's like a river between the stationary banks of the horizon. It excites me the way this picture does. What a terrible burden it must be to carry that kind of genius round in your mind. It never surprises me when brilliant men destroy themselves.'

'It's all Pasmore at home,' she said. 'Later Pasmore, of *course*.

Pasmore and Pop Art and experiments in pure white light. They tend to forget I've got to discover it all for myself and in my own way.'

'You'll be all right with me then,' I said. 'I still get very uneasy about experiments in pure white light.'

It was better here. I was all hers here, not half lost in some intensely personal future. I shouldn't have taken her to Westminster. It seemed thoughtless to the point of callousness in retrospect. We should have gone to the Tate with Martin or we should have come directly here.

Anyway, she'd enjoy half the afternoon at least. We were back together, back to that warily intense relationship we'd come to accept as normal. She looked happier than she'd looked all day.

And if we hadn't made a start in one of the French rooms she would have enjoyed it. But that particular room contained *La Première Sortie*. I'd seen it several times before, never since Emma had grown into childhood. And pictures were like books—they meant different things as you grew older. The young girl on her first visit to the theatre might have been Emma herself as she would be—she had the same prettiness and the same delicate colouring, and she gave the same trusting impression of a secure home-life. The flowers and bonnet were the trappings of a woman, but the excitement could only have been a child's. I couldn't take my eyes from it and for a while I couldn't bring myself to speak.

Her voice trailed off, but I was only half-aware of the fact. Suddenly she turned away and walked out of the room. It was a quarter of an hour later before I found her again, in that labyrinth. We walked about for the rest of the time almost in silence.

First my ambition, then my family. She'd had a lousy afternoon.

I let myself into the room I shared with Martin; a maid touched my arm. 'Mr. Robert Saxby?'

I nodded.

'Mr. Emmott said an' to be sure you got this, sorr.'

I gave her half a crown wrapped up in a crinkly smile and tore open the envelope.

Bob—Sorry, old son, but Monica rang to say she's started her labour pains—a fortnight too soon. I'll be on the Pullman when you get this. Hard cheese about Fiddler. *The tickets are on the dressing-table. I suggest you sell mine to an American and sock Esther to dinner at Kettners on the proceeds. Hope you enjoy it. See you Monday. M.*

P.S. My copy of the Harris List of Covent Garden Ladies *is in the bedside cupboard in case of what Boswell delicately referred to as 'exigency'.*

I moved slowly into the room. He'd gone. My keeper. I stared at my reflection in the handbasin mirror, at a face blank with uncertainty. I was alone with her two hundred miles from home. No Martin, no Gwen, nothing as an extra safeguard to our own obsessive caution.

But did it matter? Hadn't it been our own system of checks and balances that had really counted in the end? The certain knowledge that adultery could only have brought us more unhappiness than the uneasy relationship we'd finally established.

I glanced at my watch—two and a half hours till the show started. I hadn't much time, we'd have to set out for dinner soon. If we were staying. And if we didn't stay we'd have to go North on a crawling train.

Disappointment hit me. I worked very hard, seven days a week, year in, year out. It was a self-imposed discipline but for once the idea of uncomplicated pleasure had been very sweet—food, wine, a show; a brief rest on a ledge in the unremitting ascent of my personal Eiger.

I wondered what Gwen would have said. I couldn't ring her because I knew she was out until the late evening, and Emma at Pop's. I was almost certain she'd say stay. She trusted both of us now. She'd think it pointless to come back home at this stage.

She opened the door as if she'd been waiting. She'd put on a dress clearly bought for the occasion—mini, sleeveless and black. There was a slight flush in her cheeks; she gave me a rare natural smile.

'Yes—I'm ready.'

'Martin's had to go home. Monica's on the point of having the baby.'

'Oh.'

It could have been Bob through the looking-glass again. First blankness, then disappointment. Nothing else. No sudden eagerness or hope. Just the same disappointment as mine, based on the same wary disciplines. Ought we to go home and give up our gay night out?

171

'Well,' I said. 'If you're ready, let's go and eat.'

She began to smile, a wide toothy smile. Without a word, as if even the most cautious choice of words might make me think twice, she caught up a black leather coat, pulled it quickly on and joined me in the corridor.

It set the evening's mood. We were on the town. We walked out into the crowds and flashing lights of what American magazines were beginning to call swinging London, and for once we weren't a single girl and a mature married man but just any couple out for a bit of harmless fun.

We had dinner at a small English restaurant on Shaftesbury Avenue, sitting in half-light at a corner table—the sort of elaborate meal the pace of my life and my prudent habits normally excluded : a bottle of wine, thick soup, fish, duckling, sweet pancakes, cheese, fruit.

For a long time we hardly talked at all. We ate and drank and watched soundless black cabs plunge down to Piccadilly and brightly dressed Saturday people drift endlessly past the window. She looked even younger than usual in the indirect lighting in her simple black dress. Perhaps the light helped me too; I carried my age well.

It was as if by not speaking she could see me as the sort of man she so much wanted me to be, just as I could suspend the crowded years that separated me from her. Without words there could be no false notes about politics or ambition. Without words we were that happy couple out on the town, who had no past and no future.

When we did talk we talked about books. It was my choice and it was probably instinctive. Books seemed safe, they brought my youth nearer. After I married I never opened another novel. There was no place for them then, those stories of Frederic and Catherine together on a mountain, and Brett's love for poor Jake, and Cheri going back to Lea and finding her suddenly old, and there was no place for all those films about young men making the grade and walking towards sunshine and music with Elizabeth Taylor.

We talked about the kind of women men had written about; she asked me which I liked best. I told her Holly Golightly.

'Where is she now?' I said. 'And what was she searching for? What did she do in the parts of her life the story leaves blank? She belongs to no one but herself and no woman I've ever read about equals her for glamour. She lives in the mind.'

Myself when young. An old excitement had crept into my voice. The girl watched me impassively in the half-light.

'Holly deliberately concealed parts of her life because they were too painful to talk about. It's the pain that stays in my mind, not the glamour.'

We shouldn't have talked at all. We should simply have eaten our dinner and looked at each other. She turned away, I saw a faint familiar wretchedness. I didn't seem to be able to do or say anything today that didn't somehow hurt her.

Later, I found I'd left the tickets at the hotel. I'd grown so used to Gwen or Esther or Martin looking after the trivia that I'd never given them a thought.

Like so many of the things that had happened between us it couldn't be analysed rationally. It wasn't just because I'd forgotten the tickets and it wasn't just because I'd cast a shadow over the meal.

It was the two things happening together.

I'd left her in the foyer and gone up to my room in one of the automatic lifts. It could have taken barely a minute for me to walk from the lift to my room, to open the door, pick up the tickets and start back to the door again.

But as I reached it, so did she, from the corridor. She must have come up in the next lift. She came in rapidly, pushed the door closed and stared at me with her back to it. Then she put her arms round me and kissed me.

It caught me off-guard. I'd known all along how much at risk we were, but I'd been certain the dangerous high tide would come after the theatre when I'd be ready for it. It caught me off-guard and at a time when my defences had been weakened with unaccustomed glasses of wine. I crushed her body in my arms, kissed her so hard teeth ground against teeth. I was off-guard and I'd not laid a finger on her for the whole of a long summer.

But it was soon over. I remembered it all too well, the strain and worry that followed that time at Chelifer House, the near panic.

I pushed her away, gently but firmly. 'All right.' I said, 'I'll write that one off. But now it's back to the evening as planned. It's got to be, Esther.'

'I know,' she said quickly. 'I know, Bob. I'm sorry. I'm terribly sorry. But please don't take me to the theatre. I couldn't face it.'

'We ought to stick to the schedule. I might be asked about the show.'

'I'd like to talk to you. There won't be another chance. Not now.'

'Talking's no *good* . . .'

'I'm going away.'

'Oh.'

'When we go back. I'm leaving Fisher's.'

She moved slowly past me further into the room, sat down heavily on the bed and took out cigarettes.

I glanced at my watch. There was only time now to get to the theatre if we set off directly and by cab. She looked so miserable I decided to abandon it.

'It's the best thing,' I said at last. 'You've got your own life to live.'

I sat down beside her on Martin's bed.

'I'm in love with you.' She turned away. 'What does it matter now if I say it? You know it anyway. I . . . I've reached the stage where seeing you every day is going to be worse than not seeing you at all.'

She got up, stubbed her cigarette out, crossed to the window. She pulled the net curtains a little to one side, looked out at the bright oblongs of light of windows at the other side of the well.

'Let's find a little pub in Bloomsbury. Let's walk. Surely we can have a little time together. What difference can it make—we're in London legitimately.'

But what about when we got back from some little pub in Bloomsbury? I got up and joined her at the window. She didn't look at me. Pain had scored a single crease across the unlined skin of her forehead. The black leather coat hung open on the new dress she didn't care about any more. I stroked her long dark hair; she pushed her head against my hand like a cat seeking comfort.

But what did it matter if we slept together? Chelifer House had been an obvious risk, but this was a massive impersonal hotel. To Gwen we were staying on in London to give Esther her night out. She trusted us. We were safer here than we'd ever been. And she did want me to sleep with her. Before she left me for good.

The phone suddenly gave an odd half-ring.

I crossed over to it. 'Robert Saxby here.'

'Oh . . . I'm sorry, sir,' a polite female voice replied. 'This is the switchboard . . . I pressed your bell by mistake—I do apologise.'

But it was enough. Enough to remind me of the call to Gwen I'd deliberately placed for eleven-fifteen. Enough to remind me what Gwen's cheerful tones would remind me of—the night I'd almost retched at the idea of the machine dropping me like a stone. They all seemed to sit watching me from behind the long table at the clubhouse, Pop and Delgin and Mrs. Telleyman, their faces hostile and cold.

I watched the girl. She said she was going, but she'd said that before. Maybe she really was going this time, I believed it, but what if we made love again, would she still go? And what about me? Would I let her? Or would I try to make her stay?

She pulled on the cord that drew the heavy night-curtains, turned to me. I'd meant only to comfort her. I'd meant to talk to her about being sensible, about helping each other to keep to the old friendship, about not damaging our futures, but she lunged forward again, putting her arms round me and pushing her face against my shoulder.

This time, it was too much for me.

I pulled her face backwards by her hair and began to kiss her again and again. I drew her towards the nearest bed and half-lifted her on to it, mouth still crushed against hers. I covered her body with mine.

I'd never known that particular kind of conflict. I had a body I'd made healthy by exercise and diet, I had a mind I'd made strong by the disciplines of hard regular work. They fought each other with the calculated savagery of trained athletes of equal weight and skill who had too much to lose.

I struggled against myself, she struggled against me; suddenly she managed to jerk her mouth away.

'Oh, Bob, I know,' she said hoarsely. 'I know. Turn the light off. Please. Oh, *Bob* . . .'

She gazed up at me, flushed, tousled, breathless. I got up and turned off the light and locked the door. I heard her get off the bed, heard the sound of zips, the scratch of nylon. I stripped off my own clothes and waited in the total darkness, trembling with frustration.

Her body touched mine; first I felt her pubic hair faintly harsh against my thigh and then her breasts against my shoulder. I saw that line of cold Selection Committee faces, heard Vereburn say :

'Look, Bob, I'm sorry about this, but we've decided unanimously that you're not the right man to contest South for us.'

Our teeth ground together. I grasped her so hard the breath was forced out of her lungs like a groan. I dragged the sheets back, lowered her on to the bed again. I thrust my hand between her thighs and began a series of hard regular caresses.

Even she began to understand then. Her body stiffened and she began to shake her head violently till her mouth was free from mine.

'No! No! Please, no! Bob . . . *Bob* . . . *why*, Bob?'

But I didn't stop. I went on and on until her odour seeped out in waves and the irregular liquid noises in the silence were like the snapping of a wood fire. At last her abdomen began to push back of its own accord against my relentless palm. Suddenly her legs opened as if they were on a spring. Even before they'd finished moving I was positioning my body above hers. Within seconds I was into the rhythm of a rapid act.

But how my body craved languor. How I longed to stroke her for minutes on end, to kiss her breasts, to run my hands through her hair, to make sexual love a gradual process that drew us both into the same tender oblivion. But mind fought body and neither would accept defeat.

I knew I was hurting her. Her head moved from side to side, her hands never stopped pushing against my abdomen. There were no yelps of ecstasy this time, just rasping explosions of breath. If I could have seen her eyes I knew there'd be no bands of white round the iris, they'd be tight shut in a face haggard with pain.

But I didn't stop and suddenly she lurched into a jagged orgasm that almost threw me off her. It triggered my own orgasm—which spent itself at just the moment our bodies lost contact.

It was a pyrrhic victory for the flesh.

We lay absolutely still in the darkness, the only sounds the hum of the hotel's plant down in the well and our breathing.

I got out of bed, put on a shirt and trousers and lit the bed-lamp above the vacant bed. There was a half of brandy and some small sodas in the wardrobe. I poured myself a stiff one and sat down with my back to her.

'I want a drink, please.'

I got up and poured her one.

'You hurt me.'

I came back with the toothglass. Her eyes were heavy with pain and incomprehension. I remembered how they'd looked the last time I'd seen them, just before I'd switched off the lights, the near rapture. In a couple of weeks she'd be gone for good and I could barely stop myself from kneeling down in front of her, from begging her to forgive me.

But I couldn't do that. It could only make complications. God knows, I hadn't wanted it to be like that, but now it was done it had to be used. If the break was coming it had better be conclusive.

'I once told you,' I said, 'about not playing with the big rough boys.'

'Why did you do that to me? You almost seemed to be trying to hurt me.'

'It can be painful when you're not used to it.'

'Is that all you wanted? Sex.'

'I hadn't wanted anything till you started rubbing yourself against me.'

She shrank into herself like a shell-fish touched with a knife-edge. I had to force myself not to put my arm round her.

'Bob . . .' she said after a while. 'I'm going. I told you I was going. Couldn't you have been kind to me?'

'Look, Esther, you wanted to go to bed so I took you to bed. You've been wanting me to do it all summer. You nearly had me fooled. The kid's really trying, I thought. But it was just the old waiting game. You played it the clever way, like you did at Miss Charlotte's. Believe me, you're just about the sharpest woman I've ever known, and I've known plenty of women.'

'Oh, do stop.' Her eyes glistened with tears in the half-light. 'You're so wrong. I just wanted to be alone with you. It didn't *matter* about going to bed.'

'Look, I wouldn't *mind* an affair with you if you were older and you weren't so emotional.'

She closed her eyes. 'Oh, *stop!*'

'As long as it's quite safe and doesn't interfere with my career I've absolutely nothing against a bit on the side.'

'STOP . . . STOP . . . STOP !'

She hit me then, over the face with her clenched fist, and went on hitting. The blows had an astounding force and I had to act, fast. It wasn't so much the pain as the fear of returning home bruised.

I positioned my open hand slowly, then hit her very hard and very carefully across the cheekbone.

Her head flew round almost in a semicircle. She nearly over-balanced and fell backwards over the bed, but saved herself in time. She became quite still, propping herself on her hand, her face obscured by skeins of hair, like a rag doll.

'Now get dressed,' I said, 'and get out.'

I got up.

'You're a monster,' she whispered. 'You're a *monster*!'

'I'll take your word for it.'

'You can't be the same *man*. You can't, it's not possible.'

It was time to end all that too. I crossed to the dressing-table and poured another drink. The things she knew about me had been part of that strange summer, intangible and powerful. So much so that I'd deliberately wanted to preserve her enigma. But unexplained she'd live on too vividly in the mind.

I came back to the bed, sat down.

'Right,' I said. 'Let's get all this about the old Bob off our chest, shall we?'

She pushed her hair back, looked out at me with apprehensive eyes. Then she smiled, sourly, the large prominent teeth exposed for once, and almost rat-like.

'Why—can't you even remember the old Bob? When you used to play tennis in Westbury Park with Maggie. You used to call her Maggie-O, but I suppose you've forgotten that too. And you used to talk about politics with Brian Stokes, only in those days it was a kind of politics that was actually about people. Not comfortable middle-class people, but people like your own parents, the sort of people you came from and understood so well. And could have helped so much.'

I began to tremble, tremble as I'd trembled on a hot spring after-noon when a woman in a Victorian dress had stepped out of a Hill-man. How? Who? Could it be Maggie? Surely not Maggie herself.

Her eyes never left mine.

'Shall I tell you how the old Bob used to talk? He wasn't just clever—he cared. He was saying things then that a lot of socialists have only got around to saying now. He didn't simply talk about more money for the workers. He talked about standards and life in real terms. A lot of workers *were* getting more money. They had to, because in this kind of society consumers had to consume. A lot

178

of them could afford things like television and washing-machines and cars. But still nobody cared much how they lived or gave them any worthwhile standards to live by. They were simply producers and purchasers of goods. A lot of them earned almost middle-class money but there was no question of the middle-class trying to integrate them or letting them in on middle-class attitudes. Nothing had really changed for the workers—it was still them and us.'

She stared at me with a hard smile.

'That was the old Bob,' she said. 'He put it a lot better than I could, but those were the sort of things he used to say.'

Hairs prickled in my neck; waves of gooseflesh passed over my body. It was fear now. It couldn't be Maggie, not that sort of detail. And it couldn't be Brian Stokes, because he'd lived in the United States for the past eight years.

'How do you *know*?' I cried. 'How *can* you know?'

My tone scared her again; her mouth began to twitch at the corners.

'*How do you know?*'

'I . . . I can't tell you.'

'Who've you been talking to?'

'I haven't been talking to anyone. I don't need to. I just *know*.'

By what human agency? Suddenly I grasped her shoulders, and it wasn't curiosity any more, it was the urge to master a fear as basic as the fear I'd had of dark attics as a child. I almost had to clench my teeth to get the words out.

'Look,' I muttered, 'you're not leaving this room till I know the truth.'

'Oh, please.' She closed her eyes. 'Please don't hurt me again.'

'Then *speak*.'

'I can't. I can't talk about it.'

'*Who told you about me?*'

First there was alarm, when she opened her eyes, and then panic. I realised how hard I was shaking her, how precariously I was balanced on the edge of self-control. I didn't just scare her, I scared myself and a moment later would have stopped.

But she cried out then : '*Because I knew you!* Because one summer I sat and watched you in Westbury Park nearly every day. Because I was *there* !'

14

My grip loosened on her shoulders. I sat staring at her hard glittering eyes.

'You . . . were . . . *there*?'

The words seemed to drop into the silence from other lips.

'On the benches by the tennis courts.'

'But how *old* were you, for Christ's sake? You could only have been twelve or thirteen.'

'Twelve.'

'You were just a *kid*.'

'I sat with other kids. They watched the tennis and I watched you.'

I got up and stood with my back to her. I tried to think about what she'd told me, but for once my mind had had too much too quickly. It seemed heavy and sluggish, as if it couldn't cope with any new demands. She began to talk again in a soft low tone.

'In between games you'd sit on the benches with some of your friends,' she said. 'Often I'd only be a few feet away from you, on the same bench. Or behind you on one of the higher ones. I'd never seen anyone like you. It wasn't just the way you looked in your tennis clothes, it was how you talked about what you believed in. About people, and how they should live together and care for each other and be helped to live lives that had meaning. And how they should be given a lead by men they could trust and understand. No one I've ever known affected me like you did that summer.'

I turned back to her. She gazed straight forward, holding an unlit cigarette, hunched slightly so that her hair fell down the sides of her face like blinkers and the leather coat hung open on white underclothes.

'Most young girls admire someone—a teacher or a Guide mistress or their father. Someone they can look up to. *You* were the person I admired. More than anyone else I'd known you seemed to have genuine goodness, to . . . to care. Not even Father made an impression on me like you did, and he often said similar things.'

She laughed shortly. 'But Father's the one who still says them and means them. He doesn't sound as inspiring or as warm as you did, but *he* hasn't changed.'

She looked up at me, focussed her eyes. 'I never saw you again from that year to this. And it was true—about seeing your name in Father's papers.'

She watched me steadily. 'I had to see you again. I'd tried to live my life by the things I'd heard you say. You seemed to care so much about people, and it coloured the whole of my thinking. I simply couldn't believe you'd gone from left to right. I still can't. Even now. Even *now*.'

Her eyes had begun to glisten in the half-light : I heard her gulp.

'Oh, Bob, can't you see what it's been like for me this year, re-membering that summer? When I've seen you doing your talking head and tricking people on doorsteps and making Breasey weep. It's the little bits of the man you used to be that upset me so much. Like this afternoon when you talked about Pugin and the Van Gogh —that was the old Bob. And that's how it is all the time, little bits of the old Bob, and then it's back to the vote-catching and all that careful charm.

'It's horrible ! It's ghastly ! Everybody believes in you, like I once did, but all you want are their votes. It's all just a fix to get you in control of everything. You're not going to give them anything *back*.'

She began to cry silently, the tears dripped steadily down her cheeks. I sat on the opposite bed. I didn't know what to do or say. I was completely at a loss. I'd made a hundred guesses about how she'd found out so much about me, but this was beyond imagina-tion. I remembered that long dry summer of the mid-'fifties—God, how I remembered it. We'd played tennis every night for weeks. And talked for hours, on those viewing benches. I could remember the scents of dry earth and the taste of sweat and the puffs of red dust on the courts. I could remember the slow flawless dusks and the way the coolness had dropped and the endless thock of ball against racket. Maggie in white. Poor sweet Maggie in white.

I couldn't stop shivering at the eeriness of being watched as Esther had watched me, noting every action, every word, for a hundred and one nights.

'Now look, Esther,' I said. 'Now look, I'm very very sorry to see you so upset about me, but people change. There's a ten-year gap between now and then and a lot's happened. A hell of a lot, believe me.'

'I know that now. It took me a long time to understand it. It's because your looks haven't changed much. You're Dorian Gray, Bob, aren't you? You look the same as you did then and you still sound as if you care. But somewhere there's an attic with a portrait of you, and the face is slowly going cold and evil and hard with all the vile things you've done to get power.'

'Esther, you're being absurd . . .'

'What you did to her was part of what changed you, wasn't it? Maggie. I was jealous of her even then, all those years ago, but I knew she loved you. She couldn't take her eyes off you . . .'

'Esther . . .'

'Have you seen her lately? I have. By chance. I wouldn't have noticed her, but she was wearing the sort of clothes women wore in the 'fifties. Women sometimes do that, you know, go on wearing clothes that remind them of when they were happy. The clothes made me look at her face. She was fat and shapeless, but I knew it was her. She's married to a fat bald-headed little man, Bob, and she wears old-fashioned clothes and her eyes are dull.'

We watched each other across the space between the beds in the half-light.

'Do you know why?' I said at last, in a low voice. 'Do you know *anything* of what's happened to Maggie or me since that summer? When you've lived another ten years, Esther, you might have a past of your own to come to terms with.'

She suddenly flinched away as if I'd made to strike her again.

'Oh, Bob, she loved you. And you left her for Gwen. Why? Why, Bob? It's her that's changed you, isn't it? She's what's happened to you.'

I went across to the dressing-table for another drink. It was a mistake, I'd already drunk too much for a man of my sober habits. It blunted my thinking. I'd had a bad shock. I'd instinctively tried to say as little as possible until I'd adjusted to what she'd told me, but perfectly sober I'd have known to end it now, to send her back to her own room, to retreat into silence until I'd come to terms with it all. Words at this stage could only compound the original confusion.

'It works,' I said slowly. 'My marriage works very well. You'll learn as you get older never to knock a marriage that hangs together, however empty it seems. I'll tell you something, Gwen doesn't even know there's anything wrong with it, and neither does Emma.'

'But what about later? When Emma's old enough to judge it against real marriages.'

'I . . . shouldn't go on about Emma if I were you.'

The coldness of my tone scared her, but she didn't pause. Her face was slightly distorted with fear, and still wet, but the teeth were bared and rat-like in a smile of triumph.

'It went home, didn't it? It doesn't matter about me or Maggie or all the people you've trampled over, but you couldn't bear to have Emma stand in judgement on you and find you lacking.'

'Be careful. Be very careful.'

'She's all that matters to you, isn't she? Even though you use her like you use everyone else.'

'*Not . . . one . . . more . . . word.*'

'Oh, she'll find you out one day, like I did. She'll see through the wit and the charm. She'll begin to realise you never get enthusiastic about people—never even *talk* about them—only about buildings and paintings and new ideas.'

I got up abruptly and stood over her.

'How will it be then, Bob, when she begins to watch you in silence, when she doesn't laugh at your jokes any more? If you get a seat in the Commons she'll meet other Members, won't she, men who are at Westminster for the right reasons—because they feel and care and have genuine motives. And she'll start comparing them to the cardboard cut-out you are.'

Suddenly I cried: 'Well, she won't spoil her life getting kinky about older men, I know that.'

It was as if I'd been blundering in a dark room, trying to defend myself against an attacker who never hit twice from the same direction. It was as if I'd picked up the first heavy object that came to hand and struck out blindly with it. And connected. Damagingly.

She didn't just seem to shrink into herself this time, she actually drew her limbs close to her body in a protective ball. Her legs had come up on to the bed beneath the black coat; her arms flew round them. She became perfectly still, her head lowered and almost touching her knees.

It all clicked then. Those random memories were all gathered together as if the correct code had been fed to the selecting mechanism—memories of clawlike hands, upward light on an old wrinkled face, the way she shuddered whenever Dowling touched her.

I knew it all now.

'Well, well,' I said, in a low rasping voice. 'You're another Cynthia, aren't you? Amazing how often it happens to pretty girls.'

'Don't ... please.'

She looked up at me, mouth open and eyes wide with fear.

'Cynthia played tennis too, with that old group of mine. Tall, pale, natural blonde. Do you remember? Hair almost down to her waist. Very pretty. But uneasy, Esther, with men her own age. She married a solicitor of fifty at the full height of his earning powers. Oh, after he'd tidily divorced some dull, faithful, earlier wife, of course. She's radiantly happy now—wears dramatic hats and gives gay little dinners for lots of other elderly solicitors.'

'*Don't!*'

An etching of lines suddenly scored her forehead. They were so deep they seemed artificial, as if she'd been aged for a theatre play.

'It begins to make sense now. The way you chased me and all the trouble you took to get me into bed that time. I couldn't understand why you were a virgin—it seemed so odd. I can see just how odd it was now. Or is the word *unnatural*?'

She swung round on the bed, until her feet were back on the floor, and began to inch rapidly away from the point where I stood over her.

'Because it isn't natural, is it, Esther, for a girl of twelve to be attracted to a man ten years older and not grow out of it?'

'Don't be silly.' Her voice was so raucous I could hardly make the words out. 'I've gone out with men my own age all the time, just like everyone else.'

'But it's me you chased after. Bob Saxby—presentable, clever, mature, reasonably well-heeled. But above all, *older*. Not too much older, just old enough to make you feel you're always an innocent child in a corrupt world. It'll always be Westbury Park when you're with me, won't it—hope and sunshine and games of tennis.'

'*No!*' She got up and began to back away to where the rest of her clothes were on a chair near the window. '*No!*'

'Oh, yes, I see it all now. Men your own age terrify you. They bruise those exquisite sensibilities of yours. They haven't much money and they're full of themselves and they make marriage seem so appallingly prosaic. All that scratching round for a mortgage, all the things you'd be expected to see to, like furniture and curtains and washing-machines. Where would your shining world be then? And babies, Esther, little kids twenty-five years younger than you, needing to be fed and cleaned and stuck on pots. Babies—tying you to the house and destroying your youth. Some man your own age griping because his dinner wasn't ready. Those frightful changes, changes and adjustments a man your own age won't bother trying to make easier for you, changes that'll take you further and further away from those fine girlhood visions of life's perfectibility.'

I'd only seen that kind of terror once before—when a woman had stepped on to the road against the lights and I'd only managed to brake my shrieking car a foot away from her.

She tore off the leather coat and began to drag her dress on. I believe I'd have let it go then if the sight of her thighs and the flesh between the white underclothes hadn't made me want her again.

'It won't be any good, Esther, we all have to face the complexities in the end. It's all those days we've lived through and all the things we can remember. And the more intelligent you are the worse it is, you see, because you can't forget anything. You've heard about the burden of memory, haven't you? Men like Scott Fitzgerald drink themselves to death because of it.'

She put her hands over her ears, but had to take them away again to pull her shoes on.

'It never stops, Esther, that's the trouble, once you've worn out one year there's another all ready and waiting, to take you further and further away from Westbury Park. It goes on and on till you're old, old and withered and bent like Miss Charlotte. No wonder she scares you so much.'

Fully dressed, she gave me a glance of utter panic. She picked up her gloves and bag and ran to the door. But I'd bolted it. She scrabbled at it and I said : 'But she was just as young and pretty as you once, Esther, wasn't she—we saw that old photo. And now the poor thing's waiting to die—just like you'll be in a few short decades.

'And then that's it, Esther. It's as if all that beautiful thinking had never been. You die like a dog dies. And there's nothing out there, nothing, nothing, nothing, nothing, *nothing!*'

It was like a frozen-frame in a television feature; she became quite still against the door. And then she began to turn round, so slowly that every nerve in my body seemed to prickle. Her mouth was wide open and I realised afterwards she was already moaning, even though I couldn't hear anything. But then the sound came, a low gargling wail that lasted for seconds and seemed to go on quivering in the silence even when it was over, like the reverberations of a gong.

It was the most dreadful sound I'd ever heard.

15

It took me an hour to calm her. She never stopped sobbing; at times she seemed on the verge of hysteria. She refused to let me near her or touch her, again and again she would knock my hand savagely away, but later, probably from sheer exhaustion, she let me put my arm round her and began to rest her body against mine. I gave her three lots of brandy, lit cigarettes for her between my own lips before putting them between hers. Finally, when the last spasm had shaken her body, I laid her gently on the bed. She fell asleep within seconds. I put out the light and laid at her side.

I too must have dozed after that long strange day. When I awoke I sensed her leaning over me. Shortly afterwards she kissed me, her lips very soft and salty with dried tears.

'I'm sorry,' I said. 'I'm very very sorry.'

I believe it was the first time I'd ever made love to her. In that curtained bed at Chelifer House it was her body I'd held but it was Maggie I'd remembered. And in this hotel room, a couple of hours ago, I'd not made love to her at all, her body had been a battlefield for my private war.

But this time it was Esther Moore—the woman I'd shared that long sad summer with, the woman who'd known me all those years ago, who'd wept so bitterly in my arms. This was her tousled hair, these were her breasts and legs. It was her lips and tongue that met mine, her arms round my shoulders, her thighs I began to penetrate, her odour.

I scarcely moved, inside her body, because she was Esther Moore and I was Bob Saxby, and we'd come together across an empty decade and emptiness stretched away from this perfect instant when every atom of ourselves belonged to each other. She lay beneath me, her wet mouth clamped against mine, her arms like metal bands round my shoulders, her open thighs completely still. Time seemed elongated, the seconds gathered and fell as slowly as rain-drops falling from canvas.

Minutes, endless minutes later, our bodies began to move, almost imperceptibly and of their own volition. Her breath exploded against my ear; the yelping sounds began. I'd never known a climax that gathered as that one did, it was a climax that followed a summer of desperation and longing, and it surged over me like the slow powerful wave of a spring tide. Orgasm was a blinding yellow light that seemed to cover us both in the same radiance.

We didn't want to sleep but sleep would sometimes overcome us. Never for long because the movements of one would waken the other and she would begin to kiss me, or I would stroke her body. Sometimes we talked, because talking helped to keep us awake, but often the one who listened would sleep.

Once I said : 'Why don't you tell me about it?'

'About what?'

'About what scares you so much.'

'I can't.'

'What happened? Something must have happened to make you so scared. Tell me. It might help to talk about it.'

'I can't talk about it.'

'That kind of fear borders on neurosis.'

'I can't talk about it. Please don't ask me to.'

'You'll have to come to terms with it . . .'

'*Please.*'

I left it then. I could remember being her age and I could remember the things I'd begun to discover about myself I'd not wanted to face. The girl fell asleep, her breathing became regular in the total darkness, her head rested heavily on my shoulder. And then she spoke; her voice gave me a slight shock.

'Why have you changed so much from what you were?'

'Ten years is a long time.'

'Why did you leave Maggie?'

'I'm . . . afraid we had nothing in common.'

'Then . . . why did you marry Gwen?'

I laughed shortly. 'Oddly enough, it was *because* we had nothing in common.'

187

'I don't understand.'

'You might, one day.'

'Please tell me why you changed so much.'

'Perhaps I didn't change. Perhaps when you saw me that summer I was simply acting out of character.'

'No . . .'

'What if Martin Emmott suddenly began to work like I do, and stopped eating elaborate meals, and took an active part in local politics. Would you say *he* was acting out of character?'

'I suppose so. I don't understand.'

'It's a complicated story. You learn to live with complications as you get older. You don't believe me, of course, people your age never do.'

'Please tell me about it. I'll try to understand.'

'Simon Fisher, Martin Emmott, Maggie Cattrell. In that order. If I'd never known them who would I be, Esther? Tell me who I'd be?'

'You don't like Simon Fisher.'

'I once loathed and despised him. There was a time when I used to tremble with loathing whenever he came near me.'

'Why?'

'It was something we sensed in each other. He was wealthy and I was poor, but it wasn't that. I've never cared much about money, I think you know that now. It was . . . it was as if he could sense the potential buried in me and I could sense the waste hidden behind the Fisher mystique.'

'If you hated him so much, why didn't you leave?'

'Quite. Enter Martin Emmott. Distinguished wool trade background—what the trade used to call the nice end. Large Victorian houses, large black motors, beautiful glass, wine cellars, fly-fishing. The nice end went to the wall in the 'fifties, they were no match for the new men. The Emmotts were bought out; not long after, Martin's father died.

'Martin had what was left of the money. It was a decent sum, but not quite enough to buy him the life he was used to. Anyway, he needed an occupation. He knew the Fishers; they offered him accountancy. He's jogged along ever since. He's enough money now to live the way he always lived. That's his trouble, he likes ease.

'But inside him, struggling against the fine wines and the leather bindings and the grouse moors, there used to be an ambition like mine trying to get out. But he never made it and he lives it all through me now. Politics, creative accountancy, action—I'm getting everything he always longed for.'

'Did he talk you into staying?'

'He did more,' I said, after a while. 'He was older and shrewder and he had the objective wisdom of his class. When he saw that I hated Simon he told me to use the hate as a kind of booster fuel to push me into a position where the Fishers couldn't do without me. Revenge.

'I was idle. A dreamer. Hate was the only thing I had going for me. The idea nauseated me at first. And then it fascinated me. And here I am, the power behind the Fisher throne.'

She said nothing. Perhaps she slept. I wondered what had made me tell her things I'd sworn I'd never tell another living soul. Was it disorientation? Or was it pity, crumbs of comfort for that wretched creature who'd wept in my arms—she wasn't alone.

Or was the urge still there to convince her I'd made a worthwhile job of my own difficult nature? Nostalgia was almost certainly part of it, a longing for those good simple days when I'd been the white knight of the tennis courts.

She stirred, reached out for my hand. 'But Westbury Park . . . ?'

'That . . . extreme left-wing phase was a reaction to misery. My working life was hell that summer, real life only started when work was over, in the park and then in the pub. In fact most of that summer I was looking for another job. I was from a working-class home, remember, working for a middle-class firm. Looking back, I honestly believe going left wing was a kind of retreat, a sort of return to my origins. Security . . . the womb, if you like.

'Oh, I believed it at the time. I was young, imaginative. Too imaginative. As you know, I throbbed with passion. I cared so much about a mental concept I labelled people I could almost bring myself to the edge of tears with my own rhetoric.'

I believe I slept myself then. At any rate I had a sudden vivid picture of Maggie. She was sitting by the tennis courts in all the prettiness of her thick curly hair and her deliquescent brown eyes, smiling and silent as always. Poor Maggie. Poor sweet Maggie, secure in those bright innocent yesterdays.

'She was a figment of my imagination,' I said suddenly. 'Maggie. She was part of my search for mystery and colour. I used to believe she was *thinking*. I used to believe she understood what Stokes and

189

I were arguing about. She was so intuitive. She should have been an actress. She was as empty as a really first-class actress. Sometimes, at exactly the right moment, she'd start talking about the things she'd heard her father say about being out of work before the war. There'd be long pauses, dying falls. She could project a kind of sadness that could even make Stokes look uneasy, and they didn't come any tougher than him. I could hardly speak when she'd finished.

'But she was simply responding to me. She didn't really feel any of it, all she knew was that it pleased me when she behaved in a certain way. I soon knew it, that she wasn't really mysterious at all —most of the time she was just thinking about clothes and engagement rings and dream kitchens.

'It couldn't have lasted. At the end of that summer I dropped her.'

The girl turned to me; I felt her hand on my face.

'I . . . I hadn't meant to hurt her like that. I thought she'd get over it. But she didn't. Three months later she made the worst possible marriage. I spoiled her life. If she'd never gone out with me she'd have married someone as decent and dim and good-hearted as herself and been happy.'

We lay for a long time in an almost cosmic silence.

'And if you'd never gone out with her you'd not have married Gwen.'

'I suppose not.'

'Oh, Bob, that wasn't the answer. Getting out of people . . .'

'When that summer was over I had to face the fact that I wasn't the kind of man I'd thought I was. Maggie couldn't play the part I cast her in so I dropped her. And Simon—I hated him but instead of leaving Fisher's I couldn't resist using the hate to spur myself on.

'It was the beginning of self-awareness. Not long after I began to realise I wasn't really a left-winger either. The idealism was false, it was my own grievances going into all that passion about Chartists and Peterloo. I wasn't really a people's man at all. I'd been born into a working family but my instinctive place was in the professional middle class where everyone cheerfully uses everyone else and if you aren't making the grade no one wants to know. I had no genuine feeling for work-people, and I wasn't the man to help them to achieve fuller or richer lives. I was best at complex administration, long-term planning, big structures. It seemed sterile and it wasn't what I'd really wanted, but it was what I was best at. I didn't get out of people, I'd never really been one of them.'

'Oh, Bob...'

'Martin once said some people are made by the people they come into contact with. I suppose I'm one of them. Without Simon and Martin and Maggie I'd have been nicer but I wouldn't have done anything. They brought out the man I really was, those three.'

'Oh, Bob, politics is about *people*.'

'It's also about efficient administration and new industry. I'm more head than heart, Esther. I admit it. I've little feeling for people as such. I've done the best I could with the kind of man I am. You used to say some lousy things about me, and all of them were true. But take my word for it, you've never been as hard on me as I've been on myself.'

I suddenly awoke to find her lying half across me, almost attacking my mouth with hard wet kisses. Sleep had freshened my senses; the smell and feel of her body gave me a spasm of pure happiness. She moved until she covered me completely and I grasped her and crushed her body against mine as if I could submerge myself in her moist flesh.

It was she who made love this time. It was she who handled me, and it was her body that began to move over mine. It was she who kissed me and who controlled me with her thighs and who was silent with an almost masculine concentration.

And it was I who seemed to give, who abandoned myself to her hot weight and knew the peculiar ecstasy of yielding and being carried towards a climax that she induced, of being consumed and possessed.

Afterwards, she still lay over me.

All at once she whispered : 'You're wrong, you're wrong. I know you are.

'You're *still* the same man. Start again! You want to, I can tell you do. Start again! You've so much to give. *Please* start again.'

16

It was a difficult journey. Driving would have been easier; I could have done a steady ninety along the motorway, pretending I needed to be silent in order to concentrate. As it was we went by slow Sunday train and we couldn't sit without speaking for five hours.

But we couldn't talk about that night. At six in the morning, weeping, she'd made me promise we'd never talk about it. It was over and she was leaving Beckford; in a couple of weeks we'd be living separate lives.

I'd never been more aware of the difference in our ages in all the months I'd known her, not even when she'd danced Beatle tunes with Dowling, than I was that morning. I seemed to put back the preoccupations of my daily life with the clean shirt and the dark suit. The hotel restaurant smelt of bacon and fresh rolls, and I was very hungry and ate well. She ate nothing and sipped black coffee.

There were dusty shafts of autumn sunlight across the foyer of the Regent Palace and it made me think of the days when I'd be living the parliamentary week in London. I had my normal well-being and energy, despite my broken night. Soon I'd be back in Beckford and I was automatically thinking how best I could use the late afternoon and evening.

Her, her body, every moment of that night, were fresh and deep in my mind, but my life went on of its own relentless volition.

I could sense the faint callousness of my every routine action—the square meal, the scanning of headlines, the diary notes, the mechanical charm as I handed out lavish tips. I knew it, it was almost an affront to her pale silence and her inability to eat and her large sad eyes.

She sat dejected and still as we were driven across Bloomsbury. She stirred only once, and then to look at a fountain playing thinly near a mound of dead leaves in a corner of the gardens in Russell Square. I could remember it then, briefly but vividly, the strange delicate fatigue that followed the first night of emotion and physical love. I could remember the inexplicable wistfulness and the startling definition given to trees and fountains and piles of bright dead leaves, the fragility and the beauty and the thingness of things.

And then it passed, just as rapidly, because I was thirty-four and I fixed on ambition and I had a bagful of work at my feet.

And we couldn't sit without speaking for five hours.

But why not? Why couldn't I have left her in her own private world for the whole of the journey? Why couldn't I have just read the papers or written up the London trip or let her speak only if she felt like it?

My politics. My future. With her, talking about them had become a compulsion, it was like an aching tooth. We could have made the break right there, if I had kept silent, if I could have accepted what the night with her had made so obvious.

If I could have accepted the truth I'd have known it had already ended.

She would scarcely listen to me as it was. First there had been a blankness in her eyes, and then pain. I had upset her enough with my briskness at the hotel; I should have sat in bleak wretched silence, unable to eat. But if I was incapable of sharing her mood the least I could do was to leave her to the colours and shapes of her inner world, to the soothing sounds of carriage wheels and now and then the plaintive wail of a diesel horn.

But I persisted. I showed her the photograph. Several months ago a young architect in the Planning Department had written a respectful but shrewdly critical article for the *Standard* about Beckford's central buildings. I'd taken him to lunch. I'd told him that if he would design and construct a scale model of the city centre he envisaged I'd pay him well.

'I'd walked round the centre again and again, trying to be lenient, but in the end I could only agree with Betjeman and Nairn. This is a picture of the model he made.'

It had always excited me, and it excited me now despite her apathy. It had a tower and a floating cube and a dramatic shallow dome, it had walkways and fountains and an odd unsymmetrical pool. At first the juxtaposition of shapes was as strange as new music, it took time before you were seized by its felicity, by the way it sent space surging across open areas.

She turned abruptly away to gaze at dead fields and bare trees and sheets of oily-looking water.

'Of course, it's an impossible dream. Cities are at the mercy of development companies and Whitehall, planning departments, retired fishmongers. Perhaps we get the kind of city we deserve. But to me,' I tapped the picture, 'this is how it ought to look. It's an ideal to live by. When I'm on the council I'll measure every proposed development against this kind of perfection. It'll force me into fighting tooth and nail for the highest possible standards. With luck I'll be on the council for thirty years; in the end no other Beckford layman will have as much authority. So I start from the word go by demanding the impossible. Who knows, I might actually *work* in a Town Hall that looks like this before I retire.'

'A perfect machine for a perfect machine,' she said harshly.

I watched her. Her eyes had looked misty and unfocussed before; now they had become hard and intent and her lips had fallen back from the teeth in that almost rat-like snarl.

'For God's sake!' she cried. 'Where do *people* come into it? You don't go into it to build monuments to yourself.'

I hadn't wanted to provoke her, I knew how utterly insensitive I must have seemed at that moment, but I couldn't stop myself— two separate urges fought each other, the way mind had fought body the first time I'd made love to her last night. She wanted only peace, reverie, and I wanted her to have it, but I had to justify myself. There'd never been the need to justify myself to anyone before I'd known her, but I was that kind of man, I'd not known what hate was before Simon Fisher nor ambition before Martin.

'The model's a mental yardstick,' I said. 'If I'm going to be any good at talking industrialists into considering the area for new factories I have to convince myself my city's on the up and up, and I have to convince them that given time and money I can get things done.'

'It's all so . . . so *icy*! You dream of a perfect city, bright new factories—what about *them*?'

'It's for them. New factories mean more work. That's the whole bloody point, we're a city in decline.'

'You should be helping to build lives, not factories.'

'Esther, I'm just not a man of the people.'

'You could be. You could be if you wanted to.'

'But why? With my kind of brain? Look, Beckford needs exactly what I've got. I'm exactly right for the job. There'll be plenty of others to help people to get their lives right.'

'Is there *anything* as sickening as an idealist who turns material-ist the minute he gets on?'

The train lurched, came to a standstill. A porter barked an unintelligible word. An elderly woman with a small dog stepped into our compartment and beamed encouragingly at us. I beamed back; a moment later we were on our way to the restaurant car.

I got two brandies and two coffees. The train vibrated steadily. A handful of people drifted towards the barrier and an old white-haired man swung a little boy on to a pile of cases. A guard talked to a policeman near a boarded-up W. H. Smith's, their breath hanging about them in the cold still air.

Then the train began to move again out into the flat dead fields. She lit a cigarette and gazed through the window—at the rise and sag of hanks of wire on telegraph poles, at thin copses of silver birch, and pools, and distant cricket ovals shielded by misty lines of poplar, at steeples across meadows and neat estates glimpsed from above, full of toy houses and painted toy gardens and bright toy cars. The sun gleamed like an old coin. 'Esther . . .'

She sighed and fell back in her seat. She looked drained, as if the broken night had caught up with her, as if the effort of talking any more, of even raising her eyes to mine, was too much. The train curved inwards, drummed over points—I could scarcely hear her. I leaned across the narrow table.

'Politics, Bob—it's *people*. It's immigrants and broken families and the half-educated and the poor and the old. Which is the best achievement—to develop a town that has the best social conscience in the country, or raising all that pre-stressed concrete?'

'There's no question which the best would be. The point is that I'm the best fitted to concrete. Look, perhaps right now there's a Beckford man whose ambition to work purely in human terms is as strong as mine is to develop a new industrial atmosphere. Surely there's a viable place for us both.'

'But how often does a man as clever and single-minded as you crop up in local politics? Oh, Bob, you're so *good* with people, you can rouse them and charm them and touch their emotions. And you've come up the hard way. They'd trust you. No one could mould a finer society than you, if you went about it the way you go about your planning and your smelly little intrigues.'

'No, Esther, it's not in me.'

'It won't do. It isn't good enough . . .'

'Look,' I said. 'I *know* I've used people. I know how dubious my motives are. I know I've got grave faults. But I've focussed the whole of my ambitions on making the city a going concern. And if you're going to judge me, be fair. If I can pull any of it off, won't I have put as much into society as a man who works in pure humanist terms out of sincere idealism?'

'No.'

'Look, can't you see that fate provided Beckford with me, just as I am, to administer to its particular illness.'

'No.'

'Esther, *please* believe in me. Just a little, just as I am.'

'Oh, Bob, *please* let me be with you in London.'

Her eyes were brimming in the watery light. Suddenly her hand went over mine on the table and she clenched it so hard I felt her nails enter my skin.

'If you get the seat. No one would ever know. It's a long time off, but I could stand it if we could be together for a few years. I could get work in London, a flat—you could stay now and then. No one would ever know. Please. *Please*, Bob.'

Depression settled over me like old age. I must have known. I'd not let myself admit it, but I must have known it wasn't me she was in love with. It was some man she thought she'd known ten years ago she was in love with, a man she was positive still existed in my body, could still somehow be made to feel and think and talk like the man in Westbury Park.

She couldn't love the man I really was, that was the truth of it.

17

'Daddy...'

She launched herself off the garden wall, a second later her grinning face was inches from mine, her arms clamped round my neck.

'Hello, Em.'

'Daddy! Oh, Daddy, I *did* miss you.'

I could hardly meet her eyes. I'd be able to meet Gwen's without thinking, without the remotest pang of remorse; it was Emma I felt I'd betrayed, who made me feel ashamed and disappointed.

I remembered how strangely reluctant she'd been to see me leave

Beckford, it was as if she'd sensed the threat to her security. I remembered standing in front of Renoir's exquisite young girl for minutes on end.

I forced a gay smile.

'Did Mummy hear the alarm all right? She's not at her best first thing, is she?'

'Yes, and she made me omelettes every morning.' She lowered her voice. 'They weren't *quite* as nice as yours, Poppa, but you won't tell her I said so, will you?'

I laughed genuinely. I couldn't have combined flattery, charm and discretion better myself.

'I wouldn't think of it.'

'I mean, she did jolly well to hear the alarm at all, didn't she?'

'Jolly well!'

I'd told myself that when Emma was as old as the girl in *La Première Sortie* she too would crane eagerly forward, waiting for a curtain to rise. Books, music, art, theatre, travel. And then journalism or television or politics or the stage. We'd be the kind of father and daughter people talked wistfully about—we'd be household names, admired, envied, legendary.

It had been like an examination of first principles, looking at that picture, it had been like a reappraisal of that inflexible code I'd tried to live by.

But it hadn't been proof against Esther.

'I'm sorry.'

'Why? Why are you sorry, Poppa?'

I'd spoken without thinking.

'Oh . . . because I couldn't take you and Mummy to London with me.'

'And Genghis.'

'Oh, and Genghis, of *course*. For his knighthood.' I lowered her to the ground. 'Here you are—a present.'

I gave her the fashion watch with the big face, a present too expensive for a week's absence : conscience money.

'Daddy! Oh, Daddy! Golly! Oh, *thank you!*'

She began to dance round the pool in triumph. I felt better. It was over now, anyway. Esther was leaving Beckford. It was out of the question we'd ever live together in London. I'd made it absolutely clear before we'd got off the train.

'How did London go?'

'Very well. Look, Gwen, I'd better tell you right away that Martin came back yesterday. Monica started the baby. After a great deal of thought I decided that Esther and I were safe to stay down for the show. I'd have rung you, but I knew you'd be out. I actually booked a late call and then cancelled it—it seemed a pity to disturb you if you'd gone straight to bed.'

'Oh. And was it safe to stay down?'

'We were so formal it was ridiculous.'

'I'm sure you were. Really, Bob, you'd no need to rattle it all out like that. I trust you.'

But she was very pleased I had rattled it out like that. Dear Gwen —if you were guilty you tried to conceal things, if you were innocent you spoke openly. She inhabited a straightforward world.

'Bob, come and have a drink. I've got splendid news.'

I followed her quickly into our nice living-room, with its walnut and mahogany and its amusing Victorian water-colours of ladies drinking afternoon tea—an inner privacy extending through leaded glass to an outer privacy of the trees and high fencing of the back garden. There were two glasses and a bottle of dry sherry on a small wine-table, and the room throbbed to the slow grandeur of the overture to *Tannhäuser*. She'd always turned to Wagner at the high moments.

'Celebration.'

'Gwen . . .'

'Oh, Bob, it's in the bag. They're all absolutely for you!'

'Even Oliver?'

'Even Oliver.'

I felt my heart quicken and the pulsing of my blood. As so often before, my vitality began to flush it all away, the girl's wretchedness, the guilt about Emma, the shabby lies.

'Telleyman,' I said. 'Tell me of Telleyman.'

'Your *slave*! Babbled, absolutely babbled about your talks to her ladies and your deep love of Proust.'

'Vereburn?'

'Says we can *win* South with you up. And that was before he'd had a single drink.'

'Fantastic! Dowling?'

'Hasn't even bothered to canvas the U.T.s. They simply take it as read you want the nomination and are bound to get it.'

'Norman?'

'Oh, come on, old chum, I can't work miracles. But he did go as far as to say you stood a good chance.' She suddenly gave way to helpless laughter. 'Unless . . . unless the committee strongly favours someone else.'

I couldn't remember the last time I'd laughed so hard.

'Bob, it's sewn up for you. The only X-factor is the man they send from London. And even if *he* doesn't think you're the right man he'll have to accept you. No one from Headquarters can really dictate to a machine as powerful as ours.'

That was really it, to get the machine in your pocket, to win over those several hundred grey, touchy, unfulfilled people who sold jumble and addressed manifestos and listened to pep-talks in draughty halls, whose individual atoms of power could suddenly coalesce every few years into such an astounding force.

I drank some of the chilled, almost colourless wine, felt it pass down into my belly—one sensation enhancing another.

'Great work, Gwen! You're the best in the business.'

'This is it, Bob. You're their man. They'll back you again and again. They're a tough bunch, but they're loyal. I know them.'

She did too. I couldn't remember her happier, not even on her wedding day. But Gwen was an Endersby girl, she'd had politics ever since she could walk. She'd been just six when she'd taken numbers at polling-station doors and learned to smile appealingly at householders Pop was chatting up. And now it looked as if one day she might well have a real live walking talking M.P. of her very own. I smiled at her. I was my own complex man, but I was also their creature in a way—hers and Pop's—and they'd made a first-class job of me. They'd had the potential to go at, of course, but the difference between the raw material and the man with the crinkly smile and the warm hand and the Kenneth More delivery was ten years of ceaseless Endersby toil.

'You're going to win South, Bob, I *know* you are. You're going to get everything you ever wanted.'

How quaint, how naïve that sounded. How sad.

'I fancy you'll just about have everything you want, Bob lad, if you win that seat yon committee want you to stand for.'

After all these years I took his omniscience for granted. Even so, it gave me a slight shock to hear him talk about something I'd imagined was known only to Gwen, myself, and a discreet handful of party members.

'Percy, I don't suppose in this isolated instance, you could possibly expose the source of that remarkable piece of information?'

'Ah . . . well, just happened to be passing Martin's office, do you see, as the Governor was telling him as a gentleman called Mr. Vereburn down the Chamber had mentioned you'd most likely be adopted for Beckford South. Asked what the Governor thought, evidently, and the Governor said he had nothing but the most high praise for you, both as a person and as our chief administrator, nothing but the most high praise.'

'You must have been rushing past at the rate of two foot a minute to hear all that.'

'Ah, but his voice *booms*, Bob. And just as I got to the door, I very foolishly dropped some samples.'

'One day you'll be passing a door and you'll hear someone say that Percy Lambert is an idle, useless, ignorant old git who's ready for the chop.'

He smiled down on me benignly, blew ash off his cigarette without taking it from his mouth.

'I'm proud of thee, Bob. You were nothing when you came here, and now you're the main man. And on top of that, they want you up in Parliament. And your father just a working-class chap, no more than meself. Used to see him down the Harp of Erin of a Sunday night before he went to Morecambe. Have I ever mentioned it?'

'On average, about three times a week.'

'Nice, quiet-spoken chap, your dad. *He* must be proud of you. It's like doing two jobs, really, this and politics. It takes most people all their time to do one.'

'Not surprising if they pillock about as much as you do.'

'Strange, Bob, isn't it, to think you had nothing and Simon had the lot. My word, everybody thought he was going to be all spit and ginger like his dad, here there and everywhere, eyes in his backside. But it's you who ends up running it all. Course, *he's* got the money, but money's not the same as doing what you're best at, is it? Money's not much good to a man who's made nothing of hisself.'

I pretended to read a letter; I knew he knew I was listening. I wasn't encouraging him, but I wasn't getting rid of him either.

But for once, and almost without guilt, I went on indulging myself. Even though I knew full well he was creating pure working-class mythology. Bob Saxby had shown 'em—collapse of boss's son. How potent that clean soap-opera story-line still was, with Percy Lambert, like a character from Coronation Street, to recount it.

How seductive, how heady it seemed by the side of the bitterness and complexities and shabbiness of the real struggle—it was like those lives of famous men as Emma's picture-books outlined them —an impossibly tough beginning, a decisive and industrious middle, a triumphant, table-turning end. As if nothing else happened after that moment of victory. As if life, for me and Simon, was immutably frozen at that joyous moment where I was up and he down.

Once, at one of those lavish dockside parties shipowners throw for importers, I'd seen a man fill a dinner-plate with ten different kinds of ice-cream. He'd noticed me watching him wolf it down.

'Throwback to a foolishly indulged childhood,' he'd said guiltily. 'Sort of swan-song. I'm retiring from business soon. I'll never have another chance of eating so many different dollops at one go.'

So with me. The adoption was all but nailed on. The machine was in my pocket, a successful campaign could win me South. And I was indispensable to Singleton Fisher. Didn't I deserve to indulge myself just once more in that intensely satisfying legend before I stepped firmly without any more nonsense into the sensible, impersonal world of Martin Emmott?

'Interesting news, Bob. The Governor popped in this morning . . .'

'And told you the Selection Committee will probably find for me.'

He stared at me, a forkful of egg à la Dijon suspended in mid-air. 'Percy scooped you by fully two hours, old lad.'

'The sod must have us all wired up for sound. It's incredible.'

'How did the Governor seem?'

'Pleased. For the firm's prestige. But wistful behind the façade. I know him. Wishing it were the Only Begotten.'

'I knew yesterday, in fact. Gwen's had her ear to the ground. They all more or less told her it was sewn up for me.'

'So it should be, too. If you don't deserve to be adopted no one does.'

I looked at him across the small window-table, at the deep-set reflective eyes, the long, lined face, the wings of hair, the old good suit cut in a timeless style that could only now be achieved by certain elderly tailors in Leeds. He also was wistful behind the façade. Because of the elaborate meals and the deer-shooting and the lengthy holidays in the Rhône valley. Because he lacked drive, because the vulgarity and the cut and thrust of politics would have been too much for his sensibilities, because hate and bitterness and anger had never forced him to concentrate his mind. I felt an urge to squeeze his arm. We both knew our failings.

'Well, son of a churl, how does it feel to be getting everything you wanted?'

'Ask me that when we've actually had the General Election.'

He shook his head. 'You're going to win South, Bob. I feel it in here. Always did about you. You've got the kind of luck that comes in a solid chunk. Poor Beckford—I feel I ought to warn people Saxby is coming. If you want to know what he'll do to your city, come and see what he's done to Singleton Fisher. Even so, dear boy, I feel I must salute your achievement for some reason.'

'I wouldn't be where I am today without you, Martin.'

'Rubbish!' He drank some wine, smiled. 'Sophisticated roughnecks like you get on come what may. I merely dropped an occasional hint when your uncouthness got too much. As I've said before, we were all full of *My Fair Lady* in those dear dead days, and the idea of constructing a gentleman from a lump of working-class clay fascinated me. But the thing backfired. I'm beginning to feel like the professor who built a life-size mechanical doll that ran out of control and danced his daughter to death, all the while uttering a stream of elegant civilities.'

It was a revealing analogy. I saw the same pride in his glance that I'd seen last night in Gwen's. It was not my future, but ours, and it would be our seat in that palace by the river, and our sure steady rise to prominence as Yorkshire's greatest living son—all the things he'd wanted so much and couldn't have because life had been too good to him.

Sometimes I had the feeling that if I ever failed to accomplish all the things we both wanted me to do, I'd be able to face my own disappointment better than I could face his.

'Be flippant,' I said. 'But if it hadn't been for you, I'd probably still be adding ledgers.'

'Dear me, how misty-eyed we're getting. A change of subject is urgently called for. Devaluation, Bob—the rumours get stronger. You will watch Master Simon with those rands, won't you?'

'I've made a note to raise it with him after the sale.'

'Good man!'

'Ah—afternoon, Robert.'

'Governor! How nice to see you. My word, you *do* look well.'

'Not bad for an old man.'

'Governor, I simply can't think of you as an old man. You look exactly the same to me as the day I joined the firm—a gentleman in the prime of life.'

His face darkened with pleasure. He eased himself gradually into a swivel chair, joints clicking like caps.

'Well, Robert, Albert Vereburn was talking about you the other day. I understand you've been shaking things up in Westbury almost as vigorously as you have in here.'

'Such exaggeration!' I laughed boyishly. 'Perhaps I've streamlined a committee or two . . .'

'That's not what I heard. He told me that whenever you sat on a committee down there they found decisions being taken on the spot that normally take several weeks.

' "Ah!" says I, "that's young Saxby, Albert. How well I remember when my management committee decided to make the clerical offices open plan to speed the workflow. God bless me soul, the architects were round next morning with their tape-measures. And if *that* wasn't bad enough the bounders had the face to ask me to give my room up so they could make the area even. Albert," I said, "I hardly dare enter my own premises in case I'm under young Saxby's feet." '

I gave a sudden shout of laughter that brought a scowl of delight to his austere, ancient face.

'Governor, you'll be the death of me!'

He helpfully busied himself relighting his cigar to give me chance to collect myself.

'However, Robert,' he went on, his voice falling sonorously into the November gloom. 'You'll be pleased to know I assured him how rapidly you'd always been able to assimilate my thinking, even if you did tend to act a little precipitately. It's not a bad fault in a boy your age. I was able to tell him I could always count on you to execute our decisions to my complete satisfaction. I told him that so far as I could judge you'd make an excellent politician. He . . . he appeared to think the nomination was already yours.'

'Governor.' I dropped my eyes, allowed the smallest catch into my voice. 'I . . . I can't begin to thank you. A man who has your recommendation needs no other.'

I'd been shovelling flattery into him for a decade; today I hit the jackpot. Grim-mouthed, cold-eyed, beetle-browed—he was so pleased he looked like a hanging judge.

'Well, good luck, my boy,' he boomed sombrely. 'Let's hope you can make them vote for the right party.'

'Thank you, sir.'

He began the lengthy process of relighting his cigar from a match in the gold container.

'Robert, I understand you're aware of Simon's interest in political matters.'

'Indeed I am. And very pleased about it. In fact . . .'

'Yes, yes, I know how keen you are to have him with you in Westbury. But . . . but local politics, Robert—do you not think it a waste of his talents? Oh, I know Fearnley believes one should go through the mill, as it were, but really, could you not impress on your colleagues Simon's considerable experience of the world and his keenness to serve?' He hesitated. 'We wouldn't be ungenerous to the campaign fund, you understand . . .'

I'd been waiting for it. He was old but he was a long way from senility. Praise from the Governor always involved a clawback. He needn't have told me what had passed between him and Vereburn, and if he'd not wanted something for Simon he wouldn't have done. You didn't give praise, you bartered it. It was known as handling the men.

'Governor,' I said quietly. 'Rest assured I shall do everything in my power to get Simon's considerable abilities recognised as quickly as possible. It would be a crying shame if they let that kind of talent slip through their grasp.'

'Do your best, Robert. They won't be going to the country for two or three years. Surely in that time it can be arranged for him to stand for one of the divisions.'

I stood a little stooped and obsequious, smiling into the Governor's bleak face. It was curious to think I should be standing like this at the peak of my triumph.

Because this was the moment of revenge. After all these years the Fishers needed me, and knew it. For the very first time both of them badly wanted something that only I could supply.

'Rely on me to do the best I can, sir.'

'Good man!'

'Hello, Robert.'

'Why, Simon—*hello*.'

He walked briskly across to my desk and lit one of his thick cigarettes. You hardly noticed the tremble in his hands any more. There was little about him now to reveal his past addiction. Each week saw almost startling improvements—clear, bright eyes, increased vigour, an appearance of well-being. I was old enough to have seen a number of my contemporaries fight the disease of affluence; none of them with the iron will-power of a Fisher.

'Father tells me you're almost certain to be adopted by South,' he said.

'Yes, it was awfully good of the Governor to back me up like that.'

'I must say I take a dim view of people who are forming a committee making a decision in advance. Surely it's hardly going to be fair to other candidates.'

'Oh, I think it's bound to happen to some extent, Simon, you really can't stop people putting their heads together, on a committee or off.'

'Robert, I know you have a microscopic knowledge of local matters, and I daresay you'd make a reasonable M.P., but what if a man of much wider scope and ability were to present himself? Someone, say, who hadn't immersed himself so deeply in ward work, but who would probably make a far more valuable contribution to national affairs because of it. Wouldn't it be a great pity if you were adopted simply because it had been prearranged that you should be?'

'Simon,' I said gently. 'The seat's too marginal to attract the kind of M.P. who *must* be returned. If a first-class type *did* turn up I can assure you I'd be turned down. I can only assume they're favouring me because they think I'm the best of what there is.' I chuckled in bland deprecation. 'In the kingdom of the blind, you know . . .'

Despite the failing afternoon light, I could see those spots on his cheekbones suddenly start glowing. He could think of someone much better than me to fight South. That was why I'd thought of something to say that seemed harmless but which hurt him by stealth, like infected drinking water.

But why needle him? I couldn't see why I felt I had to. I'd beaten him. I'd always said I would, and now both Fishers were queuing up for my favours.

The room went silent, all you could hear was the intermittent burr of Esther's typewriter through the partly open ante-room door. He got up abruptly and turned to the window.

'Gwen tells me you were a big success with your talk to the U.T.s,' I said. 'Allow me to congratulate you.'

'Thank you. I was led to believe they found it of some small interest.'

For once it wasn't empty flattery. According to Gwen he really had gone down rather well. Over-awed, as I saw it, for once in his life, by a roomful of people who owed him nothing, instead of talking down as he always did at the meeting, he'd talked simply and effectively about sheep-farming around the world.

'And then I understand you very kindly agreed to sit in at our little ward meeting.'

'I hadn't intended to, but Mrs. Saxby seemed to be expecting it. There was some confusion over the point.'

I smiled. Few people were proof against the inspired and enervating vagueness Gwen could project when she wanted them to do something.

'An inordinate amount of time was devoted to that meat-pie man's activities at council meetings. He was positively encouraged to waffle on.'

'In Westbury, Simon, we risk boredom in order to know exactly what our councillors are doing with their time.'

Gwen had also reported a favourable reaction to him among the seniors. He'd been remote, but he was a Fisher after all, and his formal manners had gone down well with the old ladies. He'd spoken seldom, but when he had he'd spoken sensibly and to the point.

In that moment I knew quite certainly that the tide of his affairs was on the turn. His addiction had been defeated. He'd put in six steady months of attendance at the office. He was making a sensible marriage. And he was standing quite securely on the first rung of the political ladder.

And that was why I was bitching him.

He'd a long way to go. The money would make some things easy but his late start and his ignorance would make others very hard. But he was still young enough to make a go of politics. Anything was possible to a determined man—take me. Not that he was ever

206

going to be as good as me, but he'd got the Fisher talents, he'd be able to make himself a formidable proposition in the end.

Once, many years ago, he'd given me a bad time. Martin had always said it was because he'd sensed the threat of my potential. And now my instinct was to put the boot in on him because I sensed the threat of his. Our situation had come full circle.

I almost felt close to him then. He'd got the stuff you needed. It was real life out there, where mystiques and money weren't a scrap of use, full of tough elderly men from the old back-yard, but I knew then that he had it in him to make a go of it.

'By the way, Simon, I'm sorry to be a bore about this, but you will remember about covering the rands for Wednesday's sale, won't you? There really are some ugly rumours floating about the City.'

'Yes,' he said coldly. 'I did know about the rumours, and yes, I was aware that we'd need to cover. Does that set your mind at rest?'

One day we'd both be in local politics and we'd have a genuine respect for each other. One day he might even reach the calmer waters of self-knowledge, might begin to realise the emptiness of mystiques, might finally grasp the reason for our long antagonism. One day we might even be friends.

The days of hate were over.

18

We lay together on an ancient couch before a blazing coal fire. We'd made love with our clothes on : all I'd removed was my jacket, she her black trews.

It hadn't been a success. She'd been remote, she'd gazed past me into the half-light. She'd been so still. She'd held me almost absently, scarcely moving her thighs against mine. I couldn't understand it, after a while I'd stopped. Only then had her body begun to move, but only until mine had taken up the rhythm again.

Even orgasm had scarcely broken her inertia. Her body had reacted against mine of its own volition, but instead of the old yelping abandon there'd only been the muted explosions of her rapid breathing. She'd not spoken once from beginning to end, she'd not even whispered my name. I couldn't understand it.

207

And yet she'd wanted me. I'd said goodbye in the car, but she'd told me her parents were out, she'd invited me into that gaunt house for the first time. For a drink. But inside it had been she who'd drawn me down to the couch, who'd held my hand over her breast with both her own. She'd wanted it.

I wondered if she'd fought against herself, as I once had, and lovemaking had been the last thing she'd wanted. Or was it deeper than that and more complex; was she somehow punishing me because I belonged to Emma and Gwen and politics? Because being near me upset her too much. Because I was me.

Was this the sort of contemptuous goodbye she felt I deserved?

When our shuddering bodies finally became still she turned from me to face the back of the couch. I was empty and depressed, but even then my stomach nerves fluttered at the sight of her curved body, at the firm buttocks and the flowing contour of thigh, hip and waist, at the contrast of white flesh and black cloth, at the long skeins of hair falling diagonally across her shoulders.

I lay back on the couch, suddenly plunged into melancholy, into wistful memories of hot grass and luminous skies and claret-coloured satin, of the big empty house with its ticking clocks, of tears shed over a mourning-ring and a brown-tinted photograph, of total silence and pungent loins and aqueous light. Her soft young body lay inches from mine, but she seemed more remote now than the night she'd been with Peter Dowling in her black Spanish hat.

I remembered autumn skies and the clip of our heels across Minton tiles, taxis and Van Goghs and dinner at a table for two. I thought of the total darkness of that hotel room and the way we had laid clamped together in a perfect timeless void.

I gazed at her body in the half-light; without thinking I ran my hand over the thin cloth of her sweater, over the cool smooth flesh of her thighs and buttocks, and then I leaned over and consciously inhaled the thin wisps of her odour. It filled me with an emotion halfway between pleasure and pain.

Then all at once I was glad it had ended like this, without the almost terrifying abandon of before. If it had been like that I wouldn't now be remembering to remember, or deliberately matching odour and touch with exquisite times past, pinning down the affair's smallest details for the grey lonely journey into my future.

I heard her gulp. And then again. I took her shoulder, tried to turn her towards me. At first she resisted, but finally she gave way.

She'd been weeping for some time and I began to understand then. I stroked her hair and gently kissed her wet lips.

She too. She'd also wanted to remember. If she'd given me nothing it was only because it had been so essential she took something away with her that would last. That apparent indifference, when I'd laid over her, had been a concentration as intense and deliberate as mine had been on London and Chelifer House. She'd remembered my every movement and embrace so she could live through it again and again when our time was at an end.

She smiled wanly, pushed me away, began to pull on the black pants.

'I'm sorry,' I said.

She shrugged. 'You'd better go. Gwen'll be wondering where you are.'

'It's all right. She knows I'm with you. I could go to China with you now and she'd trust us.'

'Well.' She got up. 'If you've come for a goodbye drink you'd better have one.'

She chose a bottle from a number standing on a dusty sideboard, all of an odd foreign shape, and poured from it into two plain brandy glasses. I could hardly stand to look at her with her hair down, in the tight black sweater and pants.

I gazed bleakly at the room. It was large and shabby and had an old leather suite and a faded Indian carpet. A narrow table stood near the window, piled up with exercise books and educational magazines. There was a museum-piece radiogram against the opposite wall, its storage-racks crammed solid with L.P.s in tattered sleeves. There were framed prints on every wall—Picasso and Mondrian and Nicolas de Stael, and in the recesses at the side of the fireplace were stacked hundreds of hard-cover books.

It was all exactly as I'd pictured it, on that day last spring when I'd first taken her home. Perhaps there'd have been rooms like this in my house, if I'd stayed a left-winger.

There was an enormous television with a tiny screen standing at the edge of the hearthrug. It reminded me of the thousands of days piled up behind me. It flickered in silence. It was part of our careful evidence, on the off-chance that her parents came home early, that I'd called to see my secretary for a few minutes between engagements. It was an old film, with Doris Day being terrified by phone calls and lifts that stuck between floors. The same Doris Day I used to see in colour, twice as large as life. The same Doris Day who'd once sung *Young at Heart* when I'd sat with poor Maggie in the back row at the Cosy Clifton.

She handed me the glass, sat down heavily.

'When do you leave?'

'Monday week.'

'Where are you going?'

She shrugged. 'London. Or Sydney. Or New York.'

'Does it have to be so radical?'

'Yes.'

'Why don't you go back to the University? We'd not see each other.'

She smiled bitterly. 'You might not see me, but I'd see you.'

'This is your home. I don't like to feel I'm responsible for making you go so far away.'

'You'd better get back, Bob.'

'*Please* don't go.'

I'd expected her to be surprised, as surprised as I was. But nothing altered in her face. She drank some of the brandy, put the glass down carefully on the side arm of the couch, then finally turned to me.

'Why did you say that?'

There was an odd, impersonal tone in her voice.

'I . . . I don't know. It'll be hell without you. I couldn't help it.'

'But we agreed,' she said, with the same detachment. 'We agreed it couldn't go on like this, because of your family and your politics. We talked it over at great length on the train. The only answer was for me to go right away.'

I tried to find something in her eyes that belied the peculiar coolness, to see some of the anguished longing in them I'd seen on the train; but she went on watching me steadily.

'I'm sorry,' I said in a low voice. 'I know what we agreed. I couldn't stop myself.'

'But were you serious? About me staying.'

'Yes . . . I was.'

'And would you want to go on seeing me?'

I understood then. I'd begun to forget the control she'd always had over her features. London was still too fresh in my mind, when for once the mask had been forgotten under the impact of happiness and fear and sadness and joy.

It was too much for her. It should have ended, but now I didn't want it to. It had overwhelmed her, numbed her into a sceptical caution. But the old longing was still there, under the impassive surface.

I took her hand. She let it lay motionless in mine.

'You could go on helping me. With the politics. Get a job somewhere else but carry on as an assistant.'

'Do you really mean it?'

I was right, it had been too much to take after all the ups and downs of our relationship.

'Couldn't we . . . keep it as it was? In the summer.'

'But meeting like this. The danger . . .'

'No . . . we couldn't do this any more. Not in Beckford. But if . . . if I won the seat, if I went up. Three years is a hell of a time, I know that, and . . . and anything could happen, but if I won it and we were still seeing each other, we might have the chance of . . . of *some* life together. I'd be in London four nights a week.'

'I see. We carry on exactly as we did this summer until the next General Election, and then if you win South we can both go to London and have an affair.'

I watched her. I understood the confused state she was in now. I could make allowances. There couldn't be a lousier deal for a girl her age than to be so much in love with an ambitious married man.

'Esther,' I said. 'It's only if *you* want it. Oh, look, can't we just go on as we were and see how it works out?'

She turned away. I saw her blink rapidly. She bent and picked up a packet of cigarettes from beneath the couch and lit one with sharp nervous movements. Suddenly she leapt to her feet.

'You heel!'

'Esther . . .'

'You bastard!'

She turned on me, her large teeth clenched and rat-like. It hadn't been joy she'd been trembling with, but rage.

'That was *my* idea! I said all that on the train last week. But you turned it down flat, you wouldn't hear of it. We had to finish it, there and then.

'Only that was a week ago, and since then you've had time to think it all over. You've had time to draw a Bill up and see it through the committee stage and give it a third reading . . .'

'No, Esther, you're wrong . . .'

'You *swine*, why couldn't you just say yes on the train? What difference could it possibly have made, when it's so far away anyway? Oh *God*, why couldn't you just say yes then, why for once in your life couldn't you *just—be—spontaneous!*'

She was right. I'd had a week. The nomination was practically in my pocket, and I'd had a week to think how much my life would change if I won South, how much further ambition would eat into an already crowded life. I'd had a week to find out that an uncertain handful of nights in London was all that was left to us of each other.

I'd had a week to think how much in love with her I was.

Yes, love. For the first time in my life. Reluctantly, of course, guardedly—in love as long as love never came between me and the fix, but genuinely for all that and just as obsessively.

Even though she didn't and couldn't love me, even though she'd never love anyone but that illusion in white tennis clothes—I still loved her.

And I'd had a week to think it all out. Even in terms of Emma. I'd squared my conscience—it would either be love that fitted the code or nothing. And it would fit the code. The affair would go on ice, either until I went to London or for good. In London there would be no one to know, Emma would go on being nourished by a family structure that would always seem the same. And when she had most need of me the affair would be over.

I got up. She turned away and ground out the cigarette. . . .

'Please don't go.'

'You're just seven days too late.'

'I'm sorry about the train.'

'If you'd said yes last week I'd have done anything for you. It just needed one spontaneous gesture.'

'I wasn't capable of it. You're right . . .'

'Don't. I know your way with words. I've heard you playing your nasty games with Simon Fisher.'

'That was gratuitous,' I said, after a while, in a low voice. 'You're right about me. I admit it. Don't hit me for the sake of it.'

She turned back to me in contempt.

'It's not gratuitous. Simon Fisher's what you're all about. But not the way you pretend. You're a failure, but it's nothing to do with him. You've just made yourself believe it's him. He's a scape-goat. You can't face your guilt so you blame him for what you've become. How else could you have worked for someone you loathed?

'And you still loathe him. But you need him for that . . . that repulsive career. So you had to take it out on him sneakily, you had to think it all out. And that's how you've become with everyone now—sneaky and smarmy and never saying yes or no till you've thought about it for a week. Even with me. *Me!*'

'For Christ's sake, shut up about Simon Fisher!'

I stared at her. Hard-eyed, open-mouthed—she almost seemed ready to spring at me in the black feline clothes.

'It hurts, doesn't it? The truth.'

'Look, I blame no one for what I am. All I ever said was that if I hadn't known him I'd have been different.'

'That's where it all started. With him. That's when you started covering your real emotions up. And now you can hardly feel any.'

'How can you say that? After Saturday.'

She turned away and stood looking into the reddening coals with a faint smile. 'Oh, you've still got emotions. You've still got it in you to be a decent politician. But not for much longer. In a few more years you'll have guarded your emotions so well they'll just wither and die.'

'Don't go on. It's not for you to stand in judgement.'

'Someone has to. The way you are with people all stems from the unnatural way you are with Simon Fisher. You know I'm right.'

'Very well,' I said. 'Let's talk about what's wrong with you, for a change.'

She suddenly backed away. I remembered Saturday and wished I hadn't even made the threat. Because that was all it was, a threat. I wasn't really angry, I simply didn't want to waste precious minutes talking about the decline and fall of her version of Bob Saxby. I was resigned to it now, to knowing that she saw me as an empty failure, twisted almost beyond recognition by my burden of guilt, a Dorian Gray. I thought she'd understand, she of all people, but she saw in me only what she wanted to see.

But I could take it. I'd managed to live with everyone else's picture of me—Gwen's and Martin's and Mrs. Telleyman's; why not Esther's? It was very sad, but I was a realist—I knew she only loved me at all because she was convinced the noble youth in tennis whites still feebly struggled to get out.

I turned her gently towards me.

'I don't want to fight,' I said. 'It's beside the point. Look, we're two lonely people—perhaps our only chance of happiness is what we might be able to give each other. Why don't we simply take each other as we are?'

I took her face in my hands and kissed her on the lips. But she didn't respond.

'Well?'

She gazed forlornly past me into space. 'I don't know,' she whispered.

'All right.' I looked at my watch. 'Don't decide now. I'll have to go anyway. Think about it. I don't mind *you* thinking it over, you see.'

She smiled wanly. 'Oh, Bob. If only you weren't so cautious. If only you ever did anything to show you could be silly and human. I think if I could just see you make *one* spontaneous gesture, like you might have done in Westbury Park, it . . . it might seem worth going on.'

'I must go.' I picked up my car-coat. 'But remember, I'm married and I'm almost thirty-five and I'm in the middle of a career. Three good reasons why it's hard for me to be spontaneous. Frankly, I'm rather used. And you may not believe it, but one of the reasons I thought we ought to separate was you spoiling your life. All very cautious, I agree. And now I've thought it over and changed my mind, and that seems like caution too, and you're right. But I've changed it because it honestly seems to me we'll only get any real happiness in our lives from each other. And that's why I want you to be cautious now about deciding anything.'

It was the truth. It wasn't the simple truth because I wasn't a simple man, but it was a genuine part of a complex whole. Somehow, when I wasn't immersed in politics or administration or the construction of Emma's future, I was in love with her, and it was a love that contained tenderness.

She touched me on the arm from behind.

'Do you really want me to stay with you? You wouldn't change your mind any more?'

I daren't move. I sensed a mood so delicate that a single sound delivered at the wrong pitch might break it like a wine-glass. I was aware of my heart beating, and when she touched the side of my head I was so tense the nerves prickled down my spine in waves. It needn't end.

I began to turn to her. But something caught me, some tiny nagging detail made me hesitate, a detail that couldn't be ignored even at that moment of profound relief.

It was the television. The old film. There were some words curiously superimposed across the silent faces of Rex Harrison and Doris Day. Words that looked as if they'd been pasted on a greengrocer's window.

And then I concentrated. Hard.

£ DEVALUED 14% BANK RATE UP TO 8%

'Christ!'

She gave a minute scream.

'What is it? What is it?'

'Devaluation!'

I stared at the words, my mind, like a separate entity, automatically trying to cope with their implications.

'Look.' I turned to her. 'I've got to ring Martin, Esther. It's panic stations.'

She covered her face with her hands and suddenly hunched forward. I stood and watched her in sickened silence. It was impossible for fate to have timed it better—in all the difficult months I'd known her our situation had never hung on a finer thread.

I put my hands on her shoulders.

'*Go away!*' she cried. 'GO AWAY!'

19

'Daddy, you've lost *again*. Mummy, Daddy's lost at Lexicon now.'

'How very unusual, dear.'

She winked at me over the paper, but I shook my head. This time I wasn't cheating to let Emma win, I was genuinely losing. It gave me a feeling of unease, winning steadily at games of chance was accepted as being part of my normal luck, and I was as touchy about my luck as an actor.

'Last game, Emma.'

But she began to put the games away in the lacquered box.

'I don't like to see you lose *all* the time, ducky.'

It was a lie. She loved to see me lose, to cackle with glee—she'd play all day if I'd let her. But now she seemed to be affected by my own sense of foreboding. It was one of those dripping English days of white mist; the trees in the back garden looked as if they'd been sketched on drawing paper with a soft pencil, and birds perched motionless and silent among the faded branches.

'Smile,' Emma said. 'You're on *Candid Camera*.'

She climbed on to my knee.

'Don't go out.'

'I've got to, lovey.'

'Didn't know you'd much planned,' Gwen murmured.

'I'm going to the office with Martin. It's absolutely essential to know where we are with this devaluation.'

'Don't go out, Pop. Stay with Mummy and Emma and later on we'll play *The Gondoliers* and dance.'

It sounded marvellous. Just now and then in winter I'd devote an entire afternoon to her and we'd do just that—potter the hours away talking and dancing, and there'd be lemonade for Emma and dry sherries for me and Gwen, and later we'd draw the curtains and eat our dinner in the lamplight.

I'd had a long hard week and I yearned for that kind of simple time today, I craved it. The idea of going to the office and grappling with the problems of devaluation could scarcely be borne.

And Esther was leaving me.

'Sorry, Em.'

'Oh, *please*, Daddy.' She brought her face very close. 'And then *after* dinner we can watch *Steptoe*.'

'Can't be done.'

'Perhaps he'll sleep with the horse again, Daddy. Perhaps he'll put his socks in the oven.'

The memory was too much; she closed her eyes and began to giggle helplessly.

'Please stay, Pop.'

'Now don't go on, Emma.'

'Then let me come.'

'That won't do either. Martin and I have a lot of work to do. You'd be under our feet.'

'Please. I'll be as quiet as a little mouse.'

Beloved Emma. The warmth of our bodies mingled; I drew her closer. I was tempted to let her come, she'd only wander round the

offices, poking in cupboards and tapping at typewriters. I was lonely.
I was lonely and uneasy and Esther was going. I'd had a bad night.
I'd dreamt that people were rushing down to the city by the thousand, in buses, in cars, on foot, a jostling noisy mob, all bent on
getting their savings from the banks and buying goods with them,
because of a scare report that the purchasing power of the pound
would fall by half overnight. But the entire commercial centre was
at a standstill, the streets deserted before the onrushing crowd,
every door locked and barred.

I watched them milling outside the banks along Spinnergate. All
at once their mood turned ugly and they began to fight among themselves. I saw them raise sticks and umbrellas on one another, and
then I saw knives suddenly flashing like the underbellies of fish
against dark clothing. I saw blood spattering the pavement and
heard horrifying screams of terror and pain. I saw men run amok,
flailing clenched fists, their arms as rigid as truncheons.

Then I saw Esther standing nearby, watching. She slowly turned
towards me and I saw that her cheeks were wet with tears.

'You politician,' she said.

Her voice had been hoarse with revulsion. I had awoken sickened
and frightened, and oppressed by an appalling sense of guilt.

The guilt stayed with me; as the day went on I knew it had been
there in the first place, that the dream had sprung from it and somehow brought it out, like a dressing bringing out pus.

Guilt over her. Guilt because fate never punished me like it
punished them—first poor Maggie, now Esther. Guilt because I'd
still have Emma while she was friendless and alone. Guilt because
I'd always be like the onlooker in the dream, scared and pitying, but
too self-protecting, too fly by half, ever to be involved in genuine
anguish.

'Come on then, young 'un. Put your coat on.'

'What do you think, Bob?'

'It's only really South Africa we buy from in their own currency.
The rest sell to us in sterling and they should be covered. If they
aren't they're going to take a bad knock on outstanding contracts.
They'll take it damn badly. They might insist we share the loss with
them in some way.'

'More or less what the Governor thinks. He was on the phone
right after you last night. Closely followed by Garbage, stunned

into near sobriety. Simon, however, was up in the Dales with the Yorkshire Cob.'

'We'll list outstanding contracts, shall we, that'll give us something to go on. The telex'll be going like the clappers tomorrow, so we'd better be ready.'

'It was going like the clappers as I came across General. I shuddered and passed on. The Governor thinks Australia and New Zealand may do a parallel or even bigger devaluation.'

'It would help.' I hesitated. 'How about South Africa?'

'Your guess is as good as mine.'

We looked at each other.

'Are you thinking what I'm thinking?' he said at last.

'Don't let's even consider it. Buying rands was the one thing he really liked doing.'

'The last Cape sale was Wednesday.'

'I handed him the figures on Thursday morning.'

'So I should have a contract from the Standard Bank in my IN-tray. Hold on.'

He began to work through his papers. I crossed to the window and looked out over the square, at bare wet trees, at buildings so faint in the mist they were like shapes in an under-exposed photograph. It was a city that seemed as deserted and locked-up and inimical as the Beckford of my dream. It deepened my unease. At any moment the mob would come charging along Cloth Hall Street.

'No contract.'

'Perhaps it's in the pipe-line.'

I turned to him, willing him to agree. He sensed it and hesitated, as if he wished he could.

'I . . . don't honestly believe it can be, Bob. They get them off the minute they give verbal confirmation.'

'Has he ever let a weekend pass with a sale uncovered before?'

He bent over a book, straightened up, sighed. 'Once.'

I whispered, 'Holy Mother of God', but I was too stunned for anger, too overwhelmed by the scale of it, too involved in mental arithmetic. I wondered if there was a way out. I'd had twenty years in commerce, I'd come to know there were few mishaps that were totally irreversible.

Martin shook his head. He'd read my thoughts with an accuracy that came of our long collaboration.

'It's like death,' he said. 'I remember the last time they devalued.

If there's anything you haven't done before there's not the remotest chance of doing it after.'

'All right,' I said flatly. '*If* he hasn't covered it we've lost a straight seven thousand.'

He came across to the window.

'Now look, perhaps it's in the post. There's a chance. But if not, then there's nothing more to be done.'

'I reminded the bastard too—the same day you brought it up.'

He took my arm. 'Well, Bob, it's his firm and it's his money, and if he has forgotten to cover his pocket'll suffer most. It'll do him no harm to feel the consequences of a serious error. It was his job and his responsibility.'

'Oh, come off it. We're the accountancy chappies. The cardinal fact of life in this bloody place is that a Fisher's never wrong, even when he's flagrantly, blatantly wrong. Do you want to bet where the meeting, as one man, including Simon himself, will put the boot in? Christ, they'll *slaughter* us !'

'I *know* that,' he said. 'That's just something we'll have to accept —we've made an utter balls of it. Ten to one it'll be Simon himself who gives us the worst drubbing. But it'll not happen again, mark my words. He'll never make the kind of mistake again that'll cost him hard cash, even though he won't admit he's made this one.'

'Martin, I'm not going to let that lot crap all over us because of his incompetence.'

'Yes, you are,' he said quietly. 'You know perfectly well they'll crap on us whatever you say, so you might as well accept it. The cash department's blundered—you mustn't attempt to blame Simon. If you do you'll put both their backs up—at a very delicate stage in your own career. You've got to bite on the bullet *and* you know it. Don't bother about Garbage. He'll know. Behind all that righteous indignation he'll know where the blame really lies. You let Simon go free, you need them too much.'

I brought a fist down with all my force on top of a filing cabinet; the noise boomed across the high silent room. He was right, of course. He was always right. There was no question of me putting the finger on Simon. It was a charade, a ritual. He was a stalking horse for the real enemy—exhausting my fire so the Fishers would go unscathed.

'Forget it, old son,' he said. 'I know how you must feel; you just don't make mistakes. It's a lot of money, but the firm makes a lot —seven thousand won't make much difference to the year-end figures. At least we're forewarned, at least you've got time to think out how we should play it at the meeting.'

'Oh—all right.' I forced a smile.

'Come on, let's go through the contracts and sod off home. I've had a bellyful.'

We passed from his office to the little room connecting his and mine. I'd forgotten about Emma. She sat at Esther's desk, laboriously pecking at typewriter keys, red-faced with concentration. She wore a Fair Isle sweater and trews and a blue cap with a pom-pom. It gave me a sudden shock of pleasure to see her there, but then the old depression seemed to grow deeper—there were only five more days to see Esther herself sit there.

'Well, young lady, this *is* a funny way to spend Sunday afternoon.'

'I like to be with Daddy,' she told him. 'I hardly see him during the week.'

'Really.'

'It's because he has to do a lot of politics during the week.'

'Ah.'

'Ever such a lot of politics. And Sunday's really the only day I can be with him.'

'Never mind. Perhaps when you're a big girl you'll be able to help him to do his politics.'

'Oh *yes*! Like Esther. She does *such* a lot of politics with him. Is she coming soon, Daddy?'

'I'm . . . afraid not.'

'I only wish she were, my dear. We could do with her for the listing, eh, Bob?'

'Are you *sure* she's not coming? Why don't you ring her up and tell her I'm here?'

Martin smiled. 'She must be a special friend of yours.'

'Oh, she is. She sometimes comes to tea, doesn't she, Daddy? And once we all went to Daisy Edge Woods . . .'

'She's going away, Em. She has to leave Beckford soon.'

Her mouth fell open.

'*Going away*. Why?'

'I don't know. Perhaps she's tired of dirty old Beckford.'

'But what about your politics? What about *me*? Won't she come and see me any more?'

'She'll come to say goodbye to you and Mummy, of course, but after that . . .'

I picked her up and held her on my arm. I rubbed my cheek against hers, filled with the same urge for sanctuary as when we'd sat looking at motionless birds on sodden, faded trees. There'd always be Emma, to remind me of the happy times the three of u' had spent together.

I forced a cheerful tone. 'Well, we'll just have to get along without her as best we can. You, me and Martin.'

I caught his glance moving with embarrassment from mine. He'd been surprised that I'd brought her to the office at all; I'd noticed the uneasiness when she'd told him she'd come so as to be with me. Such a statement from one of his own children would have struck him as disturbingly excessive.

I knew he'd have liked to mould my private life as effectively as he'd moulded my professional career—to see my daughter given the same impersonal upbringing all Emmott children were given, in an atmosphere of private boarding-schools and cordial affection.

No doubt he actually loved his children, but it hadn't the remotest connection with the sort of love I shared with Emma, the sort of naked, unabashed love that he was able to equate only too well with the working-class novels and films of the late 'fifties he'd disliked so intensely, the sort of love he knew and feared as being in the same dangerous category as the hate I'd once had for Simon.

But then, it had been all those naked, unrefined emotions, the love and the hate and the egocentricity, that had forced me into achieving all the things he'd wanted in the first place.

20

I walked slowly across the big open-plan office. The manager, a quiet, industrious little man called Golding—immortalised in office-lore by Martin as The Lord of the Files—was standing with two or three young clerks.

I crossed to them, smiled, talked for a while about the economic crisis. For once I almost felt a nostalgia for General, for the camaraderie and the uncomplicated slog. Up there, in those daunting carpeted rooms, lay trouble—trouble, acrimony and humiliation. Up there lay the tangle of the devalued pound. Up there, perhaps an hour from detonation, lay a seven-thousand-pound time-bomb.

For once in my life I envied them, those clean-cut hand-picked boys of mine, envied them the comforting runs of routine work, the regular hours, the bright bubble-cut girls they took out in their old bangers, the Saturday night rave-ups. For once I longed for their simple, ordered day as much as they longed for my lengthy, complex, pressure-filled, highly paid one.

'Hello. You're early.'

'I'd like to leave a straight edge for my successor.'

She was wearing the usual grey woollen dress with the white collar and cuffs.

'You're definitely going?'

She nodded without speaking.

'Will *nothing* make you stay?'

She gave a single shake of her head, turned to the papers in my basket. 'The new girl's coming this afternoon. I'll show her exactly how you like things done . . .'

'I don't blame you,' I said in a low voice. 'It's a rotten deal. But please stay with me. Please.'

She closed her eyes, turned away.

'It's . . . it's no good, Bob. I can . . . I can just stand coming after your family, and I know what your work means to you, it's . . . it's just that I think I ought to have come somewhere between them and it, not . . . not after *everything*.'

'I can't tell you how sorry I am about Saturday. It was so unexpected. You can't believe I'd want to upset you like that. It was spontaneous. You said it was impossible for me to be spontaneous, but . . .'

I suddenly realised what I was saying. She nodded.

'About your work. You can be spontaneous about your work. But not about me.'

My eyes fell from her steady gaze. 'It's part of my fabric—work. You know that. Without work and ambition I'd be a different man altogether. If you can take me at all surely you can accept that.'

'That's it. I can't take you at all. Not any more.'

She suddenly walked away to her own room. I sat down, reached out for the letters and the telexes. But the usual concentration wouldn't come. I kept thinking of that burning June day at Chelifer House. I kept thinking of that day by the Thames when her hair had blown in the wind. I saw her in watery sunlight in the Commons Chamber, I saw her walking across Trafalgar Square, I saw her in the restaurant, in the hotel room, on a couch by a coal fire.

However hard I tried, I couldn't stem the flow of memory, my subconscious seemed to be making a last desperate bid to force me to try again, to convince me there must be a way of keeping her, must be some gesture I could make even now that would make her change her mind.

I got up. She hadn't gone yet; there was still a week left. It wasn't over until I actually saw her train pull out.

I opened her door. '*Please* don't go, Esther.'

She shook her head without looking up.

'*Please*, Esther. Tell me what I can do to make you stay and I'll try to do it. You'd have stayed on Saturday if it hadn't been for the news-flash. I know you would. I'll make it up to you, I promise. We'll go everywhere together. It'll be just like last summer. We were happy then.'

She closed her eyes, put a hand to her forehead; at that moment my office door opened.

' 'Morning, Bob. Monday again. Ah well, what I say is, you wouldn't enjoy Friday night down the boozer a quarter as much if you hadn't spent all week getting over Monday morning in this bloody hole.'

I sighed, came back into my office.

' 'Morning, Percy.'

'How about devaluating the pound then? Be like Germany after the war soon. You'll be taking a tatchy-case full of fivers to buy twenty Embassy. Inflationary roundabout, you watch. 'Course, beer and fags'll go up again if I'm any judge. Working-man's pleasures. They'd tax ferret if they could find out how many times you had it.'

'Percy, if you don't mind. I'm up to me ears in it this morning.'

He watched me in concern. I always gave him his five or ten minutes, however busy I was, it was one of the privileges of his special position.

'Bob lad,' he said in a hoarse gentle voice. 'Aren't you so good?'

His warmth only increased my utter desolation. It took me back

223

to my origins, reminded me of my father and the fishermen uncles, the smoke and the beer, the parcels of fish and chips, the love, the powerful bonds. People asking you how you were and honestly caring.

'I'm a bit weary. Devaluations cause a lot of work and worry, I'm afraid.'

'Don't overdo it, son. You work too hard as it is. It won't run away, you know.'

My door opened again. It was Simon, looking pale and tense.

' 'Morning, *Mr.* Simon, *sir.*'

He came into the room with a curt nod.

'Lambert, I keep having to tell you about wasting Mr. Saxby's time. I will not have it. If you haven't enough work of your own I can very quickly find you some.'

'Ah, well, Mr. Simon, sir, I'd have departed some time ago, except I stayed to ask after Bob's health, as he looked a bit peaky.'

Simon's lozenges glowed faintly and I could see the muscles round his jaw twitching, but he said nothing else, aware that to reprimand him further would appear callous. Percy had scored again. He went off grinning.

'*Are* you unwell?'

'No. Just tired. I slept badly.'

'I drove in with Father. We're calling a meeting for ten-thirty.'

'I thought you might. We've prepared a summary of the financial position.'

'This morning?' he said sharply.

'No. We came in yesterday.'

He turned away. He should have been in himself and he knew it.

'A filthy business. They've signed their death-warrant as credible politicians. Every time they trick the country into returning them, they cause instant economic chaos.'

'Simon,' I said evenly. 'Last week's Cape Sale. I presume you did actually cover the rands on Friday?'

Sickened as I was by the whole dreary mess, it was impossible not to have a grudging admiration for the conditioning, for the sheer breeding and assurance that went into the way he turned back to me and looked me straight in the eye.

'No,' he said. '*I* didn't cover them.'

I knew then that it must have been the first thing he'd thought of when he'd heard the news. And that almost instantaneously the mystique had exerted its profound influence, that inevitably and to him without the slightest hypocrisy, transference of responsibility from himself to the paid hacks had been natural and complete.

A Fisher was never wrong.

'In that case,' I said, 'I'm afraid they weren't covered at all.'

'They weren't covered!' he cried. 'Ye Gods! How much was involved?'

He himself had been the last one to see the figures. But I was prepared to believe the transference of responsibility had produced genuine ignorance in him; it was Fisher double-think at its most comprehensive.

'It'll cost us an additional seven thousand,' I said evenly. 'Assuming South Africa sticks to its present parity.'

'Ye Gods! This is absolutely appalling! *Seven thousand pounds.* After all that time we spent on covering rands at the meetings. Well, *really,* I can only assume there's some kind of explanation you can give Father. *Seven thousand pounds.*'

Empty words. The Governor would fly into a monumental rage. He'd hammer the table with his cigar-case. He'd shout at us. Garbutt and his snivelling Greek chorus would begin to sneer and curse. The room would be in an uproar, heaping contumely on two silent, dejected men.

And then it would all be over. This was a crisis-prone trade. Every year saw its crop of specs that misfired, sums of money laid out that would make a layman boggle; it wouldn't make much difference to the year-end figures. Seven thousand was a drop in a bucket to a firm like this.

'Simon, I thought it was agreed among the three of us that *you'd* buy the rands,' I said mildly. 'As you've done all along.'

'Robert, I'm in your department merely to study the firm's over-all activities. I'm prepared to lend a hand now and then, but you and Martin are in charge and you and Martin should have satisfied yourselves that everything was in order before you went off on Friday.'

A scratch of guilt like a hair-clipping under a shirt collar provoked the first real irritation. He had a point. All things being scrupulously equal, I *was* in charge here and I should have checked the position myself. But I hadn't, and it was because I'd grown accustomed to delegating, and trusting my delegates. Not one of those hand-picked lads in General, for instance—who were paid a tenth of what Simon took out of the firm—would have let me down as he'd done.

'Simon, I did *ask* you if you'd covered them. You assured me it was in hand.'

'That's beside the point. The ultimate responsibility rests with Martin and you. I have a great many calls on my time from the firm as a whole; on Friday it so happened that I was too busy for bumf.'

The silence that followed seemed deeper than usual. I realised that her door was ajar and her typewriter silent. She was listening. She was listening to me being given a dressing down and taking it on the chin because the Fishers were part of the magic circle. Because I needed them to get inside the palace by the river. She was listening to Bob Saxby protecting his main chance with the usual nauseating caution.

I suddenly saw a way of keeping her. It frightened me, the mere thought of it sent a sensation like a hot needle across my guts.

But then I wondered what there was to be scared of.

I knew it would work. One burst of apparently genuine anger vented on him and I was certain she'd give me another chance, certain she'd be convinced the knight of the tennis courts still lived. Hadn't she said again and again that the way I was with all people stemmed from the unnatural way I was with Simon? And that if only I could do something to show I could be silly or human it might make it seem worth going on?

He watched me steadily; I walked across to the window to gain time to think. A controlled rollicking—what real harm could it do me now? I plotted every aspect of my career with meticulous care, but it was paranoia to think it could still be endangered by a single ill-judged word in the wrong ear.

The Fishers needed me now, both of them, to help launch Simon into politics. They also needed me to service the administrative machine I'd spent ten years putting together. They imagined it had come into being because they had willed it, but even the Governor himself was prepared to admit that no one could turn his flashes of creative thought into action as efficiently as me. They might have had the mystique bred into them, but they'd also had the ability to interpret a set of accounts bred into them, and the accounts were looking healthier every year.

So where was the harm in a carefully managed display of temper?

In the privacy of my office. Just him, me and the watchful Esther. Just a few carefully chosen harsh words which I could eat later at the meeting. She'd not mind that, my public humiliation, once I'd made that silly, human, private gesture.

I gazed out at the wet roads and the leafless trees of a bleak November morning. If I made it she'd stay. It had the precise simplicity of an equation—me plus anger equalled her.

But then I almost decided against it. Not because of the danger in that calculated risk, but because of the calculation itself, because even I could barely stomach such an abysmally contrived spontaneity.

Yet surely the end would justify the shabby means. Surely they'd be justified if we could regain some of the happiness of last summer. The gesture would be an illusion but I'd always been an illusion to her anyway.

I twitched my shoulder, turned my hard blue gaze on him.

'That's it then,' I said. 'Seven thousand pounds down the drain.'

His pale eyes flinched very slightly.

'Quite. Another blunder on that scale and we might as well close down and put our money in the savings bank.'

It was a favourite Fisher cut when stock wools had to be sold at a loss.

'Now look!' I cried. 'Enough of this, Simon. I won't have it. Buying rands has been your job since last May. *You* assured me you'd cover them, and *you* forgot. Martin and I don't *make* mistakes— not seven thousand pound ones anyway.'

The lozenges had gathered colour, the eyes had widened slightly, but beyond that the inbred detachment held.

After a while he said : 'I think I ought to remind you I am your employer, Robert.'

'I know. And because of that you're going to make my department suffer for your negligence. All right, my back's broad, but let's get it absolutely straight where the blame really belongs.'

'I'm not prepared to bandy words with you. I think we'll let the meeting decide where the responsibility lies.'

'The meeting can stuff itself ! We all know what the meeting'll say. But right here and now *I'm* telling you straight that *I* lay the blame at your door, and what's more I think it's a bloody bad show.'

Uneasiness started then. Martin was standing close by; I'd not seen him come in. And I'd not seen him come in because those last

227

words had given me a sudden dangerous thrill. For a second the years had dropped away and the anger had been genuine. For a second I really had lost my cast-iron control, forgotten that I was doing this to keep her.

'*Gentlemen!*' Martin's elegant drawl seemed almost a parody of itself. He smiled wryly at us, but when his eyes met mine I glimpsed baffled alarm. He squeezed my arm, hard. 'Don't you think there'll be enough blood, sweat and tears at the meeting itself without private fracas?'

I felt almost weak with relief. Thank God for Martin! I'd shaken myself badly. I'd been certain I could play that scene without getting involved, I'd thought the hatred was all behind me.

Thank God for Martin! Everything was under control again. In an hour or so there'd be the meeting. I'd hardly open my mouth. I'd hang my head. I'd look dejected. I'd take my punishment like an officer and a gentleman.

'Very well,' I said in a low voice. 'We'll leave it to the meeting.'

I turned away, to give a deliberate impression of defeat, but something about Simon's face held me. His pallor gave me a shock; he had the drained bloodless look of an elderly clerk I'd once visited who'd had a major heart operation.

It was rage. He was wax-white with rage. If I could have seen his hands I knew they'd be trembling. It might have been me standing there ten years ago. It was uncanny, we might have been the young men we once were, eyeing each other in General, but transposed—he the outsider, I the Fisher, he taking it, me giving it, he the nobody, me the boss. It was full vicious circle, and he didn't just dislike me any more, he hated me, hated me the way I'd once hated him.

Yet still it held, that barely human restraint. The mystique had a debit side too, and it had to balance very precisely. If you accepted that it bestowed upon you infallibility and the right to rule, you were then bound to accept that you were immune to the same emotions that afflicted ordinary men.

But the mystique concealed peculiarly damaging weapons. Speaking past me to Martin, he said quietly : 'Yes. And perhaps at the meeting we should discuss Saxby's future with this firm.'

'Simon,' I said, in a low voice. 'You can call me Robert, or you can call me Mr. Saxby, but don't ever, under any circumstances, refer to me again, in my presence, as Saxby.'

For an instant there was genuine fear in his pale eyes, fear not even the mystique could control. Martin's hand tightened on my arm like a tourniquet, almost making me gasp.

'For heaven's *sake*, Bob, what's got into you?' Martin gave a burst of frenziedly light laughter. 'Now, *please* lay off, both of you, and leave it to the meeting.'

Simon walked away to his desk, saying over his shoulder as he did so : 'I can only imagine the meeting will take the gravest possible attitude to this last affair, when it follows so many other things Saxby's done to make them dissatisfied.'

'How dare you !' I cried. 'How dare you ! I'll tell you something, Fisher, wool firms are dying like flies in this bloody town and if it hadn't been for me yours would have been the biggest, smelliest corpse of the lot !'

Martin suddenly dragged me round to face him.

'No more, Bob.'

'*Well, tell him!* For Christ's sake spell it out for him—a trading loss is one thing, but money chucked down the drain through sheer bloody brass-faced incompetence is another.'

His face seemed to age with disappointment, and that calmed me like nothing else could. I suddenly felt so ashamed I could hardly meet his eyes. I shrugged, smiled wryly at him, patted the hand that gripped my arm. But he wasn't looking at me, he was staring past me towards the door.

I swung round. It was the Governor. I'd never seen him look so angry. Motionless, framed by the doorway in his black jacket and white porcelain collar, he looked so austere, so incredibly stern, he could have been a portrait of one of his own ancestors, one of those iron men who glared down from the walls of his office.

'*What is this?*' His deep voice crashed into the silence with all the force of his ebony stick clubbing a sample-room table. 'I want a full explanation of this outburst, Robert.'

'Oh, Governor,' Martin said easily. 'I'm afraid Bob's got personal troubles, he's simply not himself today. I really believe he should go home and sort himself out. You know how unlike him it is to fly off the handle like this. Please take my word that he's under a great strain and let me handle things at the meeting.'

The old man glared at me in silent motionless rage. I believe he was having one of the hardest struggles with himself he'd ever had in his life. Finally, fully thirty seconds later, he growled : 'Very well,

I shall accept your assurance, Martin, that there is good reason for this appalling demonstration. You may go, Robert. I shall want to see you in my room tomorrow after lunch.'

'For God's *sake*!'

He closed his office door, leaned against it.

'Don't go on, Martin. Nothing you could say could make me feel more rotten about it.'

'But you *knew* he'd make us take the rap. We *prepared* ourselves for it. Oh, *Bob*—what on earth possessed you. They're two of the most valuable people you know. What about your politics, for Christ's sake?'

He stared at me. In all the years I'd known him I'd never seen anything remotely resembling that look of utter consternation. I felt guilt crushing me like ill-health.

'I'm sorry, old son,' I muttered.

'But *why*, Bob?'

'Migraine. The worst one I've ever had. I woke up with it.'

'You've had them before and never lost your temper.'

'Not as bad as this. And not followed by that bastard rubbing my nose in his own dirty mess.'

'You'd better see the quack if they're so bad.'

He watched me. He wasn't entirely convinced, but it was the only story I could think of. I shrugged, tried to fend off the guilt. It was done now. It was like politics itself, you did everything you could to avert a crisis, but when something did go wrong there was no point in agonising over it—you accepted it and tried to find the best solution.

'Look, Martin, I flew off the handle but he *was* wrong and he *was* shifting the blame. All right, never mind that, but let's not forget that they both know they need me now. That's why the old sod stood there chewing his tongue for so long. They need me for the firm and they need me to get that arrogant pig into politics.'

He began to think. We were both realists. He'd been profoundly disappointed, but after all he knew me, no one better, he'd known right from the start about my temper and my hate.

'The old man knows,' he said. 'But the old man's got one foot in the grave. I'm just afraid Simon's still green enough and stupid enough to kid himself any efficient administrator could do what you've done. As for the politics, all right, you've got his nose through

230

the door at Westbury. But they *have* taken to him, Bob. There's always the danger he might decide he can get along under his own steam, even though you know the short cuts.'

'Oh, come, if I get the nomination they can't do without me.'

'If.'

'Christ, it's nailed on.'

'As long as the Governor doesn't go back on what he told Vereburn about you. I'm sorry, but we've got to consider that now.'

'Vereburn's only one voice against all the rest.'

'But a very old, very respected, very powerful voice. And he's the one they'll ask for a run-down on your commercial career. Let's hope to God the Governor doesn't put the boot in. He wants to see you tomorrow—you've got to give the performance of your life. Grovel and grovel hard. Someone's ill, at home, you've been terribly worried. Tell him in twenty-five different ways it was you to blame and not Simon. That might swing it.'

'And you'll lay it on at the meeting?'

'When I've finished about your loyalty to this firm,' he said, 'they'll be dabbing their eyes.'

'What shall I do about Simon, Martin?'

He sighed. 'I don't know. You gave him a rough ride. A handsome and abject apology for a start, that's an absolute essential. Possibly backed up by concrete evidence that you're getting things moving for him in Westbury.'

'Right.'

He watched me, the faint eternal smile beginning to show again.

'Very well—don't worry too much, I'm simply taking the gloomiest view so that we leave nothing to chance. In a couple of weeks it'll probably all be forgotten. It's just that blasted pride of theirs. Can there be any other firm in town that wouldn't have chained you down with a directorship by now? They simply will not accept what you've done for the firm . . .'

The door opened. We both wheeled round, like office-boys caught doing crosswords. But it was only Esther, with letters for Martin's tray.

'I'll go then,' I said. 'It's nearly time for the meeting.'

'Yes, clear off and cool off. I'll ring you at four.'

It was only Esther. It wasn't until I was almost home that I remembered that none of it would have happened if it hadn't been for her.

And a few minutes ago I'd looked through her, she'd stood there three feet away from me and I couldn't even remember the expression on her face.

I drew up in front of the house. He'd swing it. He was one of their own kind—they'd listen to him. He'd be able to hint at domestic upheaval, to recount my past administrative successes, to remind them that I'd been born into a class notoriously lacking in self-control. They'd listen to him.

But would they? A bead of sweat began to trickle down my spine; my face burned. He was right, Christ, I was just one of the men to them, a hired brain, they might think they could replace me. And maybe they could. Those kids in General—they were Saxby trained. They'd been hand-picked for their promise, because they wanted money and power and shiny motors. What if they blew me out and brought one of them upstairs, perhaps they *could* pull through without me.

My stomach heaved. I tasted bile. I could barely stop myself from vomiting. I clawed my way out of the driving seat, put my head between my knees, sucked in air. Mother of God, it was only a *row*, a slanging match. It happened every day in the rough business world, it was the mark of an independent mind.

Only this wasn't Shell or Unilever or I.C.I., where clever independent minds were deliberately sought, this was an old, old trade, run by men who thought themselves a business aristocracy. And the Fishers thought they came right at the top even of that group, heirs to special skills.

I sat back, wiped my forehead with a handkerchief. It wasn't the money. Or the job. I could double my salary in a year outside the trade. It was the politics. And I was tied to Beckford. The sort of knowledge I had now of this region couldn't be used anywhere else in Britain, and before I could use it here I'd got to have the Fishers. It had taken a decade to spin that delicate political web; it could be destroyed by a single blow from the Governor's ebony stick.

Or a deliberate smear from Simon. 'Oh yes, quite a clever type of chap, Saxby—we find him a useful administrator. But a little . . . what shall I say . . . unsound perhaps. Tends to go to pieces under pressure.'

I could hear him saying it to that snivelling eunuch, Sir Alfred, a walking radio-station. I levered myself out of the car like an old man. I'd *got* to disarm Simon.

I didn't hear her at first. Every part of my conscious mind, every brain-cell, seemed to be focussed on the danger to my future. My body too; every muscle and fibre, every instinct, every nerve was tensed for what my imagination had almost turned into a struggle for survival.

'Daddy . . . Daddy . . . *Daddy!* It's me. Up *here.* Smile—you're on *Candid Camera.*'

I raised my eyes slowly.

'Whatever are you doing home at lunchtime? Catch !'

She came flying down from the wall; there wasn't a fraction of my attention left to cope with her.

I did act, but too late. That was the trouble. If I'd not acted at all she'd have been all right. She'd have fallen heavily on her feet and she might have sprained an ankle, but nothing more. As it was, I was separated by a split second from the right action at the right time. I put out an arm, but it was too low at the point of contact; it caught her across the legs and swung her over in flight so that she went on head first.

When she hit the pavement she made no sound, and no further movement.

21

'Bob, I eat my words. In fact I'm beginning to think you did yourself more good losing your temper than keeping it. You're in the clear. You're under a bit of a cloud, of course, but then, you often are. To paraphrase Harold—a week in business is a long time.'

You. What possible difference can it make to you if she lives or dies?

'Naturally, they'll rub it in. The Governor'll play hell because you upset Simon and Simon'll play hell because you upset the old man. But they were significantly restrained at the meeting. Almost as if they'd had a private row. It seems incredible, but I really believe you've dented the mystique. It didn't stop them from laying the entire balls-up at our door, and Simon said that the mistake was bad enough without you trying to shift the blame like that, but they took my defence of you very quietly.

233

'I didn't lay the blame anywhere, I simply stressed how badly you took it when things went wrong. If you had a fault, I said, it was that it had come to mean so much to you to make the company the best in town, you'd got to be too perfectionist, too intolerant of the slightest mistake, whoever made it.'

I won't do anything bloody stupid like praying. I'll offer you a straight deal. Let her live and I'll pack politics in. Tomorrow. The works. Everything I've worked and struggled for. No candles or praying or money, but a genuine sacrifice—my politics for her.

'But then, Bob, an astounding ally, *Garbage*! He didn't like the Fishers carving you up—that had always been his job. He sat there like a suspicious bull while they shook their heads over you, and then something snapped. What did they expect, he cried, of a man with a mind of his own? He didn't know whose bloody mistake it was, and he didn't care, but if it was yours it was the first bad one you'd ever made. And measured by what you'd saved the firm, it was tea-money. Did they want a yes-man as accountant? Did they want to be as dicey as every other firm in the trade, because without you and your methods that's what they'd be. He'd never known a man of your calibre *not* be bloody-minded, he was only surprised you'd always had so much self-control.

'God, I *wish* you could have seen their faces. Black as your hat. Not another peep out of them about rands. They were glad to turn to other things, I can tell you. You know, I believe that was the first real inkling they'd ever had that the firm needed more for its survival than the grace of the Fishers.'

Look, I'll give it to Simon. I couldn't possibly do anything that'd come harder. I throw everything I've got into getting Simon accepted for South. I make speeches for him. I sell him to the machine. I even run his campaign for him. In return for her.

'I don't know how to thank you.'

I seemed to see his face through a muslin curtain; the raised eyebrows, the pained smile. I knew. It was the toughest job he'd ever had to face, no one loathed roughness and hostility as much as he did. It was a moment for relief, for gratitude, amazement, glee.

'What's wrong, Bob?' he said quietly.

I forced myself to smile, took his arm.

'I haven't got over my own stupidity. I don't deserve you. It must have been a blow to you yesterday. I'm very very grateful.'

234

It worked. He nodded sympathetically. It was obvious he thought I'd over-reacted, but then people of my emotional origins did over-react.

'Don't take it so hard, old son. Once again you've come up smelling of roses. The luck of the Saxbys, eh?'

She'd said go to the office. No point in sitting and waiting, go to work and carry on as if nothing had happened, she might be perfectly all right. They simply can't tell with coma, they told us so. She might come out of it any minute and start to be all right. Don't *blame* yourself, you couldn't help it, heavens, didn't I once let her fall out of the push-chair? Oh, Bob, please don't blame yourself, dear. I don't. She'll be all right. She's from tough stock.

It was exactly what you'd have expected from an Endersby girl. She'd be at home now, in her trews and sweater, sorting the washing out and cutting vegetables and hoovering the carpet. I couldn't love her and I never had, but I admired her more than any woman I'd ever known.

She suffered just as badly in her own way. The cheerfulness was an act, and somehow you knew she was going through it far more than if she'd just sat in silence like me. Now and then you saw that totally alien unfocussed gaze; it was like the pleasant voice you sometimes heard at the other end of a phone, that told you the person you wanted was unavoidably absent and that this was a recording, but that otherwise it was business exactly as usual.

Like, me she was at the hospital, for all the chatty bustle with coffee and toast, like me she was in the special ward with the plastic doors, where the nurses moved round in rubberised shoes, so that when the doors swung to behind you it was like seeing a film with no soundtrack. She was where I was, gaze fixed on the pale face of our daughter, who lay as still as the day she was born, when I'd leaned over a cot labelled Baby Saxby and known for the first time in my life what love really was.

Oh, God, forgive me. I didn't mean to be clever with you. Please let her live. You wouldn't want someone as fine as Emma to die. Oh God, please don't take my daughter away, please let her live . . . please . . . please . . . please.

A phone began to ring. It startled me, it was like a fire-bell in the quiet of my office.

'Yes.'

There was a prolonged silence; then she spoke.

'It's me, Bob.' Her voice came strongly, almost breezily through the speaker. 'It's me, dear.'

The note of confidence gave me a sensation in the lungs as if the air in them had been released through a valve.

'Yes, Gwen—go on.'

'I'm . . . very sorry, Bob. It's no good. She's . . . gone. She . . . she never came round.'

The strong, appallingly confident tones vibrated in my ear during a silence that must have lasted thirty seconds. And then she sobbed, a sound like an uncontrollable belch, and then she sobbed again.

'Oh, Bob—she's *dead*!'

The rest couldn't have happened if he'd not been standing there, just inside the door. If I could have got away without seeing him, if he'd not spoken even, it couldn't have happened.

But he chose that moment to give me my talking to. I'd scarcely put the receiver down when he began. I could hear phrases about decision of the meeting and deploring my behaviour and lenient attitude and proper apology, and they went on and on, like a stream of obscenities—it was as if we were facing each other across her death-bed, and though he could see her lying there he wouldn't let it interfere with what he had to say to me.

There was hardly anything, against that first gigantic surge of pain, that could be called a mental process, but the fragment of reason I had left, in some remote part of the brain, began to shriek a warning.

But it only reached me as a whisper, like a voice shouting a message down a long-distance connection.

It cried at me to go, to ignore him, to say nothing, to make straight for the sanctuary of my house, and it was indicative of the state of shock I was in that I didn't think to turn from him, to go through Esther's ante-room and Martin's office to the corridor instead of trying to get through my own door. Perhaps I should have done if those relentlessly intoned phrases about overlooking the lapse and tasteless scenes hadn't begun to blot out everything, even the faint desperate voice of reason, except me, him and Emma's white dead face, everything except the single fact that but for him I shouldn't have dropped her and she'd be alive now.

That first jab exactly paralleled my confusion. It was hardly a blow at all, it was more a push, a rough, distracted attempt to get him away from the door so that I could get out.

But it was enough. Enough to silence that distant warning cry, enough to give the pain a sudden outlet. Yes, that's what it did, that half-meant jab, it was like drawing off electrical current from the mains, some of the pain seemed to leave me at the sound of his grunt, and it seemed that if I went on and on it would all in the end pass from me to him.

I can't remember what I did to him. I can hear his hoarse cries faintly, and those gurgling noises, and I can see the blood spattered round his nose and mouth, and my right thumb will be permanently weak as a result of the force I punched his face and chest with, but how often I hit him or how long it lasted I can't remember, and I've never been told. Perhaps it didn't last long. I hope so. I only know that if I'd been left I'd have killed him.

But a blow from behind on the back of my neck suddenly ended it. It had the bliss of morphine. I wished Martin hadn't been so skilful afterwards. I wished the punch could have been fatal, like hitting her head at the wrong spot had been fatal for Emma.

I wished it could all have finished there and not had to start again.

But it started again quite quickly. The nothingness lifted; I could hear their low shocked voices as they gathered round him, the sudden scuffling of feet as they caught him from falling. And beyond the men I could see the frightened faces of the girls from the pool, disembodied heads crowded in the door's rectangle, arranged with an almost artistic felicity. The sense of danger drew them closer together, like darkness in a side street, and they began to utter tiny involuntary screams as Simon was half-carried from the room.

A moment later, scarcely daring to look at me, they dispersed. Then silence, even with the corridor door wide open. No voices, no footsteps, no bells, no subdued laughter, no snatch of whistled song, not even the whine of a normally busy lift. It was as if most of them had fled the building, as if the handful who dared remain were terrified of making a sound that would arouse the maniac in the managers' suite.

Suddenly he appeared at the door. He paused there, staring down at me, then he almost ran across the room and fell to one knee at my side. He took me by the lapels of my jacket, pulled my face to within inches of his.

'You scum! You worthless bloody *scum*! I should have *known* you weren't worth the effort, Christ I had plenty of warning. Well, this is for not doing that to him right at the start, before I'd given you the best years of my life.'

He raised his open hand deliberately; fear seeped across my stomach like iced water. Not because he was going to hit me, but because I didn't know who it was, because in that terrifying instant I couldn't equate Martin with the dilated nostrils and the staring eyes and the wet contorted mouth of the man above me, whose entire frame shook with uncontrollable rage.

But before he could bring his hand down it was clasped in mid-air. By Esther.

'*Stop!* Oh please *stop*, Martin. You must see something's terribly wrong. I rang Gwen. It's Emma. She's just died. For God's sake, don't do anything else to him. Emma's dead!'

22

It was basically a matter of administration. The dodge, of course, was to keep your eyes and ears fully occupied so the rest of your brain was blocked off. The telly was splendid for this, and some of the really old films even gave me an illusion of happiness. As a youngster I'd gone to the threepenny rush every Saturday afternoon, and during the war years Mum and I had gone every Monday evening to the first house of a cinema everyone in our rough neighbourhood called the Colley. When the film was Errol Flynn being *Gentleman Jim*, for instance, I got this sense of return, because I'd seen and admired him as *Gentleman Jim* a number of times, both at the Colley and at the Oriental.

It was nice catching up on all the old films I'd missed through my politics. I'd not seen a film for donkey's years.

And there were so many—by switching from one channel to another you could often see fully half a dozen over the weekend alone.

Remember *A Prize of Arms*? That was a perfect brain-blocker because of the action. Remember neurotic Richard Baseheart in *14 Hours*, hanging on to that ledge, and decent solid Paul Douglas trying to talk him off it? And *Expresso Bongo*? My word, Laurence Harvey was good in that. I hadn't seen him in a film since *I Am A Camera*. And dear old Spencer Tracy in *Captains Courageous*—how Mum and I wept when his curly head went down for the last time, to save that little boy.

I really did remarkably well when you consider I had the whole of the winter to face with no outside distraction. I rapidly developed a way of life as closely geared to idleness as my previous life had been geared to action.

As usual that was the secret of my success—speed and efficiency. I made a start the same day, the moment they were all in the sitting-room, snivelling into cups of tea. I simply left them to it, went up to my study and listened to *Woman's Hour* and *Mrs. Dale's Diary* and a talk about Ethiopia.

This had a two-fold effect. It offended most of them so badly they never bothered me again, and when nothing she could say or do would make me leave my study, it drove Gwen into that long bitter silence. Which was ideal—the blocks were even intact from her.

Sleep was the danger-point. The average person needs seven hours, thirty-six minutes' sleep a night, and spends about a quarter of that time dreaming. I heard that on *Woman's Hour*. I also heard on *Woman's Hour* that alcohol or sleeping tablets can interfere with the dream-factor of sleep, a piece of information that gave me a little smile; I'd arrived at that conclusion quite empirically within two days of the funeral.

Scotch and Mandrax. I know booze seems absurdly hackneyed, but it really does work if you go at it steadily, always keeping the edge off things but never getting drunk.

Dora Bryan and Rita Tushingham were marvellous in *A Taste of Honey*. I did enjoy that. Those mean streets and those powerful working-class bonds filled me with nostalgia for my own childhood, when the uncles would all sit round our fire drinking glasses of beer, and Auntie Kitty would sing a song with a lyric that went—'Gone, alas, like our youth too soon.' Such sad wistful words among all that affection and smoke and love.

Hitchcock's *Saboteur* was interesting in that it was clearly a kind of dry run for *North by North West*, one of the few modern films

I actually saw new. With Gwen it was, on the London honeymoon. They did us proud on Hitchcock in fact, in the winter of 'sixty-seven. We got *Psycho* twice, *Saboteur*, and then *The Lady Vanishes*. During the day, when I was carrying my transistor around with me, I heard Sir Michael Redgrave being interviewed about *The Lady Vanishes*, and he said that he'd rather thrown his performance in it away, as at the time it was made he'd not been able to take films seriously; but his performance in it looked extremely clever to me.

I carried the transistor everywhere, and I had one of those matchbox ones at the bedside for when I woke up, to feed me *Ten to Eight* and Jack de Manio and the morning serial. Though during the day, even with the elaborate VHF set I bought specially, it wasn't always easy to find a programme with someone discussing the training of guide dogs, or getting rings off polished surfaces, or husbands with wives who go out to work. Sometimes it was nothing but music whichever button you pressed.

Then one December afternoon I struck gold. I discovered the travelling library. At that time, Westbury was still having its own library built; in the meantime Beckford Main sent a large van round the district twice a week. By taking out a membership for Gwen and me I could get eight books at a time. Not that I hadn't got hundreds of books of my own, but they were all non-fiction. The travelling library had things like the Whiteoak books by Mazo de la Roche. They had the entire works of Agatha Christie, Somerset Maugham, Nevil Shute, John Galsworthy and John P. Marquand. They even had a few Hall Caines. That solved the daytime problem —whenever there were no talks or films I could sit in the pale winter light and read novels.

The season was on my side. Summer would have been very difficult, what with ice-cream bells and motor-mowers, but now I hardly heard a sound from one day to the next.

I kept the downstairs rooms always at seventy degrees and the bedrooms at sixty, and I made the timer turn the heating off at eleven-forty-five, precisely fifteen minutes before I sank into drugged oblivion, and switch it back on at six-fifteen, exactly one hour before the alarm woke me for Jack de Manio. Before reaching this simple arrangement, however, I tried many elaborate programmes with the timer. It was amazing the number of operations you could make it perform over a twenty-four-hour cycle, it kept me engrossed for a week. I'd never even *known* about the timer—Gwen had always seen to all that.

So it all worked extremely well. A temperature as unvarying as amniotic fluid, books and old films, the radio, simple meals of eggs and soup or bread and cheese. I scarcely looked out of a window even, there was no need to, except when the van was round, to check if it was snowing and I'd need to put rubbers over my house shoes.

Gwen's day was quite different. It was rather a shadowy affair because I never looked fully at her, not once, not even in the early days when she'd sometimes come into the room and try to talk to me, but I'd occasionally catch a glimpse of her crossing the hall with one of Miss Charlotte's Abbotsfords, so I supposed she was pursuing her normal activities, or what activities she had left now that our politics were finished. Also the beds were made and the house kept clean and the washing done in the usual methodical way, so it looked as if she too was getting along all right. I hoped she was, anyway. It was a different approach to the problem from mine, but I imagined it was what suited her. Or maybe she hadn't worked it out as carefully as me, even though she was such a planner, but just blindly followed the routines of a decade like a farmhorse. I wished I *could* have talked to her and helped her, I felt pretty bad about that, but it was out of the question. Not for a long time. Not till my own scheme had produced results.

I felt sorry about all the people I hurt—Percy in particular. He shouldn't have got through the defence works at all. In the rare event of the door-bell chiming when Gwen was actually in, she'd deal with it. I didn't know how she got rid of them and I didn't care, but no one ever got into the sitting-room. If she was out and it rang I simply ignored it.

For once she must have forgotten to drop the latch, and one night I glanced up from *Sunset Boulevard* to see him hesitantly looking in at me from the hall.

'I rang the bell, Bob, but happen you didn't hear it, what with the telly. I hope you didn't mind me venturing in.'

Mother of God, it threw a scare in me, seeing him stand there in his old belted overcoat, twisting his tweed cap in his hands. For a second it was sheer panic, it couldn't have been worse—all that careful planning and then for someone like him to get past. Christ, I *knew* him, we were from the same class. For all the dryness, the knowing cynicism, he was from the people who wallowed in death, who liked to get plenty of mileage from it, who offered little poems in *Memoriam* columns to a God who took the evening paper—'Here's a tribute true and tender, Just to say we still remember.' And here he was, patiently waiting for me to turn the telly off so we could grieve together.

'Are you watching the film then, Bob lad?' he said, in a gentle, faintly puzzled tone.

'Yes . . . yes.' My voice cracked in alarm; I could tell from the almost ludicrous solemnity of his expression that he'd instantly interpreted it as emotion barely under control. 'It's Bill Holden. I never miss Holden films if I can possibly help it.'

'I don't blame you. The wife's particularly fond of him. Him and John Wayne. Ever see Bill Holden in *Picnic*? With Kim Novak.'

'He's a hobo. Comes to a small town, meets Kim Novak, they fall in love. They do that dance to *Moonglow*. And then he clears off again.'

'That's it! The wife thought he was champion in that. Particularly the dance. Did you see him in *Executive Suite* with . . .'

Suddenly his voice trailed off into silence; he'd remembered his mission.

I had to keep him talking. If I could divert him till Gwen got back I'd be able to get away to bed with my pills and radio and leave her to get rid of him.

'Yes, yes, I remember *Executive Suite* very clearly. Fredric March, Louis Calhern . . .'

'That's it! And they're all playing bloody hell round that table. He could play bloody hell a treat, Bill Holden.'

'Remember *Bridge on the River Kwai*, Percy?'

'*Bridge on the River Kwai*,' he murmured fondly, gazing past me with a reminiscent smile. '*What* a film that was, Bob lad. By God, it took me back. Poor old Alec Guiness building the bleeder up and them other buggers coming through the jungle to blow it to kingdom come. Saw it three times, the wife and I.'

'If you'd like to sit and watch this you're quite welcome. I've not seen it; I've been looking forward to it all afternoon.'

'Very old, this one. Gloria Swanson, isn't it? Starts off where there's just his body floating in a swimming pool?'

'That's the one! He's writing for the movies and he can't make the grade and he takes up with Gloria Swanson. She's a rich lonely old film-star. But just as you came in he's begun to fall in love with a young girl who works at the studios.'

'Ah, it all comes back now. Very sad finish. Heart-rendering.'

I turned up the volume slightly, waved him to a nearby armchair. He sat down in his top coat, apparently engrossed, and I quickly became immersed in Bill Holden being bought suits by Gloria Swanson, and the salesman making snide remarks about the lady paying. That was where I made my mistake. I should have divided my attention equally between the film and him. I shouldn't have forgotten about his sense of what was fitting.

Suddenly he said : 'He *deserved* it, Bob. Fisher. I only wish I could have seen you do it. By God, I only wish it had been me.'

'Look, Percy,' I said quickly, pointing at the screen. 'She suspects something. It looks very ominous.'

'I'm sorry about the bairn,' he said, in a low husky voice. 'I can't tell you how sorry I am about the bairn.'

I stood up, focussing the whole of my attention on the actors and the dialogue and the camera angle. I pictured the men crowded behind the camera, and imagined the tension in the studio. I wondered how long this fragment of film must have been rehearsed, how many takes there were before the words and movements of the actors had achieved such an exquisite ordinariness.

But then I felt an arm round my shoulders, smelt the beer and tobacco on his breath.

'There, son,' he said. 'Don't take on. It could happen to anyone. Don't take on.'

'Percy !' I bounded to the television and turned the sound up so loud that the noise struck out at the walls of the room and washed back against our eardrums like shock-waves. 'Are we watching this bloody film or aren't we? Will you for Christ's sake SHUT UP !'

It would all have gone for nothing if she'd not come in just then. Despite the years of self-discipline, despite a physical effort that forced sweat through every pore in my body. I could feel it slipping from my grasp, I could almost sense the turmoil and that frightful searing pain.

But just in time she was there, hands to ears at the crashing waves of sound, and I caught a single remote glimpse of the poor bastard's terror-stricken face before she put an arm round him and led him gently away. A few dreadful minutes later I managed to stop my hands shaking for long enough to pour a large Scotch and get back into the film at the point where mad Gloria Swanson returns to her old studios, chauffeured by loyal Erich von Stroheim and accompanied by poor Bill Holden looking sick at heart.

But I felt very bad about hurting him like that, particularly when he'd given up the pub on a Sunday night to come and be kind to me. Perhaps it was some consolation Gwen telling him he wasn't the only one I'd been a swine to, I'd been a swine to everyone, even my own flesh and blood.

Dear, good Percy. It didn't make a button of difference to him, and I came to owe him such a lot in the end. A fortnight later, as I sat reading *Gone With the Wind*, Gwen opened the door and made one of her rare utterances.

'Percy Lambert's in the hall,' she said flatly. 'He wants to know if he can watch the film with you as his television has broken down.'

Without looking up, I thought for a moment, then nodded, feeling almost pleased. Without doubt, he could only be here this time to actually watch the film. He came in with his old chirpy swagger, smiling, his head on one side.

'It's *Criss Cross*, Bob. Burt Lancaster and Yvonne de Carlo. Remember seeing it back in 'forty-nine.'

'Is that the one where he comes back to his home town and she's taken up with Dan Duryea?'

'That's the feller! And they all plan a pay-roll job together, but she's double-crossing him. Good-looking girl, Yvonne de Carlo.'

'Take your coat off and sit down. What will you have to drink? Whisky . . . beer? There's Diana Dors and Rod Steiger in the *Midnight Movie*, by the way—the name escapes me. Perhaps you'd like to stay for that too. We could get you a taxi to go home in. I'll pay.'

'Oh, right you are then. He was good in *On The Waterfront*—Steiger.'

He came to be a constant visitor. One night he told me that once he and his wife had gone to the pictures two or three times a week. The cinemas had begun to close down; now his wife played bingo. Percy couldn't abide bingo. At the same time contemporary films were beginning to disappoint—'There's no proper tale to them, you just seem to be getting the hang of them when they finish. And them thrillers, half of it's happening while they put the film people's names on, and I can't follow them. I can either watch the picture or read the bloody names, but I can't do both. They never have it like the leaves of a book turning over these days, or just white satin behind the words. And the stars aren't what they were. Gary Cooper and Humphrey Bogart and Clark Gable and them, they're all dying of cancer or getting heart attacks from bothering with young women. These new lads are nothing. They never say a bloody word. Steve McQueen particular, never opens his bloody mouth. He doesn't say a dozen words a picture. And then he mutters it. *That's* not acting, Bob, is it, lad?

'And then there's these pictures making game of everything, war and crime and that. It's not right, Bob, I fought in that war and it was no laughing matter.'

He sought a vanished world, the simple world of his early manhood, a world in which people had fought together and rebuilt together, and all been together in that dark cosy cavern, full of beautiful men and women living lives of incredible colour and happiness to the sound of violins. He sought a personal golden age.

Like me.

We divined it in each other; it brought us to an almost desperate closeness as we sat there, three or four nights a week, week in, week out, as winter merged slowly into spring. It went unanalysed and unspoken, as we lay watching the flickering screen in our easy chairs, among the antiques and the oil-paintings, only acknowledged in an occasional smile or a patted arm or a solicitously poured drink.

'Remember John Garfield in *Body and Soul*?'

'John Wayne in *The Searchers*?'

'Van Johnson in *The Last Time I Saw Paris*?'

'Alan Ladd in *Shane*?'

'James Stewart in *Rear Window*?'

'Hitchcock! Don't set me off on Hitchcock. Seen the bloody lot. *Strangers on a Train*, Bob. By, *what* a moving-picture that was They all go on about *Psycho*, but that's what I mean about everything altering. Nice girl like Janet Leigh, in the old days you'd know perfectly well she'd get into serious bother, get out of it, and get married. But in *Psycho* it's *her* that's murdered. And then the private eye. The *private eye*, Bob, dead as cold mutton. I ask you, where's the sense of turning everything upside down like that?'

One night in March he came in with a bundle of old seventy-eight-speed records tucked under his arm, and while we waited for the film we played them on the radiogram that resembled a Queen Anne cabinet. They were things like poor Judy Garland singing *Meet Me in St. Louis* and *The Trolley Song*, and Bing singing *The Bells of St. Mary's*, and Fred Astaire singing *You Were Never Lovelier*, and the Glen Miller orchestra playing *Sunrise Serenade*.

And from then on, whenever we were just drinking and talking about films, we'd sit there with the records sizzling, and it might have been yesterday when I'd walked through the narrow streets of the district of my childhood, hearing those tunes coming out of people's open doorways on bright mornings in June.

In fact, in the end, it was as if the long years had never been since that simple happy time when they'd made decent films and written tunes you could tap your foot to.

23

'Hello.'

'. . . Hello.'

I slid on to the bench opposite her in the breakfast annexe. She was eating toast and marmalade; she stopped and watched my hands as I put a slice of bread in the toaster.

'Do you want an egg? The water's boiled.'

'No. Just toast.'

It was the first time I'd looked directly at her since the twenty-fifth of November, nineteen-sixty-seven. I was ready for the changes but I still got a mild shock. They were almost indefinable—her hair hadn't altered, or her colour, and there were no new lines in her face; it was something about the way she sat, there was a curious settled quality about her body. She was like an animated young actress who'd been called on to create a demanding portrayal of middle age, and who was doing it very cleverly by subtle hints of heaviness and deliberation.

But Endersbys were never obvious. They led lives based on superb health and sensible relationships in which things went right as a matter of course, but when things did go wrong you might know they'd face it with the usual lack of fuss. Those almost imperceptible signs of maturity told far more about what had happened to her than any physical changes could.

'Did you . . . want something?'

'To talk.'

She poured coffee into thick Greenwheat cups, put one before me. Her eyes rested on mine with a look of complete detachment.

In all the time I'd known her I'd never seen her uninvolved, never seen her standing back from her current activity—her voting-lists or her club work, her love-making, her antiques, her housework even. I'd never seen her simply watching life.

'First,' I said slowly, 'I want to say sorry. About the funeral, and letting you do the dirty work, and because of the way I've been all winter. I want to say how sorry I am about that sordid mess at Fisher's and about the politics being finished.' I paused and drank some of the coffee. 'And . . . and I want to say how terribly sorry I am about Emma.'

Tears welled slowly in eyes which continued to look detached, and began trickling steadily down her cheeks. The skin round her eyes instantly became swollen and red, evidence that she'd wept often and at length. She'd taken her grief on the chin the Endersby way; no obliteration techniques for her.

I'd never wept. Of course, I'd had the pills and the alcohol, the solitude, the old films, the luck even to have found a friend on the same flight from reality. I'd extinguished my grief with the same ruthless efficiency I'd turned Singleton Fisher into the *Q.E.2* of the wool trade.

But at what cost. I'd seen myself in the bathroom mirror this morning; I'd stared out almost in terror at the hot spring sunshine. The cure had been as drastic as the illness. Not that it mattered.

After a few moments she calmly took a handkerchief from her pinafore pocket and dried her eyes.

'I never blamed you for it. And I never will. I thought you behaved abominably after the funeral, but I never blamed you for her.'

I nodded slowly. 'What did you tell them? The parents?'

'That you'd had a breakdown. They were so heart-broken about Emma they accepted it at the time. Pop drove them home. They've written every week, and every week I've told them you'll go over and see them when you're fully recovered. They can't understand what's happened, but . . . they trust me.'

'Poor old Mum. We were so close once. During the war we used to go to the pictures every Monday night.'

She watched me steadily. 'Pop accepted it at the funeral, but not after he found out about Simon Fisher. It never got into the papers or anything like that, but of course everyone knows. When Pop got to know he wanted to have it out with you. I refused to let him see you. He . . . he doesn't ever want to see you again.'

I drank the rest of my coffee and looked out through the window at the laburnums, now in full exuberant bloom. Well, whatever the price, I *was* cured. I could actually talk about her now, I no longer needed to block my mind off against memories of her dancing near the pool. Not that any memories actually came.

'Why did you do all that?' I said. 'Keep them at arm's length. Why didn't you let me face the music? I caused it all.'

She shrugged and also looked out over the garden. If anything had been capable of surprising me any more it would have been her indifference to it. I'd never seen her look at that stretch of lawn on a fine day, and those ornamental trees, without a beam of pleasure, without, as often as not, being unable to contain herself from rushing out to prune a rose-bush or fill the hall-table bowl with sweet peas.

'I was very disappointed and hurt about the funeral,' she said. 'I thought it was utterly despicable, refusing all responsibility like that. I thought you just weren't facing up to it. I thought you'd simply given in.'

She hesitated. 'I . . . I was determined to leave you to it as soon as things were settled.

'But there were a lot of details to attend to, and I *had* to stay on for a few weeks. I began to watch you. I watched you staring at the telly and walking round with that expensive radio. I watched you reading those rubbishy books, and getting whisky delivered by the carton, and fiddling about with the time-clock for the heating.

'I thought about it a lot. I thought about the way you pushed everything from you, every single thing that might remind you of her. I watched you fill every moment of every day with the telly and the radio and the books. Then one night I came back and found you screaming at Percy Lambert and I knew he must have said something about her.'

She turned back to me.

'You're not a cowardly man. You've worked hard to provide for us and you've done it with spirit. You never shirked anything or gave in when we were up against it. But you wouldn't face her death, wouldn't even start to face it.

'Emma . . .' She blinked rapidly and began to swallow. 'It was frightful. I didn't know there could be such pain. But . . . but if you had to go to such fantastic lengths to . . . to push it away, it must have been even worse for you. It must have been indescribable. I decided that whatever happened afterwards I'd see you through that.'

The sun cast a diagonal shaft of light through the annexe window; I could feel its heat through my shirt sleeve. The garden droned with insects. It was almost impossible to connect the still, pensive woman opposite with the one who'd not been able to sit down on a day like this, who'd have been out there now, forking borders and playing Knock-knock with Emma and singing *Strephon's a Member of Parliament* tonelessly beneath her breath.

I wondered how she'd contrived to adjust to a life in which there were no elections to work towards, or pep-talks to deliver, or U.T.s to recruit, a life in which day followed empty day. I pictured her trying to harness her vast energy to something, anything, that would give her a brief illusion of a time when every second mattered, when every hour was stuffed like a case that could only be closed by being sat on. I pictured her watching me through half-open doors, restless, silent, setting uneasily out across uncharted seas of thought.

'Well,' she said evenly. '*Are* you through it?'

'Yes, I'm through it. It's like having an armful of something so a surgeon can cut you open. You don't feel the pain, but your body knows you've had it.'

She scrutinised my face. I'd seen it myself this morning for the first time—I'd shaved by electric razor through the winter. When I'd shaved. Yes, my body knew I'd had it. I couldn't take it on the chin, the discreet Endersby way, it had to be pills and a sea of alcohol for me.

Getting used to it had taken rather a time—the yellowy eyes and the waxy skin, the soiled-looking teeth, the hair that had the texture of dried grass. Not that it bothered me particularly, in fact I'd found the vulgar lack of subtlety and the crudeness of the changes mildly amusing. It was merely that it had taken rather a long time to get used to them.

249

'I wish I'd gone through it properly,' I said. 'Like you. I wish I'd done it the hard way now. Can you understand that? It works, you see, pushing it out. If you do it for long enough your mind accepts that you won't have it. You win. I can think of her now and nothing happens. Nothing at all.'

'Well,' she said, in the same flat voice. 'You had to do it the best way you could.'

She poured more coffee, we sat for a long time in silence, a silence in which the drone of insects and the twittering of birds seemed to reach an almost deafening intensity. Apple blossom drifted across the lawn, now and then a single laburnum raceme would be stirred by a razor-thin breeze. This was what age was like then. An empty house, a life that had been lived, fatigue, a sense of waiting and futility. And against it the fresh vertical light of a June sun, the cheerful mockery of a new spring.

'You'll want a divorce,' I said. 'I'll make it painless and fast. I'll arrange it and I'll see you right for money. It won't begin to make up for the work you've done, but it'll be something.'

'Do *you* want a divorce?'

'It's a matter of total indifference to me.'

'You think it would be better for me?'

'Yes. You could go back to Pop's and do your antiques from there. Without me the machine would welcome you back with open arms. You're only thirty-four and you're a popular, good-looking woman. You could re-marry, make a completely fresh-start.'

'What about you?'

'Christ, what does that matter?'

'What about *us*, then?'

I looked at her irritably, but there was an almost childlike look of curiosity on her face. I had to remind myself that there was nothing simple and obvious about it to her, that she was still valiantly striving to cope with sudden new dimensions, with aspects of life nothing in the Endersby environment or upbringing had prepared her for. I knew of no Endersby who hadn't married sensibly and stayed married.

'Us?' I laughed shortly. 'I'll tell you about us. Our marriage worked because Bob Saxby was a commercial and political success. It was like gold being valuable because everyone thinks it is. Well, I'm still Bob Saxby, but now I'm a commercial and political failure.

And as me being a going concern was the whole basis of our marriage, that too must obviously be finished. Apart from which we've no ties now.'

'Is that so, Bob?' she said earnestly, like a student striving to open her mind to a revolutionary new concept. 'Is that really all that made it work? What about sex?'

'What about it? We were normal and we enjoyed it. And if you remarried I suppose you'd enjoy it just as much with some other normal male.'

'But you. Wouldn't you miss sleeping with me and having me around?'

'For God's sake, Gwen, what does it *matter*? Let's get the divorce fixed up. You ought to have married a U.T. and groomed him for stardom, but you married me by mistake. Let's not waste any more of your life.'

She listened intently, gazing past me with a slight frown; again I regretted being short with her. She was still moving gingerly into a country without maps, into a land that must have seemed as strange as the inside of a political family, with its plotting and attitudes, had once seemed to me.

'It's strange you should say that,' she said. 'About me marrying you instead of a party member. I suppose it *was* rather odd, when you think about it. After all, when we met, you weren't a political, and I couldn't imagine marrying a man who wasn't. Though you soon were, of course. A few months ago I began to wonder if I'd have married you if you hadn't wanted to join the party.'

She hesitated. I could see her stopped in her tracks, perhaps while programming that elaborate washer or making beds, standing for minutes in the winter silence as she struggled to accommodate the astounding idea that youth was really an Etoile, from which led a dozen possible routes, rather than a smooth straight coach-road that swept rapidly and directly to a clean white city, visible from a great distance.

'Why *did* you want to marry me, Bob? We never went in for soppy talk and mooning about over each other, but I always assumed you'd married me because you liked me better than any other girl. But ... now I don't think it was that.'

I shook my head, gave her a faint wry smile.

'No. I married you *because* there wouldn't be any soppy talk or mooning about. And because you were a walking political machine,

251

of course. But mainly because you wouldn't want nights out or any of my time, like other women.'

'But not because I was me?'

'I've always thought of you as a good friend, Gwen. Nothing more. I'm sorry.'

She pursed her lips.

'It only bears out what I'd thought myself. You know, I used to have *such* a simple outlook on people. And I thought I was so sound. I suppose we all tend to think our outlook is the right one. I'd meet people and I'd think that that one's a worker and this one's an idler and that one's an arty type and this one's a misfit. And even the more unusual types like you I thought I was clever enough to put a label on. You were the bright, hard-working type who'd developed your ambitions because of your working-class origins. You'd risen above your background. So naturally you'd be a little different from me, who'd had Pop for a father. But there was nothing you did that I didn't seem able to understand, even when you slept with Esther. You liked sex, you wanted a change—it was as simple as that.'

She watched me in silence.

'I'm lost, Bob. I've lived with you ten years and I don't know anything about you. I can't begin to understand a man who can work like you've worked and have your kind of ambition, and then do a thing like that to Simon Fisher. It's beyond me. And the way you've been about Emma's beyond me too. I've tried. I've tried so very hard these past months. But it's no good.'

Up to then I'd felt compassion for her remotely, the compassion you felt for the tragedy that occasionally befell a public figure you'd admired. I'd watched her without emotion, feeling sorry I couldn't feel sorrow. The enormity of what I'd done to her had been too much; like the aborigines in Botany Bay simply ignoring Cook's vessel because its concept could not be coped with, my mind and instincts had not been able to accept the fact of her shattered life. I was here this morning to make a token apology, to iron out prac-ticalities. Sorrow and remorse seemed ludicrously beside the point.

But I felt genuine pity for her then, brief but overwhelming in its sudden intensity. It was as startling as if sensation had been dis-covered by chance in a paralysed limb. No one could take it like an Endersby, they could take anything you could dish out. All they wanted to know was why they were taking it. It was little enough,

I put my hand briefly over hers; she looked down at it with forlorn baffled eyes. Then she looked at my face again.

'I suppose there *were* things about you that should have given me a clue if there hadn't always been so little time. You could make such cruel jokes about people. It never struck me until recently that I didn't know anyone else who could be as cruel about people, even when you were being funny.

'And then sometimes late at night, when we were having a brandy, there'd be a sort of sadness in your face. I used to pass it off as depression—what could you possibly have to be sad about?

'And Esther—that was the biggest clue of all, I suppose. Men, the sort of men I'd always known—U.T.s and councillors and so on, if *they'd* gone into politics seriously they might have had an affair, but none of them would have done it without the utmost discretion. But you, the most professional of the lot, when you were tempted, there was such a . . . such a flashiness about Chelifer House and Esther in Victorian clothes, such a strange foolishness.'

I stared at her.

'Oh, yes,' she said. 'I did check her afternoon out, after all. Curiosity more than anything else.'

She got up and collected the few bits of crockery on to a tray, took it across to the sink, began to run water. She was wearing a yellow summer dress she'd bought a year ago, she wore her short black hair in the same style she'd had ever since I'd met her, and her strong, vital body had neither gained nor lost weight during the past months. Yet from behind, because of the deliberation in the way she began to wash up, she seemed like a total stranger. It must have been an instinctive reaction, on being denied the endless activity she lived for—to spin out what activity there was as elaborately as possible, to make it somehow try and meet those long thought-heavy hours.

At length, when each teaspoon had been individually dried and replaced carefully in the correct section of the drawer, she turned to me.

'I don't think I want a divorce.'

'For God's sake, why not?'

'I don't know. I suppose I ought to have one.'

'Definitely.'

She nodded, hung the tea-cloth over the rail so it lay perfectly flat.

'I don't understand you. Everything about you seems different from the person I thought I knew so well . . .'

She came back across to the annexe and stood above me, looking out into the blazing garden. 'And yet . . . you're still the man I married ten years ago. You attracted me then right away, the minute we started dancing together, before I knew a thing about you. Surely that must mean something.'

She shrugged, looked down at me.

'I don't honestly think I want to know why you attacked Simon Fisher, even if you could tell me, or why you had to get over Emma the way you did. I don't suppose I'd be able to understand it. We just seem to be totally different kinds of people. And yet, I was attracted to you. I wanted to marry you for my own good reasons. Perhaps . . . perhaps one of them was to be here when all this went wrong for you. I don't know, I just don't know . . .'

I got up, feeling my sight darken slightly under the pressure of sluggish blood. I felt tired most of the time these days. It no longer felt odd to stand up and not sense the old bubbling energy. But of course the old energy had made me very restless. I could sit quite comfortably for hours now with the novels. I wanted to go and sit with the novels at this moment, in a shady corner of the sitting-room. I hadn't bargained on complications and prolonged discussion. Oh, I knew how decent and good she was being, Endersby heart was legendary. Endersby girls could be ruthless in the efficient, cheerful way they'd dismiss the idea of marriage to any man who had less than their own rude health, or who didn't look certain to deliver the material goods, and yet—*noblesse oblige*—they didn't run out on the chosen one when the scene cooled. She was being just as fine and large as you could expect an Endersby girl to be, and God knows I didn't deserve it, after all the trouble I'd caused. But I didn't damned well want it either, I wanted to get things settled.

'Then if you don't want to divorce me we'll just have to separate.'

'But why, Bob, simply for the sake of it?'

'You're thirty-four,' I said wearily. 'You'll live to be ninety, like all the Endersbys. That means you've got fifty-odd years left that I can't spoil, if you make a clean break.'

She put a hand on my arm. 'Does it mean so much to you, me having another chance?'

'Don't! Don't try and endow me with Endersby honour. I simply don't *care*, Gwen. You were the best political wife in the business and we both had Emma. And now there's no Emma and no politics, and as far as I'm concerned that's that. I'm sorry, but there's no point in pretending I feel anything for you beyond friendship. And for Christ's sake don't kid yourself I'm saying that so it'll make it easier for you to go. I'm saying it because its the hard, bitter truth.'

'But if I go, what will you *do*?'

'What does it matter . . . ?'

'You'll drift. You'll just go on doing what you've done this past six months.'

'Do you think it'll be any different if you stay? I'm unemployable, remember. I keep smashing the boss's teeth in. Of course, there's always window-cleaning or the building sites, if they're not too choosey.'

'Let's go to Harrogate, Bob.'

I wanted to go away, to settle in my peaceful corner and read about Jim and Joe and Bella Brill and Cousin Clothilde. I was tired and it was beyond me, the conversation had taken on the surrealism of those you were inveigled into by tattered wretches who asked you for beer money on traffic islands.

'We can sell up here,' she said, when I didn't reply, 'and buy a small house and shop.'

'You've lost me. Is that your idea of a bright new dawn—a sweets and tob in Harrogate?'

'Don't be silly, Bob—*antiques*. There's still a good two-thirds of Miss Charlotte's collection in store. We could set up with that, it'd be a good start. And Harrogate's such a centre, full of tourists in season. One of us could look after the shop, the other could search for pieces. I've got dozens of contacts now; with two of us working at it, and your charm and organising ability . . .'

'No!'

'Oh, come—you've always liked antiques. You'd soon develop an eye. With our combination of talents we couldn't miss.'

'No!' I shook my head violently. 'Don't go on, Gwen, you're wasting your breath.'

'Why not? Find me one good reason why we shouldn't have a crack at it.'

Incredibly, astoundingly, an eagerness had begun to creep into her voice that I remembered from the days when we'd formed our plans to win friends and influence selection committees. It made me feel so exhausted even drawing breath seemed an effort. Was there anything, any mortal thing, that could keep an Endersby down for long? Oh, I knew them, knew how they reacted—stubborn about mastering their difficulties they were never, like all natural politicians, so stubborn that they couldn't occasionally accept defeat, and turn rapidly to the next move without recrimination. But it was the complexity of my nature she'd failed to master, not just why Westbury couldn't be coaxed into a higher poll. It was why I'd turned into a different man and why her daughter had been taken from her and why her entire world had been upended. How could even an Endersby girl find the courage to cut losses on that stupendous scale?

I didn't know. And much as I admired her, wanly, from beneath my blanket of lassitude, I wished she'd leave me alone. Had she learned nothing along those disturbing new pathways of thought? She knew now that I was different, hadn't she at least learned that because of that I'd not be able to turn to Harrogate and fan-back Windsors with her indestructible verve?

'Please, Gwen, just take the money and let's go our own ways. I don't want to make a fresh start with you at all, let alone in a junk-shop.'

'Oh, come, you've licked your wounds long enough. You've got to do something and you've got to have a partner, otherwise you'll simply rot.'

Her eyes had begun to shine in the sunlight; even as I stood watching her I could sense the heaviness lifting from her, as if the actress who'd portrayed middle age so skilfully was slowly assuming her true identity. How she longed to hurl herself into intensive work again, to stretch the hours once more to meet an impossible schedule. Her enforced voyage of discovery had ended, she'd tried hard to learn from it and profit by it, but it was a terrific relief to step on to firm earth again, of a country that didn't seem too different from the one she'd left.

'Gwen, how can you be so damned insensitive?'

'I could say that about you for leaving me to do all the dirty work last November.'

'Do I have to spell it out? I've ruined your life. Look, *you* might be able to face soldiering on with me, but I couldn't. Can't you see what a swine I'd feel every time I saw you trying to make antiques fill the gap everything else left?'

Her old cheerful smile flashed almost subliminally. 'Oh, come, it's past now, nothing's ever going to alter it. What's the good of moping about and sending me away and taking a hack job in an office someone with a tenth of your ability wouldn't put up with, just to punish yourself?'

Like so many people of her uncomplicated nature, like Garbutt for instance, she could often make an exact hit on a painful truth. Her words pierced deeply, almost through the barriers of my indifference and fatigue. Suddenly I had an overwhelming urge to lie in her strong arms, to put my head against her large heavy breasts. I wanted her to cook me a meal, to pour me a drink, to plunge round the house singing to herself, to fill the sitting-room with Wagner, to plan my life for me in one of her big diaries.

I turned abruptly from her, thrust my hands in my pockets to stop myself from putting my arms round her. It wouldn't be any good, that was merely the child in me seeking comfort, the invalid wanting to be cocooned in the strength and vitality of the nurse. In the long run a relationship with a woman I'd nothing in common with could only fail. It would have been difficult enough trying again with a woman I'd actually loved, assuming I could bring myself to go on living with any woman I'd brought such trouble to.

'Please leave me alone,' I said, in a low voice. 'We're not all cast in the same heroic Endersby mould. Some people are queer twisted sods like me and they have queer twisted ways of getting over things.'

'The trouble with you, Bob, is that you need pushing. Look how little you'd actually done with yourself before you met me.'

'You pushed me once,' I said bitterly. 'And look where it got you.'

'Rubbish!' She took her pinafore off decisively and tossed it on to the window ledge. 'You know you've got to find something to do and right now there's no one who's going to accept you in the sort of job you could handle. So why not try this? What can you lose? Antiques are nice things to work with and Harrogate's a nice town to live in. And it's all a bit of a closed shop, so breaking into it would get you out of yourself. Oh, come on, all I'm asking you to do is go back to work.'

'No, Gwen.'

'I'm not leaving you. Not to rot. We're still young and there's *always* something else to turn to. That was the one thing Pop never stopped drumming into us. If one door shuts another door opens, even if you have to put your shoulder to it.'

'What would Pop advise you to do about a man who married you for convenience? Who then turned out to be an absolute no-good who ruined everything you'd spent ten years slogging your guts out for.'

She stood in wide-eyed silence. She hadn't seen it that way, that she herself was proposing a new deal that flew in the face of all the cast-iron principles she'd lived her entire life by. Her mouth fell open a little; I couldn't help smiling faintly. She'd imagined the time of paradox and difficult new outlooks to be over. She'd done her best to think it out, but now it was time to turn with a sigh of relief to stripping the decks for action.

'*I* know,' I said. 'I know what he'd say. He'd say take the bounder's money, get your divorce and marry a nice hard-working bank manager.'

As I watched her, all at once she began to laugh.

'Well, Pop can go to hell!' she said. 'What does he know about **anything**?'

And then, for the first time in six months, I too began to laugh.

24

'Hello, Esther.'

'Hello, Bob.'

Surprise had made her as polite as the day we'd first met. She'd been different over the phone, she'd sounded anxious and urgent, and when I'd agreed to meet her she'd not been able to keep the relief out of her voice. But she'd not been able to see me over the phone. Over the phone I'd stood erect and full of energy in a well-pressed suit. My hair had been glossy and thick and I'd had the smooth shining face of health, the clear eyes of diet and careful living.

All at once she stuck her hand out, as if she were the Queen giving me an audience.

'How . . . are you?'

'I'm well.' I smiled in faint irony. 'And you?'

'I'm very well. How's . . . Gwen?'

'She's all right. She's over it now.'

We stood for a moment, hands frozen in formal clasp, Queen and subject. She'd also changed, minutely but perceptibly. She was thinner; her eyes seemed larger in a face that looked a trifle wasted. She was wearing a new navy raincoat with military epaulettes and silver buttons. She tried to stop her glance wavering from my eyes to the pouches beneath, to the pallor and the dead-looking hair.

I let go her rigid fingers and we moved out on to the high, flagged causeway, above water that rippled sluggishly like melted lead under a heavy sky. A handful of ducks sailed fretfully near a fountain that didn't play; in the distance we could hear the steady roar of the upper reservoir endlessly debouching itself into the one we now skirted. I'd heard that sound in my car on Water Lane the first time I'd kissed her. It was fitting.

'I'm sorry,' she said suddenly. 'About not ringing before. I thought . . . with the trouble and everything . . . it wasn't a good idea.'

'What have you been doing since last winter?'

'Nothing.'

'You left Singleton's?'

'I went to the Tech. Principal's secretary. What are you doing?'

'Nothing.'

'Nothing . . . at all?'

'There's not a great deal open to a man of my unusual reputation.'

'I'm sorry. I'm dreadfully sorry.'

'I thought you were going away.'

'I was. I . . . still am. Soon. I couldn't go away at the time. Mother's been unwell.'

She was lying. She was lying and it made her walk faster. We were almost marching when we came to the steps that rose up the side of the gully down which crashed the frothing green-tinted water of the upper level. We could not talk easily then and began to climb the steps. But it was a long time since I'd had the wind to go up steps without effort, and she began to outstrip me, unaware against the ceaseless roar of cascading water, that I'd fallen behind.

And then she realised and halted. She turned round, far enough above me to be entirely in perspective. She was pink-faced with exertion, her mouth was slightly open on large square teeth, her long hair fell to the shoulders of the neat military coat—she stood out as strikingly as a photographer's model against the dull greens and browns of an overcast summer day.

When she saw me, her face briefly distorted with shock. Then she smiled, politely. When I reached her, she carefully adopted my pace.

At the top of the steps there was a causeway that ran between the two sheets of water. On one side, water lapped a few inches below us, on the other it lay a hundred feet below, at the bottom of the steep grassy hillside we'd just climbed.

As we walked on to it I had a sudden picture of the way we must have looked against the grey, even sky to anyone standing halfway down the steps, a kind of mental long-shot of Esther, looking so healthy and fresh and clean, walking slowly with a worn-looking man in a crumpled suit. It was an image that flashed as inexplicably as the one when I'd seemed to stand outside myself in the Commons Chamber, looking down at a confident politician and a wretched young girl.

Six short months ago.

The image faded and I passed on, trying to decide the best way to punish her.

Because she had to be punished too. And I wasn't angry and I wasn't being vicious. It was simply that I owed it to them—to Emma and Gwen and Martin and Pop—to make sure she fully understood the hand she'd had in it.

God knows, it wasn't load-shifting. It was me who'd nurtured the hate object, who'd let Emma fall, who'd smashed Simon Fisher. All those things had happened, could only have happened, because I was me, and because an entire way of life had been based on hate.

And because of all that I'd been punished. Deservedly.

But none of it, not one single reaction in that appalling chain could have triggered the next if it hadn't been for her.

I'd thought about it very carefully because I'd wanted to be absolutely certain it hadn't happened *only* because I was me, that it couldn't just as easily have happened if I'd never known her, or if it had been any other woman I'd had an affair with.

And I'd gone to great lengths to err on the side of leniency. I'd dismissed the fact of the affair itself out of hand, and her long ruthless pursuit of me—I was a fully-grown male and I knew my way around; I accepted that it had been half her fault and half mine.

But I couldn't overlook the tampering. I couldn't forgive her for not being able to accept me as I was, for that desperate struggle—

once we were lovers—to make me into the man who only lived in her mind. But for her and her illusions I'd not have pretended, however briefly, to be the man she'd so much wanted me to be. And if I hadn't made that pretence I shouldn't have blamed Simon for his own mistakes, shouldn't have got carried away, shouldn't have upset myself so badly I hadn't been able to act fast enough when Emma had jumped off the wall. It had all started from the moment I'd tried to be the man I was not.

And she'd got to know it. That was all. That was to be her punishment. She'd got to know she'd struck the spark that had burnt my life out.

But for her and what she'd demanded of me I'd still be *the* Bob Saxby, still be Fisher's accountant, still be South's potential candidate, still be the embryo man of the region. Still have Emma. Yes, she had to know.

At the end of the causeway there was a bench beneath a chestnut tree at the corner of the reservoir.

'Shall we sit down?'

She glanced uneasily at her watch.

'I don't think I can, Bob. I haven't much time.'

I glanced at her; her eyes met mine and then flicked away like tropical fish.

'I work . . . peculiar hours. I'm invigilating an exam later this afternoon.'

I was puzzled. It was she who'd rung me, she who'd arranged the place and the hour. Why had she given herself so little time for a meeting she'd waited so long for?

'Then . . . shall we meet again when you have more time?' I said at last.

She gave me another darting glance and then stared back across the water, her old impassivity gone, her bottom lip trembling nervously.

'I . . . I only wanted to see you. To tell you how sorry I was.'

She was lying. That voice over the wire had almost pleaded with me to see her, as one day I'd always known it would. Sometimes it had seemed to be the only thing that had kept me going, the necessity of making sure she got her share.

She'd sounded exactly as I'd expected her to—like a woman who wanted to start again. She'd allowed the long interval of decency, but she couldn't live without me and she wanted me back. Not that it mattered, it didn't matter a damn to me any more, but that's what the phone call had told me, and I couldn't understand what had happened between the phone call and now.

I sat down heavily. It still tired me to stand or walk for very long. She turned back from the water, eyes swivelling past mine, and after a moment's hesitation, also sat down. But well apart from me. And that gave me the clue.

I should have guessed, I suppose, from the extreme formality of that first greeting, from the way her face had distorted when she'd turned to me on the steps; but I'd been sure that that had simply been pity. Now I wasn't so sure.

And yet . . . she was in love with me. It didn't matter any more, but she'd been so much in love with me she'd come to work at Fisher's because I was there. She'd kept herself a virgin for me. She'd been willing to accept what scraps of my life all the other things left. And she wasn't the kind who loved easily or changed— Christ, she'd been stuck on me since she was twelve. It didn't matter any more, but I couldn't bring myself to believe she didn't love me as she'd loved me a year ago. Or an hour ago, over the phone.

But she was sitting a foot away from me. I felt a sudden anger, a curious emotion after all those months, but it died as rapidly as it sparked. I simply could not believe what I suspected. Not yet.

'I'd been waiting for you to ring, Es,' I said, deliberately using a diminutive I'd once whispered at a moment of supreme closeness.

I sensed her body stiffen. All at once, jerkily, as if she had a disease that was slowly paralysing her nerve centres, she began to claw at the narrow bag for the inevitable gold packet. It must have taken fully a minute for her to take a cigarette out and get it lit.

'I . . . I couldn't go without seeing you. Without telling you how sorry I was.'

'That's not the real reason, Es, is it?' I murmured gently. 'You're not really going away, are you?'

'Yes . . . yes . . . I'm going very soon, Bob. I only stayed on because of Mother not being well.'

She was lying to me. It wasn't in her to lie easily; the words came out with the emphasis wrong, as if she were reading them from a script for the first time.

'Oh, no,' I said. 'If you'd been going you'd have gone months ago.'

'I am. Really I am. Try to make a fresh start. It's the only way, it's what we always said.'

I heard the faintest note of panic in her voice.

'Oh, come, Es, no need to pretend. The trouble's over now. Of course I know why you wanted to see me. It's . . . it's because of us, isn't it?'

The cigarette fell on to her new raincoat, and for a moment she simply stared at it smouldering there, as if she'd lost the use of her hands altogether. And then she shook it away, oblivious to the scorched and melted fibres.

'No . . . no. You were right before. We both have our lives to live. You were so right. I was a fool.'

'Oh, come. It's us, isn't it? I could tell the minute I picked the phone up.'

'Please.' Her eyes slid past mine and down to her watch. 'I must go.'

'Oh, Es . . .'

'I'll see you again,' she said quickly. 'If you really want me to. When I've got a clear afternoon.'

Panic had given way to relief; I knew why. She'd get away from me now by the promise of another meeting later. A promise she hadn't the remotest intention of keeping.

I was convinced then. But confused. This meeting had seemed as if it would run on such predictable lines, had been so carefully planned, so minutely rehearsed and timed, that this astounding new aspect had made my mind reel. My old deft mastery of situations had slipped from me through lack of practice.

'Please don't go,' I said uncertainly. 'Cut your invigilation. They'll dig up some old dear from the Tech Office. Stay here and talk things over.'

I placed my hand over hers. I didn't need any more proof—she wrenched hers away, and it was the horrified instinctive reaction of a woman touched by a stranger in a darkened cinema. She leapt to her feet, her face almost ugly with taut, clenched muscle.

I got up too. '*Es!*' I said, only just containing the anger behind the bemused tenderness. 'What's *wrong*? Surely you can tell me. Me, of all people. I know we've been apart a long time, but . . .'

I caught hold of her in a rapid embrace and brought my lips down to hers, but she pushed me away so hard I almost missed my footing near the edge of the reservoir. I regained my balance clumsily and watched her in silence. It was sheer terror this time. This time it wasn't a stranger who'd touched her in a cinema, it was someone who'd tried to assault her in a dark street. She was breathing so rapidly she could hardly get a word out, but finally I managed to catch a few whispered phrases—'. . . must go now . . . so sorry . . . no one else to do it except me.'

She turned then and was gone, almost running round the wide curve of the reservoir. I began to tremble. I'd thought I was beyond that kind of emotion any more. Blood began to throb so heavily in my temples I had to close my eyes for a moment and suck in air to steady my heart.

I set off after her then, pounding heavily over the flagstones. She glanced back, her face like white wax with fear, and then she began to run properly. But I was oblivious to fatigue now and muscles that screamed from lack of condition, and I began to gain on her.

All at once, as instinctively as a hunted animal trying to create a diversion, she ran off the walkway and on to the earth path that went at a tangent into the woodland surrounding the reservoir.

It was midsummer, and it was dark with the leaf-cover of oak and beech and sycamore, and we crashed through the fern and the rhododendrons that bushed out across the path like actors in some scene of tropical adventure.

I caught hold of her by the shoulder; she began to flap desperately back and forwards in my grip, like a butterfly held by a single wing, and then she began picking savagely at my clenched fist with her nails until it was scored with thin streaks of blood. But when she saw that nothing could make me release her she became totally still, eyes open so wide there were thick white bands round the iris. Her hair had become tangled across her face where the bushes had caught at it, her mouth was pulled down at the corners with the effort of running. I looked at terror so absolute it had produced the frozen acceptance of a cornered rabbit. And I was glad. I was delighted. I exulted in it.

'You bitch,' I whispered. 'You *bitch*.'

It was to have been an exercise as impartial and disinterested as the dispensation of justice in a court-room. Anger hadn't come into it, I'd simply decided to punish her in a modest and fitting way not for myself but for those who'd helped to make me. But now I wanted to hurt her as she'd never known she could be hurt. And by God I knew the ways, I knew her fears and weaknesses. I could inflict such damage on her in five minutes she'd have mental scars that wouldn't heal in a lifetime.

'You lousy bitch—you can't stand the bloody sight of me now, can you, now I'm freely available. It was only when I was a going concern you wanted me, wasn't it, when you couldn't have me.'

'No,' she said hoarsely. 'No.'

'Look.' I pulled her close to me, so close I could smell her fear, an odour as sharp and nauseous as burnt plastic. 'Look, you're supposed to be in love with me. You told me, remember, you told me you'd loved me ever since Westbury Park. But there hadn't been any trouble then, had there, I wasn't a nothing man with nowhere to go?'

Suddenly she closed her eyes and went so limp I had to use all my strength to keep her from falling. I began to shake her in exasperation. She'd beaten me again. Not only had she stopped being in love with me, she'd fainted before I could exact the retribution she deserved.

But she just hung on my hands, her head drooping forward, a weight that was rapidly becoming too much for someone as out of condition as I was. Our surroundings began to press in on me—the cloying scent of flowering bushes, subdued bird-song, the distant sound of falling water.

Just as I was about to let her down to the ground, she broke away again. She pulled herself free with a single jerk and was yards away even as I stood there, arms held out into empty space.

She didn't get far. She would have done, sheer frenzy would have got her through the wood this time, but by a fluke a strong thin branch entered one of her epaulettes and dragged her to a sudden halt, holding her as securely as a snare till I had chance to catch up with her.

'Isn't that strange?' I said, taking hold of her again. 'It's almost symbolic. Because you'll never get away from me, even if you run forever. You hunted me once, didn't you, when I was worth having? Well, I'm going to hunt you now. From this day on, wherever you are, or whatever you're doing, I'll be around there somewhere, watching you.'

I could hardly tell she was speaking for a moment, I thought her lips were working with fear.

'Please,' she whispered. 'Oh, please. You've a right to despise me, but don't twist it. I ran away . . . I despise myself as much as you do, but don't . . . don't twist it into all those other things. They're not true, they're not true . . .'

'You lying bitch . . .'

'No . . . No. Nothing's really changed. *Please*. I know it must upset you because I can't stand you to touch me, but I can't *help* it. I tried, but I can't, it's no use. It's nothing to do with *you*, with who you really are. You *must* believe me.'

'Christ, I'm the same man I was twelve months ago . . .'

'Oh, *please* ! I'm sorry, I'm sorry, I'm *sorry*, but I can't stand you near me. You look so *queer*. You look so queer and tired and old, and I can't stand you touching me. Not yet. Not now. *Oh, God, you look so OLD!*'

Her voice had gathered strength; the last words were a scream which echoed in the silence. I stepped back involuntarily and caught my heel in an exposed root. I seemed to fall in slow motion, but I suppose it was because I didn't feel the ground as I struck it. I felt as little physical pain as a drunk falling in the street feels.

I lay on my back, staring up through the lacy openings of summer foliage at the grey even sky. She knelt down at my side. Our eyes met, she began to cry; the rapid tears dripping on to my face began to mix with tears of my own, tears it had once seemed impossible to shed.

Not long ago I read about some students who volunteered for sleep experiments—they'd allowed themselves to be deliberately aroused each time they'd begun to dream. And that's what I'd done, I'd fended off memory just as deliberately, with my pills and alcohol. But when the students had been allowed to sleep undisturbed they'd had a surfeit of dreams, as if it had been imperative the mind caught up on its quota.

Perhaps with me. Perhaps it had always been certain my own mind would need to adjust its equilibrium one day by plunging me deeply and emotionally into the near past, as I should have let it do when she'd died.

I don't know. But if I'm right then something at that moment, the combination of words, or the girl's anguished voice, short-circuited the process and swung open the sealed barriers of my past as easily as an electronic impulse could release the locking mechanism of a vault-door.

And I remembered her then as she ought to have been, deserved to have been remembered. With tears and a pain that could scarcely be borne, and yet with something of the incredible release of giving in to sensible grief.

I saw her dancing in the garden, dancing in the woods, dancing on the beach. I saw her skipping and singing *Sally in the Kitchen*, I saw her at Sunday school in a white dress singing *All Things Bright and Beautiful*, I saw her scratching EMMA—SCARBOROUGH—1967 in wet sand while Gwen took a snap. I saw her tying a nail-file on Genghis Noggs and pretending it was a sword. I saw her playing Knock-knock with a circle of little girls in sunshine. I saw her shrieking with laughter because Steptoe slept with the horse. I heard the bubble of her shrill voice float down through the summer air in Daisy Edge Woods, saw her running towards Esther, saw their bodies merge again among the blinding sticks of light.

And I wept, sensibly and healthily, for my dead golden daughter, not just as she'd been but as she would have been as the poised happy creature who'd developed her talents to the full, as that dazzling blue-stocking who'd read all the books and met all the most interesting people and travelled the wide world. As that girl on a television screen whose very smile would lighten the hearts of the old and the worried and the sick. That girl who'd belong to the people as I'd never belonged.

And after I'd wept for her I wept for myself—for Bob Saxby, who'd got to look so queer and old, who'd lost his job, who'd never chair another committee, who'd never now sit in the House or grow to be the man of the Ridings. It was good. It was good to weep normally and remember the happiness of days I'd not thought happy, to lie there and grieve as I should have grieved at the beginning.

And when it was over I was almost grateful to her for finding the right combination. There was no guarantee I'd ever have found it on my own. Perhaps the capacity to mourn as others mourned would have calcified. Poor kid—she wasn't to blame and neither was I— it was simply us. Together. Apart, everything would have been the same as it was a year ago.

Later, we sat on the trunk of an oak that had blown down in a gale; she smoked a cigarette. Her eyes were swollen and her cheeks blotchy, but at least her face wasn't twisted by fear any more.

'I'm sorry,' she said. 'I can't begin to tell you. It must have been dreadful to lose someone like Emma. I'm so sorry. Do you . . . do you want to talk about it?'

I shook my head. I had. I'd wanted to tell her that if it hadn't been for her my daughter would still be alive. But not now. I couldn't bring myself to punish her now. Her future lay full of punishment.

'It's such a waste, Bob. You were so ambitious. You wanted to do so much for Beckford.'

I shrugged. 'Someone else will do it one day. Nothing's more certain. Perhaps fate decided I wasn't the man for that particular job after all.'

'You . . . hit him because you'd just heard about Emma?'

'Yes. We'd never been the closest of friends, as you know. He just happened to be saying the wrong thing at the wrong time, that's all, and he caught for the lot, poor sod.'

We sat in silence until she'd finished her cigarette. We could see the liquid metal of the reservoir rippling sluggishly through a break in the trees. She kept darting rapid glances at me.

I smiled wryly. 'If you want to run away I won't chase you any more.'

She stubbed the cigarette out carefully on the bark of the tree.

'Will you give me time? To . . . get used . . .'

'To me looking queer and tired and old?'

'It's going now,' she said quickly. 'Please believe me. You've had a frightful time, but nothing's really changed, I know that now. It was just the first shock of seeing what it had done to you.'

She touched my cheek with a hand she couldn't stop from shaking; I knew her teeth were clenched beneath the smile. But she'd stayed. I'd given her the chance to go, but she'd stayed to struggle against revulsion, to compel her shrinking flesh to accept that I really was the same man who'd shone with health and confidence, who'd kissed her and caressed her and entered her body.

'Will you . . . meet me again soon?'

Try as she might she could inject no warmth into the words, she was reading from the prepared script again.

'Of course.'

'Soon?'

'Very soon. I'll ring you next week.'

'It'll be all right again . . . Bob,' she almost whispered. 'I'll always be there, if you want me.'

I believed her absolutely, as I'd believed that Sunday in Daisy Edge Woods that she'd never use our affair as a weapon against me. She had quality; and I couldn't stand in judgement on her any more or think of punishing her, for having loved an illusion instead of a man. Hadn't I, after all, once loved a Maggie who'd only existed in my own mind?

Esther had never loved me. It was clearer to me then than it had ever been. It was the white knight of the tennis courts she'd loved, the man she'd so much wanted me to be, the man she'd been certain I could have returned to being if only I'd been true to what she'd convinced herself was my real nature. Genuine love took people as it found them, however lacking. Genuine love could also take pouch eyes and pepper and salt hair and the smell of failure.

'What shall you do? About a job?'

'Move off probably. There'll never be anything doing in Beckford. Publicity's a two-edged sword, as you once reminded me.'

'You must tell me exactly what you decide to do, Bob. I'll help. I'll do everything I can to help you.'

Remorse lent an almost convincing urgency to her voice.

'Of course.'

'You ... and Gwen. Are you ... ?'

'Separating?'

She nodded.

'I don't know. Like everything else, it's an imponderable.'

It was strange to think Gwen wouldn't go. I'd always been certain that I'd married, deliberately, against my nature and instincts when I'd married her. I'd had to start re-thinking. I'd always imagined that what I'd really wanted from a woman was what I'd found in Esther—in the poignancy and closeness of last summer, in the ever-shifting relationship, in the shared pleasure in books and pictures, in the humour and the friendship, in the total desperate involvement of our love-making. But now I couldn't be sure. Perhaps in marrying Gwen, however barren I'd been certain it would make my existence, I'd been protecting myself from the possibility of ever marrying anyone whose emotions might have been as strong as my own, whose mind might have shifted in the same restless fashion, who might have had the same imagination and self-awareness, the same craving for glamour and romantic love. Perhaps my instincts had really sought ballast, and marrying Gwen had been one of the least deliberate actions of my life.

Poor kid. She'd marry, some day, someone older who didn't look his age, from whom she'd demand an idealism that maturity wouldn't be able to muster, unless it was the maturity of a dull man. But a dull man wouldn't do for her.

It was odd to pity her so much—it was my life that had broken, not hers—but the urge to protect her from future suffering was overwhelming. Suffering seemed to lay over her like a curse, like ill-health or bad luck or melancholia hung over others. I could scarcely believe I'd wanted to actually start that process, to force a share in the responsibility for my downfall on her. She needed what shadow of happiness, what illusion of peace she could get, while youth still made sleep and regeneration an easy matter. It was ironical that for once in my complex, devious and calculated existence I should be acting from motives of genuine compassion, and that she, who'd always insisted I was incapable of it, should never know.

'I'd better be getting back, Esther.'

We moved slowly along the flagged walk and on to the causeway between the two reservoirs. There was a pale yellow light playing on the water, where the sun had finally blasted a single hole in the cloud-cap. I sensed her watching me; when I turned to her her eyes glistened slightly.

'Oh, Bob, I'm so sorry.'

I nodded.

'Have you any money? Why don't you get right away? Why don't you go to Italy or the Riviera for a few weeks?'

'Perhaps I shall.'

'Would you . . . like me . . . to come?'

I shook my head, unable to speak. I'd despised her for it at first, for being repelled by me and being unable to take the changes. But her revulsion had been genuine, I'd been able to accept that at least, so genuine she'd wanted to run away from me. Yet in spite of that, in spite of my slightest touch making her cringe, she was prepared to force herself to go away with me, to be with me all day and every day, even to offer her body to me.

'Best not,' I said at last. 'But thanks, Esther. Perhaps this is one I ought to have alone. Just eat and sleep and do a bit of swimming. Think things out.'

'Yes, that's it!' she said, genuinely eager, as if sunshine and exercise were going to bring the old Bob back intact, glossy and vital

270

and bounding with energy, as if sand and sun and clear air would wipe out her scream of horror. 'You'll feel *heaps* better!'

But then the eagerness faded, and she turned away to gaze at the swan sailing towards us. We were near the gully by now; on one side of the causeway we could see water that was polished and obsidian as it slid through the grill into the culvert, on the other, we could see it roaring and whisked into green-tinted froth as it cascaded out to crash down the steep steps of the gully.

We stood for a long time in silent contemplation of the water, sharing perhaps a similar indefinable yearning—a desire for cool, silent, green depths, an urge to slide beneath roaring spume into a buoyant silence, to be washed and washed again in the cold clean liquid, to be chilled and purified and cleansed and comforted, to be given peace and forgiveness, to weep silently and in secret.

Not very long ago, Gwen began to play her loud rousing records as she'd done in the old days—her *Lohengrin* and her *Beethoven's Seventh* and her *Lizst's Second Piano*. Finally she played the *Karelia*. I believe we'd both forgotten that the *Karelia* only filled part of the side, that it was followed by *The Swan of Tuonela*.

And as that plaintive lament, drenched in its inexplicable nostalgias, began to steal so unexpectedly across the room, it evoked with an astounding precision the confused emotions of that dark afternoon—that sliding, plunging water, that point of final and irrevocable parting, that suspended moment of endings and beginnings. And I wondered where she was and what she was doing, and what my life might have been now if I'd never known her. But only with curiosity and a brief sadness. Not with bitterness.

'Well—I'll be seeing you, Esther.'

Suddenly she swung round and kissed me fully on the lips; at the price of eyes tight shut and a nausea that almost made her retch —I heard it, the strangled sound of her gorge rising and being swallowed back. But she held her lips against mine and kept her arms round my shoulders for fully half a minute. And then, releasing me, she stood before me in silence, her head slightly bowed, her eyes not quite able to meet mine.

Finally she said : 'You must ring me soon. You must tell me what you decide to do about a holiday.'

'Yes—I'll ring you.'

'As soon as you decide?'

'Yes.'

'And . . . will you take me out one night?'

'Of course.'

'Goodbye then . . . Bob.'

'Goodbye, Esther.'

She stepped backwards, tried to smile, started to walk away. And then she stopped and turned, and began to shake her head almost imperceptibly—an involuntary action that said everything at a stroke. It was all there—the misery and the fear and the pity and the remorse, and it was the way I was always to remember her.

Then she went on again, more quickly this time, as if spurred by an instinctive relief. I watched her draw away from me, away to a life growing steadily more wretched, to painful memories and unsuitable men and the relentless process of ageing. I watched her go in profound relief that I at least had spared her pain, even if it was a pain I ought to have inflicted and which she really deserved.

I watched her out of sight, then turned away and began to walk almost briskly down the steps that ran past the booming water; back, back to Gwen and the attractive town of Harrogate, practically ready now to start clawing my way towards the glittering prizes that lay at the very top of the second-hand furniture game.